WOMEN AND MEN
TOGETHER

An Anthology of Short Fiction

WOMEN AND MEN TOGETHER

An Anthology of Short Fiction

DAWSON GAILLARD
JOHN MOSIER
Loyola University, New Orleans

HOUGHTON MIFFLIN COMPANY   BOSTON
Dallas   Geneva, Illinois   Hopewell, New Jersey   Palo Alto   London

CONTENTS

ALTERNATE TABLE OF CONTENTS
RELATIONSHIP AS METAPHOR

PREFACE

Considered in its broadest sense as a factor dominating the sub-structure of human existence, the topic of this book is inevitably a controversial one. Although we believe controversy to be healthy, some of the conflict surrounding the topic seems the result of preju-dice. There are people who reject the work of some of our most talented women because these women allegedly do not like members of their own sex. Others reject most works by men dealing with women because they have a sexually limited view of women. While some of these points of view have to be respected, they are not ours. We had no intention of recapitulating orthodoxy, of compiling a list of standard authors, or of restricting ourselves to the contem-porary American scene. This anthology contains some fiction writ-ten by women whose literary position is the subject of controversy. It contains fiction about women written by men. It also includes a good deal of material in translation. As with most anthologies, there are many omissions.

This much said, some explanations of our approach are in order. We started out trying to teach a course that would introduce stu-dents to the way that male-female relationships are handled in literature. We went into the course with an enormous list of works, and the initial group of students fought back tooth and nail. In-terestingly enough, we discovered that many students cheerfully viewed insanity as normalcy, repression as an ideal. One of us was fortunate to continue the project with a series of courses in which individual students could subject the stories to what turned out to be a depressingly withering scrutiny. Certain stories that seem to belong in this text have been left out because of negative feed-back. We listened, and we began to agree. This anthology, then, is probably as much the work of our students as of ourselves.

When we turned to the critical apparatus of the anthology, we were guided by the same experiences. Instead of making the head-notes uniform, we tried to make them responsive. In certain cases very little conventional information was needed; in others, a great deal. Mainly we wanted to supply the interested student with suggestions for further reading and some idea of how typical a se-lection was of an author's work. When we wrote the discussion questions, we tried to restrict ourselves to points with which the reader must come to terms if he or she wants to understand the story.

The selections appear in chronological order because that seemed to be the simplest, least intrusive way to present them. We have included an alternate table of contents to show ways to group the stories. The alternate table might be used by an instructor to organize a course or by a student to organize his or her own reading. We strongly encourage all users of the text to amend the table and change the lists. It is our hope that this will spark some interesting and lively discussion. The alternate table is, after all, as much of a thesis as an anthology can provide.

It should by now be obvious that the people to whom we owe the biggest debt of gratitude are our students—all of them. But without the comments of these six the book would be substantially less: Kim Bosworth, Denise Eavenson, Mary Elizabeth Finnerty, Rosalind Flynn, Sarah Elizabeth Spain, and Anne Witte. We also wish to extend our thanks to those who reviewed the manuscript critically. They include Tom Doulis, Portland State University; Stephanie Demetrakopoulos, Western Michigan University; Margaret Culley, University of Massachusetts, Amherst; Robert Canary, University of Wisconsin, Parkside; and Diane Middlebrook, Stanford University. One of us, who seemed to disappear abroad at totally inopportune moments, wishes to thank the other for forbearance. Our secretary, Sandra Ariatti, had to put up with us both and do far more than type.

D.G.
J.M.

WOMEN AND MEN
TOGETHER

An Anthology of Short Fiction

INTRODUCTION

Women and Men Together concentrates on stories that dramatize male and female relationships—parents and children, friends, wives and husbands, lovers, and enemies. Three aims guided the choice of selections: to present cross-cultural treatments of the subject, to balance the offerings by female and male authors, and to select material from some of the best Western writers in the nineteenth and twentieth centuries.

This collection is of interest not because it discusses a new subject, but because the selected works skillfully treat an old subject. People listen to and read stories about women and men together to find out how the characters develop, solve problems, and face the routine of daily living—activities that are seldom performed alone and often depend on other people for their success.

The word "together" in the title means that the characters are in physical, although not necessarily emotional, proximity. In fact, many of the selections suggest that emotional distance is often the condition of people together, as in "Daydreams of a Drunk Woman," "Bodies," "Old Mr Marblehall," "Cat in the Rain," "Wine," "Beasts of the Southern Wild," and "Giving Blood." Some stories suggest that cruelty and violence bind the characters as closely as kindness and sympathy, as in "Wine," "Giving Blood," "Her Sweet Jerome," "Dry September," and "Long Black Song." In others, the men and women misuse or misunderstand each other: "Ligeia," "The Birthmark," "Midnight Mass," "Cicely's Dream," "A Painful Case," and "The Difference." Thus, fulfillment of a relationship can be thwarted by fear, illusion, or examination. In most of these stories, we see not only the female and male characters attempting to live for and through each other but also the consequences of their desires to establish rapport.

The selections in this anthology present the social possibilities and limitations inherent in human relationships. When a member of one sex is limited or trapped by a prescribed role, the member of the opposite sex—child, spouse, lover, or friend—is equally limited. Many of these stories deal with the cultural processes that subtly relegate each sex to a particular role. Others dramatize an awakening to cultural restrictions and the consequences of that awakening.

The stories appear in chronological order; however, an alternate table of contents may serve as a guide to the reader who wants to study groups of stories that use the central relationship as a metaphor for a theme. Although the anthology may be read thematically, one might want to study the short story from its beginning. Because Edgar Allan Poe's comments have influenced modern conceptions of the well-made short story, this collection begins with a few of these remarks and a story by him.

According to Poe, every word of a short story should contribute to a unified design. His premise is that fiction making is a shaping. A selective imagination picks through the random events, objects, and people of life in order to construct an artful design. We recognize the materials as familiar not only because of the references to what we know of life but also because of the knowledge we have gained from reading other short stories.

All stories have a narrator; some have several. Someone tells the story, even if the device is a message washed ashore in a bottle. Stories may be told in the first person—as are "Ligeia" and "Beasts of the Southern Wild"—with the narrator as a participant in the action she or he relates. Or a tale may be told in the third person— as in "The Birthmark," "The Bride Comes to Yellow Sky," and "Her Sweet Jerome"—in which case the narrator is an observer of the action.

Sometimes the author limits the point of view of both third and first persons. The phrase *limited point of view* usually means that the reader and the central character simultaneously discover information about an event. However, the writer can impose other limitations on the narrator. For example, in "Midnight Mass" and "Ligeia" it is doubtful that either first-person narrator fully understands the significance of the information he has gathered. In "Cat in the Rain" and "Tuesday Siesta," both told in the third person, the narrators offer no explicit explanations about causes, effects, or significance of the actions.

Sometimes the short story relies on a narrator who seems to be omniscient; that is, the narrator shares a story that she or he fully understands, one that reveals the follies of other, lesser humans. At the end of "The Birthmark," for instance, Hawthorne's all-knowing narrator explains the significance of Aylmer's experiment.

But how are we to understand stories that set limitations on their narrators? There are at least two ways. First, because the narration of a story presupposes a listener, we can read with our ears. Just as we listen to intonations of the speaking voice, so we can listen to the narrator's tone of voice. By reading with our ears, we can infer the narrator's and the author's attitudes towards their stories. Frequently, the writer is trying to force the reader to reflect on society by implicitly raising critical questions about human behavior. The narrative tone, however, may betray no evaluation or may suggest an attitude opposite from the author's. For example, in "Old Mr Marblehall," "Permanent Wave," and "Her Sweet Jerome" the narrative tone is often sarcastic. The reader may then ask whether the sarcasm is directed towards the characters or towards the society in which they live.

Two stories in this collection use a tone that may be described as flat. Notice the tone in the following excerpt from "Cat in the Rain": "It was raining. The rain dripped from the palm trees. Water stood in pools on the gravel paths." "Tuesday Siesta" also begins with a reportorial voice describing the scenery: "The train emerged from the quivering tunnel of sandy rocks, began to cross the symmetrical, interminable banana plantations, and the air became humid and they couldn't feel the sea breeze any more. A stifling blast of smoke came in the car window." The flat tone implicitly comments on the action and characters in the stories. To make that assertion we must accept the possibility that the story is a shaped design. We may, then, read not only with our ears but also selectively with our eyes. This is the second way in which we can understand stories.

Design means the relationships among the units of a story. These units can be created within the story by descriptions that eventually form clusters of similarities (words, for example: "dry," "dusty," "barren," "hot") and can be found by asking, "What is related to what?" Other units may be discovered by asking, "What follows what," so that the reader notices not only actions that follow each other but also juxtapositions of descriptions (for example, the dry, burning wind and the people in "Tuesday Siesta").

We begin to read a short story with anticipation. "Once upon a time" is the hidden, if not explicit, formula for settling into listening or reading. We anticipate resolution, if not in the characters' lives, then at least in the structure of the story itself. The relationships among units of a story eventually satisfy our anticipations, which begin with the first few sentences of a short story. As active readers of a text, we can begin to be aware of how the story establishes and fulfills our expectations. We notice that the first paragraph of "Tuesday Siesta" ends with "It was eleven in the morning, and the heat had not yet begun." What follows what? What do we expect? More than likely that the heat will begin. We are not disappointed: "By twelve the heat had begun." And later we find that at two o'clock "weighted down by drowsiness, the town was taking a siesta" and in some of the houses "it was so hot that the residents ate lunch in the patio." We may then begin to ask questions about relationships—about the scenery, objects, the weather, and the words and phrases that describe them. Are there connections, for example, between the description of the landscape at the beginning of "Tuesday Siesta" and the description of the town or its inhabitants? If so, what is the significance of the relationship? Finding an answer to those questions should grant us satisfaction.

Conscientious readers will regard the satisfaction of their anticipation as the author's means to tell them more than the narrator, who often merely reports situations. Perhaps we can further describe the design of a story an as interaction between anticipation and satisfaction of language units. If we feel dissatisfied, we can question whether or not the design of the story led us into false expectations or whether or not the actions of the story simply are not to our liking (in which case, we may still derive satisfaction from the story's language design).

We are attempting to forestall the complaint that "nothing happens," for in García Márquez's "Tuesday Siesta" and in Hemingway's "Cat in the Rain," one may indeed find little action of the adventure story variety. Despite the slow motion, are we justified in saying that *nothing* happens? Consider the author's shaping and structuring and use of language. By means of an awareness of design, we begin to discern relationships between the choice of settings and the characters in "Tuesday Siesta" and "Cat in the Rain." We discover that the rain in Hemingway's story offers a contrast with the dry, sterile lives of the couple, while the dry, barren landscape of García Márquez's story suggests an extension of the lives of his people. A great deal is happening, then, if we note the language choices as well as the characters while reading a story.

By means of point of view, tone, and design, authors from the nineteenth through the twentieth centuries suggest, rather than shout, their visions of what it means to be human and what it means to be a shaper of language. Study questions are provided at the end of each selection to help you discover the shapes and sounds of these stories.

The study questions, headnotes, and alternate table of contents are merely guides since you will learn that each work must be met on its own grounds. Some will emphasize action; others, character. In some, tone will dominate; in others, objects. All the stories in this anthology may be considered well made; that is, they are examples of Poe's prescription that everything in the story contributes to the overall effect, emotionally and intellectually. It is hoped that you will derive pleasure from the artistry of the design of these stories as well as knowledge about the relationships they dramatize.

EDGAR ALLAN POE

1809–1849

❧ Although he was born in Boston, went to school for three years in England, and lived for a short time in New York, Poe is considered to be a Southerner. He spent his boyhood in Richmond, Virginia, and attended the University of Virginia. As a student at the university, he began writing poetry and continued a literary career by publishing poetry, short stories, reviews, and one novel, *The Narrative of Arthur Gordon Pym* (1838). He edited several literary journals, including the *Southern Literary Messenger*, which was a leading critical magazine of its day. Poe's aesthetics of the short story have influenced modern expectations regarding form. In a review of Nathaniel Hawthorne's *Twice-Told Tales*, he advises the artist to create a unified design: "If his very first sentence tend not to the outbringing of this effect, then in his very first step has he committed a blunder. In the whole composition there should be no word written, of which the tendency, direct or indirect, is not to the one pre-established design" (*The Complete Works of Edgar Allan Poe*, ed. James A. Harrison, 17 vols. [New York: The Kelmscott Society, 1902], vol. 13, p. 153). The design in Poe's own tales reveals an interconnection between human beings as well as a tension between a surface, familiar world and a symbolic, suggestive world. He is especially concerned with an overemphasis of one quality, such as intelligence, at the sacrifice of another, such as emotion. As in "Ligeia," his stories dramatize the consequence of the sacrifice as a disintegration of human relationships and values.

Ligeia

And the will therein lieth, which dieth not. Who knoweth the mysteries of the will, with its vigor? For God is but a great will pervading all things by nature of its intentness. Man doth not yield himself to the angels, nor unto death utterly, save only through the weakness of his feeble will.

JOSEPH GLANVILL

I cannot, for my soul, remember how, when, or even precisely where, I first became acquainted with the lady Ligeia. Long years have since elapsed, and my memory is feeble through much suffering. Or, perhaps, I cannot *now* bring these points to mind, because, in truth, the character of my beloved, her rare learning, her singular yet placid cast of beauty, and the thrilling and enthralling eloquence

First published in the *Baltimore American Museum*, September 18, 1838. The final text is the *Broadway Journal*, September 27, 1845.

of her low musical language, made their way into my heart by paces so steadily and stealthily progressive that they have been unnoticed and unknown. Yet I believe that I met her first and most frequently in some large, old, decaying city near the Rhine. Of her family—I have surely heard her speak. That it is of a remotely ancient date cannot be doubted. Ligeia! Ligeia! Buried in studies of a nature more than all else adapted to deaden impressions of the outward world, it is by that sweet word alone—by Ligeia—that I bring before mine eyes in fancy the image of her who is no more. And now, while I write, a recollection flashes upon me that I have *never known* the paternal name of her who was my friend and my betrothed, and who became the partner of my studies, and finally the wife of my bosom. Was it a playful charge on the part of my Ligeia? or was it a test of my strength of affection, that I should institute no inquiries upon this point? or was it rather a caprice of my own—a wildly romantic offering on the shrine of the most passionate devotion? I but indistinctly recall the fact itself—what wonder that I have utterly forgotten the circumstances which originated or attended it? And, indeed, if ever that spirit which is entitled *Romance*—if ever she, the wan and the misty-winged *Ashtophet* of idolatrous Egypt, presided, as they tell, over marriages ill-omened, then most surely she presided over mine.

There is one dear topic, however, on which my memory fails me not. It is the *person* of Ligeia. In stature she was tall, somewhat slender, and, in her latter days, even emaciated. I would in vain attempt to portray the majesty, the quiet ease of her demeanor, or the incomprehensible lightness and elasticity of her footfall. She came and departed as a shadow. I was never made aware of her entrance into my closed study save by the dear music of her low sweet voice, as she placed her marble hand upon my shoulder. In beauty of face no maiden ever equalled her. It was the radiance of an opium-dream—an airy and spirit-lifting vision more wildly divine than the phantasies which hovered about the slumbering souls of the daughters of Delos. Yet her features were not of that regular mould which we have been falsely taught to worship in the classical labors of the heathen. "There is no exquisite beauty," says Bacon, Lord Verulam, speaking truly of all the forms and *genera* of beauty, "without some *strangeness* in the proportion." Yet, although I saw that the features of Ligeia were not of a classic regularity— although I perceived that her loveliness was indeed "exquisite," and felt that there was much of "strangeness" pervading it, yet I have tried in vain to detect the irregularity and to trace home my own perception of "the strange." I examined the contour of the lofty and pale forehead—it was faultless—how cold indeed that word when applied to a majesty so divine!—the skin rivalling the purest ivory, the commanding extent and repose, the gentle prominence of the regions above the temples; and then the raven-black, the glossy, the luxuriant and naturally-curling tresses, setting forth the full force of the Homeric epithet, "hyacinthine!" I looked at the delicate outlines of the nose—and nowhere but in the graceful medallions of the Hebrews had I beheld a similar perfection. There were the same luxurious smoothness of surface, the same scarcely perceptible tendency to the aquiline, the same harmoniously curved nostrils speaking the free spirit. I regarded the sweet mouth. Here was indeed the triumph of all things heavenly—the magnificent turn of the short upper lip—the soft, voluptuous slumber of the under—the dimples which sported, and the color which spoke—the teeth glancing back, with a brilliancy almost startling, every ray of the holy light which fell upon them in her serene and placid yet most exultingly radiant of all smiles. I scrutinized the formation of the chin—and, here too, I found the gentleness of breadth, the softness and the majesty, the fullness and the spirituality, of the Greek—the contour which the god Apollo revealed but in a dream, to Cleomenes, the son of the Athenian. And then I peered into the large eyes of Ligeia.

For eyes we have no models in the remotely antique. It might have been, too, that in these eyes of my beloved lay the secret to which Lord Verulam alludes. They were, I must believe, far larger than the ordinary eyes of our own race. They were even fuller than the fullest of the gazelle eyes of the tribe of the valley of Nourjahad. Yet it was only at intervals—in moments of intense excitement— that this peculiarity became more than slightly noticeable in Ligeia. And at such moments was her beauty—in my heated fancy thus it appeared perhaps—the beauty of beings either above or apart from the earth—the beauty of the fabulous Houri of the Turk. The hue of the orbs was the most brilliant of black, and, far over them, hung jetty lashes of great length. The brows, slightly irregular in outline, had the same tint. The "strangeness," however, which I found in the eyes, was of a nature distinct from the formation, or the color, or the brilliancy of the features, and must, after all, be referred to the *expression*. Ah, word of no meaning! behind whose vast latitude of mere sound we intrench our ignorance of so much of the spiritual. The expression of the eyes of Ligeia! How for long hours have I pondered upon it! How have I, through the whole of a midsummer night, struggled to fathom it! What was it—that some- thing more profound than the well of Democritus—which lay far within the pupils of my beloved? What *was* it? I was possessed with a passion to discover. Those eyes! those large, those shining, those divine orbs! they became to me twin stars of Leda, and I to them devoutest of astrologers.

There is no point, among the many incomprehensible anomalies of the science of mind, more thrillingly exciting than the fact— never, I believe, noticed in the schools—that in our endeavors to recall to memory something long forgotten, we often find ourselves *upon the very verge* of remembrance, without being able, in the end, to remember. And thus how frequently, in my intense scrutiny of Ligeia's eyes, have I felt approaching the full knowledge of their expression—felt it approaching—yet not quite be mine—and so at length entirely depart! And (strange, oh strangest mystery of all!) I found, in the commonest objects of the universe, a circle of analogies to that expression. I mean to say that, subsequently to the period when Ligeia's beauty passed into my spirit, there dwelling as in a shrine, I derived, from many existences in the material world, a sentiment such as I felt always aroused, within me, by her large and luminous orbs. Yet not the more could I define that sentiment, or analyze, or even steadily view it. I recognized it, let me repeat, sometimes in the survey of a rapidly growing vine—in the contemplation of a moth, a butterfly, a chrysalis, a stream of running water. I have felt it in the ocean; in the falling of a meteor. I have felt it in the glances of unusually aged people. And there are one or two stars in heaven—(one especially, a star of the sixth magnitude, double and changeable, to be found near the large star in Lyra) in a telescopic scrutiny of which I have been made aware of the feeling. I have been filled with it by certain sounds from stringed instruments, and not unfrequently by passages from books. Among innumerable other instances, I well remember something in a volume of Joseph Glanvill, which (perhaps from its quaintness—who shall say?) never failed to inspire me with the sentiment;—"And the will therein lieth, which dieth not. Who knoweth the mysteries of the will, with its vigor? For God is but a great will pervading all things by nature of its intentness. Man doth not yield him to the angels, nor unto death utterly, save only through the weakness of his feeble will."

Length of years, and subsequent reflection, have enabled me to trace, indeed, some remote connection between this passage in the English moralist and a portion of the character of Ligeia. An *intensity* in thought, action, or speech, was possible, in her, a result, or at least an index, of that gigantic volition which, during our long intercourse, failed to give other and more immediate evidence of its existence. Of all the women whom I have ever known, she, the outwardly calm, the ever-placid Ligeia, was the most violently a prey to the tumultuous vultures of stern passion. And of such passion I could form no estimate, save by the miraculous expansion of those eyes which at once so delighted and appalled me—by the almost magical melody, modulation, distinctness, and placidity of her very low voice—and by the fierce energy (rendered doubly effective by contrast with her manner of utterance) of the wild words which she habitually uttered.

I have spoken of the learning of Ligeia; it was immense—such as I have never known in woman. In the classical tongues was she deeply proficient, and as far as my own acquaintance extended in regard to the modern dialects of Europe, I have never known her at fault. Indeed upon any theme of the most admired, because simply the most abstruse of the boasted erudition of the academy, have I *ever* found Ligeia at fault? How singularly—how thrillingly, this one point in the nature of my wife has forced itself, at this late period only, upon my attention! I said her knowledge was such as I have never known in a woman—but where breathes the man who has traversed, and successfully, *all* the wide areas of moral, physical, and mathematical science? I saw not then what I now clearly perceive, that the acquisitions of Ligeia were gigantic, were astounding; yet I was sufficiently aware of her infinite supremacy to resign myself, with a child-like confidence, to her guidance through the chaotic world of metaphysical investigation at which I was most busily occupied during the earlier years of our marriage. With how vast a triumph—with how vivid a delight—with how much of all that is ethereal in hope—did I *feel*, as she bent over me in studies but little sought—but less known—that delicious vista by slow degrees expanding before me, down whose long, gorgeous, and all untrodden path, I might at length pass onward to the goal of a wisdom too divinely precious not to be forbidden!

How poignant, then, must have been the grief with which, after some years, I beheld my well-grounded expectations take wings to themselves and fly away! Without Ligeia I was but as a child groping benighted. Her presence, her readings alone, rendered vividly luminous the many mysteries of the transcendentalism in which we were immersed. Wanting the radiant lustre of her eyes, letters, lambent and golden, grew duller than Saturnian lead. And now those eyes shone less and less frequently upon the pages over which I pored. Ligeia grew ill. The wild eyes blazed with a too—too glorious effulgence; the pale fingers became of the transparent waxen hue of the grave; and the blue veins upon the lofty forehead swelled and sank impetuously with the tides of the most gentle emotion. I saw that she must die—and I struggled desperately in spirit with the grim Azrael. And the struggles of the passionate wife were, to my astonishment, even more energetic than my own. There had been much in her stern nature to impress me with the belief that, to her, death would have come without its terrors; but not so. Words are impotent to convey any just idea of the fierceness of resistance with which she wrestled with the Shadow. I groaned in anguish at the pitiable spectacle. I would have soothed—I would have reasoned; but, in the intensity of her wild desire for life,—for life—*but* for life—solace and reason were alike the uttermost folly. Yet not until the last instance, amid the most convulsive writhings of her fierce spirit, was shaken the external placidity of her demeanor. Her voice grew more gentle—grew more low—yet I would not wish to dwell upon the wild meaning of the quietly uttered words. My brain reeled as I hearkened entranced, to a melody more than mortal—to assumptions and aspirations which mortality had never before known.

That she loved me I should not have doubted; and I might have been easily aware that, in a bosom such as hers, love would have reigned no ordinary passion. But in death only was I fully impressed with the strength of her affection. For long hours, detaining my hand, would she pour out before me the overflowing of a heart whose more than passionate devotion amounted to idolatry. How had I deserved to be so blessed by such confessions?—how had I deserved to be so cursed with the removal of my beloved in the hour of her making them? But upon this subject I cannot bear to dilate. Let me say only, that in Ligeia's more than womanly abandonment to a love, alas! all unmerited, all unworthily bestowed, I at length recognized the principle of her longing with so wildly earnest a desire for the life which was now fleeing so rapidly away. It is this wild longing—it is this eager vehemence of desire for life —*but* for life—that I have no power to portray—no utterance capable of expressing.

At high noon of the night in which she departed, beckoning me, peremptorily, to her side, she bade me repeat certain verses composed by herself not many days before. I obeyed her.—They were these:

> Lo! 'tis a gala night
>   Within the lonesome latter years!
> An angel throng, bewinged, bedight
>   In veils, and drowned in tears,
> Sit in a theatre, to see
>   A play of hopes and fears,
> While the orchestra breathes fitfully
>   The music of the spheres.
>
> Mimes, in the form of God on high,
>   Mutter and mumble low,
> And hither and thither fly—
>   Mere puppets they, who come and go
> At bidding of vast formless things
>   That shift the scenery to and fro,
> Flapping from out their Condor wings
>   Invisible Wo!
>
> That motley drama—oh, be sure
>   It shall not be forgot!
> With its Phantom chased forever more,
>   By a crowd that seize it not,
> Through a circle that ever returneth in
>   To the self-same spot,
> And much of Madness and more of Sin
>   And Horror the soul of the plot.
>
> But see, amid the mimic rout,
>   A crawling shape intrude!
> A blood-red thing that writhes from out
>   The scenic solitude!

It writhes!—it writhes!—with mortal pangs
The mimes become its food,
And the seraphs sob at vermin fangs
In human gore imbued.

Out—out are the lights—out all!
And over each quivering form,
The curtain, a funeral pall,
Comes down with the rush of a storm,
And the angels, all pallid and wan,
Uprising, unveiling, affirm
That the play is the tragedy, "Man,"
And its hero the Conqueror Worm.

"O God!" half shrieked Ligeia, leaping to her feet and extending her arms aloft with a spasmodic movement, as I made an end of these lines—"O God! O Divine Father!—shall these things be undeviatingly so?—shall this Conqueror be not once conquered? Are we not part and parcel in Thee? Who—who knoweth the mysteries of the will with its vigor? Man doth not yield him to the angels, *nor unto death utterly,* save only through the weakness of his feeble will."

And now, as if exhausted with emotion, she suffered her white arms to fall, and returned solemnly to her bed of death. And as she breathed her last sighs, there came mingled with them a low murmur from her lips. I bent to them my ear, and distinguished, again, the concluding words of the passage in Glanvill—"*Man doth not yield him to the angels, nor unto death utterly, save only through the weakness of his feeble will.*"

She died;—and I, crushed into the very dust with sorrow, could no longer endure the lonely desolation of my dwelling in the dim and decaying city by the Rhine. I had no lack of what the world calls wealth. Ligeia had brought me far more, very far more than ordinarily falls to the lot of mortals. After a few months, therefore, of weary and aimless wandering, I purchased, and put in some repair, an abbey, which I shall not name, in one of the wildest and least frequented portions of fair England. The gloomy and dreary grandeur of the building, the almost savage aspect of the domain, the many melancholy and time-honored memories connected with both, had much in unison with the feelings of utter abandonment which had driven me into that remote and unsocial region of the country. Yet although the external abbey, with its verdent decay hanging about it, suffered but little alteration, I gave way, with a child-like perversity, and perchance with a faint hope of alleviating my sorrows, to a display of more than regal magnificence within.— For such follies, even in childhood, I had imbibed a taste, and now they came back to me as if in the dotage of grief. Alas, I feel how much even of incipient madness might have been discovered in the gorgeous and fantastic draperies, in the solemn carvings of Egypt, in the wild cornices and furniture, in the Bedlam patterns of the carpets of tufted gold! I had become a bounden slave in the trammels of opium, and my labors and orders had taken a coloring from my dreams. But these absurdities I must not pause to detail. Let me speak only of that one chamber, ever accursed, whither, in a moment of mental alienation, I led from the altar as my bride—as the successor of the unforgotten Ligeia—the fair-haired and blue-eyed Lady Rowena Trevanion, of Tremaine.

There is no individual portion of the architecture and decoration of that bridal chamber which is not now visibly before me. Where were the souls of the haughty family of the bride, when, through thirst of gold, they permitted to pass the threshold of an apartment so bedecked, a maiden and a daughter so beloved? I have said that I minutely remember the details of the chamber—yet I am sadly forgetful on topics of deep moment—and here there was no system, no keeping, in the fantastic display, to take hold upon the memory. The room lay in a high turret of the castellated abbey, was pentagonal in shape, and of capacious size. Occupying the whole southern face of the pentagon was the sole window—an immense sheet of broken glass from Venice—a single pane, and tinted of a leaden hue, so that the rays of either the sun or moon, passing through it, fell with a ghastly lustre on the objects within. Over the upper portion of this huge window, extended the trellis-work of an aged vine, which clambered up the massy walls of the turret. The ceiling, of gloomy-looking oak, was excessively lofty, vaulted, and elaborately fretted with the wildest and most grotesque specimens of a semi-Gothic, semi-Druidical device. From out the most central recess of this melancholy vaulting, depended, by a single chain of gold with long links, a huge censer of the same metal, Saracenic in pattern, and with many perforations so contrived that there writhed in and out of them, as if endued with a serpent vitality, a continual succession of parti-colored fires.

Some few ottomans and golden candelabra, of Eastern figure, were in various stations about—and there was the couch, too—the bridal couch—of an Indian model, and low, and sculptured of solid ebony, with a pall-like canopy above. In each of the angles of the chamber stood on end a gigantic sarcophagus of black granite, from the tombs of the kings over against Luxor, with their aged lids full of immemorial sculpture. But in the draping of the apartment lay, alas! the chief phantasy of all. The lofty walls, gigantic in height—even unproportionably so—were hung from summit to foot, in vast folds, with a heavy and massive-looking tapestry—tapestry of a material which was found alike as a carpet on the floor, as a covering for the ottomans and the ebony bed, as a canopy for the bed and as the gorgeous volutes of the curtains which partially shaded the window. The material was the richest cloth of gold. It was spotted all over, at irregular intervals, with arabesque figures, about a foot in diameter, and wrought upon the cloth in patterns of the most jetty black. But these figures partook of the true character of the arabesque only when regarded from a single point of view. By a contrivance now common, and indeed traceable to a very remote period of antiquity, they were made changeable in aspect. To one entering the room, they bore the appearance of simple monstrosities; but upon a farther advance, this appearance gradually departed; and step by step, as the visitor moved his station in the chamber, he saw himself surrounded by an endless succession of the ghastly forms which belong to the superstition of the Norman, or arise in the guilty slumbers of the monk. The phantasmagoric effect was vastly heightened by the artificial introduction of a strong continual current of wind behind the draperies—giving a hideous and uneasy animation to the whole.

In halls such as these—in a bridal chamber such as this—I passed, with the Lady of Tremaine, the unhallowed hours of the first month of our marriage—passed them with but little disquietude. That my wife dreaded the fierce moodiness of my temper—that she shunned me and loved me but little—I could not help perceiving; but it gave me rather pleasure than otherwise. I loathed her with a hatred belonging more to demon than to man. My memory flew back, (oh, with what intensity of regret!) to Ligeia, the beloved, the august, the beautiful, the entombed. I revelled in recollections of her purity, of her wisdom, of her lofty, her ethereal nature, of her passionate, her idolatrous love. Now, then, did my spirit fully and freely burn with more than all the fires of her own. In the excitement of my opium dreams (for I was habitually fettered in the shackles of the drug) I would call aloud upon her name, during the silence of the night, or among the sheltered recesses of the glens by day, as if, through the wild eagerness, the solemn passion, the consuming ardor of my longing for the departed, I could restore her to the pathways she had abandoned—ah, *could* it be forever?—upon the earth.

About the commencement of the second month of the marriage, the Lady Rowena was attacked with sudden illness, from which her recovery was slow. The fever which consumed her rendered her nights uneasy; and in her perturbed state of half-slumber, she spoke of sounds, and of motions, in and above the chamber of the turret, which I concluded had no origin save in the distemper of her fancy, or perhaps in the phantasmagoric influences of the chamber itself. She became at length convalescent—finally well. Yet but a brief period elapsed, ere a second more violent disorder again threw her upon a bed of suffering; and from this attack her frame, at all times feeble, never altogether recovered. Her illnesses were, after this epoch, of alarming character and of more alarming recurrence, defying alike the knowledge and the great exertions of her physicians. With the increase of the chronic disease which had thus, apparently, taken too sure hold upon her constitution to be eradicated by human means, I could not fail to observe a similar increase in the nervous irritation of her temperament, and in her excitability by trivial causes of fear. She spoke again, and now more frequently and pertinaciously, of the sounds—of the slight sounds —and of the unusual motions among the tapestries, to which she had formerly alluded.

One night, near the closing in of September, she pressed this distressing subject with more than usual emphasis upon my attention. She had just awakened from an unquiet slumber, and I had been watching, with feelings half of anxiety, half of vague terror, the workings of her emaciated countenance. I sat by the side of her ebony bed, upon one of the ottomans of India. She partly arose, and spoke, in an earnest low whisper, of sounds which she *then* heard, but which I could not hear—of motions which she *then* saw, but which I could not perceive. The wind was rushing hurriedly behind the tapestries, and I wished to show her (what, let me confess it, I could not *all* believe) that those almost inarticulate breathings, and those very gentle variations of the figures upon the wall, were but the natural effects of that customary rushing of the wind. But a deadly pallor, overspreading her face, had proved to me that my exertions to reassure her would be fruitless. She appeared to be fainting, and no attendants were within call. I remembered where was deposited a decanter of light wine which had been ordered by her physicians, and hastened across the chamber to procure it. But, as I stepped beneath the light of the censer, two circumstances of a startling nature attracted my attention. I had felt that some palpable although invisible object had passed lightly by my person; and I saw that there lay upon the golden carpet, in the very middle of the rich lustre thrown from the censer, a shadow—a faint, indefinite shadow of angelic aspect—such as might be fancied for the shadow of a shade. But I was wild with the excitement of an immoderate dose of opium, and heeded these things but little, nor spoke of them to Rowena. Having found the wine, I recrossed the chamber, and poured out a goblet-ful, which I held to the lips of the fainting lady. She had now partially recovered, however, and took the vessel herself, while I sank upon an ottoman near me, with my eyes fastened upon her person. It was then that I became distinctly aware of a gentle foot-fall upon the carpet, and near the couch; and in a second thereafter, as Rowena was in the act of raising the wine to her lips, I saw, or may have dreamed that I saw, fall within the goblet, as if from some invisible spring in the atmosphere of the room, three or four large drops of a brilliant and ruby colored fluid. If this I saw—not so Rowena. She swallowed the wine unhesitatingly, and I forbore to speak to her of a circumstance which must, after all, I considered, have been but the suggestion of a vivid imagination, rendered morbidly active by the terror of the lady, by the opium, and by the hour.

Yet I cannot conceal it from my own perception that, immediately subsequent to the fall of the ruby-drops, a rapid change for the worse took place in the disorder of my wife; so that, on the third subsequent night, the hands of her menials prepared her for the tomb, and on the fourth, I sat alone, with her shrouded body, in that fantastic chamber which had received her as my bride.—Wild visions, opium-engendered, flitted, shadowlike, before me. I gazed with unquiet eye upon the sarcophagi in the angles of the room, upon the varying figures of the drapery, and upon the writhing of the parti-colored fires in the censer overhead. My eyes then fell, as I called to mind the circumstances of a former night, to the spot beneath the glare of the censer where I had seen the faint traces of the shadow. It was there, however, no longer; and breathing with greater freedom, I turned my glances to the pallid and rigid figure upon the bed. Then rushed upon me a thousand memories of Ligeia —and then came back upon my heart, with the turbulent violence of a flood, the whole of that unutterable woe with which I had regarded *her* thus enshrouded. The night waned; and still, with a bosom full of bitter thoughts of the one only and supremely be- loved, I remained gazing upon the body of Rowena.

It might have been midnight, or perhaps earlier, or later, for I had taken no note of time, when a sob, low, gentle, but very distinct, startled me from my revery.—I *felt* that it came from the bed of ebony—the bed of death. I listened in an agony of superstitious terror—but there was no repetition of the sound. I strained my vision to detect any motion in the corpse—but there was not the slightest perceptible. Yet I could not have been deceived. I *had* heard the noise, however faint, and my soul was awakened within me. I resolutely and perseveringly kept my attention riveted upon the body. Many minutes elapsed before any circumstance occurred tending to throw light upon the mystery. At length it became evident that a slight, a very feeble, and barely noticeable tinge of color had flushed up within the cheeks, and along the sunken small veins of the eyelids. Through a species of unutterable horror and awe, for which the language of mortality has no sufficiently energetic expression, I felt my heart cease to beat, my limbs grow rigid where I sat. Yet a sense of duty finally operated to restore my self-possession. I could no longer doubt that we had been precipitate in our preparations—that Rowena still lived. It was necessary that some immediate exertion be made; yet the turret was altogether apart from the portion of the abbey tenanted by the servants— there were none within call—I had no means of summoning them to my aid without leaving the room for many minutes—and this I could not venture to do. I therefore struggled alone in my endeavors to call back the spirit still hovering. In a short period it was certain, however, that a relapse had taken place; the color disappeared from both eyelid and cheek, leaving a wanness even more that that of marble; the lips became doubly shrivelled and pinched up in the ghastly expression of death; a repulsive clamminess and coldness overspread rapidly the surface of the body; and all the usual rigorous stiffness immediately supervened. I fell back with a shudder upon the couch from which I had been so startlingly aroused, and again gave myself up to passionate waking visions of Ligeia.

An hour thus elapsed when (could it be possible?) I was a second time aware of some vague sound issuing from the region of the bed. I listened—in extremity of horror. The sound came again—it was a sigh. Rushing to the corpse, I saw—distinctly saw—a tremor upon the lips. In a minute afterward they relaxed, disclosing a bright line of the pearly teeth. Amazement now struggled in my bosom with the profound awe which had hitherto reigned there alone. I felt that my vision grew dim, that my reason wandered; and it was only by a violent effort that I at length succeeded in nerving myself to the task which duty thus once more had pointed out. There was now a partial glow upon the forehead and upon the cheek and throat; a perceptible warmth pervaded the whole frame; there was even a slight pulsation at the heart. The lady *lived;* and with redoubled ardor I betook myself to the task of restoration. I chafed and bathed the temples and the hands, and used every exertion which experience, and no little medical reading, could suggest. But in vain. Suddenly, the color fled, the pulsation ceased, the lips resumed the expression of the dead, and, in an instant afterward, the whole body took upon itself the icy chilliness, the livid hue, the intense rigidity, the sunken outline, and all the loathsome peculiarities of that which has been, for many days, a tenant of the tomb.

And again I sunk into visions of Ligeia—and again, (what marvel that I shudder while I write?) *again* there reached my ears a low sob from the region of the ebony bed. But why shall I minutely detail the unspeakable horrors of that night? Why shall I pause to relate how, time after time, until near the period of the gray dawn, this hideous drama of revivification was repeated; how each terrific relapse was only into a sterner and apparently more irredeemable death; how each agony wore the aspect of a struggle with some invisible foe; and how each struggle was succeeded by I know not what of wild change in the personal appearance of the corpse? Let me hurry to a conclusion.

The greater part of the fearful night had worn away, and she who had been dead once again stirred—and now more vigorously than hitherto, although arousing from a dissolution more appalling in its utter hopelessness than any. I had long ceased to struggle or to move, and remained sitting rigidly upon the ottoman, a helpless prey to a whirl of violent emotions, of which extreme awe was perhaps the least terrible, the least consuming. The corpse, I repeat, stirred, and now more vigorously than before. The hues of life flushed up with unwonted energy into the countenance—the limbs relaxed—and, save that the eyelids were yet pressed heavily together, and that the bandages and draperies of the grave still imparted their charnel character to the figure, I might have dreamed that Rowena had indeed shaken off, utterly, the fetters of Death. But if this idea was not, even then, altogether adopted, I could at least doubt no longer, when, arising from the bed, tottering, with feeble steps, with closed eyes, and with the manner of one bewildered in a dream, the thing that was enshrouded advanced boldly and palpably into the middle of the apartment.

I trembled not—I stirred not—for a crowd of unutterable fancies connected with the air, the stature, the demeanor of the figure, rushing hurriedly through my brain, had paralyzed—had chilled me into stone. I stirred not—but gazed upon the apparition. There was a mad disorder in my thoughts—a tumult unappeasable. Could it, indeed, be the *living* Rowena who confronted me? Could it, indeed, be Rowena *at all*—the fair-haired, the blue-eyed Lady Rowena Trevanion of Tremaine? Why, *why* should I doubt it? The bandage lay heavily about the mouth—but then might it not be the mouth of the breathing Lady of Tremaine? And the cheeks—there were the roses as in her noon of life—yes, these might indeed be the fair cheeks of the living Lady of Tremaine. And the chin, with its dimples, as in health, might it not be hers?—but *had she then grown taller since her malady?* What inexpressible madness seized me with that thought? One bound, and I had reached her feet! Shrinking from my touch, she let fall from her head, unloosened, the ghastly cerements which has confined it, and there streamed forth into the rushing atmosphere of the chamber huge masses of long and dishevelled hair, *it was blacker than the raven wings of midnight!* And now slowly opened *the eyes* of the figure which stood before me. "Here then, at least," I shrieked aloud, "can I never—can I never be mistaken—these are the full, and the black, and the wild eyes—of my lost love—of the Lady—of the LADY LIGEIA."

Discussion of Poe's "Ligeia"

1. Remembering Poe's remarks on the importance of the initial statement in a story, notice the specific wording of the first sentence in "Ligeia." How does it contribute to the overall effect of the story?

2. Notice the emphasis on the word "Ligeia" throughout the story. What is the narrator's attitude about the limitations of language? How does Poe dramatize not only the limitations but also the possibilities of language?

3. How does the setting suggest the state of mind of the narrator? When we meet him, what is his state of mind?

4. By means of the narrator's response to his wives, what does Poe suggest about men's attitudes towards women? Compare this husband with the one created by Hawthorne in "The Birthmark."

NATHANIEL HAWTHORNE

1804–1864

In Salem, Massachusetts, there still stand the house in which Nathaniel Hawthorne was born, the "house of the seven gables," and the custom house where he worked in the 1840s. Boston, Salem, Lenox, and Concord, Massachusetts were his residences, except for a few years when he lived and traveled in England, France, and Italy. Wherever he lived, Hawthorne gathered material for his numerous stories and novels. *The Scarlet Letter* (1850) is set in colonial New England, *The House of the Seven Gables* (1851) in contemporary New England, and *The Marble Faun* (1860) in Rome. In his preface to *The House of the Seven Gables* Hawthorne maintains that art can stress a moral, but it must do so subtly: "The Author has considered it hardly worth his while, therefore, relentlessly to impale the story with its moral as with an iron rod—or rather, as by sticking a pin through a butterfly—thus at once depriving it of life, and causing it to stiffen in an ungainly and unnatural attitude" (*The Centenary Edition of the Works of Nathaniel Hawthorne,* ed. William Charvat, Roy Harvey Pearce, et al. [Columbus: Ohio State University Press, 1965], vol. 2, p. 2). Hawthorne infuses a double life into his fiction by casting the familiar, actual world in an imaginative atmosphere and thus broadening our understanding of art and life. In almost all of his writings, Hawthorne suggests that to live fully, one must always maintain sympathy for and acceptance of human fallibility.

The Birthmark

In the latter part of the last century there lived a man of science, an eminent proficient in every branch of natural philosophy, who not long before our story opens had made experience of a spiritual affinity more attractive than any chemical one. He had left his laboratory to the care of an assistant, cleared his fine countenance from the furnace smoke, washed the stain of acids from his fingers, and persuaded a beautiful woman to become his wife. In those days, when the comparatively recent discovery of electricity and other kindred mysteries of Nature seemed to open paths into the region of miracle, it was not unusual for the love of science to rival the love of woman in its depth and absorbing energy. The higher intellect, the imagination, the spirit, and even the heart might all find their congenial aliment in pursuits which, as some of their ardent votaries believed, would ascend from one step of powerful intelligence to another, until the philosopher should lay his hand

From *The Pioneer,* March 1843; collected in *Mosses from an Old Manse,* Wiley & Putnam, 1846.

on the secret of creative force and perhaps make new worlds for himself. We know not whether Aylmer possessed this degree of faith in man's ultimate control over Nature. He had devoted himself, however, too unreservedly to scientific studies ever to be weaned from them by any second passion. His love for his young wife might prove the stronger of the two; but it could only be by intertwining itself with his love of science and uniting the strength of the latter to his own.

Such a union accordingly took place, and was attended with truly remarkable consequences and a deeply impressive moral. One day, very soon after their marriage, Aylmer sat gazing at his wife with a trouble in his countenance that grew stronger until he spoke.

"Georgiana," said he, "has it never occurred to you that the mark upon your cheek might be removed?"

"No, indeed," said she, smiling; but, perceiving the seriousness of his manner, she blushed deeply. "To tell you the truth, it has been so often called a charm that I was simple enough to imagine it might be so."

"Ah, upon another face perhaps it might," replied her husband; "but never on yours. No, dearest Georgiana, you came so nearly perfect from the hand of Nature that this slightest possible defect, which we hesitate whether to term a defect or a beauty, shocks me, as being the visible mark of earthly imperfection."

"Shocks you, my husband!" cried Georgiana, deeply hurt; at first reddening with momentary anger, but then bursting into tears. "Then why did you take me from my mother's side? You cannot love what shocks you!"

To explain this conversation, it must be mentioned that in the centre of Georgiana's left cheek there was a singular mark, deeply interwoven, as it were, with the texture and substance of her face. In the usual state of her complexion—a healthy though delicate bloom—the mark wore a tint of deeper crimson, which imperfectly defined its shape amid the surrounding rosiness. When she blushed it gradually became more indistinct, and finally vanished amid the triumphant rush of blood that bathed the whole cheek with its brilliant glow. But if any shifting motion caused her to turn pale there was the mark again, a crimson stain upon the snow, in what Aylmer sometimes deemed an almost fearful distinctness. Its shape bore not a little similarity to the human hand, though of the smallest pygmy size. Georgiana's lovers were wont to say that some fairy at her birth hour had laid her tiny hand upon the infant's cheek, and left this impress there in token of the magic endowments that were to give her such sway over all hearts. Many a desperate swain would have risked life for the privilege of pressing his lips to the mysterious hand. It must not be concealed, however, that the impression wrought by this fairy sign manual varied exceedingly according to the difference of temperament in the beholders. Some fastidious persons—but they were exclusively of her own sex—

affirmed that the bloody hand, as they chose to call it, quite destroyed the effect of Georgiana's beauty and rendered her countenance even hideous. But it would be as reasonable to say that one of those small blue stains which sometimes occur in the purest statuary marble would convert the Eve of Powers to a monster. Masculine observers, if the birthmark did not heighten their admiration, contented themselves with wishing it away, that the world might possess one living specimen of ideal loveliness without the semblance of a flaw. After his marriage,—for he thought little or nothing of the matter before,—Aylmer discovered that this was the case with himself.

Had she been less beautiful,—if Envy's self could have found aught else to sneer at,—he might have felt his affection heightened by the prettiness of this mimic hand, now vaguely portrayed, now lost, now stealing forth again and glimmering to and fro with every pulse of emotion that throbbed within her heart; but, seeing her otherwise so perfect, he found this one defect grow more and more intolerable with every moment of their united lives. It was the fatal flaw of humanity which Nature, in one shape or another, stamps ineffaceably on all her productions, either to imply that they are temporary and finite, or that their perfection must be wrought by toil and pain. The crimson hand expressed the ineludible gripe in which mortality clutches the highest and purest of earthly mould, degrading them into kindred with the lowest, and even with the very brutes, like whom their visible frames return to dust. In this manner, selecting it as the symbol of his wife's liability to sin, sorrow, decay, and death, Aylmer's sombre imagination was not long in rendering the birthmark a frightful object, causing him more trouble and horror than ever Georgiana's beauty, whether of soul or sense, had given him delight.

At all the seasons which should have been their happiest he invariably, and without intending it, nay, in spite of a purpose to the contrary, reverted to this one disastrous topic. Trifling as it at first appeared, it so connected itself with innumerable trains of thought and modes of feeling that it became the central point of all. With the morning twilight Aylmer opened his eyes upon his wife's face and recognized the symbol of imperfection; and when they sat together at the evening hearth his eyes wandered stealthily to her cheek, and beheld, flickering with the blaze of the wood fire, the spectral hand that wrote mortality where he would fain have worshipped. Georgiana soon learned to shudder at his gaze. It needed but a glance with the peculiar expression that his face often wore to change the roses of her cheeks into a deathlike paleness, amid which the crimson hand was brought strongly out, like a bas-relief of ruby on the whitest marble.

Late one night, when the lights were growing dim so as hardly to betray the stain on the poor wife's cheek, she herself, for the first time, voluntarily took up the subject.

"Do you remember, my dear Aylmer," said she, with a feeble attempt at a smile, "have you any recollection, of a dream last night about this odious hand?"

"None! none whatever!" replied Aylmer, starting; but then he added, in a dry, cold tone, affected for the sake of concealing the real depth of his emotion, "I might well dream of it; for, before I fell asleep, it had taken a pretty firm hold of my fancy."

"And you did dream of it?" continued Georgiana, hastily; for she dreaded lest a gush of tears should interrupt what she had to say. "A terrible dream! I wonder that you can forget it. Is it possible to forget this one expression?—'It is in her heart now; we must have it out!' Reflect, my husband; for by all means I would have you recall that dream."

The mind is in a sad state when Sleep, the all-involving, cannot confine her spectres within the dim region of her sway, but suffers them to break forth, affrighting this actual life with secrets that perchance belong to a deeper one. Aylmer now remembered his dream. He had fancied himself with his servant Aminadab, attempting an operation for the removal of the birthmark; but the deeper went the knife, the deeper sank the hand, until at length its tiny grasp appeared to have caught hold of Georgiana's heart; whence, however, her husband was inexorably resolved to cut or wrench it away.

When the dream had shaped itself perfectly in his memory Aylmer sat in his wife's presence with a guilty feeling. Truth often finds its way to the mind close muffled in robes of sleep, and then speaks with uncompromising directness of matters in regard to which we practise an unconscious self-deception during our waking moments. Until now he had not been aware of the tyrannizing influence acquired by one idea over his mind, and of the lengths which he might find in his heart to go for the sake of giving himself peace.

"Aylmer," resumed Georgiana, solemnly, "I know not what may be the cost to both of us to rid me of this fatal birthmark. Perhaps its removal may cause cureless deformity; or it may be the stain goes as deep as life itself. Again: do we know that there is a possibility, on any terms, of unclasping the firm gripe of this little hand which was laid upon me before I came into the world?"

"Dearest Georgiana, I have spent much thought upon the subject," hastily interrupted Aylmer. "I am convinced of the perfect practicability of its removal."

"If there be the remotest possibility of it," continued Georgiana, "let the attempt be made, at whatever risk. Danger is nothing to me; for life, while this hateful mark makes me the object of your horror and disgust,—life is a burden which I would fling down with joy. Either remove this dreadful hand, or take my wretched life! You have deep science. All the world bears witness of it. You have achieved great wonders. Cannot you remove this little mark, which I cover with the tips of two small fingers? Is this beyond your power, for the sake of your own peace, and to save your poor wife from madness?"

"Noblest, dearest, tenderest wife," cried Aylmer, rapturously, "doubt not my power. I have already given this matter the deepest thought—thought which might almost have enlightened me to create a being less perfect than yourself. Georgiana, you have led me deeper than ever into the heart of science. I feel myself fully competent to render this dear cheek as faultless as its fellow; and then, most beloved, what will be my triumph when I shall have corrected what Nature left imperfect in her fairest work! Even Pygmalion, when his sculptured woman assumed life, felt not greater ecstasy than mine will be."

"It is resolved, then," said Georgiana, faintly smiling. "And, Aylmer, spare me not, though you should find the birthmark take refuge in my heart at last."

Her husband tenderly kissed her cheek—her right cheek—not that which bore the impress of the crimson hand.

The next day Aylmer apprised his wife of a plan that he had formed whereby he might have opportunity for the intense thought and constant watchfulness which the proposed operation would require; while Georgiana, likewise, would enjoy the perfect repose essential to its success. They were to seclude themselves in the extensive apartments occupied by Aylmer as a laboratory, and where, during his toilsome youth, he had made discoveries in the elemental powers of Nature that had roused the admiration of all the learned societies in Europe. Seated calmly in this laboratory, the pale philosopher had investigated the secrets of the highest cloud region and of the profoundest mines; he had satisfied himself of the causes that kindled and kept alive the fires of the volcano; and had explained the mystery of fountains, and how it is that they gush forth, some so bright and pure, and others with such rich medicinal virtues, from the dark bosom of the earth. Here, too, at an earlier period, he had studied the wonders of the human frame, and attempted to fathom the very process by which Nature assimilates all her precious influences from earth and air, and from the spiritual world, to create and foster man, her masterpiece. The latter pursuit, however, Aylmer had long laid aside in unwilling recognition of the truth—against which all seekers sooner or later stumble—that our great creative Mother, while she amuses us with apparently working in the broadest sunshine, is yet severely careful to keep her own secrets, and, in spite of her pretended openness, shows us nothing but results. She permits us, indeed, to mar, but seldom to mend, and, like a jealous patentee, on no account to make. Now, however, Aylmer resumed these half-forgotten investigations; not, of course, with such hopes or wishes as first suggested them; but because they involved much physiological truth and lay in the path of his proposed scheme for the treatment of Georgiana.

As he led her over the threshold of the laboratory, Georgiana was cold and tremulous. Aylmer looked cheerfully into her face, with intent to reassure her, but was so startled with the intense glow of the birthmark upon the whiteness of her cheek that he could not restrain a strong convulsive shudder. His wife fainted.

"Aminadab! Aminadab!" shouted Aylmer, stamping violently on the floor.

Forthwith there issued from an inner apartment a man of low stature, but bulky frame, with shaggy hair hanging about his visage, which was grimed with the vapors of the furnace. This personage had been Aylmer's underworker during his whole scientific career, and was admirably fitted for that office by his great mechanical readiness, and the skill with which, while incapable of comprehending a single principle, he executed all the details of his master's experiments. With his vast strength, his shaggy hair, his smoky aspect, and the indescribable earthiness that incrusted him, he seemed to represent man's physical nature; while Aylmer's slender figure, and pale, intellectual face, were no less apt a type of the spiritual element.

"Throw open the door of the boudoir, Aminadab," said Aylmer, "and burn a pastil."

"Yes, master," answered Aminadab, looking intently at the lifeless form of Georgiana; and then he muttered to himself, "If she were my wife, I'd never part with that birthmark."

When Georgiana recovered consciousness she found herself breathing an atmosphere of penetrating fragrance, the gentle potency of which had recalled her from her deathlike faintness. The scene around her looked like enchantment. Aylmer had converted those smoky, dingy, sombre rooms, where he had spent his brightest years in recondite pursuits, into a series of beautiful apartments not unfit to be the secluded abode of a lovely woman. The walls were hung with gorgeous curtains, which imparted the combination of grandeur and grace that no other species of adornment can achieve; and, as they fell from the ceiling to the floor, their rich and ponderous folds, concealing all angles and straight lines, appeared to shut in the scene from infinite space. For aught Georgiana knew, it might be a pavilion among the clouds. And Aylmer, excluding the sunshine, which would have interfered with his chemical processes, had supplied its place with perfumed lamps, emitting flames of various hue, but all uniting in a soft, impurpled radiance. He now knelt by his wife's side, watching her earnestly, but without alarm; for he was confident in his science, and felt he could draw a magic circle round her within which no evil might intrude.

"Where am I? Ah, I remember," said Georgiana, faintly; and she placed her hand over her cheek to hide the terrible mark from her husband's eyes.

"Fear not, dearest!" exclaimed he. "Do not shrink from me! Believe me, Georgiana, I even rejoice in this single imperfection, since it will be such a rapture to remove it."

"O, spare me!" sadly replied his wife. "Pray do not look at it again. I never can forget that convulsive shudder."

In order to soothe Georgiana, and, as it were, to release her mind from the burden of actual things, Aylmer now put in practice some of the light and playful secrets which science had taught him among its profounder lore. Airy figures, absolutely bodiless ideas, and forms of unsubstantial beauty came and danced before her, imprinting their momentary footsteps on beams of light. Though she had some indistinct idea of the method of these optical phenomena, still the illusion was almost perfect enough to warrant the belief that her husband possessed sway over the spiritual world. Then again, when she felt a wish to look forth from her seclusion, immediately, as if her thoughts were answered, the procession of external existence flitted across a screen. The scenery and the figures of actual life were perfectly represented, but with that bewitching yet indescribable difference which always makes a picture, an image, or a shadow so much more attractive than the original. When wearied of this, Aylmer bade her cast her eyes upon a vessel containing a quantity of earth. She did so, with little interest at first; but was soon startled to perceive the germ of a plant shooting upward from the soil. Then came the slender stalk; the leaves gradually unfolded themselves; and amid them was a perfect and lovely flower.

"It is magical!" cried Georgiana. "I dare not touch it."

"Nay, pluck it," answered Aylmer,—"pluck it, and inhale its brief perfume while you may. The flower will wither in a few moments and leave nothing save its brown seed vessels; but thence may be perpetuated a race as ephemeral as itself."

But Georgiana had no sooner touched the flower than the whole plant suffered a blight, its leaves turning coal-black as if by the agency of fire.

"There was too powerful a stimulus," said Aylmer, thoughtfully.

To make up for this abortive experiment, he proposed to take her portrait by a scientific process of his own invention. It was to be effected by rays of light striking upon a polished plate of metal. Georgiana assented; but, on looking at the result, was affrighted to find the features of the portrait blurred and indefinable; while the minute figure of a hand appeared where the cheek should have been, Aylmer snatched the metallic plate and threw it into a jar of corrosive acid.

Soon, however, he forgot these mortifying failures. In the intervals of study and chemical experiment he came to her flushed and exhausted, but seemed invigorated by her presence, and spoke in glowing language of the resources of his art. He gave a history of the long dynasty of the alchemists, who spent so many ages in quest of the universal solvent by which the golden principle might be elicited from all things vile and base. Aylmer appeared to believe that, by the plainest scientific logic, it was altogether within the limits of possibility to discover this long-sought medium; "but," he added, "a philosopher who should go deep enough to acquire the power would attain too lofty a wisdom to stoop to the exercise of it." Not less singular were his opinions in regard to the elixir vitae. He more than intimated that it was at his option to concoct a liquid that should prolong life for years, perhaps interminably; but that it would produce a discord in Nature which all the world, and chiefly the quaffer of the immortal nostrum, would find cause to curse.

"Aylmer, are you in earnest?" asked Georgiana, looking at him with amazement and fear. "It is terrible to possess such power, or even to dream of possessing it."

"O, do not tremble, my love," said her husband. "I would not wrong either you or myself by working such inharmonious effects upon our lives; but I would have you consider how trifling, in comparison, is the skill requisite to remove this little hand."

At the mention of the birthmark, Georgiana, as usual, shrank as if a red-hot iron had touched her cheek.

Again Aylmer applied himself to his labors. She could hear his voice in the distant furnace room giving directions to Aminadab, whose harsh, uncouth, misshapen tones were audible in response, more like the grunt or growl of a brute than human speech. After hours of absence, Aylmer reappeared and proposed that she should now examine his cabinet of chemical products and natural treasures of the earth. Among the former he showed her a small vial, in which, he remarked, was contained a gentle yet most powerful fragrance, capable of impregnating all the breezes that blow across a kingdom. They were of inestimable value, the contents of that little vial; and, as he said so, he threw some of the perfume into the air and filled the room with piercing and invigorating delight.

"And what is this?" asked Georgiana, pointing to a small crystal globe containing a gold-colored liquid. "It is so beautiful to the eye that I could imagine it the elixir of life."

"In one sense it is," replied Aylmer; "or rather, the elixir of immortality. It is the most precious poison that ever was concocted in this world. By its aid I could apportion the lifetime of any mortal at whom you might point your finger. The strength of the dose would determine whether he were to linger out years, or drop dead in the midst of a breath. No king on his guarded throne could keep his life if I, in my private station, should deem that the welfare of millions justified me in depriving him of it."

"Why do you keep such a terrific drug?" inquired Georgiana in horror.

"Do not mistrust me, dearest," said her husband, smiling; "its virtuous potency is yet greater than its harmful one. But see! here is a powerful cosmetic. With a few drops of this in a vase of water, freckles may be washed away as easily as the hands are cleansed. A stronger infusion would take the blood out of the cheek, and leave the rosiest beauty a pale ghost."

"Is it with this lotion that you intend to bathe my cheek?" asked Georgiana, anxiously.

"O, no," hastily replied her husband; "this is merely superficial. Your case demands a remedy that shall go deeper."

In his interviews with Georgiana, Aylmer generally made minute inquiries as to her sensations, and whether the confinement of the rooms and the temperature of the atmosphere agreed with her. These questions had such a particular drift that Georgiana began to conjecture that she was already subjected to certain physical influences, either breathed in with the fragrant air or taken with her food. She fancied likewise, but it might be altogether fancy, that there was a stirring up of her system—a strange, indefinite sensation creeping through her veins, and tingling, half painfully, half pleasurably, at her heart. Still, whenever she dared to look into the mirror, there she beheld herself pale as a white rose and with the crimson birthmark stamped upon her cheek. Not even Aylmer now hated it so much as she.

To dispel the tedium of the hours which her husband found it necessary to devote to the processes of combination and analysis, Georgiana turned over the volumes of his scientific library. In many dark old tomes she met with chapters full of romance and poetry. They were the works of the philosophers of the middle ages, such as Albertus Magnus, Cornelius Agrippa, Paracelsus, and the famous friar who created the prophetic Brazen Head. All these antique naturalists stood in advance of their centuries, yet were imbued with some of their credulity, and therefore were believed, and perhaps imagined themselves to have acquired from the investigation of Nature a power above Nature, and from physics a sway over the spiritual world. Hardly less curious and imaginative were the early volumes of the Transactions of the Royal Society, in which the members, knowing little of the limits of natural possibility, were continually recording wonders or proposing methods whereby wonders might be wrought.

But to Georgiana, the most engrossing volume was a large folio from her husband's own hand, in which he had recorded every experiment of his scientific career, its original aim, the methods adopted for its development, and its final success or failure, with the circumstances to which either event was attributable. The book, in truth, was both the history and emblem of his ardent, ambitious, imaginative, yet practical and laborious life. He handled physical details as if there were nothing beyond them; yet spiritualized them all and redeemed himself from materialism by his strong and eager aspiration towards the infinite. In his grasp the veriest clod of earth assumed a soul. Georgiana, as she read, reverenced Aylmer and loved him more profoundly than ever, but with a less entire dependence on his judgment than before. Much as he had accomplished, she could not but observe that his most splendid successes were almost invariably failures, if compared with the ideal at which he aimed. His brightest diamonds were the merest pebbles, and felt to be so by himself, in comparison with the inestimable gems which lay hidden beyond his reach. The volume, rich with achievements that had won renown for its author, was yet as melancholy a record as ever mortal hand had penned. It was the sad confession and continual exemplification of the shortcomings of the composite man, the spirit burdened with clay and working in matter, and of the despair that assails the higher nature at finding itself so miserably thwarted by the earthly part. Perhaps every man of genius, in whatever sphere, might recognize the image of his own experience in Aylmer's journal.

So deeply did these reflections affect Georgiana that she laid her face upon the open volume and burst into tears. In this situation she was found by her husband.

"It is dangerous to read in a sorcerer's books," said he with a smile, though his countenance was uneasy and displeased. "Georgiana, there are pages in that volume which I can scarcely glance over and keep my senses. Take heed lest it prove detrimental to you."

"It has made me worship you more than ever," said she.

"Ah, wait for this one success," rejoined he, "then worship me if you will. I shall deem myself hardly unworthy of it. But come, I have sought you for the luxury of your voice. Sing to me, dearest."

So she poured out the liquid music of her voice to quench the thirst of his spirit. He then took his leave with a boyish exuberance of gayety, assuring her that her seclusion would endure but a little longer, and that the result was already certain. Scarcely had he departed when Georgiana felt irresistibly impelled to follow him. She had forgotten to inform Aylmer of a symptom which for two or three hours past had begun to excite her attention. It was a sensation in the fatal birthmark, not painful, but which induced a restlessness throughout her system. Hastening after her husband, she intruded for the first time into the laboratory.

The first thing that struck her eye was the furnace, that hot and feverish worker, with the intense glow of its fire, which by the quantities of soot clustered above it seemed to have been burning for ages. There was a distilling apparatus in full operation. Around the room were retorts, tubes, cylinders, crucibles, and other apparatus of chemical research. An electrical machine stood ready for immediate use. The atmosphere felt oppressively close, and was tainted with gaseous odors which had been tormented forth by the processes of science. The severe and homely simplicity of the apartment, with its naked walls and brick pavement, looked strange, accustomed as Georgiana had become to the fantastic elegance of her boudoir. But what chiefly, indeed almost solely, drew her attention, was the aspect of Aylmer himself.

He was pale as death, anxious and absorbed, and hung over the furnace as if it depended upon his utmost watchfulness whether the liquid which it was distilling should be the draught of immortal happiness or misery. How different from the sanguine and joyous mien that he had assumed for Georgiana's encouragement!

"Carefully now, Aminadab; carefully, thou human machine; carefully, thou man of clay," muttered Aylmer, more to himself than his assistant. "Now, if there be a thought too much or too little, it is all over."

"Ho! ho!" mumbled Aminadab. "Look, master! look!"

Aylmer raised his eyes hastily, and at first reddened, then grew paler than ever, on beholding Georgiana. He rushed towards her and seized her arm with a gripe that left the print of his fingers upon it.

"Why do you come hither? Have you no trust in your husband?" cried he, impetuously. "Would you throw the blight of that fatal birthmark over my labors? It is not well done. Go, prying woman! go!"

"Nay, Aylmer," said Georgiana with the firmness of which she possessed no stinted endowment, "it is not you that have a right to complain. You mistrust your wife; you have concealed the anxiety with which you watch the development of this experiment. Think not so unworthily of me, my husband. Tell me all the risk we run, and fear not that I shall shrink; for my share in it is far less than your own."

"No, no, Georgiana!" said Aylmer, impatiently; "it must not be."

"I submit," replied she, calmly. "And, Aylmer, I shall quaff whatever draught you bring me; but it will be on the same principle that would induce me to take a dose of poison if offered by your hand."

"My noble wife," said Aylmer, deeply moved, "I knew not the height and depth of your nature until now. Nothing shall be concealed. Know, then, that this crimson hand, superficial as it seems, has clutched its grasp into your being with a strength of which I had no previous conception. I have already administered agents powerful enough to do aught except to change your entire physical system. Only one thing remains to be tried. If that fails us we are ruined."

"Why did you hesitate to tell me this?" asked she.

"Because, Georgiana," said Aylmer, in a low voice, "there is danger."

"Danger? There is but one danger—that this horrible stigma shall be left upon my cheek!" cried Georgiana. "Remove it, remove it, whatever be the cost, or we shall both go mad!"

"Heaven knows your words are too true," said Aylmer, sadly. "And now, dearest, return to your boudoir. In a little while all will be tested."

He conducted her back and took leave of her with a solemn tenderness which spoke far more than his words how much was now at stake. After his departure Georgiana became rapt in musings. She considered the character of Aylmer and did it completer justice than at any previous moment. Her heart exulted, while it trembled, at his honorable love—so pure and lofty that it would accept nothing less than perfection nor miserably make itself contented with an earthlier nature than he had dreamed of. She felt how much more precious was such a sentiment than that meaner kind which would have borne with the imperfection for her sake, and have been guilty of treason to holy love by degrading its perfect idea to the level of the actual; and with her whole spirit she prayed that, for a single moment, she might satisfy his highest and deepest conception. Longer than one moment she well knew it could not be; for his spirit was ever on the march, ever ascending, and each instant required something that was beyond the scope of the instant before.

The sound of her husband's footsteps aroused her. He bore a crystal goblet containing a liquor colorless as water, but bright enough to be the draught of immortality. Aylmer was pale; but it seemed rather the consequence of a highly-wrought state of mind and tension of spirit than of fear or doubt.

"The concoction of the draught has been perfect," said he, in answer to Georgiana's look. "Unless all my science have deceived me, it cannot fail."

"Save on your account, my dearest Aylmer" observed his wife, "I might wish to put off this birthmark of mortality by relinquishing mortality itself in preference to any other mode. Life is but a sad possession to those who have attained precisely the degree of moral advancement at which I stand. Were I weaker and blinder, it might be happiness. Were I stronger, it might be endured hopefully. But, being what I find myself, methinks I am of all mortals the most fit to die."

"You are fit for heaven without tasting death!" replied her husband. "But why do we speak of dying? The draught cannot fail. Behold its effect upon this plant."

On the window seat there stood a geranium diseased with yellow blotches which had overspread all its leaves. Aylmer poured a small quantity of the liquid upon the soil in which it grew. In a little time, when the roots of the plant had taken up the moisture, the unsightly blotches began to be extinguished in a living verdure.

"There needed no proof," said Georgiana, quietly. "Give me the goblet. I joyfully stake all upon your word."

"Drink, then, thou lofty creature!" exclaimed Aylmer, with fervid admiration. "There is no taint of imperfection on thy spirit. Thy sensible frame, too, shall soon be all perfect."

She quaffed the liquid and returned the goblet to his hand.

"It is grateful," said she, with a placid smile. "Methinks it is like water from a heavenly fountain; for it contains I know not what of unobtrusive fragrance and deliciousness. It allays a feverish thirst that had parched me for many days. Now, dearest, let me sleep. My earthly senses are closing over my spirit like the leaves around the heart of a rose at sunset."

She spoke the last words with a gentle reluctance, as if it required almost more energy than she could command to pronounce the faint and lingering syllables. Scarcely had they loitered through her lips ere she was lost in slumber. Aylmer sat by her side, watching her aspect with the emotions proper to a man the whole value of whose existence was involved in the process now to be tested. Mingled with this mood, however, was the philosophic investigation characteristic of the man of science. Not the minutest symptom escaped him. A heightened flush of the cheek, a slight irregularity of breath, a quiver of the eyelid, a hardly perceptible tremor through the frame,—such were the details which, as the moments passed, he wrote down in his folio volume. Intense thought had set its stamp upon every previous page of that volume; but the thoughts of years were all concentrated upon the last.

While thus employed, he failed not to gaze often at the fatal hand, and not without a shudder. Yet once, by a strange and unaccountable impulse, he pressed it with his lips. His spirit recoiled, however, in the very act; and Georgiana, out of the midst of her deep sleep, moved uneasily and murmured as if in remonstrance. Again Aylmer resumed his watch. Nor was it without avail. The crimson hand, which at first had been strongly visible upon the marble paleness of Georgiana's cheek, now grew more faintly outlined. She remained not less pale than ever; but the birthmark, with every breath that came and went lost somewhat of its former distinctness. Its presence had been awful; its departure was more awful still. Watch the stain of the rainbow fading out of the sky, and you will know how that mysterious symbol passed away.

"By Heaven! it is well nigh gone!" said Aylmer to himself, in almost irrepressible ecstasy. "I can scarcely trace it now. Success! success! And now it is like the faintest rose color. The lightest flush of blood across her cheek would overcome it. But she is so pale!"

He drew aside the window curtain and suffered the light of natural day to fall into the room and rest upon her cheek. At the same time he heard a gross, hoarse chuckle, which he had long known as his servant Aminadab's expression of delight.

"Ah, clod! ah, earthly mass!" cried Aylmer, laughing in a sort of frenzy, "you have served me well! Matter and spirit—earth and heaven—have both done their part in this! Laugh, thing of the senses! You have earned the right to laugh."

These exclamations broke Georgiana's sleep. She slowly unclosed her eyes and gazed into the mirror which her husband had arranged for that purpose. A faint smile flitted over her lips when she recognized how barely perceptible was now that crimson hand which had once blazed forth with such disastrous brilliancy as to scare away all their happiness. But then her eyes sought Aylmer's face with a trouble and anxiety that he could by no means account for.

"My poor Aylmer!" murmured she.

"Poor? Nay, richest, happiest, most favored!" exclaimed he. "My peerless bride, it is successful! You are perfect!"

"My poor Aylmer," she repeated, with a more than human tenderness, "you have aimed loftily; you have done nobly. Do not repent that, with so high and pure a feeling, you have rejected the best the earth could offer. Aylmer, dearest Aylmer, I am dying!"

Alas! it was too true! The fatal hand had grappled with the mystery of life, and was the bond by which an angelic spirit kept itself in union with a mortal frame. As the last crimson tint of the birthmark—that sole token of human imperfection—faded from her cheek, the parting breath of the now perfect woman passed into the atmosphere, and her soul, lingering a moment near her husband, took its heavenward flight. Then a hoarse, chuckling laugh was heard again! Thus ever does the gross fatality of earth exult in its invariable triumph over the immortal essence which, in this dim sphere of half development, demands the completeness of a higher state. Yet, had Aylmer reached a profounder wisdom, he need not thus have flung away the happiness which would have woven his mortal life of the selfsame texture with the celestial. The momentary circumstance was too strong for him; he failed to look beyond the shadowy scope of time, and, living once for all in eternity, to find the perfect future in the present.

Discussion of Hawthorne's "The Birthmark"

1. How does the emblem of the birthmark suggest the nature of being human? By eradicating the birthmark, what in essence is Aylmer doing? What is the result of his meddling?

2. Into what setting does Aylmer place Georgiana? What significance, if any, do you find in that setting?

3. Some critics contend that the story is an allegory of the destructive powers of analytical science. What in the story implies that it may also be a commentary on nineteenth-century relationships between men and women?

THEODOR STORM

1817–1888

Theodor Storm, a master of short fiction in German and a major writer of the nineteenth century, is probably best known in North America for his symbolic parables based on North German folklore: *Immensee* (1849), *Aquis Submersus* (1876), and *The Rider on the Pale Horse* (1886). Unlike his colleagues in England and on the Continent, Storm concentrated almost exclusively on brief stories and short novels, all of which display great psychological insight. "Veronika," *Viola Tricolor* (1873), and *Curator Carsten* (1877) are skillful investigations into familial relationships. Even though the situations in these three works are partially autobiographical, Storm's point of view is always impartial. A successful magistrate and jurist, he presents his characters in such a way that the motives of each one are made clear. The reader, then, is placed in the role of a judge or juror who must listen to the testimony, weigh the evidence, and judge the actions revealed by the story. This process of judgment is essential to reading Storm, because the morality of human behavior—no matter how irrational that behavior may seem to be—is always at the root of his fiction.

Veronika

AT THE WATER MILL

It was the beginning of April, the day before Palm Sunday. The late afternoon sun shone mildly on the new grass beside the path which sloped gradually down and along the mountainside. At this moment one of the most distinguished jurists of the city, a middle-aged man with reserved but pronounced features, was slowly walking, pausing only now and then to speak a word to the clerk who accompanied him. The object of their stroll was one of our outlying water mills, whose owner, bothered by advancing age and illness, desired to make over the property to his son according to the best legal procedures.

Another pair followed a few paces behind. Beside a young man, whose face shone with liveliness and intelligence, walked a lovely young woman. He said something to her, but she seemed not to hear him. She stared straight in front of her with her dark eyes, unheeding and alone.

When the mill came into view in the valley below them, the attorney turned his head. "Well, cousin," he called back, "your

From *The Rider on the White Horse and Selected Stories* by Theodor Storm translated by James Wright. Copyright © 1964 by James Wright. By arrangement with The New American Library, Inc., New York, N.Y.

handwriting is tolerable; what would you think of learning a bit about writing contracts?"

But the cousin waved his hand in objection. "Never mind!" he said, and turned questioning eyes on his companion. "While we're walking, I'll have a lesson in conversation from your wife."

"All right. But don't train him too well, Veronika!"

The young woman merely nodded. Behind them, from the city towers, the evening bells sounded over the landscape. Her hand had just stroked back the black hair under her dark satin hat, and now it slid down to her bosom. She made the sign of the cross, and began quietly to speak the Angelus. Like his cousin, the young man was a Protestant; he watched the regular motion of her lips, and his face betrayed a faint impatience.

A few months previously, he had come to the city as an architect, to work on the addition to a church. Since that time, he had been a guest almost every day in his cousin's home. He had become a lively and close friend of his cousin's wife almost from the very first moment of his arrival. The two of them were drawn together by the youth which they shared, and by his skill in drawing, a craft which she also practiced with pleasure and a certain flair. She had found in him a friend and a teacher at the same time. Before long, however, as they sat together through the evenings, he paid less and less attention to the drawings which lay in front of her, and more and more to her small energetic hand. And she, who had been accustomed to drop her pencil at any moment, now silently and obediently went on with her drawing without once looking up. She seemed fixed in his gaze. Perhaps they themselves did not realize that, in saying good night, their hands clung together a little longer every evening.

As for the attorney, he was absorbed in his business affairs. He was pleased that his young wife had found inspiration and understanding in her favorite pastime, which he himself had never found the time to cultivate. Once, shortly after the young architect had departed, the far-off expression in her eyes surprised her husband.

"Vroni," he remarked, restraining her gently with his hand as she tried to step past him, "is it really true, what your sisters have been saying?"

"Is what true, Franz?"

"Certainly, certainly," he said, "now I can understand it! It's just that your eyes are very spiritual." She flushed, and yielded in silence as he embraced and kissed her.

Today, since the weather was fair, she and Rudolf had been asked to go along with the attorney on his formal visit to the nearby water mill.

Since the social gathering on the previous evening, when she had displayed at her husband's request a drawing which she had completed under his very eyes, everything had changed. Rudolf remembered only too well that he had objected to the extreme praise of the other guests, and had himself offered only the harshest and most intense criticism.

Veronika had long ended her prayer, but he waited in vain for her to look at him.

"You're angry, Veronika," he said finally. She nodded vaguely, but her lips remained firmly closed.

He glanced at her. She still looked stubborn.

"I should have thought," he said, "that you, of all people, would understand how such a thing happened! Or don't you?"

"All I know is that you've caused me pain. And," she added, "that you did so deliberately."

For a while he said nothing. Then he asked hesitantly, "Did you notice the rather knowing glance of the old man who stood near you?"

She glanced at him quickly.

"Don't you see, Veronika? I had to do it first, myself. Forgive me! I can't stand the thought of hearing you criticized by others."

A veil seemed to fall over her eyes, and her long black lashes sank on her cheeks; but she said nothing.

Shortly thereafter, they came to the mill. The miller's son led the attorney into the house; Rudolf and Veronika went into the garden that lay alongside, and continued to walk silently up the long slope. They seemed so angry with each other that they had to stop for breath when they tried now and then to speak a single word.

After passing through the garden, they went over a narrow footbridge into the lower door of the mill, which stood by a rapid stream at the edge of the garden. Through the noise of the mill-works and the falling water which obliterated all outside sounds, a strange sense of separation filled the twilit room. Veronika had walked over to the door which led to the millrace, and she was gazing down into the whirling wheels where the water gleamed in the sunlight. Rudolf let her go alone. He stood inside beside the enormous cogwheel, gazing after her unhappily. At last she turned her head. She said something, he saw her lips move, but he could not catch the words.

"I can't understand you!" he said. And he shook his head.

He was just on the point of joining her, when she stepped back into the room. As she passed, she came so close to the wheel beside him that the teeth of the cogs nearly brushed her hair. She did not see the wheel, for she was still nearly blinded by the evening sun; but she felt her hands seized and her whole body quickly drawn to one side. When she looked up, her eyes met his. The two said nothing; a sudden abandonment fell over them like a shadow. The mill machinery thundered against their heads; from outside, the waters roared monotonously, plunging, plunging over wheels, plunging into the deep places. Very slowly the young man's lips began to move, and, protected by the deafening noise, where his voice was utterly lost, he said the things that are drunken and insane. Her ears heard nothing; but she read his lips, and she read the passionate anguish of his face. She tossed back her head and closed her eyes. But he smiled. She betrayed life.

And so she stood there, her helpless face turned to him, her hands, lying in his, forgetting and forgotten.

Suddenly the noise stopped. The mill stood silent. They could hear the mill workers walking over their heads; and, outside, the dripping water fell from the wheels into the pond like tiny bells. The young man's lips became dumb; and when Veronika drew away from him, he did not restrain her. She hastened out through the door, and then he seemed to regain the power of speech. He called her name and held out his arms, pleading. But she shook her head without turning around. Then she walked slowly through the garden to the house.

The door had been left open, and, as she entered, she saw opposite her the old miller lying in bed, his hands folded. Above him hung a wooden crucifix with an attached rosary. By his bedside, a young woman with a child in her arms was leaning over the blankets. "All he needs is air," she said. "He likes his food well enough."

The attorney was standing nearby, holding a document. He asked, "Who is your doctor?"

"Doctor? We have no doctor."

"You're making a mistake."

The young woman tittered with embarrassment. "He's just old," she said, as she cleaned the fat little boy's nose with her apron. "The doctor can't do anything about old age."

Veronika listened to these words without breathing. The old man started coughing and held his hand up to his eyes.

"Is this your will, Martin, just as I have it here?" the attorney asked next. But the sick old man seemed to pay no attention.

"Father," said the young woman, "is that the right will? Just as the counselor read it?"

"Certainly," said the old man. "Everything's just fine."

"And have you taken everything into consideration?" asked the attorney.

The old man nodded. "Yes, yes. I've worked very hard. But my son shouldn't have to do that."

Until now, the son had been smoking in the corner. "Of course, you have to think about the part that still belongs to the old man, too," he said, and cleared his throat a few times. "The old man is still bound to live out a good deal of the money."

The attorney paused, and gazed down with his gray eyes upon the rough peasant. "Is that your son, Wiesmann?" he asked, pointing at the child who played by the bed. "If you want to do any more talking, get the child out of this room!"

The man was silent, but he glared almost threateningly back at the attorney.

The old man's gnarled hand stroked the blanket. Then he said softly, "Oh, patience, patience, Jacob, it won't be long now. But," he added to the attorney, "he'll have to live up to the village customs and see to it that I'm properly buried. And that's going to be another expense."

Veronika vanished without a sound, just as she had come.

Outside she saw Rudolf on the other side of the garden, talking with a mill worker, but she turned aside and went along a footpath which led from the mill down to the stream. She gazed absently into the distance. She did not really notice how twilight was falling, nor how, very slowly and steadily, as she walked up and down, the moon was rising behind the mountains and pouring light out over the still valley. For the first time she was facing life directly, in all its barren poverty: it was a path that seemed endless, dry; until, suddenly, it did end: you died.

She felt as though she had been living in a dream; and now as if she had suddenly come, without consolation, into reality, and was lost.

It was quite late when she heard her husband calling her back to the mill, where he met her at the door. On the way home she walked in silence beside him, unaware of his understanding glances. "They frightened you, Veronika," he said, and touched her face. "But these people live by different standards. They're hard on their relatives, but they're also hard on themselves."

She turned and looked at her husband's calm face for an instant. Then she looked at the ground and walked humbly beside him.

Just as silently, Rudolf walked along beside the elderly clerk. He gazed steadily at the woman's hand, which shone in the moonlight; only a little while ago that hand had rested weakly in his own. He hoped to hold it again, if only to say good night. But that was not to be. As they drew near the city, he saw the small hands, one after the other, slip into a pair of dark gloves that, he knew well, Veronika usually left unworn.

They reached the house at last. Before he knew it, he felt the rapid touch of her gloved fingers against his hand. With a clear good night, Veronika opened the door and vanished into the dark hallway ahead of her husband.

PALM SUNDAY

Palm Sunday had come. The city streets were crowded with people from the neighboring villages of the countryside. Here and there in the sunlight in front of the houses one could see the Protestant children, gazing in the direction of the open door of the Catholic church. It was the day of the great Easter procession. Now the bells were ringing, and the procession came into view beneath the Gothic arch and surged forth into the street. First the orphan boys with black crosses, and then the white-veiled Sisters of Mercy, the various public schools and, finally, the endless train of people from country and city, the men, the women, the children, the old people, singing, praying, as beautifully dressed as possible, the men and boys bareheaded, their hats in their hands. Overhead, at measured intervals, carried on shoulders, the magnificent religious pictures: Christ at Calvary, Christ jeered at by the soldiers, and, high above all the rest, the enormous cross, and, at last, the Holy Sepulcher.

The ladies of the city did not customarily take part in such festivities. Veronika sat in her bedroom at a small dressing table. Before her was a small, open, gilt New Testament in the Catholic version. She seemed lost in her reading, for her long dark hair hung down over her white gown. Her hand, holding a tortoiseshell comb, lay motionless in her lap. She raised her head and listened as the noise of the procession reached her. The sounds became clearer and clearer: the paces of the feet, the singing, regular murmur of the prayers. "Holy Mary, Mother of Mercy." The sound came from outside, and from the rear of the procession an answer: "Pray for us sinners, now and in the hour of our death!"

Veronika gently recited the familiar words. She pushed back her chair. Her arms hanging loose, she stood now in the back of the room, looking steadily toward the window. New figures continuously passed, new voices spoke, one picture after another went by. Then, suddenly, a new sound cut the air, and cut the heart. The *castrum doloris* approached, with the sound of horns and followed by crowds of people, acolytes, and priests ceremonially dressed. Ribbons fluttered, the black covering of the canopy floated in the air. Beneath it, covered with flowers, lay the dead Christ. The iron clang of the horns was a summons to the Day of Judgment.

Veronika stood still. Her knees shook. Under the sharp, blackened eyebrows the fire of her eyes burned to ashes in her white face.

When the procession was gone, she sank to the floor beside the chair, and, covering her face with her hands, she cried out, in the words of Saint Luke, "Father, I have sinned against Heaven, and I am not worthy to be called Thy child!"

IN THE CONFESSIONAL

The attorney belonged to the growing community of people who saw in Christianity not a supernatural sign but rather the natural result of man's spiritual development. He therefore refrained from attending church. For all that, he allowed his wife to continue the customs of her childhood and first home. Perhaps he took it for granted that she would gradually break free from those customs on her own.

Since their wedding two years earlier, Veronika had gone to

confession and communion only at Easter. And now the Easter holiday had arrived again. Her husband was familiar with her way of going about the house on preceding days. She was silent, and apparently indifferent. For this reason, he had not been particularly struck by the cessation of the drawing lessons which had been originally undertaken with such enthusiasm; it never occurred to him to see anything strange in her giving up the lessons ever since that evening walk. But time went by, the May sunlight shone warmly into their living room, and Veronika put off her confession again. Finally he could no longer ignore the daily increasing pallor of her face and the shadows of sleeplessness under her eyes. She looked like that when, one morning, he entered her room unnoticed and found her standing by the window.

"Vroni," he said as he put his arm around her, "won't you try to hold up your head again?'

She trembled, as if he had stumbled upon some of her unguarded thoughts and surprised her, but she tried to regain control of herself. "Leave me for a while now, Franz," she said, leading him gently by the hand toward the door. When she was alone, she dressed and then left the house, carrying her prayer book.

A short time later she stepped into St. Lambert's Church. The morning was coming on, and outside the windows of the enormous church, the leaves of the linden trees were throwing their shadows. In the choir, on the doors of the reliquary, the broken rays of sunlight fluttered through the stained glass. In the nave, near the confessionals, people were scattered about, sitting or kneeling before open prayer books, getting ready for confession. From the confessionals no sound came except whispering, deep breaths, the rustling of clothing, the striking of a foot on the flagstones. Soon Veronika too was kneeling in a confessional, near a picture of the Blessed Mother, who smiled down at her sympathetically. Veronika's wholly black clothing made the pallor of her face stand out all the more strikingly. The strong, middle-aged priest leaned his head against the screen which separated him from the penitent.

Veronika began to speak half-aloud the words of the introductory formula: "I, a poor sinful human being!" And with an uncertain voice she continued: "I recognize before God and before you, the priest in the place of God . . ." But her words moved ever more slowly, were more and more difficult to understand. At last, she was dumb.

The priest's dark eyes gazed straight down upon her. He looked tired. He had been hearing confessions for a very long time. "Turn to the Lord," he said gently. "Sin kills, but repentance giveth life."

She tried to collect her thoughts. And again, as so often since that hour, she heard the terrible mill roaring in the silence of her inner ear; and again, she stood before him in that secret twilight, clasping his hands, closing her eyes under the pressure of unendurable passion, stabbed through by embarrassment, not daring to flee, daring even less to remain. Her lips moved, but she couldn't say anything. It was no use.

The priest let his silence continue for another moment. "Courage, daughter!" he said and lifted up his head, with its flowing black hair. "Meditate on the words of the Lord: 'Receive ye the Holy Spirit. Those whom you release, their sins shall be forgiven!'"

She looked up at him. The flushed face, the enormously strong bull neck of the priest were right before her eyes. She tried again; but suddenly she was overwhelmed by resentment and a reluctance to speak, as in the presence of something unchaste, worse than the thing she had come here to confess. She was frightened. What was this revolt in her? Was it a temptation of the deadly sin from which she cried to be freed? Struggling in silence, she bowed her head over the prayer book. Meanwhile, the signs of weariness had vanished from the priest's face. He began seriously and powerfully to speak. He continued, with all his subtle magic of persuasion; softly, sonorously, the tone of his voice touched her. On another occasion she would have bowed down with rapture; but this time a sudden and newly awakened feeling proved stronger than all the force of rhetoric and all the custom of childhood. Her hand fumbled with the veil and flung it back over her cap.

"Forgive me, Father," she faltered. Then, shaking her head silently, she drew the veil back down without having received the sign of the cross, she stood up, and she hurried down the aisle. Her dress rustled as she passed the benches, so she gathered the hem up in her hand. She felt as though invisible hands were clutching to keep her there.

Once outside, she stood, taking deep breaths, under the high doorway. Her spirit was troubled. The redeeming hand, which had guided her since childhood, had been offered her, and she had rejected it. Now she knew of no other hand she could grasp.

As she stood, confused, in the sunlit square, she heard a small child's voice near her. A small brown hand offered her some primroses. It was spring in the outside world, and suddenly, like a messenger from an unsuspected place, it came home to her.

She leaned down and bought flowers from the child. Then, carrying the bouquet, she walked down the street toward the city gate. The sun shone on the cobbles; from an open window a canary sang loudly and clearly. She walked on deliberately, and soon came to the last houses. From that point, a footpath off to one side led up into the hills which surrounded the city. Veronika breathed more easily. She let her eyes pause on the green fields along the path; sometimes the air moved and brought her the fragrance of the cowslips that grew at the foot of the mountain. Farther on, where the forest began at the edge of the fields, the path became steeper, and a greater effort had to be made, even though Veronika had been accustomed to mountain climbing since her childhood. Occasionally she stopped and gazed down from the evergreen shadows into the sun-filled valley, which was sinking deeper and deeper beneath her.

When she reached the summit, she sat down among the wild thyme, which at this particular place was spun out all over the mountain. She sat breathing the spicy air of the trees, and gazed off toward the blue mountain range, a haze on the horizon. Behind her, irregularly, the spring breeze moved through the tips of the pines. A blackbird called out of the deepest reaches of the forest; above her, a bird of prey cried and floated out of sight into the measureless hugeness of space.

Veronika took off her hat and put her hand to her head.

Time passed in solitude and silence. Nothing came near her but the pure moving air that sometimes lightly touched her forehead, or the calls of birds from the distance. Sometimes her cheeks flushed brightly, and her eyes shone and became larger.

Now she heard bells ascending from the city. She looked up and listened. The bells rang shrill and impatient. "Requiescat," she said softly. She had recognized the bell from the tower of St. Lambert's Church, informing the neighborhood that the grim messenger of the Lord had entered beneath one of its roofs.

The cemetery lay at the foot of the mountain. She could see the stone cross over the grave of her father, who, a few years earlier, had died in her arms as a priest murmured his prayers. Farther on, where the water shone, was that bleak, ugly patch of ground which she had so often entered as a child, shy and curious, a place where, according to the commandment of the church, those who had not received the sacrament were buried with those who had killed themselves. Now she would lie there, too; for Easter confessions, in her life, were now over and done with.

Pain crawled for an instant around her mouth, and then vanished. She rose, a decision strong and clear in her mind. She looked down for another moment at the city, over the sunlit roofs, as though searching for something. Then she turned and went through the pines, down the mountain path, the same way she had come. Soon she was in the green fields again. She seemed in a hurry, and she walked erectly, with firm steps.

She reached her house. The maid told her that her husband was in his room. She opened the door and saw him sitting quietly at his desk. She hesitated.

"Franz," she said softly.

He laid down his pen.

"Vroni? Why, you're late! Did you have to go through such a long list of sins?"

"Please don't joke!" she pleaded, as she stepped forward and took his hand. "I did not confess."

He looked up, surprised. But she knelt before him and kissed his hand.

"Franz," she said. "I've hurt you."

"Me, Veronika?" He took her face gently between his hands. "And now you've come to confess to your husband?"

"No, Franz, not to confess, but to entrust myself to you, only to you. Help me, if you can—forgive me!"

He gazed at her seriously for a moment; then he lifted her up with both arms and let her head rest against him. "Talk to me, Veronika."

She did not move, but she spoke; and, as his eyes clung to her lips, she felt his arms tightening about her.

Discussion of Storm's "Veronika"

1. This short story is made even shorter by the divisions of the text. What functional importance do these divisions have?

2. Veronika chooses to confess to her husband rather than to her priest. In the context of the story do you feel this decision is constructive?

3. The relationship of young wife–older husband–attractive younger man is widely used in literature. Frequently writers explore the comic overtones or reduce the humanity of one of the characters in the triangle. How does Storm avoid the latter? Do you feel that there is any value in the way he handles the relationships?

MARY E. WILKINS FREEMAN

1852–1930

❦ Born in Randolph, Massachusetts, Mary Wilkins Freeman moved with her family to Brattleboro, Vermont, when she was fourteen and lived there until her early thirties. Thus she established ties with New England that she never broke, even when she married Charles Manning Freeman at age forty-nine and moved to his home in Metuchen, New Jersey. After several years of alcoholism and confinements in sanitariums, Mr. Freeman died in 1923, leaving one dollar to his wife. Among her many writings are short stories—*A Humble Romance and Other Stories* (1887), *A New England Nun and Other Stories* (1891), *Silence and Other Stories* (1898)—and novels—*Pembroke* (1894), *Madelon* (1896), *Jerome, a Poor Man* (1897). She was planning a sequel to *Pembroke* the year before she died. Comparing her with Ellen Glasgow, whose story "The Difference" also appears in this collection, Perry D. Westbrook says that both writers exhibit "manifestations of the Calvinist will" (Perry D. Westbrook, *Mary Wilkins Freeman* [New York: Twayne Publishers, 1967], p. 20). The endurance and toughness of that will are central characteristics of many of Freeman's people.

A New England Nun

It was late in the afternoon, and the light was waning. There was a difference in the look of the tree shadows out in the yard. Somewhere in the distance cows were lowing and a little bell was tinkling; now and then a farm-wagon tilted by, and the dust flew; some blue-shirted laborers with shovels over their shoulders plodded past; little swarms of flies were dancing up and down before the peoples' faces in the soft air. There seemed to be a gentle stir arising over everything for the mere sake of subsidence—a very premonition of rest and hush and night.

This soft diurnal commotion was over Louisa Ellis also. She had been peacefully sewing at her sitting-room window all the afternoon. Now she quilted her needle carefully into her work, which she folded precisely, and laid in a basket with her thimble and thread and scissors. Louisa Ellis could not remember that ever in her life she had mislaid one of these little feminine appurtenances, which had become, from long use and constant association, a very part of her personality.

Louisa tied a green apron round her waist, and got out a flat

"A New England Nun" (pp. 1–17) in *A New England Nun and Other Stories* by Mary E. Wilkins Freeman (Harper & Row).

straw hat with a green ribbon. Then she went into the garden with a little blue crockery bowl, to pick some currants for her tea. After the currants were picked she sat on the back door-step and stemmed them, collecting the stems carefully in her apron, and afterwards throwing them into the hen-coop. She looked sharply at the grass beside the step to see if any had fallen there.

Louisa was slow and still in her movements; it took her a long time to prepare her tea; but when ready it was set forth with as much grace as if she had been a veritable guest to her own self. The little square table stood exactly in the centre of the kitchen, and was covered with a starched linen cloth whose border pattern of flowers glistened. Louisa had a damask napkin on her tea-tray, where were arranged a cut-glass tumbler full of teaspoons, a silver cream-pitcher, a china sugar-bowl, and one pink china cup and saucer. Louisa used china every day—something which none of her neighbors did. They whispered about it among themselves. Their daily tables were laid with common crockery, their sets of best china stayed in the parlor closet, and Louisa Ellis was no richer nor better bred than they. Still she would use the china. She had for her supper a glass dish full of sugared currants, a plate of little cakes, and one of light white biscuits. Also a leaf or two of lettuce, which she cut up daintily. Louisa was very fond of lettuce, which she raised to perfection in her little garden. She ate quite heartily, though in a delicate, pecking way; it seemed almost surprising that any considerable bulk of the food should vanish.

After tea she filled a plate with nicely baked thin corn-cakes, and carried them out into the back-yard.

"Cæsar!" she called. "Cæsar! Cæsar!"

There was a little rush, and the clank of a chain, and a large yellow-and-white dog appeared at the door of his tiny hut, which was half hidden among the tall grasses and flowers. Louisa patted him and gave him the corn-cakes. Then she returned to the house and washed the tea-things, polishing the china carefully. The twilight had deepened; the chorus of the frogs floated in at the open window wonderfully loud and shrill, and once in a while a long sharp drone from a tree-toad pierced it. Louisa took off her green gingham apron, disclosing a shorter one of pink and white print. She lighted her lamp, and sat down again with her sewing.

In about half an hour Joe Dagget came. She heard his heavy step on the walk, and rose and took off her pink-and-white apron. Under that was still another—white linen with a little cambric edging on the bottom; that was Louisa's company apron. She never wore it without her calico sewing apron over it unless she had a guest. She had barely folded the pink and white one with methodical haste and laid it in a table-drawer when the door open and Joe Dagget entered.

He seemed to fill up the whole room. A little yellow canary that had been asleep in his green cage at the south window woke up and fluttered wildly, beating his little yellow wings against the wires. He always did so when Joe Dagget came into the room.

"Good-evening," said Louisa. She extended her hand with a kind of solemn cordiality.

"Good-evening, Louisa," returned the man, in a loud voice.

She placed a chair for him, and they sat facing each other, with the table between them. He sat bolt-upright, toeing out his heavy feet squarely, glancing with a good-humored uneasiness around the room. She sat gently erect, folding her slender hands in her white-linen lap.

"Been a pleasant day," remarked Dagget.

"Real pleasant," Louisa assented, softly. "Have you been haying?" she asked, after a little while.

"Yes, I've been haying all day, down in the ten-acre lot. Pretty hot work."

"It must be."

"Yes, it's pretty hot work in the sun."

"Is your mother well to-day?"

"Yes, mother's pretty well."

"I suppose Lily Dyer's with her now?"

Dagget colored. "Yes, she's with her," he answered, slowly.

He was not very young, but there was a boyish look about his large face. Louisa was not quite as old as he, her face was fairer and smoother, but she gave people the impression of being older.

"I suppose she's a good deal of help to your mother," she said, further.

"I guess she is; I don't know how mother'd get along without her," said Dagget, with a sort of embarrassed warmth.

"She looks like a real capable girl. She's pretty-looking too," remarked Louisa.

"Yes, she is pretty fair looking."

Presently Dagget began fingering the books on the table. There was a square red autograph album, and a Young Lady's Gift-Book which had belonged to Louisa's mother. He took them up one after the other and opened them; then laid them down again, the album on the Gift-Book.

Louisa kept eying them with mild uneasiness. Finally she rose and changed the position of the books, putting the album underneath. That was the way they had been arranged in the first place.

Dagget gave an awkward little laugh. "Now what difference did it make which book was on top?" said he.

Louisa looked at him with a deprecating smile. "I always keep them that way," murmured she.

"You do beat everything," said Dagget, trying to laugh again. His large face was flushed.

He remained about an hour longer, then rose to take leave. Going out, he stumbled over a rug, and trying to recover himself, hit Louisa's work-basket on the table, and knocked it on the floor.

He looked at Louisa, then at the rolling spools; he ducked himself awkwardly toward them, but she stopped him. "Never mind," said she; "I'll pick them up after you're gone."

She spoke with a mild stiffness. Either she was a little disturbed, or his nervousness affected her, and made her seem constrained in her effort to reassure him.

When Joe Dagget was outside he drew in the sweet evening air with a sigh, and felt much as an innocent and perfectly well-intentioned bear might after his exit from a china shop.

Louisa, on her part, felt much as the kind-hearted, long-suffering owner of the china shop might have done after the exit of the bear.

She tied on the pink, then the green apron, picked up all the scattered treasures and replaced them in her work-basket, and straightened the rug. Then she set the lamp on the floor, and began sharply examining the carpet. She even rubbed her fingers over it, and looked at them.

"He's tracked in a good deal of dust," she murmured. "I thought he must have."

Louisa got a dust-pan and brush, and swept Joe Dagget's track carefully.

If he could have known it, it would have increased his perplexity and uneasiness, although it would not have disturbed his loyalty in the least. He came twice a week to see Louisa Ellis, and every time, sitting there in her delicately sweet room, he felt as if surrounded by a hedge of lace. He was afraid to stir lest he should put a clumsy foot or hand through the fairy web, and he had always the consciousness that Louisa was watching fearfully lest he should.

Still the lace and Louisa commanded perforce his perfect respect and patience and loyalty. They were to be married in a month, after a singular courtship which had lasted for a matter of fifteen years. For fourteen out of the fifteen years the two had not once seen each other, and they seldom exchanged letters. Joe had been all those years in Australia, where he had gone to make his fortune, and where he had stayed until he made it. He would have stayed fifty years if it had taken so long, and come home feeble and tottering, or never come home at all, to marry Louisa.

But the fortune had been made in the fourteen years, and he had come home now to marry the woman who had been patiently and unquestioningly waiting for him all that time.

Shortly after they were engaged he had announced to Louisa his determination to strike out into new fields, and secure a competency before they should be married. She had listened and assented with the sweet serenity which never failed her, not even when her lover set forth on that long and uncertain journey. Joe, buoyed up as he was by his sturdy determination, broke down a little at the last, but Louisa kissed him with a mild blush, and said good-by.

"It won't be for long," poor Joe had said, huskily; but it was for fourteen years.

In that length of time much had happened. Louisa's mother and brother had died, and she was all alone in the world. But greatest happening of all—a subtle happening which both were too simple to understand—Louisa's feet had turned into a path, smooth maybe under a calm, serene sky, but so straight and unswerving that it could only meet a check at her grave, and so narrow that there was no room for any one at her side.

Louisa's first emotion when Joe Dagget came home (he had not apprised her of his coming) was consternation, although she would not admit it to herself, and he never dreamed of it. Fifteen years ago she had been in love with him—at least she considered herself to be. Just at that time, gently acquiescing with and falling into the natural drift of girlhood, she had seen marriage ahead as a reasonable feature and a probable desirability of life. She had listened with calm docility to her mother's views upon the subject. Her mother was remarkable for her cool sense and sweet, even temperament. She talked wisely to her daughter when Joe Dagget presented himself, and Louisa accepted him with no hesitation. He was the first lover she had ever had.

She had been faithful to him all these years. She had never dreamed of the possibility of marrying any one else. Her life, especially for the last seven years, had been full of a pleasant peace, she had never felt discontented nor impatient over her lover's absence; still she had always looked forward to his return and their marriage as the inevitable conclusion of things. However, she had fallen into a way of placing it so far in the future that it was almost equal to placing it over the boundaries of another life.

When Joe came she had been expecting him, and expecting to be married for fourteen years, but she was as much surprised and taken aback as if she had never thought of it.

Joe's consternation came later. He eyed Louisa with an instant confirmation of his old admiration. She had changed but little. She still kept her pretty manner and soft grace, and was, he considered, every whit as attractive as ever. As for himself, his stent was done; he had turned his face away from fortune-seeking, and the old winds of romance whistled as loud and sweet as ever through his ears. All the song which he had been wont to hear in them was Louisa; he had for a long time a loyal belief that he heard it still, but finally it seemed to him that although the winds sang always that one song, it had another name. But for Louisa the wind had never more than murmured; now it had gone down, and everything was still. She listened for a little while with half-wistful attention; then she turned quietly away and went to work on her wedding-clothes.

Joe had made some extensive and quite magnificent alterations in his house. It was the old homestead; the newly-married couple would live there, for Joe could not desert his mother, who refused to leave her old home. So Louisa must leave hers. Every morning, rising and going about among her neat maidenly possessions, she felt as one looking her last upon the faces of dear friends. It was true that in a measure she could take them with her, but, robbed of their old environments, they would appear in such new guises that they would almost cease to be themselves. Then there were some peculiar features of her happy solitary life which she would probably be obliged to relinquish altogether. Sterner tasks than these graceful but half-needless ones would probably devolve upon her. There would be a large house to care for; there would be company to entertain; there would be Joe's rigorous and feeble old mother to wait upon; and it would be contrary to all thrifty village traditions for her to keep more than one servant. Louisa had a little still, and she used to occupy herself pleasantly in summer weather with distilling the sweet and aromatic essences from roses and peppermint and spearmint. By-and-by her still must be laid away. Her store of essences was already considerable, and there would be no time for her to distil for the mere pleasure of it. Then Joe's mother would think it foolishness; she had already hinted her opinion in the matter. Louisa dearly loved to sew a linen seam, not always for use, but for the simple, mild pleasure which she took in it. She would have been loath to confess how more than once she had ripped a seam for the mere delight of sewing it together again. Sitting at her window during long sweet afternoons, drawing her needle gently through the dainty fabric, she was peace itself. But there was small chance of such foolish comfort in the future. Joe's mother, domineering, shrewd old matron that she was even in her old age, and very likely even Joe himself, with his honest masculine rudeness, would laugh and frown down all these pretty but senseless old maiden ways.

Louisa had almost the enthusiasm of an artist over the mere order and cleanliness of her solitary home. She had throbs of genuine triumph at the sight of the window-panes which she had polished until they shone like jewels. She gloated gently over her orderly bureau-drawers, with their exquisitely folded contents redolent with lavender and sweet clover and very purity. Could she be sure of the endurance of even this? She had visions, so startling that she half repudiated them as indelicate, of coarse masculine belongings strewn about in endless litter; of dust and disorder arising necessarily from a coarse masculine presence in the midst of all this delicate harmony.

Among her forebodings of disturbance, not the least was with regard to Cæsar. Cæsar was a veritable hermit of a dog. For the greater part of his life he had dwelt in his secluded hut, shut out from the society of his kind and all innocent canine joys. Never had Cæsar since his early youth watched at a woodchuck's hole; never had he known the delights of a stray bone at a neighbor's kitchen door. And it was all on account of a sin committed when hardly out of his puppyhood. No one knew the possible depth of remorse of which this mild-visaged, altogether innocent-looking old dog might be capable; but whether or not he had encountered remorse, he had encountered a full measure of righteous retribution. Old Cæsar seldom lifted up his voice in a growl or a bark; he was fat and sleepy; there were yellow rings which looked like spectacles around his dim old eyes; but there was a neighbor who bore on his hand the imprint of several of Cæsar's sharp white youthful teeth, and for that he had lived at the end of a chain, all alone in a little hut, for fourteen years. The neighbor, who was choleric and smarting with the pain of his wound, had demanded either Cæsar's death or complete ostracism. So Louisa's brother, to whom the dog had belonged, had built him his little kennel and tied him up. It was now fourteen years since, in a flood of youthful spirits, he had inflicted that memorable bite, and with the exception of short excursions, always at the end of the chain, under the strict guardianship of his master or Louisa, the old dog had remained a close prisoner. It is doubtful if, with his limited ambition, he took much pride in the fact, but it is certain that he was possessed of considerable cheap fame. He was regarded by all the children in the village and by many adults as a very monster of ferocity. St. George's dragon could hardly have surpassed in evil repute Louisa Ellis's old yellow dog. Mothers charged their children with solemn emphasis not to go too near to him, and the children listened and believed greedily, with a fascinated appetite for terror, and ran by Louisa's house stealthily, with many sidelong and backward glances at the terrible dog. If perchance he sounded a hoarse bark, there was a panic. Wayfarers chancing into Louisa's yard eyed him with respect, and inquired if the chain were stout. Cæsar at large might have seemed a very ordinary dog and excited no comment whatever; chained, his reputation overshadowed him, so that he lost his own proper outlines and looked darkly vague and enormous. Joe Dagget, however, wth his good-humored sense and shrewdness, saw him as he was. He strode valiantly up to him and patted him on the head, in spite of Louisa's soft clamor of warning, and even attempted to set him loose. Louise grew so alarmed that he desisted, but kept announcing his opinion in the matter quite forcibly at intervals. "There ain't a better-natured dog in town," he would say, "and it's downright cruel to keep him tied up there. Some day I'm going to take him out."

Louisa had very little hope that he would not, one of these days, when their interests and possessions should be more completely fused in one. She pictured to herself Cæsar on the rampage through the quiet and unguarded village. She saw innocent children bleeding in his path. She was herself very fond of the old dog, because he had belonged to her dead brother, and he was always very gentle with her; still she had great faith in his ferocity. She always warned people not to go too near him. She fed him on ascetic fare of corn-mush and cakes, and never fired his dangerous temper with heating and sanguinary diet of flesh and bones. Louisa looked at the old dog munching his simple fare, and thought of her approaching marriage and trembled. Still no anticipation of disorder and confusion in lieu of sweet peace and harmony, no forebodings of Cæsar on the rampage, no wild fluttering of her little yellow canary, were sufficinet to turn her a hair's-breadth. Joe Dagget had been fond of her and working for her all these years. It was not for her, whatever came to pass, to prove untrue and break his heart. She put the exquisite little stitches into her wedding-garments, and the time went on until it was only a week before her wedding-day. It was a Tuesday evening, and the wedding was to be a week from Wednesday.

There was a full moon that night. About nine o'clock Louisa strolled down the road a little way. There were harvest-fields on either hand, bordered by low stone walls. Luxuriant clumps of bushes grew beside the wall, and trees—wild cherry and old apple-trees—at intervals. Presently Louisa sat down on the wall and looked about her with mildly sorrowful reflectiveness. Tall shrubs of blueberry and meadow-sweet, all woven together and tangled with blackberry vines and horsebriers, shut her in on either side. She had a little clear space between them. Opposite her, on the other side of the road, was a spreading tree; the moon shone between its boughs, and the leaves twinkled like silver. The road was bespread with a beautiful shifting dapple of silver and shadow; the air was full of a mysterious sweetness. "I wonder if it's wild grapes?" murmured Louisa. She sat there some time. She was just thinking of rising, when she heard footsteps and low voices, and remained quiet. It was a lonely place, and she felt a little timid. She thought she would keep still in the shadow and let the persons, whoever they might be, pass her.

But just before they reached her the voices ceased, and the foot-steps. She understood that their owners had also found seats upon the stone wall. She was wondering if she could not steal away unobserved, when the voice broke the stillness. It was Joe Dagget's. She sat still and listened.

The voice was announced by a loud sigh, which was as familiar as itself. "Well," said Dagget, "you've made up your mind, then, I suppose?"

"Yes," returned another voice; "I'm going day after to-morrow."

"That's Lily Dyer," thought Louisa to herself. The voice embodied itself in her mind. She saw a girl tall and full-figured, with a firm, fair face, looking fairer and firmer in the moonlight, her strong yellow hair braided in a close knot. A girl full of calm rustic strength and bloom, with a masterful way which might have beseemed a princess. Lily Dyer was a favorite with the village folk; she had just the qualities to arouse the admiration. She was good and handsome and smart. Louisa had often heard her praises sounded.

"Well," said Joe Dagget, "I ain't got a word to say."

"I don't know what you could say," returned Lily Dyer.

"Not a word to say," repeated Joe, drawing out the words heavily. Then there was a silence. "I ain't sorry," he began at last, "that that happened yesterday—that we kind of let on how we felt to each other. I guess it's just as well we knew. Of course I can't do anything any different. I'm going right on an' get married next week. I ain't going back on a woman that's waited for me fourteen years, an' break her heart."

"If you should jilt her to-morrow, I wouldn't have you," spoke up the girl, with sudden vehemence.

"Well, I ain't going to give you the chance," said he; "but I don't believe you would, either."

"You'd see I wouldn't. Honor's honor, an' right's right. An' I'd never think anything of any man that went against 'em for me or any other girl; you'd find that out, Joe Dagget."

"Well, you'll find out fast enough that I ain't going against 'em for you or any other girl," returned he. Their voices sounded almost as if they were angry with each other. Louisa was listening eagerly.

"I'm sorry you feel as if you must go away," said Joe, "but I don't know but it's best."

"Of course it's best. I hope you and I have got common-sense."

"Well, I suppose you're right." Suddenly Joe's voice got an undertone of tenderness. "Say, Lily," said he, "I'll get along well enough myself, but I can't bear to think—You don't suppose you're going to fret much over it?"

"I guess you'll find out I sha'n't fret much over a married man."

"Well, I hope you won't—I hope you won't, Lily. God knows I do. And—I hope—one of these days—you'll—come across somebody else—"

"I don't see any reason why I shouldn't." Suddenly her tone changed. She spoke in a sweet, clear voice, so loud that she could have been heard across the street. "No, Joe Dagget," said she, "I'll never marry any other man as long as I live. I've got good sense, an' I ain't going to break my heart nor make a fool of myself; but I'm never going to be married, you can be sure of that. I ain't that sort of a girl to feel this way twice."

Louisa heard an exclamation and a soft commotion behind the bushes; then Lily spoke again—the voice sounded as if she had risen. "This must be put a stop to," said she. "We've stayed here long enough. I'm going home."

Louisa sat there in a daze, listening to their retreating steps. After a while she got up and slunk softly home herself. The next day she did her housework methodically; that was as much a matter of course as breathing; but she did not sew on her wedding-clothes. She sat at her window and meditated. In the evening Joe came. Louisa Ellis had never known that she had any diplomacy in her, but when she came to look for it that night she found it, although meek of its kind, among her little feminine weapons. Even now she could hardly believe that she had heard aright, and that she would not do Joe a terrible injury should she break her troth-plight. She wanted to sound him without betraying too soon her own inclinations in the matter. She did it successfully, and they finally came to an understanding; but it was a difficult thing, for he was as afraid of betraying himself as she.

She never mentioned Lily Dyer. She simply said that while she had no cause of complaint against him, she had lived so long in one way that she shrank from making a change.

"Well, I never shrank, Louisa," said Dagget. "I'm going to be honest enough to say that I think maybe it's better this way; but if you'd wanted to keep on, I'd have stuck to you till my dying day. I hope you know that."

"Yes, I do," said she.

That night she and Joe parted more tenderly than they had done for a long time. Standing in the door, holding each other's hands, a last great wave of regretful memory swept over them.

"Well, this ain't the way we've thought it was all going to end, is it, Louisa?" said Joe.

She shook her head. There was a little quiver on her placid face.

"You let me know if there's ever anything I can do for you," said he. "I ain't ever going to forget you, Louisa." Then he kissed her, and went down the path.

Louisa, all alone by herself that night, wept a little, she hardly knew why; but the next morning, on waking, she felt like a queen who, after fearing lest her domain be wrested away from her, sees it firmly insured in her possssion.

Now the tall weeds and grasses might cluster around Cæsar's little hermit hut, the snow might fall on its roof year in and year out, but he never would go on a rampage through the unguarded village. Now the little canary might turn itself into a peaceful yellow ball night after night, and have no need to wake and flutter with wild terror against its bars. Louisa could sew linen seams, and distil roses, and dust and polish and fold away in lavender, as long as she listed. That afternoon she sat with her needle-work at the window, and felt fairly steeped in peace. Lily Dyer, tall and erect and blooming, went past; but she felt no qualm. If Louisa Ellis had sold her birthright she did not know it, the taste of the pottage was so delicious, and had been her sole satisfaction for so long. Serenity and placid narrowness had become to her as the birthright itself. She gazed ahead through a long reach of future days strung together like pearls in a rosary, every one like the others, and all smooth and flawless and innocent, and her heart went up in thankfulness. Outside was the fervid summer afternoon; the air was filled with the sounds of the busy harvest of men and birds and bees; there were halloos, metallic clatterings, sweet calls, and long hummings. Louisa sat, prayerfully numbering her days, like an uncloistered nun.

Discussion of Freeman's "A New England Nun"

1. What place in the total context of the story has the slow-motion effect of the first paragraphs? For example, how do those paragraphs prepare for the entrance of Joe Dagget? Notice the language that describes him: "heavy step," "seemed to fill up the whole room," and "loud voice."

2. What has happened to Louisa's feelings in the fifteen years since she has seen Joe Dagget?

3. After reading several stories that present married couples, how do you feel about Louisa's decision to remain in her own home? Do you feel pity for Louisa? What is the significance of the title? How do you think Freeman's audience in her day may have reacted?

4. In many stories, the animals provide an implicit commentary on the human characters. How do the dog and the canary serve this function in "A New England Nun"?

J. M. DE MACHADO DE ASSIS

1839–1908

🌷 Joaquim María de Machado de Assis, the pre-eminent writer of Brazil, is increasingly coming to be known as one of the major American novelists of the nineteenth century. Although his life was uneventful, it was crowned with success: shy, epileptic, self-educated, the grandson of freed slaves, he worked his way up into the highest ranks of the Brazilian civil service. From this vantage point he probed the psychology of both the nation and the individual. *Esau and Jacob* (1904) and *Counselor Ayres' Memorial* (1908), keen studies of felicitous marriages, are also novels about the political evolution of Brazil; and Machado de Assis's ability to combine the personal and social aspects of life in the novel are very much in evidence in *Posthumous Memoirs of Bras Cubas* (1880, usually known in this country as *Epitaph of a Small Winner*), *Quincus Borba* (1891), and *Dom Casmurro* (1900). One of his greatest symbols of the failures of society is the capacity of men to deceive themselves about women. By failing to see women as they really are—people—they are doomed forever to solitude, despair, or ignorance. In "Midnight Mass," one of his most popular stories, the narrator is forever condemned to this last state of mind. But the heroine, a fascinating character, manages to triumph. As in all stories by Machado de Assis, the text demands extremely close reading.

Midnight Mass

I have never quite understood a conversation that I had with a lady many years ago, when I was seventeen and she was thirty. It was Christmas Eve. I had arranged to go to Mass with a neighbor and was to rouse him at midnight for this purpose.

The two-story house in which I was staying belonged to the notary Menezes, whose first wife had been a cousin of mine. His second wife, Conceição [Conception], and her mother had received me hospitably upon my arrival a few months earlier. I had come to Rio from Mangaratiba to study for the college entrance examinations. I lived quietly with my books. Few contacts. Occasional walks. The family was small: the notary, his wife, his mother-in-law, and two female slaves. An old-fashioned household. By ten at night everyone was in his bedroom; by half-past ten the house was asleep.

I had never gone to a theater and, more than once, on hearing Menezes say that he was going, I asked him to take me along. On

From *The Psychiatrist and Other Stories* by Joaquim María de Machado de Assis translated by William L. Grossman and Helen Caldwell. Copyright © 1963 by The Regents of the University of California; reprinted by permission of the University of California Press.

these occasions his mother-in-law frowned and the slaves tittered. Menezes did not reply; he dressed, went out, and returned the next morning. Later I learned that the theater was a euphemism. Menezes was having an affair with a married woman who was separated from her husband; he stayed out once a week. Conceiçao had grieved at the beginning, but after a time she had grown used to the situation. Custom led to resignation, and finally she came almost to accept the affair as proper.

Gentle Conceição! They called her the saint and she merited the title, so uncomplainingly did she suffer her husband's neglect. In truth, she possessed a temperament of great equanimity, with extremes neither of tears nor of laughter. Everything about her was passive and attenuated. Her very face was median, neither pretty nor ugly. She was what is called a kind person. She spoke ill of no one, she pardoned everything. She didn't know how to hate; quite possibly she didn't know how to love.

On that Christmas Eve (it was 1861 or 1862) the notary was at theater. I should have been back in Mangaratiba, but I had decided to remain till Christmas to see a midnight Mass in the big city. The family retired at the usual hour. I sat in the front parlor, dressed and ready. From there I could leave through the entrance hall without waking anyone. There were three keys to the door: the notary had one, I had one, and one remained in the house.

"But Mr. Nogueira, what will you do all this while?" asked Conceição's mother.

"I'll read, Madame Ignacia."

I had a copy of an old translation of *The Three Musketeers*, published originally, I think, in serial form in *The Journal of Commerce*. I sat down at the table in the center of the room and by the light of the kerosene lamp, while the house slept, mounted once more D'Artagnan's bony nag and set out upon adventure. In a short time I was completely absorbed. The minutes flew as they rarely do when one is waiting. I heard the clock strike eleven, but almost without noticing. After a time, however, a sound from the interior of the house roused me from my book. It was the sound of footsteps, in the hall that connected the parlor with the dining room. I raised my head. Soon I saw the form of Conceição appear at the door.

"Haven't you gone?" she asked.

"No, I haven't. I don't think it's midnight yet."

"What patience!"

Conceição, wearing her bedroom slippers, came into the room. She was dressed in a white negligee, loosely bound at the waist. Her slenderness helped to suggest a romantic apparition quite in keeping with the spirit of my novel. I shut the book. She sat on the chair facing mine, near the sofa. To my question whether perchance I had awakened her by stirring about, she quickly replied:

"No, I woke up naturally."

I looked at her and doubted her statement. Her eyes were not those of a person who had just slept. However, I quickly put out of my mind the thought that she could be guilty of lying. The possibility that I might have kept her awake and that she might have lied in order not to make me unhappy, did not occur to me at the time. I have already said that she was a good person, a kind person.

"I guess it won't be much longer now," I said.

"How patient you are to stay awake and wait while your friend sleeps! And to wait alone! Aren't you afraid of ghosts? I thought you'd be startled when you saw me."

"When I heard footsteps I was surprised. But then I soon saw it was you."

"What are you reading? Don't tell me, I think I know: it's *The Three Musketeers*."

"Yes, that's right. It's very interesting."

"Do you like novels?"

"Yes."

"Have you ever read *The Little Sweetheart?*"

"By Mr. Macedo? I have it in Mangaratiba."

"I'm very fond of novels, but I don't have much time for them. Which ones have you read?"

I began to name some. Conceição listened, with her head resting on the back of her chair, looking at me past half-shut eyelids. From time to time she wet her lips with her tongue. When I stopped speaking she said nothing. Thus we remained for several seconds. Then she raised her head; she clasped her hands and rested her chin on them, with her elbows on the arms of her chair, all without taking from me her large, perceptive eyes.

"Maybe she's bored with me," I thought. And then, aloud: "Madame Conceição, I think it's getting late and I . . ."

"No, it's still early. I just looked at the clock; it's half-past eleven. There's time yet. When you lose a night's sleep, can you stay awake the next day?"

"I did once."

"I can't. If I lose a night, the next day I just have to take a nap, if only for half an hour. But of course I'm getting on in years."

"Oh, no, nothing of the sort, Madame Conceição!"

I spoke so fervently that I made her smile. Usually her gestures were slow, her attitude calm. Now, however, she rose suddenly, moved to the other side of the room, and, in her chaste disarray, walked about between the window and the door of her husband's study. Although thin, she always walked with a certain rocking gait as if she carried her weight with difficulty. I had never before felt this impression so strongly. She paused several times, examining a curtain or correcting the position of some object on the sideboard. Finally she stopped directly in front of me, with the table between us. The circle of her ideas was narrow indeed: she returned to her surprise at seeing me awake and dressed. I repeated what she

already knew, that I had never heard a midnight Mass in the city
and that I didn't want to miss the chance.

"It's the same as in the country. All Masses are alike."

"I guess so. But in the city there must be more elegance and more
people. Holy Week here in Rio is much better than in the country.
I don't know about St. John's Day or St. Anthony's . . ."

Little by little she had leaned forward; she had rested her elbows
on the marble top of the table and had placed her face between the
palms of her hands. Her unbuttoned sleeves fell naturally, and I
saw her forearms, very white and not so thin as one might have
supposed. I had seen her arms before, although not frequently, but
on this occasion sight of them impressed me greatly. The veins
were so blue that, despite the dimness of the light, I could trace
every one of them. Even more than the book, Conceição's presence
had served to keep me awake. I went on talking about holy days in
the country and in the city, and about whatever else came to my
lips. I jumped from subject to subject, sometimes returning to an
earlier one; and I laughed in order to make her laugh, so that I could
see her white, shining, even teeth. Her eyes were not really black
but were very dark; her nose, thin and slightly curved, gave her
face an air of interrogation. Whenever I raised my voice a little, she
hushed me.

"Softly! Mama may wake up."

And she did not move from that position, which filled me with
delight, so close were our faces. Really there was no need to speak
loudly in order to be heard. We both whispered, I more than she
because I had more to say. At times she became serious, very
serious, with her brow a bit wrinkled. After a while she tired and
changed both position and place. She came around the table and sat
on the sofa. I turned my head and could see the tips of her slippers,
but only for as long as it took her to sit down: her negligee was
long and quickly covered them. I remember that they were black.
Conceição said very softly:

"Mama's room is quite a distance away, but she sleeps so lightly.
If she wakes up now, poor thing, it will take her a long time to fall
asleep again."

"I'm like that, too."

"What?" she asked, leaning forward to hear better.

I moved to the chair immediately next to the sofa and repeated
what I had said. She laughed at the coincidence, for she, too, was a
light sleeper, we were all light sleepers.

"I'm just like mama: when I wake up I can't fall asleep again. I
roll all over the bed, I get up, I light the candle, I walk around, I lie
down again, and nothing happens."

"Like tonight."

"No, no," she hastened.

I didn't understand her denial; perhaps she didn't understand it either. She took the ends of her belt and tapped them on her knees, or rather on her right knee, for she had crossed her legs. Then she began to talk about dreams. She said she had had only one nightmare in her whole life, and that one during her childhood. She wanted to know whether I ever had nightmares. Thus the conversation re-engaged itself and moved along slowly, continuously, and I forgot about the hour and about Mass. Whenever I finished a bit of narrative or an explanation she asked a question or brought up some new point, and I started talking again. Now and then she had to caution me.

"Softly, softly . . ."

Sometimes there were pauses. Twice I thought she was asleep. But her eyes, shut for a moment, quickly opened: they showed neither sleepiness nor fatigue, as though she had shut them merely so that she could see better. On one of these occasions I think she noticed that I was absorbed in her, and I remember that she shut her eyes again—whether hurriedly or slowly I do not remember. Some of my recollections of that evening seem abortive or confused. I get mixed up, I contradict myself. One thing I remember vividly is that at a certain moment she, who till then had been such engaging company (but nothing more), suddenly became beautiful, so very beautiful. She stood up, with her arms crossed. I, out of respect for her, stirred myself to rise; she did not want me to, she put one of her hands on my shoulder, and I remained seated. I thought she was going to say something; but she trembled as if she had a chill, turned her back, and sat in the chair where she had found me reading. She glanced at the mirror above the sofa and began to talk about two engravings that were hanging on the wall.

"These pictures are getting old. I've asked Chiquinho to buy new ones."

Chiquinho was her husband's nickname. The pictures bespoke the man's principal interest. One was of Cleopatra; I no longer remember the subject of the other, but there were women in it. Both were banal. In those days I did not know they were ugly.

"They're pretty," I said.

"Yes, but they're stained. And besides, to tell the truth, I'd prefer pictures of saints. These are better for bachelors' quarters or a barber shop."

"A barber shop! I didn't think you'd ever been to . . ."

"But I can imagine what the customers there talk about while they're waiting—girls and flirtations, and naturally the proprietor wants to please them with pictures they'll like. But I think pictures like that don't belong in the home. That's what I think, but I have a lot of queer ideas. Anyway, I don't like them. I have an Our Lady of the Immaculate Conception, my patron saint; it's very lovely. But it's a statue, it can't be hung on the wall, and I wouldn't want it here anyway. I keep it in my little oratory."

The oratory brought to mind the Mass. I thought it might be time to go and was about to say so. I think I even opened my mouth but shut it before I could speak, so that I could go on listening to what she was saying, so sweetly, so graciously, so gently that it drugged my soul. She spoke of her religious devotions as a child and as a young girl. Then she told about dances and walks and trips to the island of Paquetá, all mixed together, almost without interruption. When she tired of the past she spoke of the present, of household matters, of family cares, which, before her marriage, everyone said would be terrible, but really they were nothing. She didn't mention it, but I knew she had been twenty-seven when she married.

She no longer moved about, as at first, and hardly changed position. Her eyes seemed smaller, and she began to look idly about at the walls.

"We must change this wallpaper," she said, as if talking to herself.

I agreed, just to say something, to shake off my magnetic trance or whatever one may call the condition that thickened my tongue and benumbed my senses. I wished and I did not wish to end the conversation. I tried to take my eyes from her, and did so out of respect; but, afraid she would think I was tired of looking at her, when in truth I was not, I turned again towards her. The conversation was dying away. In the street, absolute stillness.

We stopped talking and for some time (I cannot say how long) sat there in silence. The only sound was the gnawing of a rat in the study; it stirred me from my somnolescence. I wanted to talk about it but didn't know how to begin. Conceição seemed to be abstracted. Suddenly I heard a beating on the window and a voice shouting:

"Midnight Mass! Midnight Mass!"

"There's your friend," she said, rising. "It's funny. You were to wake him, and here he comes to wake you. Hurry, it must be late. Goodbye."

"Is it time already?"

"Of course."

"Midnight Mass!" came the voice from outside, with more beating on the window.

"Hurry, hurry, don't make him wait. It was my fault. Goodbye until tomorrow."

And with her rocking gait Conceição walked softly down the hall. I went out into the street and, with my friend, proceeded to the church. During Mass, Conceição kept appearing between me and the priest; charge this to my seventeen years. Next morning at breakfast I spoke of the midnight Mass and of the people I had seen in church, without, however, exciting Conceição's interest. During the day I found her, as always, natural, benign, with nothing to suggest the conversation of the prior evening.

A few days later I went to Mangaratiba. When I returned to Rio in March, I learned that the notary had died of apoplexy. Conceição was living in the Engenho Novo district, but I neither visited nor met her. I learned later that she had married her husband's apprenticed clerk.

Discussion of Machado de Assis's "Midnight Mass"

1. This story, like "Veronika," is concerned with an event that is not consummated, yet both characters seem in some way changed by the events. Explain how this is so.

2. Conceição's entrance into the room and the dialogue that follows are good examples of a man and a woman trying to define—and to redefine—their roles. What are these roles? How do they contrast with the roles defined by the conversations in "Psychology"? "Cat in the Rain"? "Wine"?

3. Conceição is similar also to the women in the stories by Chopin and Oates in that she is willing to cross a conventional moral line, for example, entertaining a relationship with a man other than her husband. The central male in each case reacts strongly to this possibility. Can you see further similarities in their reactions?

4. A superficial reading of this story often stereotypes the heroine as an aggressive older woman attempting to seduce a young and naive man. What details in the story establish that this is not really the case?

KATE CHOPIN

1851–1904

❦ Kate Chopin was born in St. Louis, but the bulk of her writings deal with life in southern Louisiana, where she lived from 1870 until 1884, a year after the death of her husband. She contributed numerous stories to standard American periodicals such as *Atlantic Monthly, Vogue,* and *Saturday Evening Post.* The published stories established her as a local colorist, a writer whose main talents lay in the descriptions of the exotic life of the inhabitants of southern Louisiana, but this complacent misconception was rudely shattered by the publication of her first novel, *The Awakening* (1899). The novel was frequently pulled off the shelves, its author virtually ostracized in her native St. Louis. It has been only in recent years that the novel has been discussed seriously as a major work of fiction dealing with the awakening of a young married woman to life, particularly the sexual awakening that Edna Pontellier, the heroine, experiences. Although it is tempting to dismiss the adverse reactions as yet another instance of Victorian prudery—and to see *The Awakening* as a sort of early *Lady Chatterley's Lover*—earlier critics seized on a feature of her writing now often ignored, her moral objectivity. Chopin's stories usually present a set of alternative realities to the reader. The author refuses to editorialize, but forces the audience to confront their own assumptions about the ethical norms of human behavior. The situations themselves, as in "The Storm," are quite simple. But the thoughts that they provoke and the author's refusal to judge the action evoke strong reactions. Underlying the issues are central questions: To what extent are men and women actually free and to what extent are their actions conditioned by society?

The Storm

I

The leaves were so still that even Bibi thought it was going to rain. Bobinôt, who was accustomed to converse on terms of perfect equality with his little son, called the child's attention to certain sombre clouds that were rolling with sinister intention from the west, accompanied by a sullen, threatening roar. They were at Friedheimer's store and decided to remain there till the storm had passed. They sat within the door on two empty kegs. Bibi was four years old and looked very wise.

"Mama'll be 'fraid, yes," he suggested with blinking eyes.

Reprinted by permission from *The Complete Work of Kate Chopin* edited by Per Seyersted, copyright © 1969, by Louisiana State University Press.

"She'll shut the house. Maybe she got Sylvie helpin' her this evenin'," Bobinôt responded reassuringly.

"No; she ent got Sylvie. Sylvie was helpin' her yistiday," piped Bibi.

Bobinôt arose and going across to the counter purchased a can of shrimps, of which Calixta was very fond. Then he returned to his perch on the keg and sat stolidly holding the can of shrimps while the storm burst. It shook the wooden store and seemed to be ripping great furrows in the distant field. Bibi laid his little hand on his father's knee and was not afraid.

II

Calixta, at home, felt no uneasiness for their safety. She sat at a side window sewing furiously on a sewing machine. She was greatly occupied and did not notice the approaching storm. But she felt very warm and often stopped to mop her face on which the perspiration gathered in beads. She unfastened her white sacque at the throat. It began to grow dark, and suddenly realizing the situation she got up hurriedly and went about closing windows and doors.

Out on the small front gallery she had hung Bobinôt's Sunday clothes to air and she hastened out to gather them before the rain fell. As she stepped outside, Alcée Laballière rode in at the gate. She had not seen him very often since her marriage, and never alone. She stood there with Bobinôt's coat in her hands, and the big rain drops began to fall. Alcée rode his horse under the shelter of a side projection where the chickens had huddled and there were plows and a harrow piled up in the corner.

"May I come and wait on your gallery till the storm is over, Calixta?" he asked.

"Come 'long in, M'sieur Alcée."

His voice and her own startled her as if from a trance, and she seized Bobinôt's vest. Alcée, mounting to the porch, grabbed the trousers and snatched Bibi's braided jacket that was about to be carried away by a sudden gust of wind. He expressed an intention to remain outside, but it was soon apparent that he might as well have been out in the open: the water beat in upon the boards in driving sheets, and he went inside, closing the door after him. It was even necessary to put something beneath the door to keep the water out.

"My! what a rain! It's good two years sence it rain' like that" exclaimed Calixta as she rolled up a piece of bagging and Alcée helped her to thrust it beneath the crack.

She was a little fuller of figure than five years before when she married; but she had lost nothing of her vivacity. Her blue eyes still retained their melting quality; and her yellow hair, dishevelled by the wind and rain, kinked more stubbornly than ever about her ears and temples.

The rain beat upon the low, shingled roof with a force and clatter that threatened to break an entrance and deluge them there. They were in the dining room—the sitting room—the general utility room. Adjoining was her bed room, with Bibi's couch along side her own. The door stood open, and the room with its white, monumental bed, its closed shutters, looked dim and mysterious.

Alcée flung himself into a rocker and Calixta nervously began to gather up from the floor the lengths of a cotton sheet which she had been sewing.

"If this keeps up, *Dieu sait* if the levees goin' to stan' it!" she exclaimed.

"What have you got to do with the levees?"

"I got enough to do! An' there's Bobinôt with Bibi out in that storm—if he only didn' left Friedheimer's!"

"Let us hope, Calixta, that Bobinôt's got sense enough to come in out of a cyclone."

She went and stood at the window with a greatly disturbed look on her face. She wiped the frame that was clouded with moisture. It was stiflingly hot. Alcée got up and joined her at the window, looking over her shoulder. The rain was coming down in sheets obscuring the view of far-off cabins and enveloping the distant wood in a gray mist. The playing of the lightning was incessant. A bolt struck a tall chinaberry tree at the edge of the field. It filled all visible space with a blinding glare and the crash seemed to invade the very boards they stood upon.

Calixta put her hands to her eyes, and with a cry, staggered backward. Alcée's arm encircled her, and for an instant he drew her close and spasmodically to him.

"*Bonté!*" she cried, releasing herself from his encircling arm and retreating from the window, "the house'll go next! If I only knew w'ere Bibi was!" She would not compose herself; she would not be seated. Alcée clasped her shoulders and looked into her face. The contact of her warm, palpitating body when he had unthinkingly drawn her into his arms, had aroused all the old-time infatuation and desire for her flesh.

"Calixta," he said, "don't be frightened. Nothing can happen. The house is too low to be struck, with so many tall trees standing about. There! aren't you going to be quiet? say, aren't you?" He pushed her hair back from her face that was warm and steaming. Her lips were as red and moist as pomegranate seed. Her white neck and a glimpse of her full, firm bosom disturbed him powerfully. As she glanced up at him the fear in her liquid blue eyes had given place to a drowsy gleam that unconsciously betrayed a sensuous desire. He looked down into her eyes and there was nothing for him to do but to gather her lips in a kiss. It reminded him of Assumption.

"Do you remember—in Assumption, Calixta?" he asked in a low voice broken by passion. Oh! she remembered; for in Assumption he had kissed her and kissed and kissed her; until his senses would well nigh fail, and to save her he would resort to a desperate flight. If she was not an immaculate dove in those days, she was still inviolate; a passionate creature whose very defenselessness had made her defense, against which his honor forbade him to prevail. Now—well, now—her lips seemed in a manner free to be tasted, as well as her round, white throat and her whiter breasts.

They did not heed the crashing torrents, and the roar of the elements made her laugh as she lay in his arms. She was a revelation in that dim, mysterious chamber; as white as the couch she lay upon. Her firm, elastic flesh that was knowing for the first time its birthright, was like a creamy lily that the sun invites to contribute its breath and perfume to the undying life of the world.

The generous abundance of her passion, without guile or trickery, was like a white flame which penetrated and found response in depths of his own sensuous nature that had never been reached.

When he touched her breasts they gave themselves up in quivering ecstasy, inviting his lips. Her mouth was a fountain of delight. And when he possessed her, they seemed to swoon together at the very borderland of life's mystery.

He stayed cushioned upon her, breathless, dazed, enervated, with his heart beating like a hammer upon her. With one hand she clasped his head, her lips lightly touching his forehead. The other hand stroked with a soothing rhythm his muscular shoulders.

The growl of the thunder was distant and passing away. The rain beat softly upon the shingles, inviting them to drowsiness and sleep. But they dared not yield.

The rain was over; and the sun was turning the glistening green world into a palace of gems. Calixta, on the gallery, watched Alcée ride away. He turned and smiled at her with a beaming face; and she lifted her pretty chin in the air and laughed aloud.

III

Bobinôt and Bibi, trudging home, stopped without at the cistern to make themselves presentable.

"My! Bibi, w'at will yo' mama say! You ought to be ashame'. You oughtn' put on those good pants. Look at 'em! An' that mud on yo' collar! How you got that mud on yo' collar, Bibi? I never saw such a boy!" Bibi was the picture of pathetic resignation. Bobinôt was the embodiment of serious solicitude as he strove to remove from his own person and his son's the signs of their tramp over heavy roads and through wet fields. He scraped the mud off Bibi's bare legs and feet with a stick and carefully removed all traces from his heavy brogans. Then, prepared for the worst—the meeting with an over-scrupulous housewife, they entered cautiously at the back door.

Calixta was preparing supper. She had set the table and was dripping coffee at the hearth. She sprang up as they came in.

"Oh, Bobinôt! You back! My! but I was uneasy. W'ere you been during the rain? An' Bibi? he ain't wet? he ain't hurt?" She had clasped Bibi and was kissing him effusively. Bobinôt's explanations and apologies which he had been composing all along the way, died on his lips as Calixta felt him to see if he were dry, and seemed to express nothing but satisfaction at their safe return.

"I brought you some shrimps, Calixta," offered Bobinôt, hauling the can from his ample side pocket and laying it on the table.

"Shrimps! Oh, Bobinôt! you too good fo' anything!" and she gave him a smacking kiss on the cheek that resounded. *"J'vous réponds*, we'll have a feas' to night! umph-umph!"

Bobinôt and Bibi began to relax and enjoy themselves, and when the three seated themselves at table they laughed much and so loud that anyone might have heard them as far away as Laballière's.

IV

Alcée Laballière wrote to his wife, Clarisse, that night. It was a loving letter, full of tender solicitude. He told her not to hurry back, but if she and the babies liked it at Biloxi, to stay a month longer. He was getting on nicely; and though he missed them, he was willing to bear the separation a while longer—realizing that their health and pleasure were the first things to be considered.

V

As for Clarisse, she was charmed upon receiving her husband's letter. She and the babies were doing well. The society was agreeable; many of her old friends and acquaintances were at the bay. And the first free breath since her marriage seemed to restore the pleasant liberty of her maiden days. Devoted as she was to her husband, their intimate conjugal life was something which she was more than willing to forego for a while.

So the storm passed and every one was happy.

Discussion of Chopin's "The Storm"

1. A cursory reading of this story usually disappoints because everything seems to be right there on the page. Yet it raises some

very profound questions about the need for sexual expressions in human relationships. List these questions and their implications.

2. To what extent is Calixta a free agent in this story?

3. "The Storm" is a continuation of or sequel to another Chopin story, "The 'Cadian Ball." Before reading the latter, construct a scenario, or even a story, to which "The Storm" would be an appropriate conclusion.

4. Chopin, Hemingway, and Lessing all relate in a matter-of-fact way important incidents in their characters' lives. How do these incidents stand as variations on the same theme?

STEPHEN CRANE

1871–1900

❧ Crane's reputation was established by *The Red Badge of Courage* (1895), which generations of North Americans have regarded as the most realistic and moving story ever written about the Civil War. Not only was Crane born after the end of the war, but he also did not have the experience of combat until after he wrote the novel—facts that stand as strong witness to the powers of the artist to create experiences outside of his or her own life. Crane's brief career as a journalist allowed him to cover warfare in Cuba and Greece, observe life in the slums of New York, and study the frontier of the American Southwest in its halcyon days. Crane was even more influenced by naturalism than was his contemporary, Kate Chopin: His characters seem inevitably trapped by circumstance and unable to triumph over it. *Maggie, a Girl of the Streets* (1893) is a bitter and somewhat pathetic portrait of a young woman whose life never rises above the prostitution into which her environment propels her. Maggie, in fact, is as battered and bewildered by the urban sprawl as the wife in "The Bride Comes to Yellow Sky" is by her new environment. But the bride finds strength in her husband, while Maggie never has the chance. Ironically, Potter's wife is both his entrapment and his salvation. Even though the reader may question the institution of marriage as it appears in this story, its influence on the frontier was at least as dramatic as Crane describes it to have been.

The Bride
Comes to Yellow Sky

I

The great Pullman was whirling onward with such dignity of motion that a glance from the window seemed simply to prove that the plains of Texas were pouring eastward. Vast flats of green grass, dull-hued spaces of mesquit and cactus, little groups of frame houses, woods of light and tender trees, all were sweeping into the east, sweeping over the horizon, a precipice.

A newly married pair had boarded this coach at San Antonio. The man's face was reddened from many days in the wind and sun, and a direct result of his new black clothes was that his brick-colored hands were constantly performing in a most conscious fashion. From time to time he looked down respectfully at his attire. He sat with a hand on each knee, like a man waiting in a barber's

From *The Open Boat and Other Tales of Adventure*, New York, 1898.

shop. The glances he devoted to other passengers were furtive and shy.

The bride was not pretty, nor was she very young. She wore a dress of blue cashmere, with small reservations of velvet here and there, and with steel buttons abounding. She continually twisted her head to regard her puff sleeves, very stiff, straight, and high. They embarrassed her. It was quite apparent that she had cooked, and that she expected to cook, dutifully. The blushes caused by the careless scrutiny of some passengers as she had entered the car were strange to see upon this plain, under-class countenance, which was drawn in placid, almost emotionless lines.

They were evidently very happy. "Ever been in a parlor-car before?" he asked, smiling with delight.

"No," she answered; "I never was. It's fine, ain't it?"

"Great! And then after a while we'll go forward to the diner, and get a big lay-out. Finest meal in the world. Charge a dollar."

"Oh, do they?" cried the bride. "Charge a dollar? Why, that's too much—for us—ain't it, Jack?"

"Not this trip, anyhow," he answered bravely. "We're going to go the whole thing."

Later he explained to her about the trains. "You see, it's a thousand miles from one end of Texas to the other; and this train runs right across it, and never stops but for four times." He had the pride of an owner. He pointed out to her the dazzling fittings of the coach; and in truth her eyes opened wider as she contemplated the sea-green figured velvet, the shining brass, silver, and glass, the wood that gleamed as darkly brilliant as the surface of a pool of oil. At one end a bronze figure sturdily held a support for a separated chamber, and at convenient places on the ceiling were frescos in olive and silver.

To the minds of the pair, their surroundings reflected the glory of their marriage that morning in San Antonio; this was the environment of their new estate; and the man's face in particular beamed with an elation that made him appear ridiculous to the negro porter. This individual at times surveyed them from afar with an amused and superior grin. On other occasions he bullied them with skill in ways that did not make it exactly plain to them that they were being bullied. He subtly used all the manners of the most unconquerable kind of snobbery. He oppressed them; but of this oppression they had small knowledge, and they speedily forgot that infrequently a number of travellers covered them with stares of derisive enjoyment. Historically there was supposed to be something infinitely humorous in their situation.

"We are due in Yellow Sky at 3:42," he said, looking tenderly into her eyes.

"Oh, are we?" she said, as if she had not been aware of it. To evince surprise at her husband's statement was part of her wifely amiability. She took from a pocket a little silver watch; and as she held it before her, and stared at it with a frown of attention, the new husband's face shone.

"I bought it in San Anton' from a friend of mine," he told her gleefully.

"It's seventeen minutes past twelve," she said, looking up at him with a kind of shy and clumsy coquetry. A passenger, noting this play, grew excessively sardonic, and winked at himself in one of the numerous mirrors.

At last they went to the dining-car. Two rows of negro waiters, in glowing white suits, surveyed their entrance with the interest, and also the equanimity, of men who had been forewarned. The pair fell to the lot of a waiter who happened to feel pleasure in steering them through their meal. He viewed them with the manner of a fatherly pilot, his countenance radiant with benevolence. The patronage, entwined with the ordinary deference, was not plain to them. And yet, as they returned to their coach, they showed in their faces a sense of escape.

To the left, miles down a long purple slope, was a little ribbon of mist where moved the keening Rio Grande. The train was approaching it at an angle, and the apex was Yellow Sky. Presently it was apparent that, as the distance from Yellow Sky grew shorter, the husband became commensurately restless. His brick-red hands were more insistent in their prominence. Occasionally he was even rather absent-minded and far-away when the bride leaned forward and addressed him.

As a matter of truth, Jack Potter was beginning to find the shadow of a deed weigh upon him like a leaden slab. He, the town marshal of Yellow Sky, a man known, liked, and feared in his corner, a prominent person, had gone to San Antonio to meet a girl he believed he loved, and there, after the usual prayers, had actually induced her to marry him, without consulting Yellow Sky for any part of the transaction. He was now bringing his bride before an innocent and unsuspecting community.

Of course people in Yellow Sky married as it pleased them, in accordance with a general custom; but such was Potter's thought of his duty to his friends, or of their idea of his duty, or of an unspoken form which does not control men in these matters, that he felt he was heinous. He had committed an extraordinary crime. Face to face with this girl in San Antonio, and spurred by his sharp impulse, he had gone headlong over all the social hedges. At San Antonio he was like a man hidden in the dark. A knife to sever any friendly duty, any form, was easy to his hand in that remote city. But the hour of Yellow Sky—the hour of daylight—was approaching.

He knew full well that his marriage was an important thing to his town. It could only be exceeded by the burning of the new hotel.

His friends could not forgive him. Frequently he had reflected on the advisability of telling them by telegraph, but a new cowardice had been upon him. He feared to do it. And now the train was hurrying him toward a scene of amazement, glee, and reproach. He glanced out of the window at the line of haze swinging slowly in toward the train.

Yellow Sky had a kind of brass band, which played painfully, to the delight of the populace. He laughed without heart as he thought of it. If the citizens could dream of his prospective arrival with his bride, they would parade the band at the station and escort them, amid cheers and laughing congratulations, to his adobe home.

He resolved that he would use all the devices of speed and plains-craft in making the journey from the station to his house. Once within that safe citadel, he could issue some sort of vocal bulletin, and then not go among the citizens until they had time to wear off a little of their enthusiasm.

The bride looked anxiously at him. "What's worrying you, Jack?"

He laughed again. "I'm not worrying, girl; I'm only thinking of Yellow Sky."

She flushed in comprehension.

A sense of mutual guilt invaded their minds and developed a finer tenderness. They looked at each other with eyes softly aglow. But Potter often laughed the same nervous laugh; the flush upon the bride's face seemed quite permanent.

The traitor to the feelings of Yellow Sky narrowly watched the speeding landscape. "We're nearly there," he said.

Presently the porter came and announced the proximity of Potter's home. He held a brush in his hand, and, with all his airy superiority gone, he brushed Potter's new clothes as the latter slowly turned this way and that way. Potter fumbled out a coin and gave it to the porter, as he had seen others do. It was a heavy and muscle-bound business, as that of a man shoeing his first horse.

The porter took their bag, and as the train began to slow they moved forward to the hooded platform of the car. Presently the two engines and their long string of coaches rushed into the station of Yellow Sky.

"They have to take water here," said Potter, from a constricted throat and in mournful cadence, as one announcing death. Before the train stopped his eye had swept the length of the platform, and he was glad and astonished to see there was none upon it but the station-agent, who, with a slightly hurried and anxious air, was walking toward the water-tanks. When the train had halted, the porter alighted first, and placed in position a little temporary step.

"Come on, girl," said Potter, hoarsely. As he helped her down they each laughed on a false note. He took the bag from the negro, and bade his wife cling to his arm. As they slunk rapidly away, his hang-dog glance perceived that they were unloading the two trunks, and also that the station-agent, far ahead near the baggage car, had turned and was running towards him, making gestures. He laughed, and groaned as he laughed, when he noted the first effect of his marital bliss upon Yellow Sky. He gripped his wife's arm firmly to his side, and they fled. Behind them the porter stood, chuckling fatuously.

II

The California express on the Southern Railway was due at Yellow Sky in twenty-one minutes. There were six men at the bar of the Weary Gentleman Saloon. One was a drummer who talked a great deal and rapidly; three were Texans who did not care to talk at that time; and two were Mexican sheep-herders, who did not talk as a general practice in the Weary Gentleman Saloon. The barkeeper's dog lay on the board walk that crossed in front of the door. His head was on his paws, and he glanced drowsily here and there with the constant vigilance of a dog that is kicked on occasion. Across the sandy street were some vivid green grass-plots, so wonderful in appearance, amid the sands that burned near them in a blazing sun, that they caused a doubt in the mind. They exactly resembled the grass mats used to represent lawns on the stage. At the cooler end of the railway station, a man without a coat sat in a tilted chair and smoked his pipe. The fresh-cut bank of the Rio Grande circled near the town, and there could be seen beyond it a great plum-colored plain of mesquit.

Save for the busy drummer and his companions in the saloon, Yellow Sky was dozing. The newcomer leaned gracefully upon the bar, and recited many tales with the confidence of a bard who has come upon a new field.

"—and at the moment that the old man fell downstairs with the bureau in his arms, the old woman was coming up with two scuttles of coal, and of course—"

The drummer's tale was interrupted by a young man who suddenly appeared in the open door. He cried: "Scratchy Wilson's drunk, and has turned loose with both hands." The two Mexicans at once set down their glasses and faded out of the rear entrance of the saloon.

The drummer, innocent and jocular, answered: "All right, old man. S'pose he has? Come in and have a drink, anyhow."

But the information had made such an obvious cleft in every skull in the room that the drummer was obliged to see its importance. All had become instantly solemn. "Say," said he, mystified, "what is this?" His three companions made the introductory gesture of eloquent speech; but the young man at the door forestalled them.

"It means, my friend," he answered, as he came into the saloon, "that for the next two hours this town won't be a health resort."

The barkeeper went to the door, and locked and barred it; reaching out of the window, he pulled in heavy wooden shutters, and barred them. Immediately a solemn, chapel-like gloom was upon the place. The drummer was looking from one to another.

"But say," he cried, "what is this anyhow? You don't mean there is going to be a gun-fight?"

"Don't know whether there'll be a fight or not," answered one man, grimly; "but there'll be some shootin'—some good shootin'."

The young man who had warned them waved his hand. "Oh, there'll be a fight fast enough, if any one wants it. Anybody can get a fight out there in the street. There's a fight just waiting."

The drummer seemed to be swayed between the interest of a foreigner and a perception of personal danger.

"What did you say his name was?" he asked.

"Scratchy Wilson," they answered in chorus.

"And will he kill anybody? What are you going to do? Does this happen often? Does he rampage around like this once a week or so? Can he break in that door?"

"No; he can't break down that door," replied the barkeeper. "He's tried it three times. But when he comes you'd better lay down on the floor, stranger. He's dead sure to shoot at it, and a bullet may come through."

Thereafter the drummer kept a strict eye upon the door. The time had not yet been called for him to hug the floor, but, as a minor precaution, he sidled near to the wall. "Will he kill anybody?" he said again.

The men laughed low and scornfully at the question.

"He's out to shoot, and he's out for trouble. Don't see any good in experimentin' with him."

"But what do you do in a case like this? What do you do?"

A man responded: "Why, he and Jack Potter —"

"But," in chorus the other men interrupted, "Jack Potter's in San Anton'."

"Well, who is he? What's he got to do with it?"

"Oh, he's the town marshal. He goes out and fights Scratchy when he gets on one of these tears."

"Wow!" said the drummer, mopping his brow. "Nice job he's got."

The voices had toned away to mere whisperings. The drummer wished to ask further questions, which were born of an increasing anxiety and bewilderment; but when he attempted them, the men merely looked at him in irritation and motioned him to remain silent. A tense waiting hush was upon them. In the deep shadows of the room their eyes shone as they listened for sounds from the street. One man made three gestures at the barkeeper; and the latter moving like a ghost, handed him a glass and a bottle. The man poured a full glass of whiskey, and set down the bottle noiselessly. He gulped the whiskey in a swallow, and turned again toward the door in immovable silence. The drummer saw that the barkeeper, without a sound, had taken a Winchester from beneath the bar. Later he saw this individual beckoning to him, so he tiptoed across the room.

"You better come with me back of the bar."

"No, thanks," said the drummer, perspiring; "I'd rather be where I can make a break for the back door."

Whereupon the man of bottles made a kindly but peremptory gesture. The drummer obeyed it, and, finding himself seated on a box with his head below the level of the bar, balm was laid upon his soul at sight of various zinc and copper fittings that bore a resemblance to armor-plate. The barkeeper took a seat comfortably upon an adjacent box.

"You see," he whispered, "this here Scratchy Wilson is a wonder with a gun—a perfect wonder; and when he goes on the war-trail, we hunt our holes—naturally. He's about the last one of the old gang that used to hang out along the river here. He's a terror when he's drunk. When he's sober he's all right—kind of simple —wouldn't hurt a fly—nicest fellow in town. But when he's drunk—whoo!"

There were periods of stillness. "I wish Jack Potter was back from San Anton'," said the barkeeper. "He shot Wilson up once —in the leg—and he would sail in and pull out the kinks in this thing."

Presently they heard from a distance the sound of a shot, followed by three wild yowls. It instantly removed a bond from the men in the darkened saloon. There was a shuffling of feet. They looked at each other. "Here he comes," they said.

III

A man in a maroon-colored flannel shirt, which had been purchased for purposes of decoration, and made principally by some Jewish women on the East Side of New York, rounded a corner and walked into the middle of the main street of Yellow Sky. In either hand the man held a long, heavy, blue-black revolver. Often he yelled, and these cries rang through a semblance of a deserted village, shrilly flying over the roofs in a volume that seemed to have no relation to the ordinary vocal strength of a man. It was as if the surrounding stillness formed the arch of a tomb over him. These cries of ferocious challenge rang against walls of silence. And his boots had red tops with gilded imprints, of the kind beloved in winter by little sledding boys on the hillsides of New England.

The man's face flamed in a rage begot of whiskey. His eyes, rolling, and yet keen for ambush, hunted the still doorways and windows. He walked with the creeping movement of the midnight cat. As it occurred to him, he roared menacing information.

The long revolvers in his hands were as easy as straws; they were moved with an electric swiftness. The little fingers of each hand played sometimes in a musician's way. Plain from the low collar of the shirt, the cords of his neck straightened and sank, straightened and sank as passion moved him. The only sounds were his terrible invitations. The calm adobes preserved their demeanor at the passing of this small thing in the middle of the street.

There was no offer of fight—no offer of fight. The man called to the sky. There were no attractions. He bellowed and fumed and swayed his revolvers here and everywhere.

The dog of the barkeeper of the Weary Gentleman Saloon had not appreciated the advance of events. He yet lay dozing in front of his master's door. At sight of the dog, the man paused and raised his revolver humorously. At sight of the man, the dog sprang up and walked diagonally away, with a sullen head, and growling. The man yelled, and the dog broke into a gallop. As it was about to enter an alley, there was a loud noise, a whistling, and something spat the ground directly before it. The dog screamed, and, wheeling in terror, galloped headlong in a new direction. Again there was a noise, a whistling, and sand was kicked viciously before it. Fear-stricken, the dog turned and flurried like an animal in a pen. The man stood laughing, his weapons at his hips.

Ultimately the man was attracted by the closed door of the Weary Gentleman Saloon. He went to it and, hammering with a revolver, demanded drink.

The door remained imperturbable, he picked a bit of paper from the walk, and nailed it to the framework with a knife. He then turned his back contemptuously upon this popular resort, and, walking to the opposite side of the street and spinning there on his heel quickly and lithely, fired at the bit of paper. He missed it by a half-inch. He swore at himself, and went away. Later he comfortably fusilladed the windows of his most intimate friend. The man was playing with this town; it was a toy for him.

But still there was no offer of fight. The name of Jack Potter, his ancient antagonist, entered his mind, and he concluded that it would be a glad thing if he should go to Potter's house, and by bombardment induce him to come out and fight. He moved in the direction of his desire, chanting Apache scalp-music.

When he arrived at it, Potter's house presented the same still front as had the other adobes. Taking up a strategic position, the man howled a challenge. But this house regarded him as might a great stone god. It gave no sign. After a decent wait, the man howled further challenges, mingling with them wonderful epithets.

Presently there came the spectacle of a man churning himself into deepest rage over the immobility of a house. He fumed at it as the winter wind attacks a prairie cabin in the North. To the distance there should have gone the sound of a tumult like the fighting of two hundred Mexicans. As necessity bade him, he paused for breath or to reload his revolvers.

IV

Potter and his bride walked sheepishly and with speed. Sometimes they laughed together shamefacedly and low.

"Next corner, dear," he said finally.

They put forth the efforts of a pair walking bowed against a strong wind. Potter was about to raise a finger to point the first appearance of the new home when, as they circled the corner, they came face to face with a man in a maroon-colored shirt, who was feverishly pushing cartridges into a large revolver. Upon the instant the man dropped his revolver to the ground, and, like lighting, whipped another from its holster. The second weapon was aimed at the bridegroom's chest.

There was a silence. Potter's mouth seemed to be merely a grave for his tongue. He exhibited an instinct to at once loosen his arm from the woman's grip, and he dropped the bag to the sand. As for the bride, her face had gone as yellow as old cloth. She was a slave to hideous rites, gazing at the apparitional snake.

The two men faced each other at a distance of three paces. He of the revolver smiled with a new and quiet ferocity.

"Tried to sneak up on me," he said. "Tried to sneak up on me!" His eyes grew more baleful. As Potter made a slight movement, the man thrust his revolver venomously forward. "No; don't you do it, Jack Potter. Don't you move a finger toward a gun just yet. Don't you move an eyelash. The time has come for me to settle with you, and I'm goin' to do it my own way, and loaf along with no interferin'. So if you don't want a gun bent on you, just mind what I tell you."

Potter looked at his enemy. "I ain't got a gun on me, Scratchy," he said. "Honest, I ain't." He was stiffening and steadying, but yet somewhere at the back of his mind a vision of the Pullman floated: the sea-green figured velvet, the shining brass, silver, and glass, the wood that gleamed as darkly brilliant as the surface of a pool of oil—all the glory of the marriage, the environment of the new estate. "You know I fight when it comes to fighting, Scratchy Wilson; but I ain't got a gun on me. You'll have to do all the shootin' yourself."

His enemy's face went livid. He stepped forward, and lashed his weapon to and fro before Potter's chest. "Don't you tell me you ain't got no gun on you, you whelp. Don't tell me no lie like that. There ain't a man in Texas ever seen you without no gun. Don't take me for no kid." His eyes blazed with light, and his throat worked like a pump.

"I ain't takin' you for no kid," answered Potter. His heels had not moved an inch backward. "I'm takin' you for a——fool. I tell you I ain't got a gun, and I ain't. If you're goin' to shoot me up, you better begin now; you'll never get a chance like this again."

So much enforced reasoning had told on Wilson's rage; he was calmer. "If you ain't got a gun, why ain't you got a gun?" he sneered. "Been to Sunday school?"

"I ain't got a gun because I've just come from San Anton' with my wife. I'm married," said Potter. "And if I'd thought there was going to be any galoots like you prowling around when I brought my wife home, I'd had a gun, and don't you forget it."

"Married!" said Scratchy, not at all comprehending.

"Yes, married. I'm married," said Potter, distinctly.

"Married?" said Scratchy. Seemingly for the first time, he saw the drooping, drowning woman at the other man's side. "No!" he said. He was like a creature allowed a glimpse of another world. He moved a pace backward, and his arm, with the revolver, dropped to his side. "Is this the lady?" he asked.

"Yes; this is the lady," answered Potter.

There was another period of silence.

"Well," said Wilson at last, slowly, "I s'pose it's all off now."

"It's all off if you say so, Scratchy. You know I didn't make the trouble." Potter lifted his valise.

"Well, I 'low it's off, Jack," said Wilson. He was looking at the ground. "Married!" He was not a student of chivalry; it was merely that in the presence of this foreign condition he was a simple child of the earlier plains. He picked up his starboard revolver, and, placing both weapons in their holsters, he went away. His feet made funnel-shaped tracks in the heavy sand.

Discussion of Crane's "The Bride Comes to Yellow Sky"

1. Notice the man in the second paragraph. Does he seem to be comfortable in the situation and in his attire? If you look at the first sentence of the story (and remember Edgar Allan Poe's dictum about unity), how do the pieces fit into the total fabric of "The Bride Comes to Yellow Sky"? What might Crane be suggesting about societal change? How might we see the marriage as other than literal?

2. Whose story is this? Support your answer.

3. What is the effect of Crane's use of a drummer (a traveling salesman) in the story? Of Scratchy Wilson? Describe the other characters' responses to him. Because of the language choices made by the narrator to describe him, what are your responses? What is the effect of the final image of the story?

ANTON CHEKHOV

1860–1904

🌷 Chekhov was born in Taganrog, a small town in provincial Russia. His grandfather was a serf who had purchased his own freedom, and his father ran a grocery store. Chekhov studied medicine, contracted tuberculosis, and died established as a major literary talent. His reputation as a dramatist frequently overshadows his six hundred short stories, of which North American readers usually know only a handful of extremely short tales. But Chekhov is often at his best in the seven short novels: *The Duel* (1891), *Ward No. 6* (1892), *A Woman's Kingdom* (1893), *Three Years* (1894), *My Life* (1896), *Peasants* (1897), and *In the Ravine* (1899). The progression in these works is towards complexity, social awareness, and narrative experimentation. Although Chekhov is regarded by many as an artist pure and simple, not as a political man, his works draw increasingly gloomy pictures of the quality of life in Russia. Stories such as "Ana on the Neck," "At Home," and "Christmas Time" give us striking portraits of lost and alienated women, as does "The Darling." But Olga seems to flourish in this world, and the relationships in "The Darling" are complex. It is interesting to speculate what sort of a man Sasha, a contemporary of Pasternak's Yuri Zhivago, would become in October 1917.

The Darling

Olenka Plemyannikova, the daughter of a retired collegiate assessor, was sitting on her porch, which gave on the courtyard, deep in thought. It was hot, the flies were persistent and annoying, and it was pleasant to think that it would soon be evening. Dark rainclouds were gathering in the east and there was a breath of moisture in the wind that occasionally blew from that direction.

Kukin, a theater manager who ran a summer garden known as The Tivoli and lodged in the wing of the house, was standing in the middle of the courtyard, staring at the sky.

"Again!" he was saying in despair. "It's going to rain again! Rain every day, every day, as if to spite me! It will be the death of me! It's ruin! Such a frightful loss every day!"

He struck his hands together and continued, turning to Olenka:

"There, Olga Semyonovna, that's our life. It's enough to make you weep! You work, you try your utmost, you wear yourself out, you lie awake nights, you rack your brains trying to make a better thing of it, and what's the upshot? In the first place, the public is ignorant, barbarous. I give them the very best operetta, an elaborate spectacle, first-rate vaudeville artists. But do you think they want that? It's all above their heads. All they want is slapstick! Give them trash! And then look at the weather! Rain almost every evening. It started raining on the tenth of May, and it has kept it up all May and June. It's simply terrible! The public doesn't come, but don't I have to pay the rent? Don't I have to pay the artists?"

The next day toward evening the sky would again be overcast and Kukin would say, laughing hysterically:

"Well, go on, rain! Flood the garden, drown me! Bad luck to me in this world and the next! Let the artists sue me! Let them send me to prison—to Siberia—to the scaffold! Ha, ha, ha!"

The next day it was the same thing all over again.

Olenka listened to Kukin silently, gravely, and sometimes tears would come to her eyes. In the end his misfortunes moved her and she fell in love with him. He was a short, thin man with a sallow face, and wore his hair combed down over his temples. He had a thin tenor voice and when he spoke, his mouth twisted, and his face perpetually wore an expression of despair. Nevertheless he aroused a genuine, deep feeling in her. She was always enamored of someone and could not live otherwise. At first it had been her papa, who was now ill and sat in an armchair in a darkened room, breathing with difficulty. Then she had devoted her affections to her aunt, who used to come from Bryansk every other year. Still earlier, when she went to school, she had been in love with her French teacher. She was a quiet, kind, soft-hearted girl, with meek, gentle eyes, and she enjoyed very good health. At the sight of her full pink cheeks, her soft white neck with a dark birthmark on it, and the kind artless smile that came into her face when she listened to anything pleasant, men said to themselves, "Yes, not half bad," and smiled too, while the ladies present could not refrain from suddenly seizing her hand in the middle of the conversation and exclaiming delightedly, "You darling!"

The house in which she lived all her life and which was to be hers by her father's will, was situated on the outskirts of the city on what was known as Gypsy Road, not far from The Tivoli. In the evening and at night she could hear the band play and the sky-rockets go off, and it seemed to her that it was Kukin fighting his fate and assaulting his chief enemy, the apathetic public. Her heart contracted sweetly, she had no desire to sleep, and when he returned home at dawn, she would tap softly at her bedroom window and, showing him only her face and one shoulder through the curtain, give him a friendly smile.

He proposed to her, and they were married. And when he had a good look at her neck and her plump firm shoulders, he struck his hands together, and exclaimed, "Darling!"

He was happy, but as it rained on their wedding day and the night that followed, the expression of despair did not leave his face.

As a married couple, they got on well together. She presided over the box office, looked after things in the summer garden, kept accounts and paid salaries; and her rosy cheeks, the radiance of her sweet artless smile showed now in the box office window, now in the wings of the theater, now at the buffet. And she was already telling her friends that the theater was the most remarkable, the most important, and the most essential thing in the world, and that it was only the theater that could give true pleasure and make you a cultivated and humane person.

"But do you suppose the public understands that?" she would ask. "What it wants is slapstick! Yesterday we gave 'Faust Inside Out,' and almost all the boxes were empty, and if Vanichka and I had put on something vulgar, I assure you the theater would have been packed. Tomorrow Vanichka and I are giving 'Orpheus in Hell.' Do come."

And what Kukin said about artists and the theater she would repeat. Like him she despised the public for its ignorance and indifference to art; she took a hand in the rehearsals, correcting the actors, kept an eye on the musicians, and when there was an unfavorable notice in the local paper, she wept and went to see the editor about it.

The actors were fond of her and called her "the darling," and "Vanichka-and-I." She was sorry for them and would lend them small sums, and if they cheated her, she cried in private but did not complain to her husband.

The pair got on just as well together when winter came. They leased the municipal theater for the season and sublet it for short periods to a Ukrainian troupe, a magician, or a local dramatic club. Olenka was gaining weight and beamed with happiness, but Kukin was getting thinner and more sallow and complained of terrible losses, although business was fairly good during the winter. He coughed at night, and she would make him drink an infusion of raspberries and linden blossoms, rub him with eau de Cologne and wrap him in her soft shawls.

"What a sweet thing you are!" she would say quite sincerely, smoothing his hair. "My handsome sweet!"

At Lent he left for Moscow to engage a company of actors for the summer season, and she could not sleep with him away. She sat at the window and watched the stars. It occurred to her that she had something in common with the hens: they too stayed awake all night and were disturbed when the cock was absent from the henhouse. Kukin was detained in Moscow, and wrote that he would return by Easter, and in his letters he sent instructions about The Tivoli. But on the Monday of Passion Week, late in the evening, there was a sudden ominous knock at the gate; someone was banging at the wicket as though it were a barrel—boom, boom, boom! The sleepy cook, her bare feet splashing through the puddles, ran to open the gate.

"Open, please!" someone on the other side of the gate was saying in a deep voice. "There's a telegram for you."

Olenka had received telegrams from her husband before, but this time for some reason she was numb with fright. With trembling hands she opened the telegram and read the following:

"Ivan Petrovich died suddenly today awaiting prot instructions tuneral Tuesday."

That is exactly how the telegram had it: "tuneral," and there was also the incomprehensible word "prot"; the signature was that of the director of the comic opera company.

"My precious!" Olenka sobbed. "Vanichka, my precious, my sweet! Why did we ever meet! Why did I get to know you and to love you! To whom can your poor unhappy Olenka turn?"

Kukin was buried on Tuesday in the Vagankovo Cemetery in Moscow. Olenka returned home on Wednesday, and no sooner did she enter her room than she sank onto the bed and sobbed so loudly that she could be heard in the street and in the neighboring courtyards.

"The darling!" said the neighbors, crossing themselves. "Darling Olga Semyonovna! How the poor soul takes on!"

Three months later Olenka was returning from Mass one day in deep mourning and very sad. It happened that one of her neighbors, Vasily Andreich Pustovalov, the manager of Babakayev's lumberyard, who was also returning from church, was walking beside her. He was wearing a straw hat and a white waistcoat, with a gold watch-chain, and he looked more like a landowner than a businessman.

"There is order in all things, Olga Semyonovna," he was saying sedately, with a note of sympathy in his voice; "and if one of our dear ones passes on, then it means that this was the will of God, and in that case we must keep ourselves in hand and bear it submissively."

Having seen Olenka to her gate, he took leave of her and went further. All the rest of the day she heard his sedate voice, and as soon as she closed her eyes she had a vision of his dark beard. She liked him very much. And apparently she too had made an impression on him, because a little later a certain elderly lady, whom she scarcely knew, called to have coffee with her, and no sooner was she seated at table than the visitor began to talk about Pustovalov, saying that he was a fine, substantial man, and that any marriageable woman would be glad to go to the altar with him. Three days later Pustovalov himself paid her a visit. He did not stay more than ten minutes and he said little, but Olenka fell in love with him, so deeply that she stayed awake all night burning as with fever, and in the morning she sent for the elderly lady. The match was soon arranged and then came the wedding.

As a married couple Pustovalov and Olenka got on very well

together. As a rule he was in the lumberyard till dinnertime, then he went out on business and was replaced by Olenka, who stayed in the office till evening, making out bills and seeing that orders were shipped.

"We pay twenty per cent more for lumber every year," she would say to customers and acquaintances. "Why, we used to deal in local timber, and now Vasichka has to travel to the province of Mogilev for timber regularly. And the freight rates!" she would exclaim, putting her hands to her cheeks in horror. "The freight rates!"

It seemed to her that she had been in the lumber business for ages, that lumber was the most important, the most essential thing in the world, and she found something intimate and touching in the very sound of such words as beam, log, batten, plank, box board, lath, scantling, slab . . .

At night she would dream of whole mountains of boards and planks, of endless caravans of carts hauling lumber out of town to distant points. She would dream that a regiment of beams, 28 feet by 8 inches, standing on end, was marching in the lumberyard, that beams, logs, and slabs were crashing against each other with the hollow sound of dry wood, that they kept tumbling down and rising again, piling themselves on each other. Olenka would scream in her sleep and Pustovalov would say to her tenderly: "Olenka, what's the matter, darling? Cross yourself!"

Whatever ideas her husband had, she adopted as her own. If he thought that the room was hot or that business was slow, she thought so too. Her husband did not care for entertainments and on holidays stayed home—so did she.

"You are always at home or in the office," her friends would say. "You ought to go to the theater, darling, or to the circus."

"Vasichka and I have no time for the theater," she would answer sedately. "We are working people, we're not interested in such foolishness. What good are these theaters?"

On Saturdays the two of them would go to evening service, on holidays they attended early Mass, and returning from the church they walked side by side, their faces wearing a softened expression. There was an agreeable aroma about them, and her silk dress rustled pleasantly. At home they had tea with shortbread, and various kinds of jam, and afterwards they ate pie. Every day at noon, in the yard and on the street just outside the gate, there was a delicious smell of *borshch* and roast lamb or duck, and on fast days there was the odor of fish, and one could not pass the Pustovalov gate without one's mouth watering.

In the office the samovar was always boiling and the customers were treated to tea with doughnuts. Once a week the pair went to the baths and returned side by side, both with red faces.

"Yes, everything goes well with us, thank God," Olenka would say to her friends. "I wish everyone were as happy as Vasichka and I."

When Pustovalov went off to the provinces of Mogilev for timber, she missed him badly and lay awake nights, crying. Sometimes, in the evening, a young army veterinary, by the name of Smirnin, who rented the wing of their house, would call on her. He chatted or played cards with her and that diverted her. What interested her most was what he told her about his domestic life. He had been married and had a son, but was separated from his wife because she had been unfaithful to him, and now he hated her; he sent her forty rubles a month for the maintenance of the child. And listening to him, Olenka would sign and shake her head: she was sorry for him.

"Well, God keep you," she would say to him as she took leave of him, going to the stairs with him, candle in hand. "Thank you for relieving my boredom, and may the Queen of Heaven give you health!"

She always expressed herself in this sedate and reasonable manner, in imitation of her husband. Just as the veterinary would be closing the door behind him, she would recall him and say:

"You know, Vladimir Platonych, you had better make up with your wife. You ought to forgive her, at least for your son's sake! I am sure the little boy understands everything."

And when Pustovalov came back, she would tell him in low tones about the veterinary and his unhappy domestic life, and both of them would sigh and shake their heads and speak of the boy, who was probably missing his father. Then by a strange association of ideas they would both turn to the icons, bow down to the ground before them and pray that the Lord would grant them children.

Thus the Pustovalovs lived in peace and quiet, in love and harmony for six years. But one winter day, right after having hot tea at the office, Vasily Andreich went out without his cap to see about shipping some lumber, caught a chill and was taken sick. He was treated by the best doctors, but the illness had its own way with him, and he died after four months. Olenka was a widow again.

"To whom can I turn now, my darling?" she sobbed when she had buried her husband. "How can I live without you, wretched and unhappy as I am? Pity me, good people, left all alone in the world—"

She wore a black dress with white cuffs and gave up wearing hat and gloves for good. She hardly ever left the house except to go to church or to visit her husband's grave, and at home she lived like a nun. Only at the end of six months did she take off her widow's weeds and open the shutters. Sometimes in the morning she was seen with her cook going to market for provisions, but how she lived now and what went on in her house could only be guessed. People based their guesses on such facts as that they saw her having tea with the veterinary in her little garden, he reading the newspaper aloud to her, and that, meeting an acquaintance at the post office, she would say:

"There is no proper veterinary inspection in our town, and that's why there is so much illness around. So often you hear of people getting ill from the milk or catching infections from horses and cows. When you come down to it, the health of domestic animals must be as well cared for as the health of human beings."

She now repeated the veterinary's words and held the same opinions about everything that he did. It was plain that she could not live even for one year without an attachment and that she had found new happiness in the wing of her house. Another woman would have been condemned for this, but of Olenka no one could think ill: everything about her was so unequivocal. Neither she nor the veterinary mentioned to anyone the change that had occurred in their relations; indeed, they tried to conceal it, but they didn't succeed, because Olenka could not keep a secret. When he had visitors, his regimental colleagues, she, pouring the tea or serving the supper, would begin to talk of the cattle plague, of the pearl disease, of the municipal slaughter-houses. He would be terribly embarrassed and when the guests had gone, he would grasp her by the arms and hiss angrily:

"I've asked you before not to talk about things that you don't understand! When veterinaries speak among themselves, please don't butt in! It's really annoying!"

She would look at him amazed and alarmed and ask, "But Volodichka, what shall I talk about?"

And with tears in her eyes she would hug him and beg him not to be angry, and both of them were happy.

Yet this happiness did not last long. The veterinary left, left forever, with his regiment, which was moved to some remote place, it may have been Siberia. And Olenka remained alone.

Now she was quite alone. Her father had died long ago, and his armchair stood in the attic, covered with dust and minus one leg. She got thinner and lost her looks, and passers-by in the street did not glance at her and smile as they used to. Obviously, her best years were over, were behind her, and now a new kind of life was beginning for her, an unfamiliar kind that did not bear thinking of. In the evening Olenka sat on her porch, and heard the band play at The Tivoli and the rockets go off, but this no longer suggested anything to her mind. She looked apathetically at the empty court-yard, thought of nothing, and later, when night came, she would go to bed and dream of the empty courtyard. She ate and drank as though involuntarily.

Above all, and worst of all, she no longer had any opinions whatever. She saw objects about her and understood what was going on, but she could not form an opinion about anything and did not know what to talk about. And how terrible it is not to have any opinions! You see, for instance, a bottle, or the rain, or a peasant driving in a cart, but what is the bottle for, or the rain, or the peasant, what is the meaning of them, you can't tell, and you couldn't, even if they paid you a thousand rubles. When Kukin was about, or Pustovalov or, later, the veterinary, Olenka could explain it all and give her opinions about anything you like, but now there was the same emptiness in her head and in her heart as in her courtyard. It was weird, and she felt as bitter as if she had been eating wormwood.

Little by little the town was extending in all directions. Gypsy Road was now a regular street, and where The Tivoli had been and the lumberyards, houses had sprung up and lanes had multiplied. How swiftly time passes! Olenka's house had taken on a shabby look, the roof was rusty, the shed sloped, and the whole yard was invaded by burdock and stinging nettles. Olenka herself had aged and grown homely. In the summer she sat on the porch, feeling empty and dreary and bitter, as before; in the winter she sat by the window and stared at the snow. Sometimes at the first breath of spring or when the wind brought her the chime of church bells, memories of the past would overwhelm her, her heart would contract sweetly and her eyes would brim over with tears. But this only lasted a moment, and then there was again emptiness and once more she was possessed by a sense of the futility of life; Trot, the black kitten, rubbed against her and purred softly, but Olenka was not affected by these feline caresses. Is that what she needed? She needed an affection that would take possession of her whole being, her soul, her mind, that would give her ideas, a purpose in life, that would warm her aging blood. And she would shake the kitten off her lap, and say irritably: "Scat! Scat! Don't stick to me!"

And so it went, day after day, year after year, and no joy, no opinion! Whatever Mavra the cook would say, was well enough.

One hot July day, toward evening, when the cattle were being driven home and the yard was filled with clouds of dust, suddenly someone knocked at the gate. Olenka herself went to open it and was dumfounded at what she saw: at the gate stood Smirnin, the veterinary, already gray, and wearing civilian clothes. She suddenly recalled everything and, unable to control herself, burst into tears, silently letting her head drop on his breast. She was so agitated that she scarcely noticed how the two of them entered the house and sat down to tea.

"My dear," she murmured, trembling with joy, "Vladimir Platonych, however did you get here?"

"I have come here for good," he explained. "I have retired from the army and want to see what it's like to be on my own and live a settled life. And besides, my son is ready for high school. I have made up with my wife, you know."

"Where is she?"

"She's at the hotel with the boy, and I'm out looking for lodgings."

"Goodness, Vladimir Platonych, take my house! You don't need to look further! Good Lord, and you can have it free," exclaimed Olenka, all in a flutter and beginning to cry again. "You live here in the house, and the wing will do for me. Heavens, I'm so glad!"

The next day they began painting the roof and white-washing the walls, and Olenka, her arms akimbo, walked about the yard, giving orders. The old smile had come back to her face, and she was lively and spry, as though she had waked from a long sleep. Presently the veterinary's wife arrived, a thin, homely lady with bobbed hair who looked as if she were given to caprices. With her was the little boy, Sasha, small for his age (he was going on ten), chubby, with clear blue eyes and dimples in his cheeks.

No sooner did he walk into the yard than he began chasing the cat, and immediately his eager, joyous laughter rang out.

"Auntie, is that your cat?" he asked Olenka. "When she has little ones, please give us a kitten. Mama is terribly afraid of mice."

Olenka chatted with him, then gave him tea, and her heart suddenly grew warm and contracted sweetly, as if this little boy were her own son. And in the evening, as he sat in the dining-room doing his homework, she looked at him with pity and tenderness and whispered:

"My darling, my pretty one, my little one! How blond you are, and so clever!"

"An island," he was reciting from the book, "is a body of land entirely surrounded by water."

"An island is a body of land . . ." she repeated and this was the first opinion she expressed with conviction after so many years of silence and mental vacuity.

She now had opinions of her own, and at supper she had a conversation with Sasha's parents, saying that studying in high school was hard on the children, but that nevertheless the classical course was better than the scientific one because a classical education opened all careers to you: you could be either a doctor or an engineer.

Sasha started going to high school. His mother went off to Kharkov to visit her sister and did not come back; every day his father left town to inspect herds and sometimes he stayed away for three days together, and it seemed to Olenka that Sasha was wholly abandoned, that he was unwanted, that he was being starved, and she moved him into the wing with her and settled him in a little room there.

For six months now Sasha had been living in her wing. Every morning Olenka comes into his room; he is fast asleep, his hand under his cheek, breathing quietly. She is sorry to wake him.

"Sashenka," she says sadly, "get up, my sweet! It's time to go to school."

He gets up, dresses, says his prayers, and sits down to his breakfast: he drinks three glasses of tea and eats two large doughnuts, and half a buttered French roll. He is hardly awake and consequently cross.

"You haven't learned the fable, Sashenka," says Olenka, looking at him as though she were seeing him off on a long journey. "You worry me. You must do your best, darling, study. And pay attention to your teachers."

"Please leave me alone!" says Sasha.

Then he walks down the street to school, a small boy in a big cap, with his books in a rucksack. Olenka follows him noiselessly.

"Sashenka!" she calls after him. He turns around and she thrusts a date or a caramel into his hand. When they turn into the school lane, he feels ashamed at being followed by a tall stout woman; he looks round and says: "You'd better go home, auntie; I can go alone now."

She stands still and stares after him until he disappears at the school entrance. How she loves him! Not one of her former attachments was so deep; never had her soul surrendered itself so unreservedly, so disinterestedly and with such joy as now when her maternal instinct was increasingly asserting itself. For this little boy who was not her own, for the dimples in his cheeks, for his very cap, she would have laid down her life, would have laid it down with joy, with tears of tenderness. Why? But who knows why?

Having seen Sasha off to school, she goes quietly home, contented, tranquil, brimming over with love; her face, grown younger in the last six months, beams with happiness; people meeting her look at her with pleasure and say:

"Good morning, Olga Semyonovna, darling! How are you, darling?"

"They make the children work so hard at high school nowadays," she says, as she does her marketing. "Think of it: yesterday in the first form they had a fable to learn by heart, a Latin translation and a problem for homework. That's entirely too much for a little fellow."

And she talks about the teachers, the lessons, the textbooks— saying just what Sasha says about them.

At three o'clock they have dinner together, in the evening they do the homework together, and cry. When she puts him to bed, she takes a long time making the sign of the cross over him and whispering prayers. Then she goes to bed and thinks of the future, distant and misty, when Sasha, having finished his studies, will become a doctor or an engineer, will have a large house of his own, horses, a carriage, will marry and become a father. She falls asleep and her dreams are of the same thing, and tears flow down her cheeks from her closed eyes. The black kitten lies beside her purring: Purr-purrr-purrr.

Suddenly there is a loud knock at the gate. Olenka wakes up, breathless with fear, her heart palpitating. Half a minute passes, and there is another knock.

"That's a telegram from Kharkov," she thinks, beginning to tremble from head to foot. "Sasha's mother is sending for him from Kharkov—O Lord!"

She is in despair. Her head, her hands, her feet grow chill and it seems to her that she is the most unhappy woman in the whole world. But another minute passes, voices are heard: it's the veterinary returning from the club.

"Well, thank God!" she thinks.

Little by little the load rolls off her heart and she is again at ease; she goes back to bed and thinks of Sasha who is fast asleep in the next room and sometimes shouts in his sleep:

"I'll give it to you! Scram! No fighting!"

Discussion of Chekhov's "The Darling"

1. Olga desperately needs men around her. The worst thing that happens to her after the veterinarian leaves is that "she could not form an opinion." Although the tone here is ironic, Chekhov is obviously saying something about woman's position in society. What?

2. Each of the four males in her life reacts differently to her. Chart the progression in their attitudes.

3. The image of Trot, the black kitten that rubs against Olga (page 91), is an allusion to a famous Russian short novel by Nikolai Leskov, "Lady MacBeth of the Mtensk District." Chekhov's story is a comic treatment of the same theme—woman's need for contact with humanity—and you might wish to compare the two.

4. On page 92 there is a shift in tense in the narration (the English accurately reflects the original Russian). Why?

5. Can a case be made that what Olenka really wants is not a husband but a child? Does this mean that men are not quite as indispensable to Olga as the earlier parts of the story suggest?

CHARLES WADDELL CHESNUTT

🌣 Chesnutt is a brilliant and self-educated black writer whose talents are only now beginning to be recognized. He was born in Cleveland, but grew up in North Carolina, where he became a schoolteacher at sixteen, a school principal at twenty-three. Two years later he returned to Cleveland to study law. It is convenient to see in Chesnutt the operation of such dualisms: midwesterner and southerner, teacher and lawyer. Like Kate Chopin, he was first ignored and then consigned to the status of local colorist. The neglect is most unfortunate, because Chesnutt discusses some of the most significant areas of national experience: the lifestyles of the blacks who emigrated to the North ("Wife of His Youth"), the difficulties of race relations during the Reconstruction ("The Sheriff's Children"), and the impact of the Civil War on human beings ("Cicely's Dream"). In addition to two collections of short fiction, he wrote three novels and a biography of Frederick Douglass —all between 1899 and 1905. Technically the most impressive feature of Chesnutt's writing is his ability to plot, but his most impressive achievement as a writer is his skill in exposing the close relationship between major social events and the personal lives of his characters. All of them have dreams of happy lives with the men or women they love. In each story, however, as in "Cicely's Dream," they must realize that their hopes for personal relationships are determined largely by the societies in which they live.

Cicely's Dream

I

The old woman stood at the back door of the cabin, shading her eyes with her hand, and looking across the vegetable garden that ran up to the very door. Beyond the garden she saw, bathed in the sunlight, a field of corn, just in the ear, stretching for half a mile, its yellow, pollen-laden tassels over-topping the dark green mass of broad glistening blades; and in the distance, through the faint morning haze of evaporating dew, the line of the woods, of a still darker green, meeting the clear blue of the summer sky. Old Dinah saw, going down the path, a tall, brown girl, in a homespun frock, swinging a slat-bonnet in one hand and a splint basket in the other.

"Oh, Cicely!" she called.

The girl turned and answered in a resonant voice, vibrating with youth and life,—

"Yes, granny!"

From *The Wife of His Youth and Other Stories of the Color Line*, 1899.

"Be sho' and pick a good mess er peas, chile, fer yo' gran-daddy's gwine ter be home ter dinner ter-day."

The old woman stood a moment longer and then turned to go into the house. What she had not seen was that the girl was not only young, but lithe and shapely as a sculptor's model; that her bare feet seemed to spurn the earth as they struck it; that though brown, she was not so brown but that her cheek was darkly red with the blood of another race than that which gave her her name and station in life; and the old woman did not see that Cicely's face was as comely as her figure was superb, and that her eyes were dreamy with vague yearnings.

Cicely climbed the low fence between the garden and the cornfield, and started down one of the long rows leading directly away from the house. Old Needham was a good ploughman, and straight as an arrow ran the furrow between the rows of corn, until it vanished in the distant perspective. The peas were planted beside alternate hills of corn, the corn-stalks serving as supports for the climbing pea-vines. The vines nearest the house had been picked more or less clear of the long green pods, and Cicely walked down the row for a quarter of a mile, to where the peas were more plentiful. And as she walked she thought of her dream of the night before.

She had dreamed a beautiful dream. The fact that it was a beautiful dream, a delightful dream, her memory retained very vividly. She was troubled because she could not remember just what her dream had been about. Of one other fact she was certain, that in her dream she had found something, and that her happiness had been bound up with the thing she had found. As she walked down the corn-row she ran over in her mind the various things with which she had always associated happiness. Had she found a gold ring? No, it was not a gold ring—of that she felt sure. Was it a soft, curly plume for her hat? She had seen town people with them, and had indulged in day-dreams on the subject; but it was not a feather. Was it a bright-colored silk dress? No; as much as she had always wanted one, it was not a silk dress. For an instant, in a dream, she had tasted some great and novel happiness, and when she awoke it was dashed from her lips, and she could not even enjoy the memory of it, except in a vague, indefinite, and tantalizing way.

Cicely was troubled, too, because dreams were serious things. Dreams had certain meanings, most of them, and some dreams went by contraries. If her dream had been a prophecy of some good thing, she had by forgetting it lost the pleasure of anticipation. If her dream had been one of those that go by contraries, the warning would be in vain, because she would not know against what evil to provide. So, with a sigh, Cicely said to herself that it was a troubled world, more or less; and having come to a promising point, began to pick the tenderest pea-pods and throw them into her basket.

By the time she had reached the end of the line the basket was nearly full. Glancing toward the pine woods beyond the rail fence, she saw a brier bush loaded with large, luscious blackberries. Cicely was fond of blackberries, so she set her basket down, climbed the fence, and was soon busily engaged in gathering the fruit, delicious even in its wild state.

She had soon eaten all she cared for. But the berries were still numerous, and it occurred to her that her granddaddy would like a blackberry pudding for dinner. Catching up her apron, and using it as a receptacle for the berries, she had gathered scarcely more than a handful when she heard a groan.

Cicely was not timid, and her curiosity being aroused by the sound, she stood erect, and remained in a listening attitude. In a moment the sound was repeated, and, gauging the point from which it came, she plunged resolutely into the thick underbrush of the forest. She had gone but a few yards when she stopped short with an exclamation of surprise and concern.

Upon the ground, under the shadow of the towering pines, a man lay at full length,—a young man, several years under thirty, apparently, so far as his age could be guessed from a face that wore a short soft beard, and was so begrimed with dust and incrusted with blood that little could be seen of the underlying integument. What was visible showed a skin browned by nature or by exposure. His hands were of even a darker brown, almost as dark as Cicely's own. A tangled mass of very curly black hair, matted with burs, dank with dew, and clotted with blood, fell partly over his forehead, on the edge of which, extending back into the hair, an ugly scalp wound was gaping, and, though apparently not just inflicted, was still bleeding slowly, as though reluctant to stop, in spite of the coagulation that had almost closed it.

Cicely with a glance took in all this and more. But, first of all, she saw the man was wounded and bleeding, and the nurse latent in all womankind awoke in her to the requirements of the situation. She knew there was a spring a few rods away, and ran swiftly to it. There was usually a gourd at the spring, but now it was gone. Pouring out the blackberries in a little heap where they could be found again, she took off her apron, dipped one end of it into the spring, and ran back to the wounded man. The apron was clean, and she squeezed a little stream of water from it into the man's mouth. He swallowed it with avidity. Cicely then knelt by his side, and with the wet end of her apron washed the blood from the wound lightly, and the dust from the man's face. Then she looked at her apron a moment, debating whether she should tear it or not.

"I'm feared granny'll be mad," she said to herself. "I reckon I'll jes' use de whole apron."

So she bound the apron around his head as well as she could, and then sat down a moment on a fallen tree trunk, to think what she should do next. The man already seemed more comfortable; he had ceased moaning, and lay quiet, though breathing heavily.

"What shall I do with that man?" she reflected. "I don' know whether he's a w'ite or a black man. Ef he's a w'ite man, I oughter go an' tell de w'ite folks up at de big house, an' dey'd take keer of 'im. If he's a black man, I oughter go tell granny. He don' look lack a black man somehow er nuther, an' yet he don' look lack a w'ite man; he's too dahk, an' his hair's too curly. But I mus' do somethin' wid 'im. He can't be lef' here ter die in de woods all by hisse'f. Reckon I'll go an' tell granny."

She scaled the fence, caught up the basket of peas from where she had left it, and ran, lightly and swiftly as a deer, toward the house. Her short skirt did not impede her progress, and in a few minutes she had covered the half mile and was at the cabin door, a slight heaving of her full and yet youthful breast being the only sign of any unusual exertion.

Her story was told in a moment. The old woman took down a black bottle from a high shelf, and set out with Cicely across the cornfield, toward the wounded man.

As they went through the corn Cicely recalled part of her dream. She had dreamed that under some strange circumstances—what they had been was still obscure—she had met a young man—a young man whiter than she and yet not all white—and that he had loved her and married her. Her dream had been all the sweeter because in it she had first tasted the sweetness of love, and she had not recalled it before because only in her dream had she known or thought of love as something supremely desirable.

With the memory of her dream, however, her fears revived. Dreams were solemn things. To Cicely the fabric of a vision was by no means baseless. Her trouble arose from her not being able to recall, though she was well versed in dream-lore, just what event was foreshadowed by a dream of finding a wounded man. If the wounded man were of her own race, her dream would thus far have been realized, and having met the young man, the other joys might be expected to follow. If he should turn out to be a white man, then her dream was clearly one of the kind that go by contraries, and she could expect only sorrow and trouble and pain as the proper sequences of this fateful discovery.

II

The two women reached the fence that separated the cornfield from the pine woods.

"How is I gwine ter git ovuh dat fence, chile?" asked the old woman.

"Wait a minute, granny," said Cicely; "I'll take it down."

It was only an eight-rail fence, and it was a matter of but a few minutes for the girl to lift down and lay to either side the ends of the rails that formed one of the angles. This done, the old woman easily stepped across the remaining two or three rails. It was only a moment before they stood by the wounded man. He was lying still, breathing regularly, and seemingly asleep.

"What is he, granny," asked the girl anxiously, "a w'ite man, or not?"

Old Dinah pushed back the matted hair from the wounded man's brow, and looked at the skin beneath. It was fairer there, but yet of a decided brown. She raised his hand, pushed back the tattered sleeve from his wrist, and then she laid his hand down gently.

"Mos' lackly he's a mulatter man f'om up de country somewhar. He don' look lack dese yer niggers roun' yere, ner yet lack a w'ite man. But de po' boy's in a bad fix, w'ateber he is, an' I 'spec's we bettah do w'at we kin fer 'im, an' w'en he comes to he'll tell us w'at he is—er w'at he calls hisse'f. Hol' 'is head up, chile, an' I'll po' a drop er dis yer liquor down his th'oat; dat'll bring 'im to quicker 'n anything e'se I knows."

Cicely lifted the sick man's head, and Dinah poured a few drops of the whiskey between his teeth. He swallowed it readily enough. In a few minutes he opened his eyes and stared blankly at the two women. Cicely saw that his eyes were large and black, and glistening with fever.

"How you feelin', suh?" asked the old woman.

There was no answer.

"Is you feelin' bettah now?"

The wounded man kept on staring blankly. Suddenly he essayed to put his hand to his head, gave a deep groan, and fell back again unconscious.

"He's gone ag'in," said Dinah. "I reckon we'll hafter tote 'im up ter de house and take keer er 'im dere. W'ite folks wouldn't want ter fool wid a nigger man, an' we doan know who his folks is. He's outer his head an' will be fer some time yet, an' we can't tell nuthin' 'bout 'im tel he comes ter his senses."

Cicely lifted the wounded man by the arms and shoulders. She was strong, with the strength of youth and a sturdy race. The man was pitifully emaciated; how much, the two women had not suspected until they raised him. They had no difficulty whatever, except for the awkwardness of such a burden, in lifting him over the fence and carrying him through the cornfield to the cabin.

They laid him on Cicely's bed in the little lean-to shed that formed a room separate from the main apartment of the cabin. The old woman sent Cicely to cook the dinner, while she gave her own attention exclusively to the still unconscious man. She brought water and washed him as though he were a child.

"Po' boy," she said, "he doan feel lack he's be'n eatin' nuff to feed a sparrer. He 'pears ter be mos' starved ter def."

She washed his wound more carefully, made some lint,—the art was well known in the sixties,—and dressed his wound with a fair degree of skill.

"Somebody must 'a' be'n tryin' ter put yo' light out, chile," she muttered to herself as she adjusted the bandage around his head. "A little higher er a little lower, an' you would n' 'a' be'n yere ter tell de tale. Demm clo's," she argued, lifting the tattered garments she had removed from her patient, "don' b'long 'roun' yere. Dat kinder weavin' come f'om down to'ds Souf Ca'lina. I wish Needham 'u'd come erlong. He kin tell who dis man is, an' all erbout 'im."

She made a bowl of gruel, and fed it, drop by drop, to the sick man. This roused him somewhat from his stupor, but when Dinah thought he had enough of the gruel, and stopped feeding him, he closed his eyes again and relapsed into a heavy sleep that was so closely akin to unconsciousness as to be scarcely distinguishable from it.

When old Needham came home at noon, his wife, who had been anxiously awaiting his return, told him in a few words the story of Cicely's discovery and of the subsequent events.

Needham inspected the stranger with a professional eye. He had been something of a plantation doctor in his day, and was known far and wide for his knowledge of simple remedies. The negroes all around, as well as many of the poorer white people, came to him for the treatment of common ailments.

"He's got a fevuh," he said, after feeling the patient's pulse and laying his hand on his brow, "an' we'll hafter gib 'im some yarb tea an' nuss 'im tel de fevuh w'ars off. I 'spec'," he added, "dat I knows whar dis boy come f'om. He's mos' lackly one er dem bright mulatters, f'om Robeson County—some of 'em call deyse'ves Croatan Injins—w'at's been conscripted an' sent ter wu'k on de fo'tifications down at Wimbleton er some'er's er nuther, an' done 'scaped, and got mos' killed gittin' erway, an' wuz n' none too well fed befo', an' nigh 'bout starved ter def sence. We'll hafter hide dis man, er e'se we is lackly ter git inter trouble ou'se'ves by harb'rin' 'im. Ef dey ketch 'im yere, dey's liable ter take 'im out an' shoot 'im —an' des ez lackly us too."

Cicely was listening with bated breath.

"Oh, gran'daddy," she cried with trembling voice, "don' let 'em ketch 'im! Hide 'im somewhar."

"I reckon we'll leave 'im yere fer a day er so. Ef he had come f'om roun' yere I'd be skeered ter keep 'im, fer de w'ite folks 'u'd prob'ly be lookin' fer 'im. But I knows ev'ybody w'at's be'n conscripted fer ten miles 'roun', an' dis yere boy don' b'long in dis neighborhood. W'en 'e gits so 'e kin he'p 'isse'f we'll put 'im up in de lof' an' hide 'im till de Yankees come. Fer dey're comin', sho'. I dremp' las' night dey wuz close ter han', and I hears de w'ite folks talkin' ter deyse'ves 'bout it. An' de time is comin' w'en de good Lawd gwine ter set his people free, an' it ain' gwine ter be long, nuther."

Needham's prophecy proved true. In less than a week the Confederate garrison evacuated the arsenal in the neighboring town of Patesville, blew up the buildings, destroyed the ordnance and stores, and retreated across the Cape Fear River, burning the river bridge behind them,—two acts of war afterwards unjustly attributed to General Sherman's army, which followed close upon the heels of the retreating Confederates.

When there was no longer any fear for the stranger's safety, no more pains were taken to conceal him. His wound had healed rapidly, and in a week he had been able with some help to climb up the ladder into the loft. In all this time, however, though apparently conscious, he had said no word to any one, nor had he seemed to comprehend a word that was spoken to him.

Cicely had been his constant attendant. After the first day, during which her granny had nursed him, she had sat by his bedside, had fanned his fevered brow, had held food and water and medicine to his lips. When it was safe for him to come down from the loft and sit in a chair under a spreading oak, Cicely supported him until he was strong enough to walk about the yard. When his strength had increased sufficiently to permit of greater exertion, she accompanied him on long rambles in the fields and woods.

In spite of his gain in physical strength, the newcomer changed very little in other respects. For a long time he neither spoke nor smiled. To questions put to him he simply gave no reply, but looked at his questioner with the blank unconsciousness of an infant. By and by he began to recognize Cicely, and to smile at her approach. The next step in returning consciousness was but another manifestation of the same sentiment. When Cicely would leave him he would look his regret, and be restless and uneasy until she returned.

The family were at a loss what to call him. To any inquiry as to his name he answered no more than to other questions.

"He come jes' befo' Sherman," said Needham, after a few weeks, "lack John de Baptis' befo' de Lawd. I reckon we bettah call 'im John."

So they called him John. He soon learned the name. As time went on Cicely found that he was quick at learning things. She taught him to speak her own negro English, which he pronounced with absolute fidelity to her intonations; so that barring the quality of his voice, his speech was an echo of Cicely's own.

The summer wore away and the autumn came. John and Cicely wandered in the woods together and gathered walnuts, and chinquapins and wild grapes. When harvest time came, they worked in the fields side by side,—plucked the corn, pulled the fodder, and gathered the dried peas from the yellow pea-vines. Cicely was a phenomenal cotton-picker, and John accompanied her to the fields and stayed by her hours at a time, though occasionally he would complain of his head, and sit under a tree and rest part of the day while Cicely worked, the two keeping one another always in sight.

They did not have a great deal of intercourse with other people. Young men came to the cabin sometimes to see Cicely, but when they found her entirely absorbed in the stranger they ceased their visits. For a time Cicely kept him away, as much as possible, from others, because she did not wish them to see that there was anything wrong about him. This was her motive at first, but after a while she kept him to herself simply because she was happier so. He was hers—hers alone. She had found him, as Pharaoh's daughter had found Moses in the bulrushes; she had taught him to speak, to think, to love. She had not taught him to remember; she would not have wished him to; she would have been jealous of any past to which he might have proved bound by other ties. Her dream so far had come true. She had found him; he loved her. The rest of it would as surely follow, and that before long. For dreams were serious things, and time had proved hers to have been not a presage of misfortune, but one of the beneficent visions that are sent, that we may enjoy by anticipation the good things that are in store for us.

III

But a short interval of time elapsed after the passage of the warlike host that swept through North Carolina, until there appeared upon the scene the vanguard of a second army, which came to bring light and the fruits of liberty to a land which slavery and the havoc of war had brought to ruin. It is fashionable to assume that those who undertook the political rehabilitation of the Southern States merely rounded out the ruin that the war had wrought—merely ploughed up the desolate land and sowed it with salt. Perhaps the gentler judgments of the future may recognize that their task was a difficult one, and that wiser and honester men might have failed as egregiously. It may even, in time, be conceded that some good came out of the carpet-bag governments, as, for instance, the establishment of a system of popular education in the former slave States. Where it had been a crime to teach people to read or write, a schoolhouse dotted every hillside, and the State provided education for rich and poor, for white and black alike. Let us lay at least this token upon the grave of the carpet-baggers. The evil they did lives after them, and the statute of limitations does not seem to run against it. It is but just that we should not forget the good.

Long, however, before the work of the political reconstruction had begun, a brigade of Yankee schoolmasters and schoolma'ams had invaded Dixie, and one of the latter had opened a Freedman's Bureau School in the town of Patesville, about four miles from Needham Green's cabin on the neighboring sandhills.

It had been quite a surprise to Miss Chandler's Boston friends when she had announced her intention of going South to teach the freedmen. Rich, accomplished, beautiful, and a social favorite, she was giving up the comforts and luxuries of Northern life to go among hostile strangers, where her associates would be mostly ignorant negroes. Perhaps she might meet occasionally an officer of some Federal garrison, or a traveler from the North; but to all intents and purposes her friends considered her as going into voluntary exile. But heroism was not rare in those days, and Martha Chandler was only one of the great multitude whose hearts went out toward an oppressed race, and who freely poured out their talents, their money, their lives,—whatever God had given them,—in the sublime and not unfruitful effort to transform three millions of slaves into intelligent freedmen. Miss Chandler's friends knew, too, that she had met a great sorrow, and more than suspected that out of it had grown her determination to go South.

When Cicely Green heard that a school for colored people had been opened at Patesville she combed her hair, put on her Sunday frock and such bits of finery as she possessed, and set out for town early the next Monday morning.

There were many who came to learn the new gospel of education, which was to be the cure for all the freedmen's ills. The old and gray-haired, the full-grown man and woman, the toddling infant,— they came to acquire the new and wonderful learning that was to make them the equals of the white people. It was the teacher's task, by no means an easy one, to select from this incongruous mass the most promising material, and to distribute among them the second-hand books and clothing that were sent, largely by her Boston friends, to aid her in her work; to find out what they knew, to classify them by their intelligence rather than by their knowledge, for they were all lamentably ignorant. Some among them were the children of parents who had been free before the war, and of these some few could read and one or two could write. One paragon, who could repeat the multiplication table, was immediately promoted to the position of pupil teacher.

Miss Chandler took a liking to the tall girl who had come so far to sit under her instruction. There was a fine, free air in her bearing, a lightness in her step, a sparkle in her eye, that spoke of good blood, —whether fused by nature in its own alembic, out of material despised and spurned of men, or whether some obscure ancestral strain, the teacher could not tell. The girl proved intelligent and learned rapidly, indeed seemed almost feverishly anxious to learn. She was quiet, and was, though utterly untrained, instinctively polite, and profited from the first day by the example of her teacher's quiet elegance. The teacher dressed in simple black. When Cicely came back to school the second day, she had left off her glass beads and her red ribbon, and had arranged her hair as nearly like the teacher's as her skill and its quality would permit.

The teacher was touched by these efforts at imitation, and by the intense devotion Cicely soon manifested toward her. It was not a sycophantic, troublesome devotion, that made itself a burden to its object. It found expression in little things done rather than in any words the girl said. To the degree that the attraction was mutual, Martha recognized in it a sort of freemasonry of temperament that drew them together in spite of the differences between them. Martha felt sometimes, in the vague way that one speculates about the impossible, that if she were brown, and had been brought up in North Carolina, she would be like Cicely; and that if Cicely's ancestors had come over in the Mayflower, and Cicely had been reared on Beacon Street, in the shadow of the State House dome, Cicely would have been very much like herself.

Miss Chandler was lonely sometimes. Her duties kept her occupied all day. On Sundays she taught a Bible class in the school-room. Correspondence with bureau officials and friends at home furnished her with additional occupation. At times, nevertheless, she felt a longing for the company of women of her own race; but the white ladies of the town did not call, even in the most formal way, upon the Yankee school-teacher. Miss Chandler was therefore fain to do the best she could with such companionship as was available. She took Cicely to her home occasionally, and asked her once to stay all night. Thinking, however, that she detected a reluctance on the girl's part to remain away from home, she did not repeat her invitation.

Cicely, indeed, was filling a double rôle. The learning acquired from Miss Chandler she imparted to John at home. Every evening, by the light of the pine-knots blazing on Needham's ample hearth, she taught John to read the simple words she had learned during the day. Why she did not take him to school she had never asked herself; there were several other pupils as old as he seemed to be. Perhaps she still thought it necessary to protect him from curious remark. He worked with Needham by day, and she could see him at night, and all of Saturdays and Sundays. Perhaps it was the jealous selfishness of love. She had found him; he was hers. In the spring, when school was over, her granny had said that she might marry him. Till then her dream would not yet have come true, and she must keep him to herself. And yet she did not wish him to lose this golden key to the avenues of opportunity. She would not take him to school, but she would teach him each day all that she herself had learned. He was not difficult to teach, but learned, indeed, with what seemed to Cicely marvelous ease,—always, however, by her lead, and never of his own initiative. For while he could do a man's work, he was in most things but a child, without a child's curiosity. His love for Cicely appeared the only thing for which he needed no suggestion; and even that possessed an element of childish dependence that would have seemed, to minds trained to thoughtful observation, infinitely pathetic.

The spring came and cotton-planting time. The children began to drop out of Miss Chandler's school one by one, as their services were required at home. Cicely was among those who intended to remain in school until the term closed with the "exhibition," in which she was assigned a leading part. She had selected her recitation, or "speech," from among half a dozen poems that her teacher had suggested, and to memorizing it she devoted considerable time and study. The exhibition, as the first of its kind, was sure to be a notable event. The parents and friends of the children were invited to attend, and a colored church, recently erected,—the largest available building,—was secured as the place where the exercises should take place.

On the morning of the eventful day, uncle Needham, assisted by John, harnessed the mule to the two-wheeled cart, on which a couple of splint-bottomed chairs were fastened to accommodate Dinah and Cicely. John put on his best clothes,—an ill-fitting suit of blue jeans, —a round wool hat, a pair of coarse brogans, a homespun shirt, and a bright blue necktie. Cicely wore her best frock, a red ribbon at her throat, another in her hair, and carried a bunch of flowers in her hand. Uncle Needham and aunt Dinah were also in holiday array. Needham and John took their seats on opposite sides of the cart-frame, with their feet dangling down, and thus the equipage set out leisurely for the town.

Cicely had long looked forward impatiently to this day. She was going to marry John the next week, and then her dream would have come entirely true. But even this anticipated happiness did not over-shadow the importance of the present occasion, which would be an epoch in her life, a day of joy and triumph. She knew her speech perfectly, and timidity was not one of her weaknesses. She knew that the red ribbons set off her dark beauty effectively, and that her dress fitted neatly the curves of her shapely figure. She confidently expected to win the first prize, a large morocco-covered Bible, offered by Miss Chandler for the best exercise.

Cicely and her companions soon arrived at Patesville. Their entrance into the church made quite a sensation, for Cicely was not only an acknowledged belle, but a general favorite, and to John there attached a tinge of mystery which inspired a respect not bestowed upon those who had grown up in the neighborhood. Cicely secured a seat in the front part of the church, next to the aisle, in the place reserved for the pupils. As the house was already partly filled by townspeople when the party from the country arrived, Needham and his wife and John were forced to content themselves with places somewhat in the rear of the room, from which they could see and hear what took place on the platform, but where they were not at all conspicuously visible to those at the front of the church.

The schoolmistress had not yet arrived, and order was preserved in the audience by two of the elder pupils, adorned with large rosettes of red, white, and blue, who ushered the most important visitors to the seats reserved for them. A national flag was gracefully draped over the platform, and under it hung a lithograph of the Great Emancipator, for it was thus these people thought of him. He had saved the Union, but the Union had never meant anything good to them. He had proclaimed liberty to the captive, which meant all to them; and to them he was and would ever be the Great Emancipator.

The schoolmistress came in at a rear door and took her seat upon the platform. Martha was dressed in white; for once she had laid aside the sombre garb in which alone she had been seen since her arrival at Patesville. She wore a yellow rose at her throat, a bunch of jasmine in her belt. A sense of responsibility for the success of the exhibition had deepened the habitual seriousness of her face, yet she greeted the audience with a smile.

"Don' Miss Chan'ler look sweet," whispered the little girls to one another, devouring her beauty with sparkling eyes, their lips parted over a wealth of ivory.

"De Lawd will bress dat chile," said one old woman, in soliloquy. "I t'ank de good Marster I 's libbed ter see dis day."

Even envy could not hide its noisome head: a pretty quadroon whispered to her neighbor:—

"I don't b'liebe she's natch'ly ez white ez dat. I 'spec, she's be'n powd'rin'! An' I know all dat hair can't be her'n; she's got on a switch, sho 's you bawn."

"You knows dat ain' so, Ma'y 'Liza Smif," rejoined the other, with a look of stern disapproval; "you *knows* dat ain' so. You'd gib yo' everlastin' soul 'f you wuz ez white ez Miss Chan'ler, en yo' ha'r wuz ez long ez her'n."

"By Jove, Maxwell!" exclaimed a young officer, who belonged to the Federal garrison stationed in the town, "but that girl is a beauty." The speaker and a companion were in fatigue uniform, and had merely dropped in for an hour between garrison duty. The ushers had wished to give them seats on the platform, but they had declined, thinking that perhaps their presence there might embarrass the teacher. They sought rather to avoid observation by sitting behind a pillar in the rear of the room, around which they could see without attracting undue attention.

"To think," the lieutenant went on, "of that Junonian figure, those lustrous orbs, that golden coronal, that flower of Northern civilization, being wasted on these barbarians!" The speaker uttered an exaggerated but suppressed groan.

His companion, a young man of clean-shaven face and serious aspect, nodded assent, but whispered reprovingly,—

"Sh! some one will hear you. The exercises are going to begin."

When Miss Chandler stepped forward to announce the hymn to be sung by the school as the first exercise, every eye in the room was fixed upon her, except John's, which saw only Cicely. When the teacher had uttered a few words, he looked up to her, and from that moment did not take his eyes off Martha's face.

After the singing, a little girl, dressed in white, crossed by ribbons of red and blue, recited with much spirit a patriotic poem.

When Martha announced the third exercise, John's face took on a more than usually animated expression, and there was a perceptible deepening of the troubled look in his eyes, never entirely absent since Cicely had found him in the woods.

A little yellow boy, with long curls, and a frightened air, next ascended the platform.

"Now, Jimmie, be a man, and speak right out," whispered his teacher, tapping his arm reassuringly with her fan as he passed her.

Jimmie essayed to recite the lines so familiar to a past generation of schoolchildren:—

> "I knew a widow very poor,
>   Who four small children had;
> The eldest was but six years old,
>   A gentle, modest lad."

He ducked his head hurriedly in a futile attempt at a bow; then, following instructions previously given to him, fixed his eyes upon a large cardboard motto hanging on the rear wall of the room, which admonished him in bright red letters to

"ALWAYS SPEAK THE TRUTH"

and started off with assumed confidence—

> "I knew a widow very poor,
>   Who"—

At this point, drawn by an irresistible impulse, his eyes sought the level of the audience. Ah, fatal blunder! He stammered, but with an effort raised his eyes and began again:

> "I knew a widow very poor,
>   Who four"—

Again his treacherous eyes fell, and his little remaining self-possession utterly forsook him. He made one more despairing effort:—

> "I knew a widow very poor,
>   Who four small"—

and then bursting into tears, turned and fled amid a murmur of sympathy.

Jimmie's inglorious retreat was covered by the singing in chorus of "The Star-spangled Banner," after which Cicely Green came forward to recite her poem.

"By Jove, Maxwell!" whispered the young officer, who was evidently a connoisseur of female beauty, "that isn't bad for a bronze Venus. I'll tell you"—

"'Sh!" said the other. "Keep still."

When Cicely finished her recitation, the young officers began to applaud, but stopped suddenly in some confusion as they realized that they were the only ones in the audience so engaged. The colored people had either not learned how to express their approval in orthodox fashion, or else their respect for the sacred character of the edifice forbade any such demonstration. Their enthusiasm found vent, however, in a subdued murmur, emphasized by numerous nods and winks and suppressed exclamations. During the singing that followed Cicely's recitation the two officers quietly withdrew, their duties calling them away at this hour.

At the close of the exercises, a committee on prizes met in the vestibule, and unanimously decided that Cicely Green was entitled to the first prize. Proudly erect, with sparkling eyes and cheeks flushed with victory, Cicely advanced to the platform to receive the coveted award. As she turned away, her eyes, shining with gratified vanity, sought those of her lover.

John sat bent slightly forward in an attitude of strained attention; and Cicely's triumph lost half its value when she saw that it was not at her, but at Miss Chandler, that his look was directed. Though she watched him thenceforward, not one glance did he vouchsafe to his jealous sweetheart, and never for an instant withdrew his eyes from Martha, or relaxed the unnatural intentness of his gaze. The imprisoned mind, stirred to unwonted effort, was struggling for liberty; and from Martha had come the first ray of outer light that had penetrated its dungeon.

Before the audience was dismissed, the teacher rose to bid her school farewell. Her intention was to take a vacation of three months; but what might happen in that time she did not know, and there were duties at home of such apparent urgency as to render her return to North Carolina at least doubtful; so that in her own heart her *au revoir* sounded very much like a farewell.

She spoke to them of the hopeful progress they had made, and praised them for their eager desire to learn. She told them of the serious duties of life, and of the use they should make of their acquirements. With prophetic finger she pointed them to the upward way which they must climb with patient feet to raise themselves out of the depths.

Then, an unusual thing with her, she spoke of herself. Her heart was full; it was with difficulty that she maintained her composure; for the faces that confroned her were kindly faces, and not critical, and some of them she had learned to love right well.

"I am going away from you, my children," she said; "but before I go I want to tell you how I came to be in North Carolina; so that if I have been able to do anything here among you for which you might feel inclined, in your good nature, to thank me, you may thank not me alone, but another who came before me, and whose work I have taken up where *he* laid it down. I had a friend,—a dear friend,—why should I be ashamed to say it?—a lover, to whom I was to be married,—as I hope all you girls may some day be happily married. His country needed him, and I gave him up. He came to fight for the Union and for Freedom, for he believed that all men are brothers. He did not come back again—he gave up his life for you. Could I do less than he? I came to the land that he sanctified by his death, and I have tried in my weak way to tend the plant he watered with his blood, and which, in the fullness of time, will blossom forth into the perfect flower of liberty."

She could say no more, and as the whole audience thrilled in sympathy with her emotion, there was a hoarse cry from the men's side of the room, and John forced his way to the aisle and rushed forward to the platform.

"Martha! Martha!"

"Arthur! O Arthur!"

Pent-up love burst the flood-gates of despair and oblivion, and caught these two young hearts in its torrent. Captain Arthur Carey, of the 1st Massachusetts, long since reported missing, and mourned as dead, was restored to reason and to his world.

It seemed to him but yesterday that he had escaped from the Confederate prison at Salisbury; that in an encounter with a guard he had received a wound in the head; that he had wandered on in the woods, keeping himself alive by means of wild berries, with now and then a piece of bread or a potato from a friendly negro. It seemed but the night before that he had laid himself down, tortured with fever, weak from loss of blood, and with no hope that he would ever rise again. From that moment his memory of the past was a blank until he recognized Martha on the platform and took up again the thread of his former existence where it had been broken off.

And Cicely? Well, there is often another woman, and Cicely, all unwittingly to Carey or to Martha, had been the other woman. For, after all, her beautiful dream had been one of the kind that go by contraries.

Discussion of Chesnutt's "Cicely's Dream"

1. This story is largely about Cicely's education, which consists of a literal education by Martha as well as a shattering of her dreams

regarding her life with John. Cicely believes that this literal education will be the freedmen's salvation. To what extent is this actually true?

2. Chesnutt, Walker, and Chopin all deal with sexual relationships that cross class boundaries. Many sociologists argue that in such cases there will be conflict caused by the widely differing backgrounds. To what extent do these three stories support this contention?

3. To what extent is this story a political fable about events in the South after the Civil War? If one considers the story from this point of view, it is interesting that it is the women who are the most actively engaged in the struggle. What are the implications?

4. When Martha speaks metaphorically of her students as "my children" (page 110), another interpretation of the story is suggested, one that is psychological and familial. Discuss it.

SIGRID UNDSET

1882–1949

🌷 Although Sigrid Undset was born in Denmark, she is usually regarded as a Norwegian, and justly so, for her themes are deeply rooted in the development of modern Norway. Undset shares playwright Henrik Ibsen's interest in the hypocrisy and vanity of the middle classes, and also composer Edvard Grieg's interests in Scandinavian myths. Her early novel, *Jenny* (1911), established her reputation in Scandinavia, but American readers are probably more familiar with her work through the trilogy *Kristin Lavransdatter* (1929). Undset received a Nobel Prize in 1929. Although many of the characters of "Simonsen" are pretentious bourgeoisie, Simonsen himself rises above them. Like the heroine of "Tuesday Siesta," he endures, and his conscious affirmation of faith in the world gives the story an optimistic and, perhaps, even a mystical tone.

Simonsen

Simonsen stopped in the gateway and dug out his worn, greasy old wallet, meaning to slip into it the testimonial he had in his hand. But first he unfolded the grimy paper and read it through, although he knew it by heart:

"Storeman Anton Simonsen has been with our firm for three years. During this time he has shown himself to be a sober, hard-working, and willing man.

N. Nielsen
Hercules Engineering Works."

No, indeed; that reference wouldn't do him much good. Damn the fellow, it was a shabby way to treat him. The chief had never minded pitching the tale to customers about delivery dates and things like that—but write the sort of reference that would get a poor devil a job—not likely! "Well, I can't state that you've carried out your work to our satisfaction," he'd said, the so-and-so. But at least he'd had to put "sober." He hadn't at first, but Simonsen had insisted. "Seems to me I've smelled drink on you from time to time, Simonsen." But Simonsen had spoken up. "I do take a nip now and again, sir," he'd said. "And I believe you would too, if you had to spend your days rummaging about in that cold warehouse. But nobody can say Anton Simonsen was ever the worse for drink at his work—no, not even tipsy. Not once." So then his lordship

From *Four Stories*, by Sigrid Undset, translated by Naomi Walford. Copyright © 1959 by Alfred A. Knopf, Inc. Reprinted by permission of the publisher.

had to give in and the secretary lady had to write it out again with "sober" in it. And now here it was—such as it was; no great shakes, but he had nothing better to show.

"Look out, blast you—fathead!"

Simonsen jumped aside against the wall as a cartload of clattering iron girders swung into the gateway. Steam rose from the horses' damp backs as they threw themselves into the collar to drag the sleigh over the bare paving-stones under the arch. The driver shouted something else after him, but Simonsen couldn't hear it for the din of the clashing girders.

He put away his testimonial and slipped the wallet into his breast pocket. Then he glanced indignantly after the sleigh. It was standing in the yard in front of the warehouse, under the crane which projected with its chain and pulley from a dark hole above the barred windows in the blackish-red wall. White steam was rising from the horses' backs, and their coats were matted into little wet, frosty tufts. The carter hadn't put their rugs on them; he was talking to another man.

Simonsen buttoned up his winter overcoat, which was fairly new and tidy, straightened himself up, and threw out his stomach. A sense of dignity as a citizen arose in him; he was, after all, a respectable member of society, and that ruffian of a driver had bawled at him. And with this feeling something else stirred within him at the sight of the two cart horses, which had hauled their load until the muscles of their sweating loins were tense. He stepped back into the yard.

"You ought to cover those horses of yours, you know. Why d'you let 'em stand in the cold like that, in a muck sweat?"

The carter—a tall lout of a fellow—turned and looked down at him.

"Is that any o' your business, fellow?"

"They'd have something to say to you, wouldn't they, if I was to go up to the office and tell 'em how you treat their animals?"

"Just you get out—and quick about it! What the hell's it got to do with you, eh? Shoving your nose in—" and he took a step toward Simonsen.

Simonsen withdrew a little—but of course the fellow would never dare touch him here in the yard. He stuck out his stomach even farther, saying: "Don't forget they can see you from the office windows, that's all—see how you look after the firm's horses."

With that he turned. And at once the feeling of self-confidence ebbed away. For as he was passing through the gateway a man ran down the steps and shot past him, a gentleman, wearing an astrakhan cap and a fur coat, and carrying a black stick with a silver handle —a red-and-white, fair-haired man, the man he had spoken to when he applied for the job.

Dusk was falling. It was nearly four o'clock. Olga would have something to say about it when he arrived back so late for dinner. Well, he'd just have to tell her he'd been kept late at the warehouse.

Simonsen padded quickly along Torv Street. He both shuffled and hopped, and with his big round belly and little curved arms he looked rather like a rubber ball rolling and bouncing along. He was a little, short-necked man with a pouchy, fat face and watery eyes hidden far in behind their lids, red-veined cheeks, and a rather blue blob of a nose above the bristly, grayish-yellow moustache.

It was a raw Saturday afternoon early in December, and the air was thick with gray frost-fog that smelled and tasted of gas and soot. Out in the street the sleighs swung from side to side over the ploughed-up, potholed, hard-frozen snow, while on the pavement the stream of people flowed black and heavy past the illuminated, frosted shopwindows. Somebody bumped into Simonsen every moment, and looked back at him angrily as he bumbled along deep in his own thoughts.

Not that many thoughts were stirring in his mind, for he thrust them away. He'd find something, somehow, somewhere. So he needn't tell Olga that he'd been sacked at last, and was to leave on New Year's Day. Heigh-ho—the battle of life.

There was no great hurry. He had nearly a month. But if it came to the pinch, he'd have to write to Sigurd. Sigurd would always be able to find him a job. It wasn't too much to ask of one's own son —when the son was in Sigurd's position. Still, he didn't care for the idea; it would be for the fourth time. The fourth time in eight whole years, though—eight years exactly at the New Year, since Sigurd had got him into the office because his smart new daughter-in-law, the bitch, didn't think he was good enough to live with them in Fredrikstad. It was a pity he'd lost all three jobs—but that wasn't his fault. At the office it was the girls who'd done for him, cheeky little sluts. As if it mattered to them what he was like so long as he did his work properly—and he had. And he'd taken no liberties with them—as if he would, with such stuck-up, white-faced shrews. And then there was the timber yard. In those days he'd been really neat and respectable, for it was then he had ...oved to Olga's. He wasn't used to that sort of job, of course; but if it hadn't been for the foreman's malice he would never have lost it. And then he was taken on by the engineering works. And what sort of situation was that for a man nearing sixty, having to learn about a whole lot of queer new things he'd never heard of, and dispatching and packing and invoicing and all the rest of it. The chief storeman was a lazy devil; Simonsen was blamed for everything, and they'd always treated him badly—all of them, from the manager and the chief clerk (who kept reminding him that he'd only been taken on temporarily and asking him whether he had anything else in view) to the head storeman and the foreman and the drivers—*and* the cashier: how sour and cross she'd been every time he went up to her to ask for an advance!

All these things went round and round in his head, rolled up in a gray, woolly fog of anxiety and depression: Olga would nag at him when he got home, Sigurd and his wife would make themselves most unpleasant when they heard he'd been dismissed, and he would have to make a fresh start in a new job where he would dither, frightened and uncomprehending and woolly-minded, faced with new work that he knew nothing about and would never learn, in a new warehouse or perhaps a new office full of strange, hostile things, cowering under constant correction and rebuke, dully awaiting a fresh dismissal—just as he had dithered and cowered, heavy and old and stupid, through his previous situations.

But Simonsen had had a certain amount of practice in keeping gloomy thoughts at bay. He had dithered through his whole life in just the same way; he had cowered and expected dismissal and reprimand and nagging and unpleasantness as something inevitable. So it had been at sea, so it had been on Consul Isachsen's wharf, and so it had been at home while his wife was alive. She had been ill-tempered and sour and strict and cross-grained—and his daughter-in-law was not so very different.

Yes, Sigurd had been paid out for marrying that shabby-genteel daughter of Captain Myhre's. What good times Simonsen had had at home after Laura's death! The boy had come on well: he'd been good to his old dad—paid his way and everything. Not that it had been so bad here in town either, for the first few years, when he'd been a gay bachelor again, going out and about and having fun. And since he'd taken up with Olga he'd really been very comfortable—on the whole. She hadn't been too easy the time she became pregnant, but that was understandable, and she had calmed down the moment he promised to marry her. Sometimes she went on at him to keep his word, and of course he fully intended to marry her sometime; he'd have done it long ago if he hadn't known what trouble he'd have over it with Sigurd and his wife. But one day he'd find a good, easy job that he could keep, and when Olga expanded her dressmaking business, and her boy Henry went into the office—he was errand-boy there now, and shaping well—they would all be happy and comfortable together. He would sit on the sofa with his toddy and his pipe, and Olga would flit in and out seeing to things, and Svanhild would sit beside him and do her homework. For Olga was a decent, steady person, and nobody should have a chance to call Svanhild a bastard when she started school.

Simonsen had reached Ruseløk Road. The fog lay heavy and raw in the narrow street, and was barred with light—yellowish-green light from the frozen panes of the little shopwindows. In all of these, visible where gas jet or lamp had thawed a clear patch, hung a cluster of paper Christmas-tree baskets, whether it was a draper's or a delicatessen store or a tobacco shop. The reddish glow from the big windows of the market hall on the other side of the street flowed oilily out into the fog; the gas lamps on the terrace above could just be glimpsed, but the big private houses up there were invisible; not a gleam of light came from them, though one could sense them like a wall high up in the fog, pressing down upon the street that ran like a ditch at their foot.

Simonsen toddled and trudged along; the pavement was slippery in many places where the sheet-ice had not been chipped away. Children swarmed in and out of the dark gateways, and in the street among carts and sleighs they tried to slide, wherever there was as much as a slippery runner-track through the bumpy, brown layer of hard-frozen snow.

"Svanhild!"

Simonsen called sharply to a little girl in a dirty white hood. She had clambered up on to the piled-up snow along the edge of the pavement, and from there slid down to the roadway on tiny skis that were black with dirty snow and had hardly any curve left in them.

The child stood still in the middle of the street, looking up at Simonsen, who had stepped over the heap of snow to her. Her blue eyes were conscience-stricken, as she brushed her fair hair up under her hood and wiped her nose on her red-mittened hand.

"How many times have you been told not to run out into the street, Svanhild! Why can't you be a good girl and play in the yard?"

Svanhild looked up fearfully.

"I can't ski in the yard; there isn't any slope."

"And suppose a cart came along and ran over you—or a drunken man carried you off—what d'you think Mum and Dad would say then, eh?"

Svanhild, ashamed, was silent. Simonsen helped her on to the pavement, and they tripped along together hand in hand, her little sticks of skis clattering on the snowless path.

"Do you think Dad'll take you for a walk this evening, when you're such a naughty, disobedient girl, and don't do what you're told? Finished dinner, I suppose, have they?"

"Mummy and Henry and me had dinner a long time ago."

"H'm." Simonsen trudged in through the gateway. MRS. OLGA MARTINSEN. DRESSMAKING. CHILDREN'S AND BOYS' CLOTHES. 3RD FLOOR, ENTRANCE IN YARD was the legend on a white enamel plate. Simonsen crossed the courtyard and glanced up at the lighted window, where some fashion magazines were propped up against the panes. Then he took Svanhild's skis under his arm and led the child up the narrow stairs at the back of the yard.

Outside Olga's door some little boys were reading a comic by the light of a kitchen lamp that hung there. Simonsen growled something and let himself in.

It was dark in the hall. At the farther end, light shone through the glass pane in the sitting-room door. Simonsen went into his own room. It was dark in there too, and cold. Damn it, she'd let the stove go out. He lit the lamp.

"Run in to Mummy, Svanhild, and tell her I'm back."

He opened the door into the next room. At the table, which

overflowed with half-finished sewing, pieces cut out and scraps left over, Miss Abrahamsen sat bowed over her work. She had fastened a newspaper to one side of the lamp, so that all the light fell upon her yellow little old-maid's face and brown, rat's paw hands. The steel of the two sewing-machines glinted a little, and against the wall Olga's and Svanhild's white-covered beds could just be discerned.

"Hard at it, then, Miss Abrahamsen!"

"Yes, well—you got to be."

"Funny, this Christmas business. You'd think the world was coming to an end."

Svanhild crept into the room.

"Mum says your dinner's in the oven."

"I shall sit here and enjoy your company, Miss Abrahamsen. It's cold in my room."

Miss Abrahamsen silently cleared a corner of the table while Simonsen fetched his meal: white cabbage soup and sausage.

H'm. Good. If only he'd had—Simonsen rose and knocked at the sitting-room door.

"I say, Olga—"

"Why, good evening, Mr. Simonsen! How are you keeping?"

He opened the door and looked in.

"So it's you! Another new dress, Miss Hellum?"

Olga was standing with her mouth full of pins, fitting her customer. She arranged the folds at Miss Hellum's breast, in front of the wall mirror.

"Like that, I thought." Olga took the lamp from the nickel stand beside her and held it up.

"Ye—es. You're sure its not lopsided at the back, now, Mrs. Martinsen?"

Two girls who were sitting and waiting in the half light over on the plush sofa put down a fashion journal, glanced at each other and smiled, looked at Miss Hellum and smiled at each other again. "Gracious!" one whispered audibly. They were dressed almost exactly alike, in three-quarter-length coats with a little strip of fur at the neck, and respectable felt hats trimmed with a bird's wing. Simonsen paused in the doorway; he was a little shy of them.

"What do you think of it, Mr. Simonsen? Is it going to look nice?"

"How well that color suits you, Miss Hellum! But to beauty all is becoming, as they say."

"Ah, go on with you!" Miss Hellum laughed. Pretty girl, that. Olga was cutting round the neck, and her customer bent her head a little and shivered at the touch of the cold scissors. She had a pretty, plump neck with curly yellow hair growing low on it, and soft round arms.

"I expect this costs a bit," said Simonsen, feeling the silk—and then feeling her arm, as Olga went to fetch the sleeve.

"Shame on you, Mr. Simonsen!" laughed Miss Hellum. Olga looked annoyed; she shoved him aside and pulled on the sleeve.

"What was I going to say? . . . Oh, yes, Olga. Do you think Henry could nip down and borrow a couple of beers?"

"Poor Henry had to go back to the office; there was an estimate to be copied, he said."

"Oh, did he? Too bad. It's the same every Saturday evening nowadays, seems to me. Yes, it's a grind all right. And it was nearly four before I could get away from the warehouse. Oh, to be young and lovely, Miss Hellum!"

Svanhild looked in.

"Come along, Svanhild. Do you remember my name today?"

"Miss Hellum." Svanhild smiled obediently.

"Would you like some sweets again today?" Miss Hellum looked into her handbag and brought out a paper cornet.

"What do you say now, Svanhild? Your right hand, mind, and a pretty curtsy."

Svanhild whispered thank you, gave her right hand, and curtsied. Then she began breaking apart the camphor-drop sweets that had stuck together in the paper bag.

Miss Hellum dressed and talked and laughed.

"I'll be along for the final fitting on Tuesday, then, at the same time. You won't let me down, Mrs. Martinsen, will you? Good-by, then. Good-by, Mr. Simonsen. 'Bye, Svanhild."

Simonsen gallantly opened the door for her, and she swept out with waving feathers, the muskrat stole flung stylishly back over her shoulder.

"Gosh," said one of the young girls on the sofa. "Not bad."

"Hee-hee! No, she's a one, all right."

Simonsen went back to Miss Abrahamsen and his dinner, which had grown cold. Olga came in soon afterwards, fetched the coffee, and poured it out.

"I don't understand you, Anton, playing the fool like that! What can you be thinking of—in front of other people, too."

"Who cares about those little baggages?"

"It was the pastor's daughter from the Terrace and her friend. You make things hard enough for me as it is, without carrying on so silly with Miss Hellum. Yes, that's given them something to talk about—as if they hadn't enough already!"

"Ah, go on—it wasn't as bad as that."

The front doorbell rang. Miss Abrahamsen went to answer it.

"It's Miss Larsen."

Olga put down her cup and laid a tacked-up dress over her arm. "Never any peace—"

Miss Abrahamsen bent over her sewing again.

Mrs. Martinsen and Miss Abrahamsen sat sewing all that Sunday. They put off dinner until it was too dark to work; afterwards Olga lit the lamp and they started again.

"That plastron for Miss Olsen's dress, Miss Abrahamsen—you were working on it just now, weren't you?"

Miss Abrahamsen buzzed away at the machine.

"I put it on the table."

Olga searched, and looked about the floor.

"Svanhild, you haven't seen a little piece of white lace, have you?"

"No," said Svanhild from the window. She crept out and began searching too—but first she laid her doll on the upturned stool that was its bed, and covered it up well.

"Astrid's asleep—she's got diphtheria and scarlet fever," Svanhild protested, as her mother hunted through the doll's things. But relentlessly Olga lifted the patient—it was wrapped in white, ruched lace fastened carefully with safety pins.

"Good gracious! The child must be out of her mind! And I do declare you've torn a hole in it with the pins—you naughty, wicked girl—" she smacked her "—oh, what *shall* I do? Miss Olsen's expensive lace . . ."

Svanhild howled.

"Haven't I told you never to take anything that's on the floor? You're a wicked, mischievous little girl!"

Miss Abrahamsen inspected the plastron.

"I can unpick the pleats and press it and pleat it again so's to hide the tear in a fold. I don't think it'll show—"

Svanhild was yelling at the top of her voice. Simonsen opened the door a crack.

"What on earth's the matter, Svanhild—screaming like that when you know Daddy's taking his nap?"

Olga explained, vehemently.

"Oh, what a bad girl, Svanhild, to play such a nasty trick on your mother. You're not my Svanhild any more."

"I think you might take her out for a bit, Anton. It can't be good for you to lie in bed and sleep all day."

Simonsen scolded the child vigorously as he set off with her. But when they got as far as the hall and he helped her into her outdoor things, he comforted her.

"Don't cry any more now—oh, what an ugly noise! We'll go and toboggan in the Palace Park. It was very wrong of you, you know. Blow your nose now—there. You and I will go off and toboggan now—come along, Svanhild love."

Olga was really too strict with the child sometimes. Not that children shouldn't be punished when they did wrong—but Svanhild took things to heart so. There she was, still sobbing on the sled behind him—poor little mite.

The evening sky was dark purple above the towers and spires of the Terrace. The weather had cleared, and only a thin, sooty frost-haze hung in the streets round the lamps when Simonsen trudged uphill dragging his daughter on the sled.

It was so pretty in the park. Thick white hoarfrost lay on all the trees and bushes, so that they sparkled in the lamplight. But what crowds of children everywhere! On every smallest slope they were sledding or skiing; in the big avenue were swarms of big, rough boys, five or six of them on a fish sledge, yelling and shrieking as they whizzed down over the frozen snow with a long, thin rat's tail of sticks behind them. But Simonsen knew of a nice, quiet little slope; he and Svanhild had often tobogganed there in the evenings. It was fun for her there; Daddy stood at the top and gave her a shove, Svanhild shouted: "Way!" till her thin little voice nearly cracked, and Simonsen roared: "Way!" from right down in his stomach, although the only other people there were two little boys in ski-runners' shoes and woolen caps. Simonsen spoke to them; their names were Alf and Johannes Hauge, and their father was head of a government office and lived in Park Road. Simonsen gave all three children a shove—they were going to see whose sled ran fastest—but he shoved Svanhild hardest so that she won. Then he trotted down after them and helped Svanhild up again, for otherwise her feet broke through the frozen crust of the snow and she got stuck.

But presently Svanhild began to whimper.

"Daddy, my feet are so cold."

"Run then, my dear—come along, we'll go up on to the path and run."

Svanhild ran and cried; her toes hurt her so.

"Come now, you must run faster than that—much, much faster, Svanhild. Try and catch me!"

Simonsen bounced along with little tiny steps, like a rubber ball. And Svanhild ran after him as hard as she could and caught him up—again and again until she was warm and cheerful again, and laughing.

But then they couldn't find the sled. Simonsen hunted above the slope and below the slope and in among the bushes, but it was gone. Alf and Johannes had seen it standing over by the big tree near the path a little while before, but that was all they knew. Yes, and some big, rough boys had passed—Simonsen remembered that. It must have been they who took it.

Svanhild cried bitterly. Simonsen thought of Olga—oh, she really ought to be kinder; she was so snappy all day. Nasty, bad boys to steal a poor little girl's sled. How could children be so cruel.

"Don't cry, sweetheart, we'll find it again, you'll see."

Simonsen trotted about from slope to slope asking if anyone had seen a little blue sled. Svanhild went with him, holding his hand and crying; Alf and Johannes came too, clutching their sled ropes as with wide eyes they told Simonsen all the dreadful things they had heard about big, nasty boys who stole sleds and tobogganed into little children and threw lumps of ice in the Palace Park.

There was no sign of the sled. And up in the main avenue they met a grand, angry lady who turned out to be Alf's and Johannes' nanny, and she scolded them for not having come in half an hour before, and promised them they would catch it from Mummy and Daddy. She wasn't a bit interested to hear that the little girl was called Svanhild and that she had lost her sled; she went on scolding and scolding as she shuffled away holding the little boys' hands in a nurse's iron grasp. And Simonsen nearly got a steering-stick in his eye and the tip of a sled on his shin.

"Well, I'm afraid they've taken your sled, Svanhild; I don't think we shall see *that* again." Simonsen sighed dejectedly. "Hush now, don't cry so, my darling. Daddy'll give you a fine new sled for Christmas. There! Come along, we'll go down Karl Johan and look at the shops—they're wonderful tonight—and perhaps we'll see a fine new sled for you there," he said, brightening.

So Svanhild and her daddy went and looked at the shops. And when they came to a window where the crowds had halted and clustered in a big, black, jostling mass, Simonsen lifted her up on his arm and wriggled and shoved until they got right up to the shining window, and there they stood until there wasn't a single thing in it about which they hadn't talked and wondered how much it cost. In some places there were decorated Christmas trees with electric lights on their branches—and Svanhild was going to have a tree too, on Christmas Eve. In one shop there was a Christmas party, with tremendously grand lady dolls—just like Svanhild would be when she grew up. And in a shop where they sold trunks and suitcases, there was a tiny, tiny crocodile in a tiny, tiny pool; they had to wait a long time—could it be alive? And at last it blinked one eye the teeniest bit. Fancy, it *was* alive! A little crocodile like that would grow up to be so big that it could eat up a whole Svanhild at one gulp—"but this one can't bite, can it?" "No, this one couldn't do you any harm."

Up in Ekertorvet there was a movie camera in the window, among advertisements in photographs. And Svanhild had been to a movie with Daddy—three times—and they had to go over all they had seen there: the two little girls who had been kidnapped by kidnappers in a motor car, and a lot more. The lost sled was quite forgotten—and so was Mummy, sitting with pursed lips at her sewing until she grew tired and cross—everything was forgotten except that Svanhild was Daddy's little girl and that in seventeen days it would be Christmas.

There was a sports shop with sleds in the window, sleds large and small—but the finest of all, the scarlet one with rose-painting on it and a bronzed iron back-rest—that was the one Daddy would give Svanhild on Christmas Eve.

But after all this they needed something hot inside them. Simonsen knew of a snug little temperance café; it was Sunday, so the licensed ones were closed. There were no other customers, and the lady behind the counter was not insensible to Simonsen's gallant conversation while he had his coffee and sandwich and Svanhild a cream cake and a sip from Daddy's cup now and again.

"Not a word to Mummy!" Simonsen said with a wink. But Svanhild knew better than to tell Mummy when she and Daddy popped in here and there on their evening walks, and Svanhild had a stick of barley-sugar although Mummy believed it gave little girls worms in their teeth, and Daddy had something to drink which Mummy thought gave him worms in the stomach. But Mummy was always busy and it made her very cross—and Daddy was busy too when he was in the warehouse, and Henry at the office—When people were grown-up they had to work terribly hard. Svanhild knew that.

But after Sunday came Monday and five other gray week-days. Svanhild sat on the floor in the sewing-room and played, for Daddy came back so late in the evenings now that he had no time to take her for a walk. Daddy was cross too, now, she noticed; perhaps because he had so much work to do at the warehouse, or because Mummy had so much work that she hardly had time to get dinner or supper until late. And Henry was cross as well, for ladies had fittings until late at night in the room where he slept, so that he couldn't get to bed. But Svanhild consoled herself with the thought of the wonderful sled she was going to have for Christmas.

On the fifteenth Anton wrote to his son. He was sick of running after jobs in vain. After that he took a calmer view of the future, and had time once more to go out with Svanhild in the evenings and drag her along on her skis in the park; and they talked about the fine sled she was going to have.

But on the morning of the eighteenth, as Simonsen was nailing up a crate of machinery parts, the chief storeman came to tell him that he was wanted on the telephone. It was Sigurd; he was in town. Would his father drop in at the Augustin for coffee—take a couple of hours off that afternoon so that they could have a talk?

"How's Mossa and the children?"

The children were very well. Mossa was in town too; she had a bit of Christmas shopping to do.

"I've just remembered, son—I haven't a chance of getting even an hour off now, with Christmas coming on."

Sigurd said he'd have a word with the manager.

Well, thanks. Love to Mossa.

How like her! Ask him to dinner? Not on your life! Damned if he wouldn't get himself a skinful before he went to that *party*.

"Do you think you must?" Mrs. Carling asked her husband, who was uncorking a bottle of punch.

"Yes, I really think we can stand the old man a glass of punch."

"Well, well, just as you like, dear." Mossa Carling displayed all the double chins at her command. She was not pretty: her eyelids thickened toward the temples, so that her stabbing little gray eyes seemed to creep toward the bridge of her nose; her face was fat and fresh-colored but her mouth small and pinched, with thin lips.

Her chest was narrow and cramped, but the lower half of her body was broad and bulky.

She sat in the middle of the plush sofa under the electric chandelier, whose three lights splendidly illuminated the hotel room with its two iron beds, two mahogany washstands, two bedside tables, the wardrobe with the mirror, and the two armchairs in front of the table, on which an ash tray stood on a mat in the middle of the chenille cloth.

There was a timid knock on the door, and Simonsen stepped warily into the room. He shook hands.

"Well, Sigurd, nice to see you again, my boy. How are you, Mossa? Glad to see you again too—young and pretty as ever, I see."

Mossa rang for coffee and poured it out while Sigurd filled the glasses.

While he talked to Sigurd, Simonsen glanced at his daughter-in-law, who sat mute with a pinched mouth. Slowly and deviously the conversation turned toward the purpose of the meeting.

"We may smoke, mayn't we, my dear? Here, Father, have a cigar. Now, about what you said in your letter. I went up to the office this morning and had a word with your boss. He agreed with me: you don't fit in here in town. The work's too hard for a man of your age. And I can't get you anything else."

Simonsen said nothing. But Mossa took over.

"You must remember that Sigurd's in a subordinate position himself—in a way, that is. The board of directors wouldn't like him to keep bothering their business connections to give you a job. He's done it three times now, and each time you've lost your position. I must tell you that Sigurd was in quite serious trouble after getting you into this last place, which it seems you've now lost—"

"Yes, I was. No, as I say, you don't fit in here, Father. And you're too old to start anything new. So there's only one way I can help you. I can get you a job at the Mensted works up in Øimark—it's nice easy work. Of course, the wages aren't high: sixty crowns to start with, I believe. But, as I say, I can get you that."

Simonsen was silent.

"Yes, well—that's the only way I can help you," said Sigurd Carling.

"Do you want me to get it for you then, Father?" he asked after a while.

His father cleared his throat once or twice.

"Yes. Well, now. There's one thing, Sigurd—I don't know whether you've heard anything about it, but I'm engaged to be married—to the lady I've been lodging with these last six years. So I shall have to talk this over with Olga first and see what she thinks. Her name's Olga," he explained: "Mrs. Olga Martinsen, a widow."

There was a horribly long pause. Simonsen fidgeted with the tassels on the armchair.

"She's a real, good, respectable, decent person in every way,

Olga is. And she's got a big, expanding dressmaking business here in town, so it's quite a question whether she'd care much about moving into the wilds. Her boy's got an office job here, too."

"Is that the lady—" Sigurd spoke very slowly, "—who's said to have a child by you?"

"We've got a little girl, yes; her name's Svanhild—she'll be five in April."

"Oh." This was Mossa. "So you have a daughter by the woman you lodge with—the woman who's such a good, respectable, decent person in every way."

"And so she is—decent and respectable. And hard-working too. And kind."

"Then it's odd, father-in-law—" Mrs. Carling's voice was very sweet and smooth "—that you didn't marry this wonderful Mrs. Martinsen long ago. You had every reason."

"Well, I'll tell you, Mossa my dear." Simonsen perked up as he thought of what to say. "I didn't want to see any wife of mine toiling and slaving so hard, so I waited until I could find something better. But marry her I will. I've promised her that all along, and I'll keep my word as sure as my name's Anton Simonsen."

"Ye—es." Mossa grew sweeter and smoother. "Sixty crowns a month isn't much to marry on, and keep wife and child. And Mrs. Martinsen can hardly hope to build up a very extensive connection in Øimark."

"The worst part of it is this child of yours, Father," said Sigurd. "But no doubt Mrs. Martinsen can be brought to understand the situation, so that we can come to some arrangement."

"You must remember this about that little sister o' yours—about Svanhild. I don't want her to suffer for being illegitimate, and I think you're taking on a big responsibility, Sigurd, if you interfere in this."

Mossa snatched the word from him, and now there was no trace of gentleness in her voice.

"Responsibility! For *your* illegitimate child! That comes well from you, I *must* say! Here's Sigurd offering to get you a position—for the fourth time—in Øimark. To find one here in town is out of the question. If you don't think you can leave town because of your private affairs, you're perfectly free to stay. And if you can find a job and marry on it, we certainly shan't interfere. But naturally Sigurd can't help you in any other way. *His* responsibility, first and foremost, is to his own wife and children."

Mrs. Carling had put on her silk petticoat and draped herself in her new set of furs when on the following morning she climbed the stairs to Mrs. Martinsen's dressmaking establishment in the courtyard off Ruseløk Road. She placed a determined first finger on the bell under Simonsen's dirty visiting card.

The woman who opened the door was small, plump, and dark. She had pretty blue eyes in a face that was pale and washed-out from sitting indoors.

"Are you Mrs. Martinsen? I'm Mrs. Carling. I wanted to speak to you."

Rather hesitantly Olga opened the door of the nearest room.

"Please come in. I'm sorry there's no fire in here; we work in the other rooms."

Mrs. Carling sailed in and seated herself in the only armchair. The room was furnished as rooms to let usually are. On the chest of drawers, which was covered with a white cloth, the photographs of the late Mrs. Simonsen, of Sigurd, and of herself were conscientiously arrayed—engagement photographs—and two groups of the grandchildren.

"Well now, Mrs. Martinsen—" Olga was now standing over by the chest of drawers, observing the speaker "—there are one or two things I'd very much like to talk to you about. Won't you sit down?"

"Thank you, but I really haven't much time. What was it you wanted, Mrs. Carling?"

"Quite so. I won't keep you. We understand that Mr. Simonsen, my husband's father, has certain obligations toward you. I don't know whether he has made the present situation clear to you?"

"About the new job in Øimark? Oh, yes."

"Oh. Well, as you know, it's quite a modest position, so that for the time being he won't be able to fulfil his obligations to the child—his and yours. My husband and I have therefore decided to offer you—"

"Thank you very much." Olga spoke quickly and curtly. "We don't want to trouble you with our affairs, Mrs. Carling. We've agreed about it, Anton and I. We've agreed to get married now, right away."

"I see. Mrs. Martinsen, I must point out that Mr. Simonsen cannot expect any assistance from my husband—none whatever. He has a large family himself. And for four people to live on sixty crowns a month—I understand you have another child besides Mr. Simonsen's—"

"My boy will stay here. I have a sister in Trondhjem Road he can live with. Our plan was for us to live in Fredrikstad; I could carry on my dressmaking there, and Anton could come down to us on weekends."

"Yes, well, that *sounds* a very sensible idea. But you see, there are more than enough dressmakers in Fredrikstad already, so it's doubtful whether it would pay to give up your connection here and start all over again there, *Miss* Martinsen!"

Olga jumped.

"*Mrs.* Martinsen, I beg your pardon. That's what you call yourself, of course. Yes, you see my husband and I have been making a few inquiries. You can't be surprised that we should want to know just what sort of person it was he'd taken up with."

Olga gave a puff of scorn.

"And it's the same thing for me, Mrs. Simonsen—I beg your pardon, Mrs. *Carling*, I mean. But it so happens that Anton thinks none the worse of me because my fiancé ran away to America, leaving me to support myself and my boy the best way I could. And he's told me, Anton has, he's said it over and over again: 'I shan't let you down, Olga.' So it don't seem to me it need concern you at all, Mrs. Carling. We shan't trouble you and come running to you— and as your husband hasn't even kept his father's name—"

"My dear Mrs. Martinsen." Mossa waved her hand and displayed all her double chins. "I beg you not to get so excited. I hadn't the least idea of meddling in your affairs. Quite the contrary—I came here with the very best intentions. I simply wanted to make it quite clear to you—in case you imagined that Mr. Simonsen was any sort of catch—that if you do marry him, I believe all you'll gain will be the pleasure of supporting both him and his child. Just think for a moment. My dear father-in-law has never been exactly a model of efficiency, has he? We have no guarantee that he won't be dismissed again as usual. Yes . . . Do you think it will be easy for a man of his age—with a family—to keep on finding new situations? I've come here in a perfectly friendly way to bring you an offer from Mr. Carling. Look, my dear Mrs. Martinsen, up to now you've managed very well without a husband. Mr. Carling offers you a sum of money —we thought five hundred crowns—to compensate you for losing your lodger so suddenly. Without conditions. You understand that if later my father-in-law is so placed that he can marry we won't stand in his way. As you very rightly say, it doesn't concern us. And as for your little girl, we're prepared to offer her a home with us—"

"Never!" Olga flashed. "Let Svanhild go? That's one thing you can be certain I'll never do."

"Well, well. That's entirely as you wish, of course. You and my father-in-law will naturally please yourselves. If you like to marry on sixty crowns a month—give up your livelihood here and try to start a dressmaking business in Fredrikstad, which I assure you will never succeed . . . What baffles me is why you should want Mr. Simonsen at all. To *marry* him! In your circles people surely aren't so particular as to whether or not you've had some little affair with your lodger. How you could take up with him in the first place . . . You must forgive my saying this, but it's no recommendation in my eyes. Frankly, he's a nasty old man—"

Olga broke in: "Please say no more, Mrs. Carling. But I'll tell you just why I wanted Anton Simonsen. Maybe there *is* one or two things against him. But it didn't take me long to find out that he's a kind-hearted man—and there's not too many of that sort about. And as soon as he saw I wanted to make things snug and comfortable for him, he took to me and tidied himself up and behaved himself; and he'd a' done it before, *I* say, if he'd had any kindness or comfort where he come from. Kind and grateful always, Anton's been. And so taken up with Svanhild—almost too much of a good thing, it is—he quite spoils her. I'm fond of Anton, let me tell you, Mrs. Carling."

Mossa stood up and put the tips of her gloved fingers between the lace edges of her muff.

"Ah, well. If you *love* Mr. Simonsen, that's another matter."

Sigurd Carling had a high opinion of his wife's cleverness—he'd heard about it so often that he'd come to believe in it. As Miss Mossa Myhre she had pushed him on and made him the man he was today. Nevertheless, he had his doubts of her being the right person to come to an understanding with Mrs. Martinsen. She had very strict views, and this Olga creature had had two children in a rather irregular manner. And Mossa could make herself most unpleasant. So afterward he regretted having let her go: it had been a stupid thing to do. For an arrangement of some sort there must be. If his father were to move to Fredrikstad with a wife and child whom he couldn't support, it was as clear as daylight what would happen: Sigurd and his wife would never be safe from appeals for help, along with all the other kinds of bother his father always caused. And endless trouble with Mossa.

The matter had to be settled, and at once, before the old man had time to play them any tricks. Sigurd went to the Hercules works and ordered two new turbines, and in passing said a word or two about his father. It was arranged that Simonsen should leave for good on Christmas Eve, so that he might go home with them for the holiday.

Afterwards, he too went to see Mrs. Martinsen.

Olga was tear-stained when Simonsen came home at dinnertime. Carling had been there. He'd been quite nice; he had asked to see Svanhild and taken her on his lap, and told her she should have something special for Christmas. Afterward he had talked to Olga. It was about her debts: she owed rent, as well as sums here and there among the tradespeople. And she had accepted his money. Besides that, he had promised her fifteen crowns a month for Svanhild; that meant something steady coming in, and she had Henry too, who wouldn't be able to support himself for a while—fifteen crowns a month, he'd said, for the time being: "until my father has become self-supporting and can marry you." Olga sat on Simonsen's knee and cried; he was in the armchair in that cold room, in front of the chest of drawers with its family photographs. She cried, and he patted her.

"Oh, Anton, I don't know! What else could I a' done? If he won't help you there's nothing else for it. And I could see he wouldn't—not in any other way. If they set themselves against us, we should never make a go of it in Fredrikstad, you see—"

She blew her nose and wiped her eyes. And had another fit of crying.

"We got to accept it—you got to accept a lot of things when you're poor."

But to go home with Sigurd and Mossa for Christmas was one thing Simonsen would not do. They tempted him with a Christmas tree and grandchildren and goose and beer and spirits and pickled brawn, but the old man stood firm: he wanted to spend Christmas with Olga and the children. The most they managed to get from Simonsen was his promise to go down the day after Christmas Day. Sigurd had given him twenty-five crowns, so it was as well to get him out of town rather than let him loaf about there with money in his pocket until the New Year. Far better for the old boy to have his Christmas drinks with them, under supervision.

When Simonsen came home the evening before Christmas Eve, he had the new sled under his arm. Humming away in a deep bass voice he lit the lamp in his own room and unpacked his parcels.

There were drinks—aqua vitae and punch and brandy, and sweet port for Olga; so with a drop of beer they'd do all right. A pipe for Henry—it hadn't cost much; it was really just to show the boy he hadn't forgotten him, and it was a manly sort of thing to have. All the same he was pretty well broke now; the blouse material for Olga cost only 1 crown 45 øre, but then he'd bought her a brooch too, for 3.75, which looked more like ten crowns' worth. Simonsen took it out of its little box; he was sure she'd like it. He wanted to buy some little trifle for Miss Abrahamsen too—just a souvenir. Something quite small—he could afford that.

And then the sled, of course. Simonsen took the cloth off the table, unpacked the sled, and put it on display.

"Come and have a look, Olga love," he called into the sewing-room.

"What is it? I'm busy."

Simonsen moved the lamp over to the table.

"What do you think Svanhild will say to this, eh, Olga?"

"Mind the veneer, Anton!" and she spread newspaper under the sled and the lamp. "Yes, that's lovely—that's a beautiful sled."

"And look!" Simonsen unbuckled the cushion so that Olga could see all the rose-painting. "The cushion was extra."

"H'm. Must have been dear."

"Five crowns and twenty-five øre with the cushion," Simonsen answered briskly.

"Yes, well, that's a lot of money to spend on a thing like that, Anton. For such a little girl—she'd have been just as happy with a plainer one." Olga sighed.

"Oh, but now we got a little ready money handy, it's fun to give nice things. You've settled your debts and that. I bought something for my sweetheart too—" and he nudged her. Run and fetch a couple of glasses, Olga—I've got some port. You must taste it and see how you like it—I bought it on your account mostly."

Olga glanced at the many bottles on the chest of drawers and sighed a little. Then she fetched the glasses.

It was late on Christmas Eve when work finished at Mrs. Martinsen's. But at last all was done. Henry had gone off to deliver the last of the completed sewing, and Olga and Miss Abrahamsen had cleared away everything else, heaping it on the chairs and table in the sewing-room. Before she left, Miss Abrahamsen was given coffee and pastries and from Simonsen a bottle of eau-de-Cologne.

Then Olga went into the sitting-room. She cleared the magazines off the table, and materials and half-made garments off the chairs, and picked up the pins and buttons to drop them into the glass bowls on the console table. And she lit the candles on the Christmas tree, which she had decorated the night before.

Svanhild and Henry and Simonsen came in; the grownups sat down on the plush chairs, but Svanhild skipped and danced and rejoiced; she caught sight of the sled and shrieked with delight, then ran back to the tree again, not knowing what to do with herself for joy. Simonsen beamed and Olga smiled, though her eyes were sadly red; Simonsen had glanced at them several times during the afternoon. It would be the limit if she started to cry on this of all evenings, when they were going to have such a nice time.

He fetched his presents, smiling mischievously: she wouldn't think the blouse material was much of a gift. Then he brought out the eau-de-Cologne; for he had yielded to the temptation of doing things in style when he went into the fifty-øre bazaar after something for Miss Abrahamsen. There was also a cup to hold Olga's ball of wool when she knitted, and a little matchbox that looked like silver for Henry. The boy shook hands and laid pipe and box down by the window, where he had been lounging in a chair. But then came the brooch.

"All those was sort of practical things, Olga; you must have a little trifle just for pleasure, too."

Olga picked up the brooch and her eyes filled with tears.

"Such a lot of things, Anton!"

Simonsen threw out his hand in a magnificent gesture.

"You must think of me when you wear it, Olga love."

"Oh, I will, Anton."

"And what about that box that came for Svanhild?"

Olga fetched it. On it was written: To little Miss Svanhild, c/o Mrs. Martinsen's dressmaking establishment." Olga opened it. The card inside bore the inscription: "Merry Christmas!" It was Sigurd Carling's card. With it was a doll—but what a doll!

It had curly yellow hair and eyes that opened and shut. It was dressed in a white coat and white fur cap, and carried a little pair of skates over its arm—that was the most marvelous thing of all. Svanhild was speechless, but Simonsen talked and talked; he and the child were equally enraptured with the doll.

"Mummy must keep it for you—you'd better only play with it on Sundays."

"He's a good fellow, you know, Sigurd is," he said to Olga, who was bringing in the glasses and the jug of hot water. "It's what I always say: Sigurd's all right at heart—it's that damned hag of his who puts him up to things, for he's a good chap."

Simonsen mixed a toddy and Olga had port. Svanhild too was given a little drop of the sweet wine in her own glass as she sat on Daddy's lap.

"Come along, Henry, and mix yourself a toddy. You're a man now, you know."

Henry rose rather reluctantly, not looking at Simonsen. He had hard, pale eyes in a white, freckled face, and he looked thin and slight in his grown-up clothes.

"Well, *skål*, everybody! Isn't this jolly! Eh, Olga love?"

"Yes," she said, and bit her lip. Tears came into her eyes. "If only we knew what next Christmas was going to be like."

Simonsen lit his cigar. He looked troubled.

"Aren't you going to try your pipe, Henry my boy? You'll find some tobacco on my chest of drawers if you haven't any yourself."

"No, thanks," said Henry.

"Yes, next Christmas," said Olga, fighting with her tears.

"Hard to say when you don't know," Simonsen said. He leaned back in his chair. "Good cigar, this. Drink up, Olga. Yes, well, perhaps we'll all be celebrating Christmas together among the country bumpkins. I hear they have great goings-on at Christmas up in Øimark. I think you'd like the country, Olga. When you want a Christmas tree, all you do is walk out of the door and cut one. Not bad! How'd you like that, Svanhild—going out into the woods with your daddy to cut down a Christmas tree—and then drag it home on your sled, eh?"

Svanhild nodded, radiant.

"And Henry would get time off from the office and spend Christmas with us."

Henry smiled slightly—scornfully.

"Wouldn't that be fun, Svanhild—going to the station to meet Henry? Would you like it if you and Daddy and Mummy lived on a big farm with cows and horses and pigs and roosters and hens and all? And then kind Sigurd, who gave you your doll—he's got a little girl about your age, and a boy just a bit bigger, and a tiny, tiny baby; you could go into town and play with them."

"While I have tea with that stuck-up daughter-in-law of yours, I s'pose! That's the idea, eh, Anton?"

"Oh, well—I don't think that would be necessary—"

"How can you go on talking such nonsense!" Olga laughed—
and then burst out crying.

"Oh, now Olga, what are you crying for, love? Why do you take
it like that?"

"How do you expect me to take it? Am I supposed to be pleased
when that woman throws it in my face that Henry's father made a
fool of me, and that now you're leaving me too? And me and my
children—my by-blows—we're left with the disgrace. Perhaps you
think like they do—you think it serves me right to sit here and make
clothes for all the girls you have fun and games with. Just as if it
was all right for people to treat me as they choose. Yes, yes—good
enough for me. I ought to a' known what you was all like; soon's
you get your own way with a poor woman it's love you and leave
you—thanks and good-by!"

"But Olga, my dear!"

"Ah, it's nothing to you. No, you can move out into the country,
you can, and start all over again with your sozzling and your girls—
like you was doing when I found you. And my God, a nice fool I
was to give in to you."

"Olga, Olga—remember the children!"

"Ho, they hear enough about it, you may be sure, in the yard and
on the stairs. So they might just as well hear it from me too."

"It's Christmas Eve, Olga. Remember that, please," Simonsen
said solemnly.

Olga wept quietly with her head on the table. Simonsen laid his
hand on her shoulder.

"Now Olga, you know very well—you know very well how fond
I am of you. And there's Svanhild—d'you really think I'd forget my
own, innocent little girl? Trust me, Olga; I won't let you down or
deceive you—I'll keep my promise to you."

"Why, you poor man—" Olga sat up and blew her nose. "That's
not for you to decide."

"But you must remember one thing, Olga—" Simonsen laid one
arm round her neck and held Svanhild with the other, straightened
himself, and stuck out his stomach. "There's One Above—one
greater than either Sigurd or Mossa—who *does* decide—for us all."

"Now I think we ought to sing a carol," he said a little later. He
took a gulp of toddy and cleared his throat. " 'The Joy of Christmas'
—let's have that; Svanhild knows it, I know it, I know. Sing out,
now, Svanhild love."

Svanhild sang joyfully, and Simonsen growled too, leaving off
when the notes went too high, but beginning again with every
verse. Presently Olga joined in with a voice hoarse from weeping.
Henry alone did not sing.

Then came the last morning. In Olga's room the alarm clock
rang, but Simonsen lay dozing on in the darkness—it was so cold
getting up. And everything was dreary and comfortless. That he

should have to get up in the cold and go away—away from everything.

Never, in any place where he had lived, had he had so comfortable a bed as this, with eiderdown both under and over him.

Olga opened the door, and by the light shining through from her room she set down the tray she was carrying, lit the lamp, and took the tray over to the bed; on it were coffee and rolls.

"You'll have to get moving now, Anton."

"Yes, yes—I s'pose so."

Simonsen sighed. He drew her down on to the edge of the bed and stroked her—stroked her cheek and arm and breast and hips, as he drank the coffee and dunked the rolls in it.

"This is splendid coffee, my love. Won't you have a drop too?"

"No, I'd better go and get a bit of breakfast ready for you."

Simonsen crawled out of bed, dressed, and packed the last of his belongings. Then he locked both his boxes and went into Olga's room.

He stood by the bed where Svanhild lay asleep, looking down at her with his hands in his pockets. "My Svanhild . . ."

He peeped into the sitting-room too; it was pitch-dark and icy cold. Henry had gone off to Nordmarka with some friends on Christmas morning. Simonsen pottered about in there for a while, and in the darkness knocked against Svanhild's Christmas tree, so that the little tinsel balls tinkled together. Who knew—who knew whether he would ever come back here again?

He returned to Olga's room; it was nice and warm in there. Places were laid at the lower end of the long table where Olga and Miss Abrahamsen worked during the day. On the white cloth were brawn and beer and spirits and all the rest, and over it the lamp shone peacefully, humming softly as it burned. A light fell on Svanhild, asleep in her little bed, with her pretty hair spread over the pillow. His little, little girl . . .

There was a sweet, cosy warmth from Olga's bed, which was unmade, the covers thrown back from the hollow where she had lain. How good his life had been here with Olga and Svanhild! His eyes filled with tears; he let them run without drying them, so that Olga should see them. His pouchy, bluish-red cheeks were quite wet when Olga came in with the coffee.

"We'd better have breakfast," she said.

"Yes, we'd better. What about Svanhild? D'you think she'd like to come to the station, just for the sleigh ride?"

"I thought of that, Anton, but it's so dark and cold outside. But I might wake her now, so she can have a cup of coffee with us."

She went over to the bed and gently shook the child.

"Svanhild, would you like to get up now and have coffee with Mummy and Daddy?"

Svanhild blinked, sitting in her nightgown on Simonsen's lap. The coffee had roused her a little, but she was still quiet and subdued because the grownups were.

"Where are you going, Daddy?"

"Why, to Fredrikstad, don't you remember?"

"When are you coming back?"

"Oh, well—I expect you'll be down to see me first."

"In the country, like you talked about?"

"That's it."

"You'll be able to toboggan with me again there, won't you, Daddy?"

"Yes, that's right—I'll be able to toboggan with you again there."

The doorbell rang. Olga looked out: the sleigh had come. The carter's boy took Simonsen's boxes and went.

Simonsen kissed Svanhild, and having got up, he stood for a little with her on his arm.

"Now you must be a good girl, mind, and do as you're told while Daddy's away!"

"Yes, I will," said Svanhild.

Olga went into the kitchen to turn off the stove, as Svanhild was to be alone at home; then came in again and stood with her hands on the lamp screw.

"Well, Anton—"

He gave Svanhild a smacking kiss, laid her down in her bed, and covered her up.

"Bye-bye then, Svanhild love."

Olga put out the lamp, and they left the room. In the hall he put his arms round her and pressed her to him. They kissed.

In the sleigh they sat in silence as they jolted down through the darkness of early morning. And they still had nothing to say to each other as they wandered together round the cold, bleak station hall. But she followed at his heels when he bought his ticket and despatched his trunk; she stood behind him, a small figure in black, square in her thick outer clothes.

Then they wandered into the waiting-room and sat looking up at the clock.

"We started in good time, didn't we?" said Olga.

"Yes, we did. Best thing when you're going on a journey. Shame you had to get up so early, though, when it's a holiday."

"Oh, well," said Olga. "Perhaps we'd better go along and take a seat for you on the train."

Simonsen put his things into a smoking-compartment. He stood at the window while she remained down on the platform.

"Mind you, write often, Olga, and tell me how you're getting on."

"Yes—and you too, Anton."

Porters began slamming the carriage doors along the train. Olga got up on the step, and they kissed again.

"Thanks for everything, Olga love."

"And thanks to you, Anton. Good journey!"

The engine whistled—a jerk ran through the train, and it began to move. Olga and Simonsen pulled out their handkerchiefs and waved to each other for as long as the handkerchiefs could be seen.

The train swished away in the first pale light of dawn—past the Bekkelag villas, past Nordstrand and Ljan. There were lights in the windows here and there. Below the railway line the fjord could be glimpsed, ice-gray, with black islands on it.

Oh, it was dreary . . . Simonsen was alone in the compartment, smoking his cigar and looking out of the window. Farms and woods came up and swam past—gray-brown fields with strips of snow along their edges—black woods.

By now Olga would be at home again. What would she be doing? Dressing Svanhild, probably. Olga had to work today, so she'd said. Svanhild would sit on the floor by the window, playing with the waste scraps. Now she had no Daddy to go tobogganing with in the Palace Park.

The snug room with its two warm, white beds. And the lamp, and the sewing everywhere, and the scraps on the floor which one waded through. Svanhild over by the window—his own, precious child. He could see her sitting there so quietly with her little affairs. Now and then a Miss Hellum or someone came in and gave her sweets. She'd miss her Daddy, Svanhild would.

It was wrong. It was all wrong.

For a moment the wrongness of it struck a spark inside him and smarted and burned through all that life had left of Anton Simonsen's heart.

"Svanhild love, my own little Svanhild . . ." he whimpered.

But he thrust the thought away.

That innocent little girl, who was so good—so very good. Surely life would turn out well for her?

He wiped his eyes. There must be One Above who decided these things. That must be his consolation: that there was One who decided . . .

Discussion of Undset's "Simonsen"

1. Although the author implies that we are to accept the last paragraph of the story as an optimistic resolution, do you feel that Simonsen's faith is justified?

2. Does Simonsen's love for his children seem to be repaid? Do you feel that it should be?

3. In what ways are Simonsen's feelings for Svanhild deeper and more profound than Olenka's feelings for Sasha in "The Darling"?

SELMA LAGERLÖF

1859–1940

🌷 At the age of three Selma Lagerlöf was stricken with a disease that lamed her for life. Scholars often argue that the illness separated her from her peers, thereby causing her exhaustive interest in—and knowledge of—the legends of her native district in Sweden. She began to write poetry at fifteen, studied to be a teacher, and wrote her first major novel, *The Story of Gösta Berling* (1891), in her spare time. It promptly won Lagerlöf a literary prize in Sweden and established her reputation in the rest of Europe. A Nobel Prize followed in 1909. Although the two-part novel *Jerusalem* (1902) had the greatest impact of her early writings, *The Ring of the Löwens*kölds (1925) is the work that has made her known to many North American readers. Her style seems at times old-fashioned, and she has been criticized as a "romantic" novelist. These observations do her work serious injustice, for Lagerlöf's stature rests in large measure on her ability to combine folk tales and invented materials into constructs that establish deep and often unexplainable bonds among the characters. "Romance of a Fisherman's Wife" is one such story, taken from a collection entitled *Invisible Links* (1894). The collection title is suggestive, but the English translation of the story title is misleading. "Romance" brings to mind only "romantic" to most readers, but in Swedish, as in German, "romance" often means "novel." The story, then, is the fishwife's novel, an apt reminder that there is much more happening in this story than a casual reading would reveal.

Romance
of a Fisherman's Wife

On the outer edge of the fishing-village stood a little cottage on a low mound of white sea sand. It was not built in line with the even, neat, conventional houses that enclosed the wide green place where the brown fish-nets were dried, but seemed as if forced out of the row and pushed on one side to the sand-hills. The poor widow who had erected it had been her own builder, and she had made the walls of her cottage lower than those of all the other cottages and its steep thatched roof higher than any other roof in the fishing-village. The floor lay deep down in the ground. The window was neither high nor wide, but nevertheless it reached from the cornice to the level of the earth. There had been no space for a chimney-breast in the one narrow room and she had been obliged to add a small, square

From *Invisible Links* by Selma Lagerlöf, translated from the Swedish by Pauline B. Flach, Little, Brown and Company, 1899.

projection. The cottage had not, like the other cottages, its fenced-in garden with gooseberry bushes and twining morning-glories and elder-bushes half suffocated by burdocks. Of all the vegetation of the fishing-village, only the burdocks had followed the cottage to the sand-hill. They were fine enough in summer with their fresh, dark-green leaves and prickly baskets filled with bright, red flowers. But towards the autumn, when the prickles had hardened and the seeds had ripened, they grew careless about their looks, and stood hideously ugly and dry with their torn leaves wrapped in a melancholy shroud of dusty cobwebs.

The cottage never had more than two owners, for it could not hold up that heavy roof on its walls of reeds and clay for more than two generations. But as long as it stood, it was owned by poor widows. The second widow who lived there delighted in watching the burdocks, especially in the autumn, when they were dried and broken. They recalled her who had built the cottage. She too had been shrivelled and dry and had had the power to cling fast and adhere, and all her strength had been used for her child, whom she had needed to help on in the world. She, who now sat there alone, wished both to weep and to laugh at the thought of it. If the old woman had not had a burr-like nature, how different everything would have been! But who knows if it would have been better?

The lonely woman often sat musing on the fate which had brought her to this spot on the coast of Skone, to the narrow inlet and among these quiet people. For she was born in a Norwegian seaport which lay on a narrow strip of land between rushing falls and the open sea, and although her means were small after the death of her father, a merchant, who left his family in poverty, still she was used to life and progress. She used to tell her story to herself over and over again, just as one often reads through an obscure book in order to discover its meaning.

The first thing of note which had happened to her was when, one evening on the way home from the dressmaker with whom she worked, she had been attacked by two sailors and rescued by a third. The latter fought for her at peril of his life and afterwards went home with her. She took him in to her mother and sisters, and told them excitedly what he had done. It was as if life had acquired a new value for her, because another had dared so much to defend it. He had been immediately well received by her family and asked to come again as soon and as often as he could.

His name was Börje Nilsson, and he was a sailor on the Swedish lugger "Albertina." As long as the boat lay in the harbor, he came almost every day to her home, and they could soon no longer believe that he was only a common sailor. He shone always in a clean, turned-down collar and wore a sailor suit of fine cloth. Natural and frank, he showed himself among them, as if he had been used to move in the same class as they. Without his ever having said it in so many words, they got the impression that he was from a respectable home, the only son of a rich widow, but that his unconquerable love for a sailor's profession had made him take a place before the mast, so that his mother should see that he was in earnest. When he had passed his examination, she would certainly get him his own ship.

The lonely family who had drawn away from all their former friends, received him without the slightest suspicion. And he described with a light heart and fluent tongue his home with its high, pointed roof, the great open fireplace in the dining-room and the little leaded glass panes. He also painted the silent streets of his native town and the long rows of even houses, built in the same style, against which his home, with its irregular buttresses and terraces, made a pleasant contrast. And his listeners believed that he had come from one of those old burgher houses with carved gables and with overhanging second stories, which give such a strong impression of wealth and venerable age.

Soon enough she saw that he cared for her. And that gave her mother and sisters great joy. The young, rich Swede came as if to raise them all up from their poverty. Even if she had not loved him, which she did, she would never have a thought of saying no to his proposal. If she had had a father or a grown-up brother, he could have found out about the stranger's extraction and position, but neither she nor her mother thought of making any inquiries. Afterwards she saw how they had actually forced him to lie. In the beginning, he had let them imagine great ideas about his wealth without any evil intention, but when he understood how glad they were over it, he had not dared to speak the truth for fear of losing her.

Before he left they were betrothed, and when the lugger came again, they were married. It was a disappointment for her that he also on his return appeared as a sailor, but he had been bound by his contract. He had no greetings either from his mother. She had expected him to make another choice, but she would be so glad, he said, if she would once see Astrid.—In spite of all his lies, it would have been an easy matter to see that he was a poor man, if they had only chosen to use their eyes.

The captain offered her his cabin if she would like to make the journey in his vessel, and the offer was accepted with delight. Börje was almost exempt from all work, and sat most of the time on the deck, talking to his wife. And now he gave her the happiness of fancy, such as he himself had lived on all his life. The more he thought of that little house which lay half buried in the sand, so much the higher he raised that palace which he would have liked to offer her. He let her in thought glide into a harbor which was adorned with flags and flowers in honor of Börje Nilsson's bride. He let her hear the mayor's speech of greeting. He let her drive under a triumphal arch, while the eyes of men followed her and the women grew pale with envy. And he led her into the stately home, where bowing, silvery-haired servants stood drawn up along the side of the broad stairway and where the table laden for the feast groaned under the old family silver.

When she discovered the truth, she supposed at first that the captain had been in league with Börje to deceive her, but afterwards she found that it was not so. They were accustomed on board the boat to speak of Börje as of a great man. It was their greatest joke to talk quite seriously of his riches and his fine family. They thought that Börje had told her the truth, but that she joked with him, as they all did, when she talked about his big house. So it happened that when the lugger cast anchor in the harbor which lay nearest to Börje's home, she still did not know but that she was the wife of a rich man.

Börje got a day's leave to conduct his wife to her future home and to start her in her new life. When they were landed on the quay, where the flags were to have fluttered and the crowds to have rejoiced in honor of the newly-married couple, only emptiness and calm reigned there, and Börje noticed that his wife looked about her with a certain disappointment.

"We have come too soon," he had said. "The journey was such an unusually quick one in this fine weather. So we have no carriage here either, and we have far to go, for the house lies outside the town."

"That makes no difference, Börje," she had answered. "It will do us good to walk, after having been quiet so long on board."

And so they began their walk, that walk of horror, of which she could not think even in her old age without moaning in agony and wringing her hands in pain. They went along the broad, empty streets, which she instantly recognized from his description. She felt as if she met with old friends both in the dark church and in the even houses of timber and brick; but where were the carved gables and marble steps with the high railing?

Börje had nodded to her as if he had guessed her thoughts. "It is a long way still," he had said.

If he had only been merciful and at once killed her hope. She loved him so then. If he of his own accord had told her everything, there would never have been any sting in her soul against him. But when he saw her pain at being deceived, and yet went on misleading her, that had hurt her too bitterly. She had never really forgiven him that. She could of course say to herself that he had wanted to take her with him as far as possible so that she would not be able to run away from him, but his deceit created such a deadly coldness in her that no love could entirely thaw it.

They went through the town and came out on the adjoining plain. There stretched several rows of dark moats and high, green ramparts, remains from the time when the town had been fortified, and at the point where they all gathered around a fort, she saw some ancient buildings and big, round towers. She cast a shy look towards them, but Börje turned off to the mounds which followed the shore.

"This is a shorter way," he said, for she seemed to be surprised that there was only a narrow path to follow.

He had become very taciturn. She understood afterwards that he had not found it so merry as he had fancied, to come with a wife to the miserable little house in the fishing-village. It did not seem so fine now to bring home a better man's child. He was anxious about what she would do when she should know the truth.

"Börje," she said at last, when they had followed the shelving, sandy hillocks for a long while, "where are we going?"

He lifted his hand and pointed towards the fishing-village, where his mother lived in the house on the sand-hill. But she believed that he meant one of the beautiful country-seats which lay on the edge of the plain, and was again glad.

They climbed down into the empty cow-pastures, and there all her uneasiness returned. There, where every tuft, if one can only see it, is clothed with beauty and variety, she saw merely an ugly field. And the wind, which is ever shifting there, swept whistling by them and whispered of misfortune and treachery.

Börje walked faster and faster, and at last they reached the end of the pasture and entered the fishing-village. She, who at the last had not dared to ask herself any questions, took courage again. Here again was a uniform row of houses, and this one she recognized even better than that in the town. Perhaps, perhaps he had not lied.

Her expectations were so reduced that she would have been glad from the heart if she could have stopped at any of the neat little houses, where flowers and white curtains showed behind shining window-panes. She grieved that she had to go by them.

Then she saw suddenly, just at the outer edge of the fishing-village, one of the most wretched of hovels, and it seemed to her as if she had already seen it with her mind's eye before she actually had a glimpse of it.

"Is it here?" she said, and stopped just at the foot of the little sand-hill.

He bent his head imperceptibly and went on towards the little cottage.

"Wait," she called after him, "we must talk this over before I go into your home. You have lied," she went on, threateningly, when he turned to her. "You have deceived me worse than if you were my worst enemy. Why have you done it?"

"I wanted you for my wife," he answered, with a low, trembling voice.

"If you had only deceived me within bounds! Why did you make everything so fine and rich? What did you have to do with man-servants and triumphal arches and all the other magnificence? Did you think that I was so devoted to money? Did you not see that I cared enough for you to go anywhere with you? That you could believe you needed to deceive me! That you could have the heart to keep up your lies to the very last!"

"Will you not come in and speak to my mother?" he said, helplessly.

"I do not intend to go in there."

"Are you going home?"

"How can I go home? How could I cause them there at home such sorrow as to return, when they believe me happy and rich? But with you I will not stay either. For one who is willing to work there is always a livelihood."

"Stop!" he begged. "I did it only to win you."

"If you had told me the truth, I would have stayed."

"If I had been a rich man, who had pretended to be poor, then you would have stayed."

She shrugged her shoulders and turned to go, when the door of the cottage opened and Börje's mother came out. She was a little, dried-up old woman with few teeth and many wrinkles, but not so old in years or in feelings as in looks.

She had heard a part and guessed a part, for she knew what they were quarrelling about. "Well," she said, "that is a fine daughter-in-law you have got me, Börje. And you have been deceiving again, I can hear." But to Astrid she came and patted her kindly on the cheek. "Come in with me, you poor child! I know that you are tired and worn out. This is my house. He is not allowed to come in here. But you come. Now you are my daughter, and I cannot let you go to strangers, do you understand?"

She caressed her daughter-in-law and chatted to her and drew and pushed her quite imperceptibly forward to the door. Step by step she lured her on, and at last got her inside the house; but Börje she shut out. And there, within, the old woman began to ask who she was and how it had all happened. And she wept over her and made her weep over herself. The old woman was merciless about her son. She, Astrid, did right; she could not stay with such a man. It was true that he was in the habit of lying, it was really true.

She told her how it had been with her son. He had been so fair in face and limbs, even when he was small, that she had always marvelled that he was a poor man's child. He was like a little prince gone astray. And ever after it had always seemed as if he had not been in his right place. He saw everything on such a large scale. He could not see things as they were, when it concerned himself. His mother had wept many a time on that account. But never before had he done any harm with his lies. Here, where he was known, they only laughed at him.—But now he must have been so terribly tempted. Did she really not think, she, Astrid, that it was wonderful how the fisher boy had been able to deceive them? He had always known so much about wealth, as if he had been born to it. It must be that

he had come into the world in the wrong place. See, that was another proof,—he had never thought of choosing a wife in his own
station.

"Where will he sleep to-night?" asked Astrid, suddenly.

"I imagine he will lie outside on the sand. He will be too anxious
to go away from here."

"I suppose it is best for him to come in," said Astrid.

"Dearest child, you cannot want to see him. He can get along out
there if I give him a blanket."

She let him actually sleep out on that sand that night, thinking it
best for Astrid not to see him. And with her she talked and talked,
and kept her, not by force, but by cleverness, not by persuasion,
but by real goodness.

But when she had at last succeeded in keeping her daughter-
in-law for her son, and had got the young people reconciled, and
had taught Astrid that her vocation in life was just to be Börje
Nilsson's wife and to make him as happy as she could,—and that
had not been the work of one evening, but of many days,—then the
old woman had laid herself down to die.

And in that life, with its faithful solicitude for her son, there was
some meaning, thought Börje Nilsson's wife.

But in her own life she saw no meaning. Her husband was
drowned after a few years of married life, and her one child died
young. She had not been able to make any change in her husband.
She had not been able to teach him earnestness and truth. It was
rather in her the change showed, after she had been more and more
with the fishing people. She would never see any of her own family,
for she was ashamed that she now resembled in everything a fisherman's wife. If it had only been of any use! If she, who lived by
mending the fishermen's nets, knew why she clung so to life! If she
had made any one happy or had improved anybody!

It never occurred to her to think that she who considers her life a
failure because she has done no good to others, perhaps by that
thought of humility has saved her own soul.

Discussion of Lagerlöf's "Romance of a Fisherman's Wife"

1. Astrid comes close to total despair at the story's end; Undset's
Simonsen seems to have faith. Why should the situations not be
reversed?

2. Astrid, Simonsen, the heroine of "Her Sweet Jerome," and the
narrator of "We're Very Poor" are all members of the lower class.
Could the authors be saying something about an attitude towards
life that people in this socioeconomic group might have?

3. Astrid and the heroine of "Her Sweet Jerome" are both betrayed
by men they love. But how much of the fault for being betrayed
rests on the women themselves?

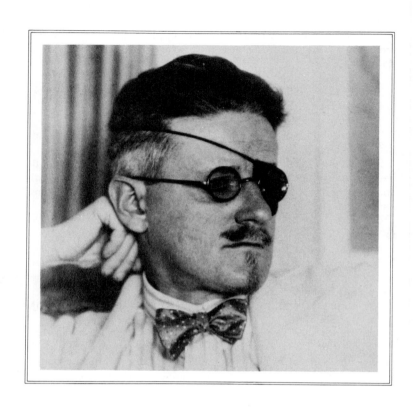

JAMES JOYCE

1882–1941

❦ Joyce is perhaps the greatest English-language novelist of the century and certainly one of the most important. His reputation rests on three novels and a collection of short stories. Of the novels, the first, *A Portrait of the Artist As a Young Man* (1916), is both the most accessible to readers and the most realistic. *Ulysses* (1922) and *Finnegans Wake* (1939) are difficult and massive landmarks in contemporary fiction. Although Joyce's stories rely heavily on myths, the recurrent image is Ireland, specifically Dublin. "A Painful Case" is taken from *Dubliners* (1914), a collection of short stories so unified by time, place, and theme that they form a closely integrated cycle. Each story, however, gives us insights into the lives of empty, alienated human beings. Joyce's protagonist in the following story is unusual only in that he reaches a conscious self-knowledge that the other characters in *Dubliners* often lack.

A Painful Case

Mr James Duffy lived in Chapelizod because he wished to live as far as possible from the city of which he was a citizen and because he found all the other suburbs of Dublin mean, modern and pretentious. He lived in an old sombre house and from his windows he could look into the disused distillery or upwards along the shallow river on which Dublin is built. The lofty walls of his uncarpeted room were free from pictures. He had himself bought every article of furniture in the room: a black iron bedstead, an iron washstand, four cane chairs, a clothes-rack, a coal-scuttle, a fender and irons and a square table on which lay a double desk. A bookcase had been made in an alcove by means of shelves of white wood. The bed was clothed with white bed-clothes and a black and scarlet rug covered the foot. A little hand-mirror hung above the washstand and during the day a white-shaded lamp stood as the sole ornament of the mantelpiece. The books on the white wooden shelves were arranged from below upwards according to bulk. A complete Wordsworth stood at one end of the lowest shelf and a copy of the *Maynooth Catechism*, sewn into the cloth cover of a notebook, stood at one end of the top shelf. Writing materials were always on the desk. In the desk lay a manuscript translation of Hauptmann's *Michael Kramer*, the stage directions of which were written in purple ink, and a little sheaf of papers held together by a brass pin. In these sheets a sentence was inscribed from time to time and, in an ironical moment, the headline of an advertisement for *Bile Beans* had been pasted on to the first sheet. On lifting the lid of the desk a faint fragrance escaped—the fragrance of new cedarwood pencils or of a bottle of gum or of an over-ripe apple which might have been left there and forgotten.

Mr Duffy abhorred anything which betokened physical or mental disorder. A mediæval doctor would have called him saturnine. His face, which carried the entire tale of his years, was of the brown tint of Dublin streets. On his long and rather large head grew dry black hair and a tawny moustache did not quite cover an unamiable mouth. His cheekbones also gave his face a harsh character; but there was no harshness in the eyes which, looking at the world from under their tawny eyebrows, gave the impression of a man ever alert to greet a redeeming instinct in others but often disappointed. He lived at a little distance from his body, regarding his own acts with doubtful side-glances. He had an odd autobiographical habit which led him to compose in his mind from time to time a short sentence about himself containing a subject in the third person and a predicate in the past tense. He never gave alms to beggers and walked firmly, carrying a stout hazel.

He had been for many years cashier of a private bank in Baggot Street. Every morning he came in from Chapelizod by tram. At midday he went to Dan Burke's and took his lunch—a bottle of lager beer and a small tray of arrowroot biscuits. At four o'clock he was set free. He dined in an eating-house in George's Street where he felt himself safe from the society of Dublin's gilded youth and where there was a certain plain honesty in the bill of fare. His evenings were spent either before his landlady's piano or roaming about the outskirts of the city. His liking for Mozart's music brought him sometimes to an opera or a concert: these were the only dissipations of his life.

He had neither companions nor friends, church nor creed. He lived his spiritual life without any communion with others, visiting his relatives at Christmas and escorting them to the cemetery when they died. He performed these two social duties for old dignity's sake but conceded nothing further to the conventions which regulate the civic life. He allowed himself to think that in certain circumstances he would rob his bank but, as these circumstances never arose, his life rolled out evenly—an adventureless tale.

One evening he found himself sitting beside two ladies in the Rotunda. The house, thinly peopled and silent, gave distressing prophecy of failure. The lady who sat next him looked round at the deserted house once or twice and then said:

—What a pity there is such a poor house to-night! It's so hard on people to have to sing to empty benches.

He took the remark as an invitation to talk. He was surprised that she seemed so little awkward. While they talked he tried to fix her permanently in his memory. When he learned that the young girl beside her was her daughter he judged her to be a year or so younger than himself. Her face, which must have been handsome, had remained intelligent. It was an oval face with strongly marked features. The eyes were very dark blue and steady. Their gaze began with a defiant note, but was confused by what seemed a deliberate swoon of the pupil into the iris, revealing for an instant a temperament of great sensibility. The pupil reasserted itself quickly, this half-disclosed nature fell again under the reign of prudence, and her astrakhan jacket, moulding a bosom of a certain fulness, struck the note of defiance more definitely.

He met her again a few weeks afterwards at a concert in Earlsfort Terrace and seized the moments when her daughter's attention was diverted to become intimate. She alluded once or twice to her husband but her tone was not such as to make the allusion a warning. Her name was Mrs Sinico. Her husband's great-great-grandfather had come from Leghorn. Her husband was captain of a mercantile boat plying between Dublin and Holland; and they had one child.

Meeting her a third time by accident he found courage to make an appointment. She came. This was the first of many meetings; they met always in the evening and chose the most quiet quarters for their walks together. Mr Duffy, however, had a distaste for underhand ways and, finding that they were compelled to meet stealthily, he forced her to ask him to her house. Captain Sinico encouraged his visits, thinking that his daughter's hand was in question. He had dismissed his wife so sincerely from his gallery of pleasures that he did not suspect that anyone else would take an interest in her. As the husband was often away and the daughter out giving music lessons Mr Duffy had many opportunities of enjoying the lady's society. Neither he nor she had had any such adventure before and neither was conscious of any incongruity. Little by little he entangled his thoughts with hers. He lent her books, provided her with ideas, shared his intellectual life with her. She listened to all.

Sometimes in return for his theories she gave out some fact of her own life. With almost maternal solicitude she urged him to let his nature open to the full; she became his confessor. He told her that for some time he had assisted at the meetings of an Irish Socialist Party where he had felt himself a unique figure amidst a score of sober workmen in a garret lit by an inefficient oil-lamp. When the party had divided into three sections, each under its own leader and in its own garret, he had discontinued his attendances. The workmen's discussions, he said, were too timorous; the interest they took in the question of wages was inordinate. He felt that they were hard-featured realists and that they resented an exactitude which was the product of a leisure not within their reach. No social revolution, he told her, would be likely to strike Dublin for some centuries.

She asked him why did he not write out his thoughts. For what, he asked her, with careful scorn. To compete with phrasemongers, incapable of thinking consecutively for sixty seconds? To submit himself to the criticisms of an obtuse middle class which entrusted its morality to policemen and its fine arts to impresarios?

He went often to her little cottage outside Dublin; often they spent their evenings alone. Little by little, as their thoughts entangled, they spoke of subjects less remote. Her companionship was like a warm soil about an exotic. Many times she allowed the dark to fall upon them, refraining from lighting the lamp. The dark discreet room, their isolation, the music that still vibrated in their ears united them. This union exalted him, wore away the rough edges of his character, emotionalised his mental life. Sometimes he caught himself listening to the sound of his own voice. He thought that in her eyes he would ascend to an angelical stature; and, as he attached the fervent nature of his companion more and more closely to him, he heard the strange impersonal voice which he recognised as his own, insisting on the soul's incurable loneliness. We cannot give ourselves, it said: we are our own. The end of these discourses was that one night during which she had shown every sign of unusual excitement, Mrs Sinico caught up his hand passionately and pressed it to her cheek.

Mr Duffy was very much surprised. Her interpretation of his words disillusioned him. He did not visit her for a week; then he wrote to her asking her to meet him. As he did not wish their last interview to be troubled by the influence of their ruined confessional they met in a little cakeshop near the Parkgate. It was cold autumn weather but in spite of the cold they wandered up and down the roads of the Park for nearly three hours. They agreed to break off their intercourse: every bond, he said, is a bond to sorrow. When they came out of the Park they walked in silence towards the tram; but here she began to tremble so violently that, fearing another collapse on her part, he bade her good-bye quickly and left her. A few days later he received a parcel containing his books and music.

Four years passed. Mr Duffy returned to his even way of life. His room still bore witness of the orderliness of his mind. Some new pieces of music encumbered the music-stand in the lower room and on his shelves stood two volumes by Nietzsche: *Thus Spake Zarathustra* and *The Gay Science*. He wrote seldom in the sheaf of papers which lay in his desk. One of his sentences, written two months after his last interview with Mrs Sinico, read: Love between man and man is impossible because there must not be sexual intercourse and friendship between man and woman is impossible because there must be sexual intercourse. He kept away from concerts lest he should meet her. His father died; the junior partner of the bank retired. And still every morning he went into the city by tram and every evening walked home from the city after having dined moderately in George's Street and read the evening paper for dessert.

One evening as he was about to put a morsel of corned beef and cabbage into his mouth his hand stopped. His eyes fixed themselves on a paragraph in the evening paper which he had propped against the water-carafe. He replaced the morsel of food on his plate and read the paragraph attentively. Then he drank a glass of water, pushed his plate to one side, doubled the paper down before him between his elbows and read the paragraph over and over again. The cabbage began to deposit a cold white grease on his plate. The girl came over to him to ask was his dinner not properly cooked. He said it was very good and ate a few mouthfuls of it with difficulty. Then he paid his bill and went out.

He walked along quickly through the November twilight, his stout hazel stick striking the ground regularly, the fringe of the buff *Mail* peeping out of a side-pocket of his tight reefer overcoat. On the lonely road which leads from the Parkgate to Chapelizod he slackened his pace. His stick struck the ground less emphatically and his breath, issuing irregularly, almost with a sighing sound, condensed in the wintry air. When he reached his house he went up at once to his bedroom and, taking the paper from his pocket, read the paragraph again by the failing light of the window. He read it not aloud, but moving his lips as a priest does when he reads the prayers *Secreto*. This was the paragraph:

DEATH OF A LADY AT SYDNEY PARADE

A PAINFUL CASE

To-day at the City of Dublin Hospital the Deputy Coroner (in the absence of Mr Leverett) held an inquest on the body of Mrs Emily Sinico, aged forty-three years, who was killed at Sydney Parade Station yesterday evening. The evidence showed that the deceased lady, while attempting to cross the line, was knocked down by the engine of the ten o'clock slow train from Kingstown, thereby sustaining injuries of the head and right side which led to her death.

James Lennon, driver of the engine, stated that he had been in the employment of the railway company for fifteen years. On hearing the guard's whistle he set the train in motion and a second or two afterwards brought it to rest in response to loud cries. The train was going slowly.

P. Dunne, railway porter, stated that as the train was about to start he observed a woman attempting to cross the lines. He ran towards her and shouted but, before he could reach her, she was caught by the buffer of the engine and fell to the ground.

A juror—You saw the lady fall?

Witness—Yes.

Police Sergeant Croly deposed that when he arrived he found the deceased lying on the platform apparently dead. He had the body taken to the waiting-room pending the arrival of the ambulance.

Constable 57E corroborated.

Dr Halpin, assistant house surgeon of the City of Dublin Hospital, stated that the deceased had two lower ribs fractured and had sustained severe contusions of the right shoulder. The right side of the head had been injured in the fall. The injuries were not sufficient to have caused death in a normal person. Death, in his opinion, had been probably due to shock and sudden failure of the heart's action.

Mr H. B. Patterson Finlay, on behalf of the railway company, expressed his deep regret at the accident. The company had always taken every precaution to prevent people crossing the lines except by the bridges, both by placing notices in every station and by the use of patent spring gates at level crossings. The deceased had been in the habit of crossing the lines late at night from platform to platform and, in view of certain other circumstances of the case, he did not think the railway officials were to blame.

Captain Sinico, of Leoville, Sydney Parade, husband of the deceased, also gave evidence. He stated that the deceased was his wife. He was not in Dublin at the time of the accident as he had arrived only that morning from Rotterdam. They had been married for twenty-two years and had lived happily until about two years ago when his wife began to be rather intemperate in her habits.

Miss Mary Sinico said that of late her mother had been in the habit of going out at night to buy spirits. She, witness, had often tried to reason with her mother and had induced her to join a league. She was not at home until an hour after the accident.

The jury returned a verdict in accordance with the medical evidence and exonerated Lennon from all blame.

The Deputy Coroner said it was a most painful case, and expressed great sympathy with Captain Sinico and his daughter. He urged on the railway company to take strong measures to prevent the possibility of similar accidents in the future. No blame attached to anyone.

Mr Duffy raised his eyes from the paper and gazed out of his window on the cheerless evening landscape. The river lay quiet beside the empty distillery and from time to time a light appeared in some house on the Lucan road. What an end! The whole narrative of her death revolted him and it revolted him to think that he had ever spoken to her of what he held sacred. The threadbare phrases, the inane expressions of sympathy, the cautious words of a reporter won over to conceal the details of a commonplace vulgar death attacked his stomach. Not merely had she degraded herself;

she had degraded him. He saw the squalid tract of her vice, miserable and malodorous. His soul's companion! He thought of the hobbling wretches whom he had seen carrying cans and bottles to be filled by the barman. Just God, what an end! Evidently she had been unfit to live, without any strength of purpose, an easy prey to habits, one of the wrecks on which civilisation has been reared. But that she could have sunk so low! Was it possible he had deceived himself so utterly about her? He remembered her outburst of that night and interpreted it in a harsher sense than he had ever done. He had no difficulty now in approving of the course he had taken.

As the light failed and his memory began to wander he thought her hand touched his. The shock which had first attacked his stomach was now attacking his nerves. He put on his overcoat and hat quickly and went out. The cold air met him on the threshold; it crept into the sleeves of his coat. When he came to the public-house at Chapelizod Bridge he went in and ordered a hot punch.

The proprietor served him obsequiously but did not venture to talk. There were five or six working-men in the shop discussing the value of a gentleman's estate in County Kildare. They drank at intervals from their huge pint tumblers and smoked, spitting often on the floor and sometimes dragging the sawdust over their spits with their heavy boots. Mr Duffy sat on his stool and gazed at them, without seeing or hearing them. After a while they went out and he called for another punch. He sat a long time over it. The shop was very quiet. The proprietor sprawled on the counter reading the *Herald* and yawning. Now and again a tram was heard swishing along the lonely road outside.

As he sat there, living over his life with her and evoking alternately the two images in which he now conceived her, he realised that she was dead, that she had ceased to exist, that she had become a memory. He began to feel ill at ease. He asked himself what else could he have done. He could not have carried on a comedy of deception with her; he could not have lived with her openly. He had done what seemed to him best. How was he to blame? Now that she was gone he understood how lonely her life must have been, sitting night after night alone in that room. His life would be lonely too until he, too, died, ceased to exist, became a memory— if anyone remembered him.

It was after nine o'clock when he left the shop. The night was cold and gloomy. He entered the Park by the first gate and walked along under the gaunt trees. He walked through the bleak alleys where they had walked four years before. She seemed to be near him in the darkness. At moments he seemed to feel her voice touch his ear, her hand touch his. He stood still to listen. Why had he withheld life from her? Why had he sentenced her to death? He felt his moral nature falling to pieces.

When he gained the crest of the Magazine Hill he halted and

looked along the river towards Dublin, the lights of which burned redly and hospitably in the cold night. He looked down the slope and, at the base, in the shadow of the wall of the Park, he saw some human figures lying. Those venal and furtive loves filled him with despair. He gnawed the rectitude of his life; he felt that he had been outcast from life's feast. One human being had seemed to love him and he had denied her life and happiness: he had sentenced her to ignominy, a death of shame. He knew that the prostrate creatures down by the wall were watching him and wished him gone. No one wanted him; he was outcast from life's feast. He turned his eyes to the grey gleaming river, winding along towards Dublin. Beyond the river he saw a goods train winding out of Kingsbridge Station, like a worm with a fiery head winding through the darkness, obstinately and laboriously. It passed slowly out of sight; but still he heard in his ears the laborious drone of the engine reiterating the syllables of her name.

He turned back the way he had come, the rhythm of the engine pounding in his ears. He began to doubt the reality of what memory told him. He halted under a tree and allowed the rhythm to die away. He could not feel her near him in the darkness nor her voice touch his ear. He waited for some minutes listening. He could hear nothing: the night was perfectly silent. He listened again: perfectly silent. He felt that he was alone.

Discussion of Joyce's "A Painful Case"

1. Duffy comes to a series of complex self-realizations at the end of the story. To what extent does this make him superior to characters such as the men in the stories by Updike, Machado de Assis, and Lessing?

2. Both Duffy and Pauline in "Bodies" attempt to live completely private and autonomous lives. What do the authors seem to be saying about this possibility in life?

3. Do you feel that the reader is supposed to agree with Duffy's assessment of his moral predicament on page 151?

ELLEN GLASGOW

1874–1945

🌺 Ellen Glasgow was born April 22, 1874 in Virginia and although she traveled a great deal, Richmond was her home until her death in 1945. Among her many novels are *Barren Ground* (1925), *The Sheltered Life* (1932), and *Vein of Iron* (1935). *A Certain Measure* (1943) contains her prefaces to all her works, and her short stories are published in *The Collected Stories of Ellen Glasgow* (1963) edited by Richard K. Meeker. About art she says that when she discovered Chekhov, she found what was missing in Maupassant: "Here was art used by life for its own purpose, and because it had been so used, art itself had become living" (Ellen Glasgow, *The Woman Within* [New York: Harcourt Brace Jovanovich, 1954], p. 126). She assesses human relationships by declaring, "I should have found wholly inadequate the mere physical sensation, which the youth of today seek so blithely. If I were young now, I might feel differently. . . . Yet I am so constituted that the life of the mind is reality, and love without romantic illumination is a spiritless matter" (*The Woman Within*, p. 163).

The Difference

Outside, in the autumn rain, the leaves were falling.

For twenty years, every autumn since her marriage, Margaret Fleming had watched the leaves from this window; and always it had seemed to her that they were a part of her life which she held precious. As they fell she had known that they carried away something she could never recover—youth, beauty, pleasure, or only memories that she wanted to keep. Something gracious, desirable and fleeting; but never until this afternoon had she felt that the wind was sweeping away the illusion of happiness by which she lived. Beyond the panes, against which the rain was beating in gray sheets, she looked out on the naked outlines of the city: bleak houses, drenched grass in squares, and boughs of trees where a few brown or yellow leaves were clinging.

On the hearth rug the letter lay where it had fallen a few minutes—or was it a few hours ago? The flames from the wood fire cast a glow on the white pages; and she imagined that the ugly words leaped out to sting her like scorpions as she moved by them. Not for worlds, she told herself, would she stoop and touch them again. Yet what need had she to touch them when each slanting black line was etched in her memory with acid? Never, though she

From *The Shadowy Third and Other Stories* by Ellen Glasgow, copyright, 1923, by Doubleday Page & Company, Inc.; renewed 1951 by First and Merchants National Bank of Richmond. Reprinted by permission of Harcourt Brace Jovanovich, Inc.

lived a hundred years, could she forget the way the letters fell on
the white paper!

Once, twice, three times, she walked from window to door and
back again from door to window. The wood fire burned cheerfully
with a whispering sound. As the lights and shadows stirred over the
familiar objects she had once loved, her gaze followed them hun-
grily. She had called this upstairs library George's room, and she
realized now that every piece of furniture, every book it contained,
had been chosen to please him. He liked the golden brown of the
walls, the warm colours in the Persian rugs, the soft depth of the
cushioned chairs. He liked, too, the flamboyant red lilies beneath
the little Chippendale mirror.

After twenty years of happiness, of comradeship, of mutual dependence, after all that marriage could mean to two equal spirits,
was there nothing left except ashes? Could twenty years of happiness be destroyed in an afternoon, in an hour? Stopping abruptly,
with a jerk which ran like a spasm through her slender figure, she
gazed with hard searching eyes over the red lilies into the mirror.
The grave beauty of her face, a beauty less of flesh than of spirit,
floated there in the shadows like a flower in a pond.

"I am younger than he is by a year," she thought, "and yet he
can begin over again to love, while a new love for me would be
desecration."

There was the sound of his step on the stair. An instant later his
hand fell on the door, and he entered the room.

Stooping swiftly, she picked up the letter from the rug and hid it
in her bosom. Then turning toward him, she received his kiss with
a smile. "I didn't wait lunch for you," she said.

"I got it at the club." After kissing her cheek, he moved to the
fire and stood warming his hands. "Beastly day. No chance of golf,
so I've arranged to see that man from Washington. You won't get
out, I suppose?"

She shook her head. "No, I sha'n't get out."

Did he know, she wondered, that this woman had written to her?
Did he suspect that the letter lay now in her bosom? He had
brought the smell of rain, the taste of dampness, with him into the
room; and this air of the outer world enveloped him while he stood
there, genial, robust, superbly vital, clothed in his sanguine temperament as in the healthy red and white of his flesh. Still boyish at
forty-five, he had that look of perennial innocence which some
men carry untarnished through the most enlightening experiences.
Even his moustache and his sharply jutting chin could not disguise
the softness that hovered always about his mouth, where she
noticed now, with her piercing scrutiny, the muscles were growing
lax. Strange that she had never seen this until she discovered that
George loved another woman! The thought flashed into her mind
that she knew him in reality no better than if she had lived with a
stranger for twenty years. Yet, until a few hours ago, she would

have said, had any one asked her, that their marriage was as perfect as any mating between a man and a woman could be in this imperfect world.

"You're wise. The wind's still in the east, and there is no chance, I'm afraid, of a change." He hesitated an instant, stared approvingly at the red lilies, and remarked abruptly, "Nice colour."

"You always liked red." Her mouth lost its softness. "And I was pale even as a girl."

His genial gaze swept her face. "Oh, well, there's red and red, you know. Some cheeks look best pale."

Without replying to his words, she sat looking at him while her thoughts, escaping her control, flew from the warm room out into the rough autumn weather. It was as if she felt the beating of the rain in her soul, as if she were torn from her security and whirled downward and onward in the violence of the storm. On the surface of her life nothing had changed. The fire still burned; the lights and shadows still flickered over the Persian rugs; her husband still stood there, looking down on her through the cloudless blue of his eyes. But the real Margaret, the vital part of her, was hidden far away in that deep place where the seeds of mysterious impulses and formless desires lie buried. She knew that there were secrets within herself which she had never acknowledged in her own thoughts; that there were unexpressed longings which had never taken shape even in her imagination. Somewhere beneath the civilization of the ages there was the skeleton of the savage.

The letter in her bosom scorched her as if it were fire. "That was why you used to call me magnolia blossom," she said in a colourless voice, and knew it was only the superficial self that was speaking.

His face softened; yet so perfectly had the note of sentiment come to be understood rather than expressed in their lives that she could feel his embarrassment. The glow lingered in his eyes, but he answered only, "Yes, you were always like that."

An irrepressible laugh broke from her. Oh, the irony, the bitterness! "Perhaps you like them pale!" she tossed back mockingly, and wondered if this Rose Morrison who had written to her was coloured like her name?

He looked puzzled but solicitous. "I'm afraid I must be off. If you are not tired, could you manage to go over these galleys this afternoon? I'd like to read the last chapter aloud to you after the corrections are made." He had written a book on the history of law; and while he drew the roll of proof sheets from his pocket, she remembered, with a pang as sharp as the stab of a knife, all the work of last summer when they had gathered material together. He needed her for his work, she realized, if not for his pleasure. She stood, as she had always done, for the serious things of his life. This book could not have been written without her. Even his success in his profession had been the result of her efforts as well as his own.

"I'm never too tired for that," she responded, and though she smiled up at him, it was a smile that hurt her with its irony.

"Well, my time's up," he said. "By the way, I'll need my heavier golf things if it is fine to-morrow." To-morrow was Sunday, and he played golf with a group of men at the Country Club every Sunday morning.

"They are in the cedar closet. I'll get them out."

"The medium ones, you know. That English tweed."

"Yes, I know. I'll have them ready." Did Rose Morrison play golf? she wondered.

"I'll try to get back early to dinner. There was a button loose on the waistcoat I wore last evening. I forgot to mention it this morning."

"Oh, I'm sorry. I left it to the servants, but I'll look after it myself." Again this perverse humour seized her. Had he ever asked Rose Morrison to sew on a button?

At the door he turned back. "And I forgot to ask you this morning to order flowers for Morton's funeral. It is to be Monday."

The expression on her face felt as stiff as a wax mask, and though she struggled to relax her muscles, they persisted in that smile of inane cheerfulness. "I'll order them at once, before I begin the galleys," she answered.

Rising from the couch on which she had thrown herself at his entrance, she began again her restless pacing from door to window. The library was quiet except for the whispering flames. Outside in the rain the leaves were falling thickly, driven hither and thither by the wind which rocked the dappled boughs of the sycamores. In the gloom of the room the red lilies blazed.

The terror, which had clutched her like a living thing, had its fangs in her heart. Terror of loss, of futility. Terror of the past because it tortured her. Terror of the future because it might be empty even of torture. "He is mine, and I will never give him up," she thought wildly. "I will fight to the end for what is mine."

There was a sound at the door and Winters, the butler, entered. "Mrs. Chambers, Madam. She was quite sure you would be at home."

"Yes, I am at home." She was always at home, even in illness, to Dorothy Chambers. Though they were so different in temperament, they had been friends from girlhood; and much of the gaiety of Margaret's life had been supplied by Dorothy. Now, as her friend entered, she held out her arms. "You come whenever it rains, dear," she said. "It is so good of you." Yet her welcome was hollow, and at the very instant when she returned her friend's kiss she was wishing that she could send her away. That was one of the worst things about suffering; it made one indifferent and insincere.

Dorothy drew off her gloves, unfastened her furs, and after raising her veil over the tip of her small inquisitive nose, held out her hand with a beseeching gesture.

"I've come straight from a committee luncheon. Give me a cigarette."

Reaching for the Florentine box on the desk, Margaret handed it to her. A minute later, while the thin blue flame shot up between them, she asked herself if Dorothy could look into her face and not see the difference?

Small, plain, vivacious, with hair of ashen gold, thin intelligent features, and a smile of mocking brilliance, Dorothy was the kind of woman whom men admire without loving and women love without admiring. As a girl she had been a social success without possessing a single one of the qualities upon which social success is supposed to depend.

Sinking back in her chair, she blew several rings of smoke from her lips and watched them float slowly upward.

"We have decided to give a bridge party. There's simply no other way to raise money. Will you take a table?"

Margaret nodded. "Of course." Suffering outside of herself made no difference to her. Her throbbing wound was the only reality.

"Janet is going to lend us her house." A new note had come into Dorothy's voice. "I haven't seen her since last spring. She had on a new hat, and was looking awfully well. You know Herbert has come back."

Margaret started. At last her wandering attention was fixed on her visitor. "Herbert? And she let him?" There was deep disgust in her tone.

Dorothy paused to inhale placidly before she answered. "Well, what else could she do? He tried to make her get a divorce, and she wouldn't."

A flush stained Margaret's features. "I never understood why she didn't. He made no secret of what he wanted. He showed her plainly that he loved the other woman."

Dorothy's only reply was a shrug; but after a moment, in which she smoked with a luxurious air, she commented briefly, "But man's love isn't one of the eternal verities."

"Well, indifference is, and he proved that he was indifferent to Janet. Yet she has let him come back to her. I can't see what she is to get out of it."

Dorothy laughed cynically. "Oh, she enjoys immensely the attitude of forgiveness, and at last he has permitted her to forgive him. There is a spiritual vanity as well as a physical one, you know, and Janet's weakness is spiritual."

"But to live with a man who doesn't love her? To remember every minute of the day and night that it is another woman he loves?"

"And every time that she remembers it she has the luxury of forgiving again." Keenness flickered like a blade in Dorothy's gray eyes. "You are very lovely, Margaret," she said abruptly. "The years seem only to leave you rarer and finer, but you know nothing about life."

A smile quivered and died on Margaret's lips. "I might retort that you know nothing about love."

With an impatient birdlike gesture Dorothy tossed her burned-out cigarette into the fire. "Whose love?" she inquired as she opened the Florentine box, "Herbert's or yours?"

"It's all the same, isn't it?"

By the flame of the match she had struck Dorothy's expression appeared almost malign. "There, my dear, is where you are wrong," she replied. "When a man and a woman talk of love they speak two different languages. They can never understand each other because women love with their imagination and men with their senses. To you love is a thing in itself, a kind of abstract power like religion; to Herbert it is simply the way he feels."

"But if he loves the other woman, he doesn't love Janet; and yet he wants to return to her."

Leaning back in the chair, Dorothy surveyed her with a look which was at once sympathetic and mocking. Her gaze swept the pure grave features; the shining dusk of the hair; the narrow nose with its slight arch in the middle; the straight red lips with their resolute pressure; the skin so like a fading rose-leaf. Yes, there was beauty in Margaret's face if one were only artist or saint enough to perceive it.

"There is so much more in marriage than either love or indifference," she remarked casually. "There is, for instance, comfort."

"Comfort?" repeated Margaret scornfully. She rose, in her clinging draperies of chiffon, to place a fresh log on the fire. "If he really loves the other woman, Janet ought to give him up," she said.

At this Dorothy turned on her. "Would you, if it were George?" she demanded.

For an instant, while she stood there in front of the fire, it seemed to Margaret that the room whirled before her gaze like the changing colours in a kaleidoscope. Then a gray cloud fell over the brightness, and out of this cloud there emerged only the blaze of the red lilies. A pain struck her in the breast, and she remembered the letter she had hidden there.

"Yes," she answered presently. "I should do it if it were George."

A minute afterward she became conscious that while she spoke, a miracle occurred within her soul.

The tumult of sorrow, of anger, of bitterness, of despair, was drifting farther and farther away. Even the terror, which was worse than any tumult, had vanished. In that instant of renunciation she had reached some spiritual haven. What she had found, she understood presently, was the knowledge that there is no support so strong as the strength that enables one to stand alone.

"I should do it if it were George," she said again, very slowly.

"Well, I think you would be very foolish." Dorothy had risen and was lowering her veil. "For when George ceases to be desirable for sentimental reasons, he will still have his value as a good provider." Her mocking laugh grated on Margaret's ears. "Now, I must run away. I only looked in for an instant. I've a tea on hand, and I must go home and dress."

When she had gone, Margaret stood for a minute, thinking deeply. For a minute only, but in that space of time her decision was made. Crossing to the desk, she telephoned for the flowers. Then she left the library and went into the cedar closet at the end of the hall. When she had found the golf clothes George wanted, she looked over them carefully and hung them in his dressing room. Her next task was to lay out his dinner clothes and to sew the loose button on the waistcoat he had worn last evening. She did these things deliberately, automatically, repeating as if it were a formula, "I must forget nothing"; and when at last she had finished, she stood upright, with a sigh of relief, as if a burden had rolled from her shoulders. Now that she had attended to the details of existence, she would have time for the problem of living.

Slipping out of her gray dress, she changed into a walking suit of blue homespun. Then, searching among the shoes in her closet, she selected a pair of heavy boots she had worn in Maine last summer. As she put on a close little hat and tied a veil of blue chiffon over her face, she reflected, with bitter mirth, that only in novels could one hide one's identity behind a veil.

In the hall downstairs she met Winters, who stared at her discreetly but disapprovingly.

"Shall I order the car, madam?"

She shook her head, reading his thoughts as plainly as if he had uttered them. "No, it has stopped raining. I want to walk."

The door closed sharply on her life of happiness, and she passed out into the rain-soaked world where the mist caught her like damp smoke. So this was what it meant to be deserted, to be alone on the earth! The smell of rain, the smell that George had brought with him into the warm room upstairs, oppressed her as if it were the odour of melancholy.

As the chill pierced her coat, she drew her furs closely about her neck, and walked briskly in the direction of the street car. The address on the letter she carried was burned into her memory not in numbers, but in the thought that it was a villa George owned in an unfashionable suburb named Locust Park. Though she had never been there, she knew that, with the uncertain trolley service she must expect, it would take at least two hours to make the trip and return. Half an hour for Rose Morrison; and even then it would be night, and Winters at least would be anxious, before she reached home. Well, that was the best she could do.

The street car came, and she got in and found a seat behind a man who had been shooting and carried a string of partridges. All the other seats were filled with the usual afternoon crowd for the suburbs—women holding bundles or baskets and workmen returning from the factories. A sense of isolation like spiritual darkness descended upon her; and she closed her eyes and tried to bring back the serenity she had felt in the thought of relinquishment. But she could remember only a phrase of Dorothy's which floated like a wisp of thistledown through her thoughts, "Spiritual vanity. With some women it is stronger than physical vanity." Was that her weakness, vanity, not of the body, but of the spirit?

Thoughts blew in and out of her mind like dead leaves, now whirling, now drifting, now stirring faintly in her consciousness with a moaning sound. Twenty years. Nothing but that. Love and nothing else in her whole life. . . . The summer of their engagement. A rose garden in bloom. The way he looked. The smell of roses. Or was it only the smell of dead leaves rotting to earth? . . . All the long, long years of their marriage. Little things that one never forgot. The way he laughed. The way he smiled. The look of his hair when it was damp on his forehead. The smell of cigars in his clothes. The three lumps of sugar in his coffee. The sleepy look in his face when he stood ready to put out the lights while she went up the stairs. Oh, the little things that tore at one's heart!

The street car stopped with a jerk, and she got out and walked through the drenched grass in the direction one of the women had pointed out to her.

"The Laurels? That low yellow house at the end of this lane, farther on where the piles of dead leaves are. You can't see the house now, the lane turns, but it's just a stone's throw farther on."

Thanking her, Margaret walked on steadily toward the turn in the lane. Outside of the city the wind blew stronger, and the coloured leaves, bronze, yellow, crimson, lay in a thick carpet over the muddy road. In the west a thin line of gold shone beneath a range of heavy, smoke-coloured clouds. From the trees rain still dripped slowly; and between the road and the line of gold in the west there stretched the desolate autumn landscape.

"Oh, the little things!" her heart cried in despair. "The little things that make happiness!"

Entering the sagging gate of The Laurels, she passed among mounds of sodden leaves which reminded her of graves, and followed the neglected walk between rows of leafless shrubs which must have looked gay in summer. The house was one of many cheap suburban villas (George had bought it, she remembered, at an auction) and she surmised that, until this newest tenant came, it must have stood long unoccupied. The whole place wore, she reflected as she rang the loosened bell, a furtive and insecure appearance.

After the third ring the door was hurriedly opened by a dishevelled maid, who replied that her mistress was not at home.

"Then I shall wait," said Margaret firmly. "Tell your mistress, when she comes in, that Mrs. Fleming is waiting to see her." With a step as resolute as her words, she entered the house and crossed the hall to the living room where a bright coal fire was burning.

The room was empty, but a canary in a gilded cage at the window broke into song as she entered. On a table stood a tray containing the remains of tea; and beside it there was a half-burned cigarette in a bronze Turkish bowl. A book—she saw instantly that it was a volume of the newest plays—lay face downward beneath a pair of eyeglasses, and a rug, which had fallen from the couch, was in a crumpled pile on the floor.

"So she isn't out," Margaret reflected; and turning at a sound, she confronted Rose Morrison.

For an instant it seemed to the older woman that beauty like a lamp blinded her eyes. Then, as the cloud passed, she realized that it was only a blaze, that it was the loveliness of dead leaves when they are burning.

"So you came?" said Rose Morrison, while she gazed at her with the clear and competent eyes of youth. Her voice, though it was low and clear, had no softness; it rang like a bell. Yes, she had youth, she had her flamboyant loveliness; but stronger than youth and loveliness, it seemed to Margaret, surveying her over the reserves and discriminations of the centuries, was the security of one who had never doubted her own judgment. Her power lay where power usually lies in an infallible self-esteem.

"I came to talk it over with you," began Margaret quietly; and though she tried to make her voice insolent, the deep instinct of good manners was greater than her effort. "You tell me that my husband loves you."

The glow, the flame, in Rose Morrison's face made Margaret think again of leaves burning. There was no embarrassment, there was no evasion even, in the girl's look. Candid and unashamed, she appeared to glory in this infatuation, which Margaret regarded as worse than sinful, since it was vulgar.

"Oh, I am so glad that you did," Rose Morrison's sincerity was disarming. "I hated to hurt you. You can never know what it cost me to write that letter; but I felt that I owed it to you to tell you the truth. I believe that we always owe people the truth."

"And did George feel this way also?"

"George?" The flame mounted until it enveloped her. "Oh, he doesn't know. I tried to spare him. He would rather do anything than hurt you, and I thought it would be so much better if we could talk it over and find a solution just between ourselves. I knew if you cared for George, you would feel as I do about sparing him."

About sparing him! As if she had done anything for the last twenty years, Margaret reflected, except think out new and different ways of sparing George!

"I don't know," she answered, as she sat down in obedience to the other's persuasive gesture. "I shall have to think a minute. You see this has been—well, rather—sudden."

"I know, I know." The girl looked as if she did. "May I give you a cup of tea? You must be chilled."

"No, thank you. I am quite comfortable."

"Not even a cigarette? Oh, I wonder what you Victorian women did for a solace when you weren't allowed even a cigarette!"

You Victorian women! In spite of her tragic mood, a smile hovered on Margaret's lips. So that was how this girl classified her. Yet Rose Morrison had fallen in love with a Victorian man.

"Then I may?" said the younger woman with her full-throated laugh. From her bright red hair, which was brushed straight back from her forehead, to her splendid figure, where her hips swung free like a boy's, she was a picture of barbaric beauty. There was a glittering hardness about her, as if she had been washed in some indestructible glaze; but it was the glaze of youth, not of experience. She reminded Margaret of a gilded statue she had seen once in a museum; and the girl's eyes, like the eyes of the statue, were gleaming, remote and impassive—eyes that had never looked on reality. The dress she wore was made of some strange "art-cloth," dyed in brilliant hues, fashioned like a kimono, and girdled at the hips with what Margaret mistook for a queer piece of rope. Nothing, not even her crude and confident youth, revealed Rose Morrison to her visitor so completely as this end of rope.

"You are an artist?" she asked, for she was sure of her ground. Only an artist, she decided, could be at once so arrogant with destiny and so ignorant of life.

"How did you know? Has George spoken of me?"

Margaret shook her head. "Oh, I knew without any one's telling me."

"I have a studio in Greenwich Village, but George and I met last summer at Ogunquit. I go there every summer to paint."

"I didn't know." How easily, how possessively, this other woman spoke her husband's name.

"It began at once." To Margaret, with her inherited delicacy and reticence, there was something repellent in this barbaric simplicity of emotion.

"But you must have known that he was married," she observed coldly.

"Yes, I knew, but I could see, of course, that you did not understand him."

"And you think that you do?" If it were not tragic, how amusing it would be to think of her simple George as a problem!

"Oh, I realize that it appears very sudden to you; but in emotions time counts for so little. Just living with a person for twenty years doesn't enable one to understand him, do you think?"

"I suppose not. But do you really imagine," she asked in what struck her as a singularly impersonal tone for so intimate a question, "that George is complex?"

The flame, which was revealed now as the illumination of some secret happiness, flooded Rose Morrison's features. As she leaned forward, with clasped hands, Margaret noticed that the girl was careless about those feminine details by which George declared so often that he judged a woman. Her hair was carelessly arranged; her finger nails needed attention; and beneath the kimonolike garment, a frayed place showed at the back of her stocking. Even her red morocco slippers were run down at the heels; and it seemed to Margaret that this physical negligence had extended to the girl's habit of thought.

"He is so big, so strong and silent, that it would take an artist to understand him," answered Rose Morrison passionately. Was this really, Margaret wondered, the way George appeared to the romantic vision?

"Yes, he is not a great talker," she admitted. "Perhaps if he talked more, you might find him less difficult." Then before the other could reply, she inquired sharply, "Did George tell you that he was misunderstood?"

"How you misjudge him!" The girl had flown to his defense; and though Margaret had been, as she would have said "a devoted wife," she felt that all this vehemence was wasted. After all, George, with his easy, prosaic temperament, was only made uncomfortable by vehemence. "He never speaks of you except in the most beautiful way," Rose Morrison was insisting. "He realizes perfectly what you have been to him, and he would rather suffer in silence all his life than make you unhappy."

"Then what is this all about?" Though she felt that it was unfair, Margaret could not help putting the question.

Actually there were tears in Rose Morrison's eyes. "I could not bear to see his life ruined," she answered. "I hated to write to you; but how else could I make you realize that you were standing in the way of his happiness? If it were just myself, I could have borne it in silence. I would never have hurt you just for my own sake; but, the subterfuge, the dishonesty, is spoiling his life. He does not say so, but, oh, I see it every day because I love him!" As she bent over, the firelight caught her hair, and it blazed out triumphantly like the red lilies in Margaret's library.

"What is it you want me to do?" asked Margaret in her dispassionate voice.

"I felt that we owed you the truth," responded the girl, "and I hoped that you would take what I wrote you in the right spirit."

"You are sure that my husband loves you?"

"Shall I show you his letters?" The girl smiled as she answered, and her full red lips reminded Margaret suddenly of raw flesh. Was raw flesh, after all, what men wanted?

"No!" The single word was spoken indignantly.

"I thought perhaps they would make you see what it means," explained Rose Morrison simply. "Oh, I wish I could do this without causing you pain!"

"Pain doesn't matter. I can stand pain."

"Well, I'm glad you aren't resentful. After all, why should we be enemies? George's happiness means more than anything else to us both."

"And you are sure you know best what is for George's happiness?"

"I know that subterfuge and lies and dishonesty cannot bring happiness." Rose Morrison flung out her arms with a superb gesture. "Oh, I realize that it is a big thing, a great thing, I am asking of you. But in your place, if I stood in his way, I should so gladly sacrifice myself for his sake I should give him his freedom. I should acknowledge his right to happiness, to self-development."

A bitter laugh broke from Margaret's lips. What a jumble of sounds these catchwords of the new freedom made! What was this self-development which could develop only through the sacrifice of others? How would these immature theories survive the compromises and concessions and adjustments which made marriage permanent?

"I cannot feel that our marriage has interfered with his development," she rejoined presently.

"You may be right," Rose Morrison conceded the point. "But to-day he needs new inspiration, new opportunities. He needs the companionship of a modern mind."

"Yes, he has kept young at my cost," thought the older woman. "I have helped by a thousand little sacrifices, by a thousand little cares and worries, to preserve this unnatural youth which is destroying me. I have taken over the burden of details in order that he might be free for the larger interests of life. If he is young to-day, it is at the cost of my youth."

For the second time that day, as she sat there in silence, with her eyes on the blooming face of Rose Morrison, a wave of peace, the peace of one who has been shipwrecked and then swept far off into some serene haven, enveloped her. Something to hold by, that at least she had found. The law of sacrifice, the ideal of self-surrender, which she had learned in the past. For twenty years she had given freely, abundantly, of her best; and to-day she could still prove to him that she was not beggared. She could still give the supreme gift of her happiness. "How he must love you!" she exclaimed. "How he must love you to have hurt me so much for your sake! Nothing but a great love could make him so cruel."

"He does love me," answered Rose Morrison, and her voice was like the song of a bird.

"He must." Margaret's eyes were burning, but no tears came. Her lips felt cracked with the effort she made to keep them from trembling. "I think if he had done this thing with any other motive than a great love, I should hate him until I died." Then she rose and held out her hand. "I shall not stand in your way," she added.

Joy flashed into the girl's eyes. "You are very noble," she answered. "I am sorry if I have hurt you. I am sorry, too, that I called you old-fashioned."

Margaret laughed. "Oh, I am old-fashioned. I am so old-fashioned that I should have died rather than ruin the happiness of another woman."

The joy faded from Rose Morrison's face. "It was not I," she answered. "It was life. We cannot stand in the way of life."

"Life to-day, God yesterday, what does it matter? It is a generation that has grasped everything except personal responsibility." Oh, if one could only keep the humour! A thought struck her, and she asked abruptly, "When your turn comes, if it ever does, will you give way as I do?"

"That will be understood. We shall not hold each other back."

"But you are young. You will tire first. Then he must give way?" Why, in twenty years George would be sixty-five and Rose Morrison still a young woman!

Calm, resolute, uncompromising, Rose Morrison held open the door. "Whatever happens, he would never wish to hold me back."

Then Margaret passed out, the door closed behind her, and she stood breathing deep draughts of the chill, invigorating air. Well, that was over.

The lawn, with its grave-like mounds of leaves, looked as mournful as a cemetery. Beyond the bare shrubs the road glimmered; the wind still blew in gusts, now rising, now dying away with a plaintive sound; in the west the thread of gold had faded to a pale greenish light. Veiled in the monotonous fall of the leaves, it seemed to Margaret that the desolate evening awaited her.

"How he must love her," she thought, not resentfully, but with tragic resignation. "How he must love her to have sacrificed me as he has done."

This idea, she found as she walked on presently in the direction of the street car, had taken complete possession of her point of view. Through its crystal lucidity she was able to attain some sympathy with her husband's suffering. What agony of mind he must have endured in these past months, these months when they had worked so quietly side by side on his book! What days of gnawing remorse! What nights of devastating anguish! How this newer love must have rent his heart asunder before he could stoop to the baseness of such a betrayal! Tears, which had not come for her own pain, stung her eyelids. She knew that he must have fought it hour by hour, day by day, night by night. Conventional as he was, how violent this emotion must have been to have conquered him so completely. "Terrible as an army with banners," she repeated softly, while a pang of jealously shot through her heart. Was there in George, she asked now, profounder depths of feeling than she had ever reached; was there some secret garden of romance where she had never entered? Was George larger, wilder, more adventurous in imagination, than she had dreamed? Had the perfect lover lain hidden in his nature, awaiting only the call of youth?

The street car returned almost empty; and she found restfulness in the monotonous jolting, as if it were swinging her into some world beyond space and time, where mental pain yielded to the sense of physical discomfort. After the agony of mind, the aching of body was strangely soothing.

Here and there, the lights of a house flashed among the trees, and she thought, with an impersonal interest, of the neglected villa, surrounded by mounds of rotting leaves, where that girl waited alone for happiness. Other standards. This was how the newer generation appeared to Margaret—other standards, other morals. Facing life stripped bare of every safeguard, of every restraining tradition, with only the courage of ignorance, of defiant inexperience, to protect one. That girl was not wilfully cruel. She was simply greedy for emotion; she was gasping at the pretense of happiness like all the rest of her undisciplined generation. She was caught by life because she had never learned to give up, to do without, to stand alone.

Her corner had come, and she stepped with a sensation of relief on the wet pavement. The rain was dripping steadily in a monotonous drizzle. While she walked the few blocks to her door, she forced herself by an effort of will to go on, step by step, not to drop down in the street and lose consciousness.

The tinkle of the bell and the sight of Winters's face restored her to her senses.

"Shall I bring you tea, madam?"

"No, it is too late."

Going upstairs to her bedroom, she took off her wet clothes and slipped into her prettiest tea gown, a trailing thing of blue satin and chiffon. While she ran the comb through her damp hair and touched her pale lips with colour, she reflected that even renunciation was easier when one looked desirable. "But it is like painting the cheeks of the dead," she thought, as she turned away from the mirror and walked with a dragging step to the library. Never, she realized suddenly, had she loved George so much as in this hour when she had discovered him only to lose him.

As she entered, George hurried to meet her with an anxious air. "I didn't hear you come in, Margaret. I have been very uneasy. Has anything happened?"

By artificial light he looked younger even than he had seemed in the afternoon; and this boyishness of aspect struck her as strangely pathetic. It was all a part, she told herself, of that fulfilment which had come too late, of that perilous second blooming, not of youth, but of Indian Summer. The longing to spare him, to save him from the suffering she had endured, pervaded her heart.

"Yes, something has happened," she answered gently. "I have been to see Rose Morrison."

As she spoke the name, she turned away from him, and walking with unsteady steps across the room, stood looking down into the fire. The knowledge of all that she must see when she turned, of the humiliation, the anguish, the remorse in his eyes, oppressed her heart with a passion of shame and pity. How could she turn and look on his wounded soul which she had stripped bare?

"Rose Morrison?" he repeated in an expressionless voice. "What do you know of Rose Morrison?"

At his question she turned quickly, and faced not anguish, not humiliation, but emptiness. There was nothing in his look except the blankness of complete surprise. For an instant the shock made her dizzy; and in the midst of the dizziness there flashed through her mind the memory of an evening in her childhood, when she had run bravely into a dark room where they told her an ogre was hiding, and had found that it was empty.

"She wrote to me." Her legs gave way as she replied, and, sinking into the nearest chair, she sat gazing up at him with an immobile face.

A frown gathered his eyebrows, and a purplish flush (he flushed so easily of late) mounted slowly to the smooth line of his hair. She watched the quiver that ran through his under lip (strange that she had not noticed how it had thickened) while his teeth pressed it sharply. Everything about him was acutely vivid to her, as if she were looking at him closely for the first time. She saw the furrow between his eyebrows, the bloodshot stain on one eyeball, the folds of flesh beneath his jutting chin, the crease in his black tie, the place where his shirt gave a little because it had grown too tight— all these insignificant details would exist indelibly in her brain.

"She wrote to you?" His voice sounded strained and husky, and he coughed abruptly as if he were trying to hide his embarrassment. "What the devil! But you don't know her."

"I saw her this afternoon. She told me everything."

"Everything?" Never had she imagined that he could appear so helpless, so lacking in the support of any conventional theory. A hysterical laugh broke from her, a laugh as utterly beyond her control as a spasm, and at the sound he flushed as if she had struck him. While she sat there she realized that she had no part or place in the scene before her. Never could she speak the words that she longed to utter. Never could she make him understand the real self behind the marionette at which he was looking. She longed with all her heart to say: "There were possibilities in me that you never suspected. I also am capable of a great love. In my heart I also am a creature of romance, of adventure. If you had only known it, you might have found in marriage all that you have sought elsewhere . . ." This was what she longed to cry out, but instead she said merely,

"She told me of your love. She asked me to give you up."

"She asked you to give me up?" His mouth fell open as he finished, and while he stared at her he forgot to shut it. It occurred to her that he had lost the power of inventing a phrase, that he could only echo the ones she had spoken. How like a foolish boy he looked as he stood there, in front of the sinking fire, trying to hide behind that hollow echo!

"She said that I stood in your way." The phrase sounded so grotesque as she uttered it that she found herself laughing again. She had not wished to speak these ugly things. Her heart was filled with noble words, with beautiful sentiments, but she could not make her lips pronounce them in spite of all the efforts she made. And she recalled suddenly the princess in the fairy tale who, when she opened her mouth, found that toads and lizards escaped from it instead of pearls and rubies.

At first he did not reply, and it seemed to her that only mechanical force could jerk his jaw back into place and close the eyelids over his vacant blue eyes. When at last he made a sound it was only the empty echo again, "stood in my way!"

"She is desperately in earnest." Justice wrung this admission from her. "She feels that this subterfuge is unfair to us all. Your happiness, she thinks, is what we should consider first, and she is convinced that I should be sacrificed to your future. She was perfectly frank. She suppressed nothing."

For the first time George Fleming uttered an original sound. "O Lord!" he exclaimed devoutly.

"I told her that I did not wish to stand in your way," resumed Margaret, as if the exclamation had not interrupted the flow of her thoughts. "I told her I would give you up."

Suddenly, without warning, he exploded. "What, in the name of heaven, has it got to do with you?" he demanded.

"To do with me?" It was her turn to echo. "But isn't that girl—" she corrected herself painfully—"isn't she living in your house at this minute?"

He cast about helplessly for an argument. When at last he discovered one, he advanced it with a sheepish air, as if he recognized its weakness. "Well, nobody else would take it, would they?"

"She says that you love her."

He shifted his ground nervously. "I can't help what she says, can I?"

"She offered to show me your letters."

"Compliments, nothing more."

"But you must love her, or you couldn't—you wouldn't——" A burning flush scorched Margaret's body.

"I never said that I . . ." Even with her he had always treated the word love as if it were a dangerous explosive, and he avoided touching it now, "that I cared for her in that way."

"Then you do in another way?"

He glanced about like a trapped animal. "I am not a fool, am I? Why, I am old enough to be her father! Besides, I am not the only one anyway. She was living with a man when I met her, and he wasn't the first. She isn't bad, you know. It's a kind of philosophy with her. She calls it self . . ."

"I know." Margaret cut the phrase short. "I have heard what she calls it." So it was all wasted! Nothing that she could do could lift the situation above the level of the commonplace, the merely vulgar.

She was defrauded not only of happiness, but even of the opportunity to be generous. Her sacrifice was as futile as that girl's passion. "But she is in love with you now," she said.

"I suppose she is." His tone had grown stubborn. "But how long would it last? In six months she would be leaving me for somebody else. Of course, I won't see her again," he added, with the manner of one who is conceding a reasonable point. Then, after a pause in which she made no response, his stubbornness changed into resentment. "Anybody would think that you are angry because I am not in love with her!" he exclaimed. "Anybody would think—but I don't understand women!"

"Then you will not—you do not mean to leave me?" she asked; and her manner was as impersonal, she was aware, as if Winters had just given her notice.

"Leave you?" He glanced appreciatively round the room. "Where on earth could I go?"

For an instant Margaret looked at him in silence. Then she insisted coldly, "To her, perhaps. She thinks that you are in love with her."

"Well, I suppose I've been a fool," he confessed, after a struggle, "but you are making too much of it."

Yes, she was making too much of it; she realized this more poignantly than he would ever be able to do. She felt like an actress who has endowed a comic part with the gesture of high tragedy. It was not, she saw clearly now, that she had misunderstood George, but that she had overplayed life.

"We met last summer at Ogunquit." She became aware presently that he was still making excuses and explanations about nothing. "You couldn't go about much, you know, and we went swimming and played golf together. I liked her, and I could see that she liked me. When we came away I thought we'd break it off, but somehow we didn't. I saw her several times in New York. Then she came here unexpectedly, and I offered her that old villa nobody would rent. You don't understand such things, Margaret. It hadn't any more to do with you than—than——" He hesitated, fished in the stagnant waters of his mind, and flung out abruptly, "than golf has. It was just a sort of—well, sort of—recreation."

Recreation! The memory of Rose Morrison's extravagant passion smote her sharply. How glorified the incident had appeared in the girl's imagination, how cheap and tawdry it was in reality. A continual compromise with the second best, an inevitable surrender to the average, was this the history of all romantic emotion? For an instant, such is the perversity of fate, it seemed to the wife that she and this strange girl were united by some secret bond which George could not share—by the bond of woman's immemorial disillusionment.

"I wouldn't have had you hurt for worlds, Margaret," said George, bending over her. The old gentle voice, the old possessive and complacent look in his sleepy blue eyes, recalled her wandering senses. "If I could only make you see that there wasn't anything in it."

She gazed up at him wearily. The excitement of discovery, the exaltation, the anguish, had ebbed away, leaving only gray emptiness. She had lost more than love, more than happiness, for she had lost her belief in life.

"If there had been anything in it, I might be able to understand," she replied.

He surveyed her with gloomy severity. "Hang it all! You act as if you wanted me to be in love with her." Then his face cleared as if by magic. "You're tired out, Margaret, and you're nervous. There's Winters now. You must try to eat a good dinner."

Anxious, caressing, impatient to have the discussion end and dinner begin, he stooped and lifted her in his arms. For an instant she lay there without moving, and in that instant her gaze passed from his face to the red lilies and the uncurtained window beyond.

Outside the leaves were falling.

Discussion of Glasgow's "The Difference"

1. Whose point of view guides this story?

2. Margaret asks herself, "Could twenty years of happiness be destroyed in an afternoon, in an hour?" What is the answer? What does the story suggest as the character's basis for happiness? Is that basis faulty from the beginning? Support your answer (for example, notice phrases that delineate the wife's assessment of her marriage of "two equal spirits").

3. What is the significance of the title? How might it apply not only to the relationships between George and the two women but also to Margaret and her friend? Why do you think Dorothy Chambers is in the story? The crowd on the street car?

ERNEST HEMINGWAY

1899–1961

🌜 Hemingway, a successful journalist with a distinctive style that has profoundly influenced a generation of writers, wrote some of the best-known novels of modern America: *The Sun Also Rises* (1926), *A Farewell to Arms* (1929), *For Whom the Bell Tolls* (1940), *The Old Man and the Sea* (1952). These novels are deeply rooted in Hemingway's own life: He served in the Italian front in World War I, was a correspondent during the Spanish Civil War and World War II, and spent many years abroad—living in Paris and Spain, hunting and fishing in Africa and the Caribbean. One of his first books was a thematically linked collection of short fiction, *In Our Time* (1924). Although this book lacks the geographical unity of Joyce's *Dubliners*, Rulfo's *Burning Plain*, and García Márquez's *Funeral of Mama Grande*, it is nonetheless a tightly structured grouping. "Cat in the Rain," taken from *In Our Time*, is an excellent illustration of Hemingway's grasp of symbolic detail to give stories what he speaks of as a fourth or fifth dimension. A consideration of these extra dimensions is vital to "Cat in the Rain," which is a deceptively simple and innocent tale about the relationship between a husband and wife.

Cat in the Rain

There were only two Americans stopping at the hotel. They did not know any of the people they passed on the stairs on their way to and from their room. Their room was on the second floor facing the sea. It also faced the public garden and the war monument. There were big palms and green benches in the public garden. In the good weather there was always an artist with his easel. Artists liked the way the palms grew and the bright colors of the hotels facing the gardens and the sea. Italians came from a long way off to look up at the war monument. It was made of bronze and glistened in the rain. It was raining. The rain dripped from the palm trees. Water stood in pools on the gravel paths. The sea broke in a long line in the rain and slipped back down the beach to come up and break again in a long line in the rain. The motor cars were gone from the square by the war monument. Across the square in the doorway of the café a waiter stood looking out at the empty square.

The American wife stood at the window looking out. Outside right under their window a cat was crouched under one of the dripping green tables. The cat was trying to make herself so compact that she would not be dripped on.

"I'm going down and get that kitty," the American wife said.

"I'll do it," her husband offered from the bed.

"No, I'll get it. The poor kitty out trying to keep dry under a table."

The husband went on reading, lying propped up with the two pillows at the foot of the bed.

"Don't get wet," he said.

The wife went downstairs and the hotel owner stood up and bowed to her as she passed the office. His desk was at the far end of the office. He was an old man and very tall.

"Il piove," the wife said. She liked the hotel-keeper.

"Si, si, Signora, brutto tempo. It is very bad weather."

He stood behind his desk in the far end of the dim room. The wife liked him. She liked the deadly serious way he received any complaints. She liked his dignity. She liked the way he wanted to serve her. She liked the way he felt about being a hotel-keeper. She liked his old, heavy face and big hands.

Liking him she opened the door and looked out. It was raining harder. A man in a rubber cape was crossing the empty square to the café. The cat would be around to the right. Perhaps she could go along under the eaves. As she stood in the doorway an umbrella opened behind her. It was the maid who looked after their room.

"You must not get wet," she smiled, speaking Italian. Of course, the hotel-keeper had sent her.

With the maid holding the umbrella over her, she walked along the gravel path until she was under their window. The table was there, washed bright green in the rain, but the cat was gone. She was suddenly disappointed. The maid looked up at her.

"Ha perduto qualque cosa, Signora?"

"There was a cat," said the American girl.

"A cat?"

"Si, il gatto."

"A cat?" the maid laughed. "A cat in the rain?"

"Yes," she said, "under the table." Then, "Oh, I wanted it so much. I wanted a kitty."

When she talked English the maid's face tightened.

"Come, Signora," she said. "We must get back inside. You will be wet."

"I suppose so," said the American girl.

They went back along the gravel path and passed in the door. The maid stayed outside to close the umbrella. As the American girl passed the office, the padrone bowed from his desk. Something felt very small and tight inside the girl. The padrone made her feel very small and at the same time really important. She had a momentary feeling of being of supreme importance. She went on up the stairs. She opened the door of the room. George was on the bed, reading.

"Did you get the cat?" he asked, putting the book down.

"It was gone."

"Wonder where it went to," he said, resting his eyes from reading. She sat down on the bed.

"I wanted it so much," she said. "I don't know why I wanted it so much. I wanted that poor kitty. It isn't any fun to be a poor kitty out in the rain."

George was reading again.

She went over and sat in front of the mirror of the dressing table looking at herself with the hand glass. She studied her profile, first one side and then the other. Then she studied the back of her head and her neck.

"Don't you think it would be a good idea if I let my hair grow out?" she asked, looking at her profile again.

George looked up and saw the back of her neck, clipped close like a boy's.

"I like it the way it is."

"I get so tired of it," she said. "I get so tired of looking like a boy."

George shifted his position in the bed. He hadn't looked away from her since she started to speak.

"You look pretty darn nice," he said.

She laid the mirror down on the dresser and went over to the window and looked out. It was getting dark.

"I want to pull my hair back tight and smooth and make a big knot at the back that I can feel," she said. "I want to have a kitty to sit on my lap and purr when I stroke her."

"Yeah?" George said from the bed.

"And I want to eat at a table with my own silver and I want candles. And I want it to be spring and I want to brush my hair out in front of a mirror and I want a kitty and I want some new clothes."

"Oh, shut up and get something to read," George said. He was reading again.

His wife was looking out of the window. It was quite dark now and still raining in the palm trees.

"Anyway, I want a cat," she said, "I want a cat. I want a cat now. If I can't have long hair or any fun, I can have a cat."

George was not listening. He was reading his book. His wife looked out of the window where the light had come on in the square.

Someone knocked at the door.

"Avanti," George said. He looked up from his book.

In the doorway stood the maid. She held a big tortoise-shell cat pressed tight against her and swung down against her body.

"Excuse me," she said, "the padrone asked me to bring this for the Signora."

Discussion of Hemingway's "Cat in the Rain"

1. Hemingway is noted for his style. In what way does his flat reportage suggest a world deeper than the surface he describes?

2. Describe the hotel-keeper and the husband. How does their behavior towards the wife contrast? Do you find this contrast significant? If so, how?

3. Looking at the references to Americans and Italians, what political relationships do you notice? Do these seem to correspond with the sexual relationships? How?

4. Do you find it significant that the cat is female? Does there seem to be some cause-and-effect relationship between the wife's not finding the cat and her dissatisfaction with herself? If so, what?

D. H. LAWRENCE

1885–1930

Lawrence, author of twelve novels and numerous short stories, poems, essays, and plays, is one of the most controversial, as well as important, figures in English literature. Born in a small mining town in England, he fought off frequent bouts of pneumonia and managed to become a schoolteacher. But his real interest was in writing, and by the outbreak of World War I his reputation had been firmly established with the success of his third novel, *Sons and Lovers* (1913). In many respects this novel may be his finest, although it is frequently overshadowed by *Lady Chatterley's Lover* (1928). Lawrence's works reveal a deep and abiding interest in the importance of sexual expression in human relationships. "The Rocking-Horse Winner," a justly famous story, is an exploration of this area, the most obvious level being the boy's feeling of rejection by his mother. Although the elements of the irrational and bizarre make the story susceptible to many interpretations, it is quite profitable to see the young boy's demoniacal drive for success as being the paradigm of the causes for achievement in a young man, achievements bought at an extremely high price.

The Rocking-Horse Winner

There was a woman who was beautiful, who started with all the advantages, yet she had no luck. She married for love, and the love turned to dust. She had bonny children, yet she felt they had been thrust upon her, and she could not love them. They looked at her coldly, as if they were finding fault with her. And hurriedly she felt she must cover up some fault in herself. Yet what it was she must cover up she never knew. Nevertheless, when her children were present, she always felt the centre of her heart go hard. This troubled her, and in her manner she was all the more gentle and anxious for her children, as if she loved them very much. Only she herself knew that at the centre of her heart was a hard little place that could not feel love, no, not for anybody. Everybody else said of her: "She is such a good mother. She adores her children." Only she herself, and her children themselves, knew it was not so. They read it in each other's eyes.

There were a boy and two little girls. They lived in a pleasant house, with a garden, and they had discreet servants, and felt themselves superior to anyone in the neighbourhood.

Although they lived in style, they felt always an anxiety in the house. There was never enough money. The mother had a small income, and the father had a small income, but not nearly enough for the social position which they had to keep up. The father went into town to some office. But though he had good prospects, these prospects never materialised. There was always the grinding sense of the shortage of money, though the style was always kept up.

At last the mother said: "I will see if *I* can't make something." But she did not know where to begin. She racked her brains, and tried this thing and the other, but could not find anything successful. The failure made deep lines come into her face. Her children were growing up, they would have to go to school. There must be more money, there must be more money. The father, who was always very handsome and expensive in his tastes, seemed as if he never *would* be able to do anything worth doing. And the mother, who had a great belief in herself, did not succeed any better, and her tastes were just as expensive.

And so the house came to be haunted by the unspoken phrase: *There must be more money! There must be more money!* The children could hear it all the time, though nobody said it aloud. They heard it at Christmas, when the expensive and splendid toys filled the nursery. Behind the shining modern rocking-horse, behind the smart doll's house, a voice would start whispering: "There *must* be more money! There *must* be more money!" And the children would stop playing, to listen for a moment. They would look into each other's eyes, to see if they had all heard. And each one saw in the eyes of the other two that they too had heard. "There *must* be more money! There *must* be more money!"

It came whispering from the springs of the still-swaying rocking-horse, and even the horse, bending his wooden, champing head, heard it. The big doll, sitting so pink and smirking in her new pram, could hear it quite plainly, and seemed to be smirking all the more self-consciously because of it. The foolish puppy, too, that took the place of the teddy-bear, he was looking so extraordinarily foolish for no other reason but that he heard the secret whisper all over the house: "There *must* be more money!"

Yet nobody ever said it aloud. The whisper was everywhere, and therefore no one spoke it. Just as no one ever says: "We are breathing!" in spite of the fact that breath is coming and going all the time.

"Mother," said the boy Paul one day, "why don't we keep a car of our own? Why do we always use uncle's, or else a taxi?"

"Because we're the poor members of the family," said the mother.

"But why *are* we, mother?"

"Well—I suppose," she said slowly and bitterly, "it's because you father has no luck."

The boy was silent for some time.

"Is luck money, mother?" he asked, rather timidly.

"No Paul. Not quite. It's what causes you to have money."

"Oh!" said Paul vaguely. "I thought when Uncle Oscar said *filthy lucker*, it meant money."

"*Filthy lucre* does mean money," said the mother. "But it's lucre, not luck."

"Oh!" said the boy. "Then what *is* luck, mother?"

"It's what causes you to have money. If you're lucky you have money. That's why it's better to be born lucky than rich. If you're rich, you may lose your money. But if you're lucky, you will always get more money."

"Oh! Will you? And is father not lucky?"

"Very unlucky, I should say," she said bitterly.

The boy watched her with unsure eyes.

"Why?" he asked.

"I don't know. Nobody ever knows why one person is lucky and another unlucky."

"Don't they? Nobody at all? Does *nobody* know?"

"Perhaps God. But He never tells."

"He ought to, then. And aren't you lucky either, mother?"

"I can't be, if I married an unlucky husband."

"But by yourself, aren't you?"

"I used to think I was, before I married. Now I think I am very unlucky indeed."

"Why?"

"Well—never mind! Perhaps I'm not really," she said.

The child looked at her to see if she meant it. But he saw, by the lines of her mouth, that she was only trying to hide something from him.

"Well, anyhow," he said stoutly, "I'm a lucky person."

"Why?" said his mother, with a sudden laugh.

He stared at her. He didn't even know why he had said it.

"God told me," he asserted, brazening it out.

"I hope He did, dear!" she said, again with a laugh, but rather bitter.

"He did, mother!"

"Excellent!" said the mother, using one of her husband's exclamations.

The boy saw she did not believe him; or rather, that she paid no attention to his assertion. This angered him somewhere, and made him want to compel her attention.

He went off by himself, vaguely, in a childish way, seeking for the clue to 'luck'. Absorbed, taking no heed of other people, he went about with a sort of stealth, seeking inwardly for luck. He wanted luck, he wanted it, he wanted it. When the two girls were playing dolls in the nursery, he would sit on his big rocking-horse, charging madly into space, with a frenzy that made the little girls peer at him uneasily. Wildly the horse careered, the waving dark hair of the boy tossed, his eyes had a strange glare in them. The little girls dared not speak to him.

When he had ridden to the end of his mad little journey, he climbed down and stood in front of his rocking-horse, staring fixedly into its lowered face. Its red mouth was slightly open, its big eye was wide and glassy-bright.

"Now!" he would silently command the snorting steed. "Now, take me to where there is luck! Now take me!"

And he would slash the horse on the neck with the little whip he had asked Uncle Oscar for. He *knew* the horse could take him to where there was luck, if only he forced it. So he would mount again and start on his furious ride, hoping at last to get there. He knew he could get there.

"You'll break your horse, Paul!" said the nurse.

"He's always riding like that! I wish he'd leave off!" said his elder sister Joan.

But he only glared down on them in silence. Nurse gave him up. She could make nothing of him. Anyhow, he was growing beyond her.

One day his mother and his Uncle Oscar came in when he was on one of his furious rides. He did not speak to them.

"Hallo, you young jockey! Riding a winner?" said his uncle.

"Aren't you growing too big for a rocking-horse? You're not a very little boy any longer, you know," said his mother.

But Paul only gave a blue glare from his big, rather close-set eyes. He would speak to nobody when he was in full tilt. His mother watched him with an anxious expression on her face.

At last he suddenly stopped forcing his horse into the mechanical gallop and slid down.

"Well, I got there!" he announced fiercely, his blue eyes still flaring, and his sturdy long legs straddling apart.

"Where did you get to?" asked his mother.

"Where I wanted to go," he flared back at her.

"That's right, son!" said Uncle Oscar. "Don't you stop till you get there. What's the horse's name?"

"He doesn't have a name," said the boy.

"Gets on without all right?" asked the uncle.

"Well, he has different names. He was called Sansovino last week."

"Sansovino, eh? Won the Ascot. How did you know this name?"

"He always talks about horse-races with Bassett," said Joan.

The uncle was delighted to find that his small nephew was posted with all the racing news. Bassett, the young gardener, who had been wounded in the left foot in the war and had got his present job through Oscar Cresswell, whose batman he had been, was a perfect blade of the 'turf'. He lived in the racing events, and the small boy lived with him.

Oscar Cresswell got it all from Bassett.

"Master Paul comes and asks me, so I can't do more than tell him, sir," said Bassett, his face terribly serious, as if he were speaking of religious matters.

"And does he ever put anything on a horse he fancies?"

"Well—I don't want to give him away—he's a young sport, a fine sport, sir. Would you mind asking him himself? He sort of takes a pleasure in it, and perhaps he'd feel I was giving him away, sir, if you don't mind."

Bassett was serious as a church.

The uncle went back to his nephew and took him off for a ride in the car.

"Say, Paul, old man, do you ever put anything on a horse?" the uncle asked.

The boy watched the handsome man closely.

"Why, do you think I oughtn't to?" he parried.

"Not a bit of it! I thought perhaps you might give me a tip for the Lincoln."

The car sped on into the country, going down to Uncle Oscar's place in Hampshire.

"Honour bright?" said the nephew.

"Honour bright, son!" said the uncle.

"Well, then, Daffodil."

"Daffodil! I doubt it, sonny. What about Mirza?"

"I only know the winner," said the boy. "That's Daffodil."

"Daffodil, eh?"

There was a pause. Daffodil was an obscure horse comparatively.

"Uncle!"

"Yes, son?"

"You won't let it go any further, will you? I promised Bassett."

"Bassett be damned, old man! What's he got to do with it?"

"We're partners. We've been partners from the first. Uncle, he lent me my first five shillings, which I lost. I promised him, honour bright, it was only between me and him; only you gave me that ten-shilling note I started winning with, so I thought you were lucky. You won't let it go any further, will you?"

The boy gazed at his uncle from those big, hot, blue eyes, set rather close together. The uncle stirred and laughed uneasily.

"Right you are, son! I'll keep your tip private. Daffodil, eh? How much are you putting on him?"

"All except twenty pounds," said the boy. "I keep that in reserve."

The uncle thought it a good joke.

"You keep twenty pounds in reserve, do you, you young romancer? What are you betting, then?"

"I'm betting three hundred," said the boy gravely. "But it's between you and me, Uncle Oscar! Honour bright?"

The uncle burst into a roar of laughter.

"It's between you and me all right, you young Nat Gould," he said, laughing. "But where's your three hundred?"

"Bassett keeps it for me. We're partners."

"You are, are you! And what is Bassett putting on Daffodil?"

"He won't go quite as high as I do, I expect. Perhaps he'll go a hundred and fifty."

"What, pennies?" laughed the uncle.

"Pounds," said the child, with a surprised look at his uncle. "Bassett keeps a bigger reserve than I do."

Between wonder and amusement Uncle Oscar was silent. He pursued the matter no further, but he determined to take his nephew with him to the Lincoln races.

"Now, son," he said, "I'm putting twenty on Mirza, and I'll put five on for you on any horse you fancy. What's your pick?"

"Daffodil, uncle."

"No, not the fiver on Daffodil!"

"I should if it was my own fiver," said the child.

"Good! Good! Right you are! A fiver for me and a fiver for you on Daffodil."

The child had never been to a race-meeting before, and his eyes were blue fire. He pursed his mouth tight and watched. A Frenchman just in front had put his money on Lancelot. Wild with excitement, he flayed his arms up and down, yelling "*Lancelot! Lancelot!*" in his French accent.

Daffodil came in first, Lancelot second, Mirza third. The child, flushed with eyes blazing, was curiously serene. His uncle brought him four five-pound notes, four to one.

"What am I to do with these?" he cried, waving them before the boy's eyes.

"I suppose we'll talk to Bassett," said the boy. "I expect I have fifteen hundred now; and twenty in reserve; and this twenty."

His uncle studied him for some moments.

"Look here, son!" he said. "You're not serious about Bassett and that fifteen hundred, are you?"

"Yes, I am. But it's between you and me, Uncle. Honour bright?"

"Honour bright all right, son! But I must talk to Bassett."

"If you'd like to be a partner, uncle, with Bassett and me, we could all be partners. Only, you'd have to promise, honour bright, uncle, not to let it go beyond us three. Bassett and I are lucky, and you must be lucky, because it was your ten shillings I started winning with. . . ."

Uncle Oscar took both Bassett and Paul into Richmond Park for an afternoon, and there they talked.

"It's like this, you see, sir," Bassett said. "Master Paul would get me talking about racing events, spinning yarns, you know, sir. And he was always keen on knowing if I'd made or if I'd lost. It's about a year since, now, that I put five shillings on Blush of Dawn for him: and we lost. Then the luck turned, with that ten shillings he had from you: that we put on Singhalese. And since that time, it's been pretty steady, all things considering. What do you say, Master Paul?"

"We're all right when we're sure," said Paul. "It's when we're not quite sure that we go down."

"Oh, but we're careful then," said Bassett.

"But when are you *sure?*" smiled Uncle Oscar.

"It's Master Paul, sir," said Bassett in a secret, religious voice. "It's as if he had it from heaven. Like Daffodil, now, for the Lincoln. That was as sure as eggs."

"Did you put anything on Daffodil?" asked Oscar Cresswell.

"Yes, sir. I made my bit."

"And my nephew?"

Bassett was obstinately silent, looking at Paul.

"I made twelve hundred, didn't I, Bassett? I told Uncle I was putting three hundred on Daffodil."

"That's right," said Bassett, nodding.

"But where's the money?" asked the uncle.

"I keep it safe locked up, sir. Master Paul he can have it any minute he likes to ask for it."

"What, fifteen hundred pounds?"

"And twenty! And *forty*, that is, with the twenty he made on the course."

"It's amazing!" said the uncle.

"If Master Paul offers you to be partners, sir, I would, if I were you: if you'll excuse me," said Bassett.

Oscar Cresswell thought about it.

"I'll see the money," he said.

They drove home again, and, sure enough, Bassett came round to the garden-house with fifteen hundred pounds in notes. The twenty pounds reserve was left with Joe Glee, in the Turf Commission deposit.

"You see, it's all right, uncle, when I'm *sure!* Then we go strong, for all we're worth. Don't we, Bassett?"

"We do that, Master Paul."

"And when are you sure?" said the uncle, laughing.

"Oh, well, sometimes I'm *absolutely* sure, like about Daffodil," said the boy; "and sometimes I have an idea; and sometimes I haven't even an idea, have I, Bassett? Then we're careful, because we mostly go down."

"You do, do you! And when you're sure, like about Daffodil, what makes you sure, sonny?"

"Oh, well, I don't know," said the boy uneasily. "I'm sure, you know, uncle; that's all."

"It's as if he had it from heaven, sir," Bassett reiterated.

"I should say so!" said the uncle.

But he became a partner. And when the Leger was coming on Paul was 'sure' about Lively Spark, which was a quite inconsiderable horse. The boy insisted on putting a thousand on the horse, Bassett went for five hundred, and Oscar Cresswell two hundred. Lively Spark came in first, and the betting had been ten to one against him. Paul had made ten thousand.

"You see," he said, "I was absolutely sure of him."

Even Oscar Cresswell had cleared two thousand.

"Look here, son," he said, "this sort of thing makes me nervous."

"It needn't, uncle! Perhaps I shan't be sure again for a long time."

"But what are you going to do with your money?" asked the uncle.

"Of course," said the boy, "I started it for mother. She said she had no luck, because father is unlucky, so I thought if *I* was lucky, it might stop whispering."

"What might stop whispering?"

"Our house. I *hate* our house for whispering."

"What does it whisper?"

"Why—why"—the boy fidgeted—"why, I don't know. But it's always short of money, you know, uncle."

"I know it, son, I know it."

"You know people send mother writs, don't you, uncle?"

"I'm afraid I do," said the uncle.

"And then the house whispers, like people laughing at you behind your back. It's awful, that is! I thought if I was lucky——"

"You might stop it," added the uncle.

The boy watched him with big blue eyes, that had an uncanny cold fire in them, and he said never a word.

"Well, then!" said the uncle. "What are we doing?"

"I shouldn't like mother to know I was lucky," said the boy.

"Why not, son?"

"She'd stop me."

"I don't think she would."

"Oh!"—and the boy writhed in an odd way—"I *don't* want her to know, uncle."

"All right, son! We'll manage it without her knowing."

They managed it very easily. Paul, at the other's suggestion, handed over five thousand pounds to his uncle, who deposited it with the family lawyer, who was then to inform Paul's mother that a relative had put five thousand pounds into his hands, which sum was to be paid out a thousand pounds at a time, on the mother's birthday, for the next five years.

"So she'll have a birthday present of a thousand pounds for five successive years," said Uncle Oscar. "I hope it won't make it all the harder for her later."

Paul's mother had her birthday in November. The house had been 'whispering' worse than ever lately, and, even in spite of his luck, Paul could not bear up against it. He was very anixous to see the effect of the birthday letter, telling his mother about the thousand pounds.

When there were no visitors, Paul now took his meals with his parents, as he was beyond the nursery control. His mother went into town nearly every day. She had discovered that she had an odd knack of sketching furs and dress materials, so she worked secretly in the studio of a friend who was the chief 'artist' for the leading drapers. She drew the figures of ladies in furs and ladies in silk and sequins for the newspaper advertisements. This young woman artist earned several thousand pounds a year, but Paul's mother only made several hundreds, and she was again dissatisfied. She so wanted to be first in something, and she did not succeed, even in making sketches for drapery advertisements.

She was down to breakfast on the morning of her birthday. Paul watched her face as she read her letters. He knew the lawyer's letter. As his mother read it, her face hardened and became more expressionless. Then a cold, determined look came on her mouth. She hid the letter under the pile of others, and said not a word about it.

"Didn't you have anything nice in the post for your birthday, mother?" said Paul.

"Quite moderately nice," she said, her voice cold and absent.

She went away to town without saying more.

But in the afternoon Uncle Oscar appeared. He said Paul's mother had had a long interview with the lawyer, asking if the whole five thousand could not be advanced at once, as she was in debt.

"What do you think, uncle?" said the boy.

"I leave it to you, son."

"Oh, let her have it, then! We can get some more with the other," said the boy.

"A bird in the hand is worth two in the bush, laddie!" said Uncle Oscar.

"But I'm sure to *know* for the Grand National; or the Lincolnshire; or else the Derby. I'm sure to know for *one* of them," said Paul.

So Uncle Oscar signed the agreement, and Paul's mother touched the whole five thousand. Then something very curious happened. The voices in the house suddenly went mad, like a chorus of frogs on a spring evening. There were certain new furnishings, and Paul had a tutor. He was *really* going to Eton, his father's school, in the following autumn. There were flowers in the winter, and a blossoming of the luxury Paul's mother had been used to. And yet the voices in the house, behind the sprays of mimosa and almond-blossom, and from under the piles of iridescent cushions, simply trilled and screamed in a sort of ecstasy: "There *must* be more money! Oh-h-h; there *must* be more money. Oh, now, now-w!

Now-w-w—there *must* be more money!—more than ever! More than ever!"

It frightened Paul terribly. He studied away at his Latin and Greek with his tutor. But his intense hours were spent with Bassett. The Grand National had gone by: he had not 'known', and had lost a hundred pounds. Summer was at hand. He was in agony for the Lincoln. But even for the Lincoln he didn't 'know', and he lost fifty pounds. He became wild-eyed and strange, as if something were going to explode in him.

"Let it alone, son! Don't you bother about it!" urged Uncle Oscar. But it was as if the boy couldn't really hear what his uncle was saying.

"I've got to know for the Derby! I've got to know for the Derby!" the child reiterated, his big blue eyes blazing with a sort of madness.

His mother noticed how overwrought he was.

"You'd better go to the seaside. Wouldn't you like to go now to the seaside, instead of waiting? I think you'd better," she said, looking down at him anxiously, her heart curiously heavy because of him.

But the child lifted his uncanny blue eyes.

"I couldn't possibly go before the Derby, mother!' he said. "I couldn't possibly!"

"Why not?" she said, her voice becoming heavy when she was opposed. "Why not? You can still go from the seaside to see the Derby with your Uncle Oscar, if that's what you wish. No need for you to wait here. Besides, I think you care too much about these races. It's a bad sign. My family has been a gambling family, and you won't know till you grow up how much damage it has done. But it has done damage. I shall have to send Bassett away, and ask Uncle Oscar not to talk racing to you, unless you promise to be reasonable about it: go away to the seaside and forget it. You're all nerves!"

"I'll do what you like, mother, so long as you don't send me away till after the Derby," the boy said.

"Send you away from where? Just from this house?"

"Yes," he said, gazing at her.

"Why, you curious child, what makes you care about this house so much, suddenly? I never knew you loved it."

He gazed at her without speaking. He had a secret within a secret, something he had not divulged, even to Bassett or to his Uncle Oscar.

But his mother, after standing undecided and a little bit sullen for some moments, said:

"Very well, then! Don't go to the seaside till after the Derby, if you don't wish it. But promise me you won't let your nerves go to pieces. Promise you won't think so much about horse-racing and *events*, as you call them!"

"Oh no," said the boy casually. "I won't think much about them, mother. You needn't worry. I wouldn't worry, mother, if I were you."

"If you were me and I were you," said his mother, "I wonder what we *should* do!"

"But you know you needn't worry, mother, don't you?" the boy repeated.

"I should be awfully glad to know it," she said wearily.

"Oh, well, you *can*, you know. I mean, you *ought* to know you needn't worry," he insisted.

"Ought I? Then I'll see about it," she said.

Paul's secret of secrets was his wooden horse, that which had no name. Since he was emancipated from a nurse and a nursery-governess, he had had his rocking-horse removed to his own bedroom at the top of the house.

"Surely you're too big for a rocking-horse!" his mother had remonstrated.

"Well, you see, mother, till I can have a *real* horse, I like to have *some* sort of animal about," had been his quaint answer.

"Do you feel he keeps you company?" she laughed.

"Oh yes! He's very good, he always keeps me company, when I'm there," said Paul.

So the horse, rather shabby, stood in an arrested prance in the boy's bedroom.

The Derby was drawing near, and the boy grew more and more tense. He hardly heard what was spoken to him, he was very frail, and his eyes were really uncanny. His mother had sudden strange seizures of uneasiness about him. Sometimes, for half an hour, she would feel a sudden anxiety about him that was almost anguish. She wanted to rush to him at once, and know he was safe.

Two nights before the Derby, she was at a big party in town, when one of her rushes of anxiety about her boy, her first-born, gripped her heart till she could hardly speak. She fought with the feeling, might and main, for she believed in common sense. But it was too strong. She had to leave the dance and go downstairs to telephone to the country. The children's nursery-governess was terribly surprised and startled at being rung up in the night.

"Are the children all right, Miss Wilmot?"

"Oh yes, they are quite all right."

"Master Paul? Is he all right?"

"He went to bed as right as a trivet. Shall I run up and look at him?"

"No," said Paul's mother reluctantly. "No! Don't trouble. It's all right. Don't sit up. We shall be home fairly soon." She did not want her son's privacy intruded upon.

"Very good," said the governess.

It was about one o'clock when Paul's mother and father drove up to their house. All was still. Paul's mother went to her room and slipped off her white fur cloak. She had told her maid not to wait up for her. She heard her husband downstairs, mixing a whisky and soda.

And then, because of the strange anxiety at her heart, she stole upstairs to her son's room. Noiselessly she went along the upper corridor. Was there a faint noise? What was it?

She stood, with arrested muscles, outside his door, listening. There was a strange, heavy, and yet not loud noise. Her heart stood still. It was a soundless noise, yet rushing and powerful. Something huge, in violent, hushed motion. What was it? What in God's name was it? She ought to know. She felt that she knew the noise. She knew what it was.

Yet she could not place it. She couldn't say what it was. And on and on it went, like a madness.

Softly, frozen with anxiety and fear, she turned the door-handle.

The room was dark. Yet in the space near the window, she heard and saw something plunging to and fro. She gazed in fear and amazement.

Then suddenly she switched on the light, and saw her son, in his green pyjamas, madly surging on the rocking-horse. The blaze of light suddenly lit him up, as he urged the wooden horse, and lit her up, as she stood, blonde, in her dress of pale green and crystal, in the doorway.

"Paul!" she cried. "Whatever are you doing?"

"It's Malabar!" he screamed in a powerful, strange voice. "It's Malabar!"

His eyes blazed at her for one strange and senseless second, as he ceased urging his wooden horse. Then he fell with a crash to the ground, and she, all her tormented motherhood flooding upon her, rushed to gather him up.

But he was unconscious, and unconscious he remained, with some brain-fever. He talked and tossed, and his mother sat stonily by his side.

"Malabar! It's Malabar! Bassett, Bassett, I *know*! It's Malabar!"

So the child cried, trying to get up and urge the rocking-horse that gave him his inspiration.

"What does he mean by Malabar?" asked the heart-frozen mother.

"I don't know," said the father stonily.

"What does he mean by Malabar?" she asked her brother Oscar.

"It's one of the horses running for the Derby," was the answer.

And, in spite of himself, Oscar Cresswell spoke to Bassett, and himself put a thousand on Malabar: at fourteen to one.

The third day of the illness was critical: they were waiting for a change. The boy, with his rather long, curly hair, was tossing ceaselessly on the pillow. He neither slept nor regained consciousness, and his eyes were like blue stones. His mother sat, feeling her heart had gone, turned actually into a stone.

In the evening, Oscar Cresswell did not come, but Bassett sent a message, saying could he come up for one moment, just one moment? Paul's mother was very angry at the intrusion, but on second thoughts she agreed. The boy was the same. Perhaps Bassett might bring him to consciousness.

The gardener, a shortish fellow with a little brown moustache and sharp little brown eyes, tiptoed into the room, touched his imaginary cap to Paul's mother, and stole to the bedside, staring with glittering, smallish eyes at the tossing, dying child.

"Master Paul!" he whispered. "Master Paul! Malabar came in first all right, a clean win. I did as you told me. You've made over seventy thousand pounds, you have; you've got over eighty thousand. Malabar came in all right, Master Paul."

"Malabar! Malabar! Did I say Malabar, mother? Did I say Malabar? Do you think I'm lucky, mother? I knew Malabar, didn't I? Over eighty thousand pounds! I call that lucky, don't you, mother? Over eighty thousand pounds! I knew, didn't I know I knew? Malabar came in all right. If I ride my horse till I'm sure, then I tell you, Bassett, you can go as high as you like. Did you go for all you were worth, Bassett?"

"I went a thousand on it, Master Paul."

"I never told you, mother, that if I can ride my horse, and *get there*, then I'm absolutely sure—oh, absolutely! Mother, did I ever tell you? I *am* lucky!"

"No, you never did," said his mother.

But the boy died in the night.

And even as he lay dead, his mother heard her brother's voice saying to her: "My God, Hester, you're eighty-odd thousand to the good, and a poor devil of a son to the bad. But, poor devil, poor devil, he's best gone out of a life where he rides his rocking-horse to find a winner."

Discussion of Lawrence's "The Rocking-Horse Winner"

1. If the story is about Paul, as the title implies, what might be Lawrence's intention in beginning with the emphasis on Paul's mother?

2. Notice the tone of the narrator's voice; describe it. What place does it have in the total context of "The Rocking-Horse Winner"?

3. What sort of journey—other than the literal—does the boy seem to be making on his rocking horse? Support your answer. Pay attention to the demonic elements in the story. How do they affect your responses?

4. What does Lawrence suggest about the relationship among humans in a materialistic society? What does he accomplish by the choice of betting on horses as the central action of the story?

WILLIAM FAULKNER

1897–1962

❧ William Faulkner was born in New Albany, Mississippi;
in 1902 his family moved to Oxford, Mississippi, which is now
synonymous with his name and that of his fictional county,
Yoknapatawpha. Faulkner's influence on American writers, especially those in the Deep South, has been formidable. Among his
novels are *Soldier's Pay* (1926), *The Sound and the Fury* (1929),
As I Lay Dying (1930), *Absalom, Absalom!* (1936), *The Unvan-
quished* (1938), *Intruder in the Dust* (1948), and *The Reivers* (1962).
His *Collected Stories* were published in 1950, a year after he received
the Nobel Prize for literature. Faulkner's conferences with students
give us an insight into his concerns as a writer: "The story can come
from an anecdote, it can come from a character. With me, it never
comes from an idea because I don't know too much about ideas and
ain't really interested in ideas. . . . I'm interested primarily in people,
in man in conflict with himself, with his fellow man, or with his
time and place, his environment" (*Faulkner in the University*, ed.
Frederick L. Gwynn and Joseph L. Blotner [New York: Vintage
Books, 1959], p. 19).

Dry September

I

Through the bloody September twilight, aftermath of sixty-two
rainless days, it had gone like a fire in dry grass—the rumor, the
story, whatever it was. Something about Miss Minnie Cooper and
a Negro. Attacked, insulted, frightened: none of them, gathered in
the barber shop on that Saturday evening where the ceiling fan
stirred, without freshening it, the vitiated air, sending back upon
them, in recurrent surges of stale pomade and lotion, their own
stale breath and odors, knew exactly what had happened.

"Except it wasn't Will Mayes," a barber said. He was a man of
middle age; a thin, sand-colored man with a mild face, who was
shaving a client. "I know Will Mayes. He's a good nigger. And I
know Miss Minnie Cooper, too."

"What do you know about her?" a second barber said.

"Who is she?" the client said. "A young girl?"

"No," the barber said. "She's about forty, I reckon. She ain't
married. That's why I dont believe—"

"Believe, hell!" a hulking youth in a sweat-stained silk shirt said.
"Wont you take a white woman's word before a nigger's?"

"I dont believe Will Mayes did it," the barber said. "I know Will Mayes."

"Maybe you know who did it, then. Maybe you already got him out of town, you damn niggerlover."

"I dont believe anybody did anything. I dont believe anything happened. I leave it to you fellows if them ladies that get old without getting married dont have notions that man cant—"

"Then you are a hell of a white man," the client said. He moved under the cloth. The youth had sprung to his feet.

"You dont?" he said. "Do you accuse a white woman of lying?"

The barber held the razor poised above the half-risen client. He did not look around.

"It's this durn weather," another said. "It's enough to make a man do anything. Even to her."

Nobody laughed. The barber said in his mild, stubborn tone: "I aint accusing nobody of nothing. I just know and you fellows know how a woman that never—"

"You damn niggerlover!" the youth said.

"Shut up, Butch," another said. "We'll get the facts in plenty of time to act."

"Who is? Who's getting them?" the youth said. "Facts, hell! I—"

"You're a fine white man," the client said. "Aint you?" In his frothy beard he looked like a desert rat in the moving pictures. "You tell them, Jack," he said to the youth. "If there aint any white men in this town, you can count on me, even if I aint only a drummer and a stranger."

"That's right, boys," the barber said. "Find out the truth first. I know Will Mayes."

"Well, by God!" the youth shouted. "To think that a white man in this town—"

"Shut up, Butch," the second speaker said. "We got plenty of time."

The client sat up. He looked at the speaker. "Do you claim that anything excuses a nigger attacking a white woman? Do you mean to tell me you are a white man and you'll stand for it? You better go back North where you came from. The South dont want your kind here."

"North what?" the second said. "I was born and raised in this town."

"Well, by God!" the youth said. He looked about with a strained, baffled gaze, as if he was trying to remember what it was he wanted to say or to do. He drew his sleeve across his sweating face. "Damn if I'm going to let a white woman—"

"You tell them, Jack," the drummer said. "By God, if they—"

The screen door crashed open. A man stood in the floor, his feet apart and his heavy-set body poised easily. His white shirt was open at the throat; he wore a felt hat. His hot, bold glance swept

the group. His name was McLendon. He had commanded troops
at the front in France and had been decorated for valor.

"Well," he said, "are you going to sit there and let a black son
rape a white woman on the streets of Jefferson?"

Butch sprang up again. The silk of his shirt clung flat to his
heavy shoulders. At each armpit was a dark halfmoon. "That's
what I been telling them! That's what I—"

"Did it really happen?" a third said. "This aint the first man
scare she ever had, like Hawkshaw says. Wasn't there something
about a man on the kitchen roof, watching her undress, about a
year ago?"

"What?" the client said. "What's that?" The barber had been
slowly forcing him back into the chair; he arrested himself reclin-
ing, his head lifted, the barber still pressing him down.

McLendon whirled on the third speaker. "Happen? What the
hell difference does it make? Are you going to let the black sons
get away with it until one really does it?"

"That's what I'm telling them!" Butch shouted. He cursed, long
and steady, pointless.

"Here, here," a fourth said. "Not so loud. Dont talk so loud."

"Sure," McLendon said; "no talking necessary at all. I've done
my talking. Who's with me?" He poised on the balls of his feet,
roving his gaze.

The barber held the drummer's face down, the razor poised.
"Find out the facts first, boys. I know Willy Mayes. It wasn't him.
Let's get the sheriff and do this thing right."

McLendon whirled upon him his furious, rigid face. The barber
did not look away. They looked like men of different races. The
other barbers had ceased also above their prone clients. "You mean
to tell me," McLendon said, "that you'd take a nigger's word before
a white woman's? Why, you damn niggerloving—"

The third speaker rose and grasped McLendon's arm; he too had
been a soldier. "Now, now. Let's figure this thing out. Who knows
anything about what really happened?"

"Figure out hell!" McLendon jerked his arm free. "All that're
with me get up from there. The ones that aint—" He roved his
gaze, dragging his sleeve across his face.

Three men rose. The drummer in the chair sat up. "Here," he
said, jerking at the cloth about his neck; "get this rag off me. I'm
with him. I don't live here, but by God, if our mothers and wives
and sisters—" He smeared the cloth over his face and flung it to the
floor. McLendon stood in the floor and cursed the others. Another
rose and moved toward him. The remainder sat uncomfortable, not
looking at one another, then one by one they rose and joined him.

The barber picked the cloth from the floor. He began to fold it
neatly. "Boys, don't do that. Will Mayes never done it. I know."

"Come on," McLendon said. He whirled. From his hip pocket pro-
truded the butt of a heavy automatic pistol. They went out. The
screen door crashed behind them reverberant in the dead air.

The barber wiped the razor carefully and swiftly, and put it away, and ran to the rear, and took his hat from the wall. "I'll be back as soon as I can," he said to the other barbers. "I cant let—" He went out, running. The two other barbers followed him to the door and caught it on the rebound, leaning out and looking up the street after him. The air was flat and dead. It had a metallic taste at the base of the tongue.

"What can he do?" the first said. The second one was saying "Jees Christ" under his breath. "I'd just as lief be Will Mayes as Hawk, if he gets McLendon riled."

"Jees Christ, Jees Christ," the second whispered.

"You reckon he really done it to her?" the first said.

II

She was thirty-eight or thirty-nine. She lived in a small frame house with her invalid mother and a thin, sallow, unflagging aunt, where each morning between ten and eleven she would appear on the porch in a lace-trimmed boudoir cap, to sit swinging in the porch swing until noon. After dinner she lay down for a while, until the afternoon began to cool. Then, in one of the three or four new voile dresses which she had each summer, she would go downtown to spend the afternoon in the stores with the other ladies, where they would handle the goods and haggle over the prices in cold immediate voices, without any intention of buying.

She was of comfortable people—not the best in Jefferson, but good people enough—and she was still on the slender side of ordinary looking, with a bright, faintly haggard manner and dress. When she was young she had a slender, nervous body and a sort of hard vivacity which enabled her for a time to ride upon the crest of the town's social life as exemplified by the high school party and church social period of her contemporaries while still children enough to be unclassconscious.

She was the last to realize that she was losing ground; that those among whom she had been a little brighter and louder flame than any other were beginning to learn the pleasure of snobbery—male— and retaliation—female. That was when her face began to wear that bright, haggard look. She still carried it to parties on shadowy porticoes and summer lawns, like a mask or a flag, with the bafflement of furious repudiation of truth in her eyes. One evening at a party she heard a boy and two girls, all schoolmates, talking. She never accepted another invitation.

She watched the girls with whom she had grown up as they married and got homes and children, but no man ever called on her steadily until the children of the other girls had been calling her "aunty" for several years, the while their mothers told them in bright voices about how popular Aunt Minnie had been as a girl. Then the town began to see her driving on Sunday afternoons with the cashier in the bank. He was a widower of about forty—a high-colored man, smelling always faintly of the barber shop or of whisky. He owned the first automobile in town, a red runabout; Minnie had the first motoring bonnet and veil the town ever saw. Then the town began to say: "Poor Minnie." "But she is old enough to take care of herself," others said. That was when she began to ask her old schoolmates that their children call her "cousin" instead of "aunty."

It was twelve years now since she had been relegated into adultery by public opinion, and eight years since the cashier had gone to a Memphis bank, returning for one day each Christmas, which he spent at an annual bachelors' party at a hunting club on the river. From behind their curtains the neighbors would see the party pass, and during the over-the-way Christmas day visiting they would tell her about him, about how well he looked, and how they heard that he was prospering in the city, watching with bright, secret eyes her haggard, bright face. Usually by that hour there would be a scent of whisky on her breath. It was supplied her by a youth, a clerk at the soda fountain: "Sure; I buy it for the old gal. I reckon she's entitled to a little fun."

Her mother kept to her room altogether now; the gaunt aunt ran the house. Against that background Minnie's bright dresses, her idle and empty days, had a quality of furious unreality. She went out in the evenings only with women now, neighbors, to the moving pictures. Each afternoon she dressed in one of the new dresses and went downtown alone, where her young "cousins" were already strolling in the late afternoons with their delicate, silken heads and thin, awkward arms and conscious hips, clinging to one another or shrieking and giggling with paired boys in the soda fountain when she passed and went on along the serried store fronts, in the doors of which the sitting and lounging men did not even follow her with their eyes any more.

III

The barber went swiftly up the street where the sparse lights, insect-swirled, glared in rigid and violent suspension in the lifeless air. The day had died in a pall of dust; above the darkened square, shrouded by the spent dust, the sky was as clear as the inside of a brass bell. Below the east was a rumour of the twice-waxed moon.

When he overtook them McLendon and three others were getting into a car parked in an alley. McLendon stooped his thick head, peering out beneath the top. "Changed your mind, did you?" he said. "Damn good thing; by God, tomorrow when this town hears about how you talked tonight—"

"Now, now," the other ex-soldier said. "Hawkshaw's all right. Come on, Hawk; jump in."

"Will Mayes never done it, boys," the barber said. "If anybody done it. Why, you all know well as I do there aint any town where they got better niggers than us. And you know how a lady will kind of think things about men when there aint any reason to, and Miss Minnie anyway—"

"Sure, sure," the soldier said. "We're just going to talk to him a little; that's all."

"Talk hell!" Butch said. "When we're through with the—"

"Shut up, for God's sake!" the soldier said. "Do you want everybody in town—"

"Tell them, by God!" McLendon said. "Tell every one of the sons that'll let a white woman—"

"Let's go; let's go: here's the other car." The second car slid squealing out of a cloud of dust at the alley mouth. McLendon started his car and took the lead. Dust lay like fog in the street. The street lights hung nimbused as in water. They drove on out of town.

A rutted lane turned at right angles. Dust hung above it too, and above all the land. The dark bulk of the ice plant, where the Negro Mayes was night watchman, rose against the sky. "Better stop here, hadn't we?" the soldier said. McLendon did not reply. He hurled the car up and slammed to a stop, the headlights glaring on the blank wall.

"Listen here, boys," the barber said; "if he's here, don't that prove he never done it? Dont it? If it was him, he would run. Dont you see he would?" The second car came up and stopped. McLendon got down; Butch sprang down beside him. "Listen, boys," the barber said.

"Cut the lights off!" McLendon said. The breathless dark rushed down. There was no sound in it save their lungs as they sought air in the parched dust in which for two months they had lived; then the diminishing crunch of McLendon's and Butch's feet, and a moment later McLendon's voice:

"Will! . . . Will!"

Below the east the wan hemorrhage of the moon increased. It heaved above the ridge, silvering the air, the dust, so that they seemed to breathe, live, in a bowl of molten lead. There was no sound of nightbird nor insect, no sound save their breathing and a faint ticking of contracting metal about the cars. When their bodies touched one another they seemed to sweat dryly, for no more moisture came. "Christ!" a voice said; "let's get out of here."

But they didn't move until vague noises began to grow out of the darkness ahead; then they got out and waited tensely in the breathless dark. There was another sound: a blow, a hissing expulsion of breath and McLendon cursing in undertone. They stood a moment longer, then they ran forward. They ran in a stumbling clump, as though they were fleeing something. "Kill him, kill the son," a voice whispered. McLendon flung them back.

"Not here," he said. "Get him into the car." "Kill him, kill the black son!" the voice murmured. They dragged the Negro to the car. The barber had waited beside the car. He could feel himself sweating and he knew he was going to be sick at the stomach.

"What is it, captains?" the Negro said. "I aint done nothing. 'Fore God, Mr John." Someone produced handcuffs. They worked busily about the Negro as though he were a post, quiet, intent, getting in one another's way. He submitted to the handcuffs, looking swiftly and constantly from dim face to dim face. "Who's here, captains?" he said, leaning to peer into the faces until they could feel his breath and smell his sweaty reek. He spoke a name or two. "What you all say I done, Mr John?"

McLendon jerked the car door open. "Get in!" he said.

The Negro did not move. "What you all going to do with me, Mr John? I aint done nothing. White folks, captains, I aint done nothing: I swear 'fore God." He called another name.

"Get in!" McLendon said. He struck the Negro. The others expelled their breath in a dry hissing and struck him with random blows and he whirled and cursed them, and swept back his manacled hands across their faces and slashed the barber upon the mouth, and the barber struck him also. "Get him in there," McLendon said. They pushed at him. He ceased struggling and got in and sat quietly as the others took their places. He sat between the barber and the soldier, drawing his limbs in so as not to touch them, his eyes going swiftly and constantly from face to face. Butch clung to the running board. The car moved on. The barber nursed his mouth with his handkerchief.

"What's the matter, Hawk?" the soldier said.

"Nothing," the barber said. They regained the highroad and turned away from town. The second car dropped back out of the dust. They went on gaining speed; the final fringe of houses dropped behind.

"Goddamn, he stinks!" the soldier said.

"We'll fix that," the drummer in front beside McLendon said. On the running board Butch cursed into the hot rush of air. The barber leaned suddenly forward and touched McLendon's arm.

"Let me out, John," he said.

"Jump out, niggerlover," McLendon said without turning his head. He drove swiftly. Behind them the sourceless lights of the second car glared in the dust. Presently McLendon turned into a narrow road. It was rutted with disuse. It led back to an abandoned brick kiln—a series of reddish mounds and weed- and vine-choked vats without bottom. It had been used for pasture once, until one day the owner missed one of his mules. Although he prodded carefully in the vats with a long pole, he could not even find the bottom of them.

"John," the barber said.

"Jump out, then," McLendon said, hurling the car along the ruts. Beside the barber the Negro spoke:

"Mr Henry."

The barber sat forward. The narrow tunnel of the road rushed up and past. Their motion was like an extinct furnace blast: cooler, but utterly dead. The car bounded from rut to rut.

"Mr Henry," the Negro said.

The barber began to tug furiously at the door. "Look out, there!" the soldier said, but the barber had already kicked the door open and swung onto the running board. The soldier leaned across the Negro and grasped at him, but he had already jumped. The car went on without checking speed.

The impetus hurled him crashing through dust-sheathed weeds, into the ditch. Dust puffed about him, and in a thin vicious crackling of sapless stems he lay choking and retching until the second car passed and died away. Then he rose and limped on until he reached the highroad and turned toward town, brushing at his clothes with his hands. The moon was higher, riding high and clear of the dust at last, and after a while the town began to glare beneath the dust. He went on, limping. Presently he heard cars and the glow of them grew in the dust behind him and he left the road and crouched again in the weeds until they passed. McLendon's car came last now. There were four people in it and Butch was not on the running board.

They went on; the dust swallowed them; the glare and the sound died away. The dust of them hung for a while, but soon the eternal dust absorbed it again. The barber climbed back onto the road and limped on toward town.

IV

As she dressed for supper on that Saturday evening, her own flesh felt like fever. Her hands trembled among the hooks and eyes, and her eyes had a feverish look, and her hair swirled crisp and crackling under the comb. While she was still dressing the friends called for her and sat while she donned her sheerest underthings and stockings and a new voile dress. "Do you feel strong enough to go out?" they said, their eyes bright too, with a dark glitter. "When you have had time to get over the shock, you must tell us what happened. What he said and did; everything."

In the leafed darkness, as they walked toward the square, she began to breathe deeply, something like a swimmer preparing to dive, until she ceased trembling, the four of them walking slowly because of the terrible heat and out of solicitude for her. But as they neared the square she began to tremble again, walking with her head up, her hands clenched at her sides, their voices about her murmurous, also with that feverish, glittering quality of their eyes.

They entered the square, she in the center of the group, fragile in her fresh dress. She was trembling worse. She walked slower and slower, as children eat ice cream, her head up and her eyes bright in the haggard banner of her face, passing the hotel and the coatless drummers in chairs along the curb looking around at her: "That's the one: see? The one in pink in the middle." "Is that her? What did they do with the nigger? Did they—?" "Sure. He's all right." "All right, is he?" "Sure. He went on a little trip." Then the drug store, where even the young men lounging in the doorway tipped their hats and followed with their eyes the motion of her hips and legs when she passed.

They went on, passing the lifted hats of the gentlemen, the suddenly ceased voices, deferent, protective. "Do you see?" the friends said. Their voices sounded like long, hovering sighs of hissing exultation. "There's not a Negro on the square. Not one."

They reached the picture show. It was like a miniature fairyland with its lighted lobby and colored lithographs of life caught in its terrible and beautiful mutations. Her lips began to tingle. In the dark, when the picture began, it would be all right; she could hold back the laughing so it would not waste away so fast and so soon. So she hurried on before the turning faces, the undertones of low astonishment, and they took their accustomed places where she could see the aisle against the silver glare and the young men and girls coming in two and two against it.

The lights flicked away; the screen glowed silver, and soon life began to unfold, beautiful and passionate and sad, while still the young men and girls entered, scented and sibilant in the half dark, their paired backs in silhouette delicate and sleek, their slim, quick bodies awkward, divinely young, while beyond them the silver dream accumulated, inevitably on and on. She began to laugh. In trying to suppress it, it made more noise than ever; heads began to turn. Still laughing, her friends raised her and led her out, and she stood at the curb, laughing on a high, sustained note, until the taxi came up and they helped her in.

They removed the pink voile and the sheer underthings and the stockings, and put her to bed, and cracked ice for her temples, and sent for the doctor. He was hard to locate, so they ministered to her with hushed ejaculations, renewing the ice and fanning her. While the ice was fresh and cold she stopped laughing and lay still for a time, moaning only a little. But soon the laughing welled again and her voice rose screaming.

"Shhhhhhhhhhh! Shhhhhhhhhhhhhhh!" they said, freshening the icepack, smoothing her hair, examining it for gray; "poor girl!" Then to one another: "Do you suppose anything really happened?" their eyes darkly aglitter, secret and passionate. "Shhhhhhhhhh! Poor girl! Poor Minnie!"

v

It was midnight when McLendon drove up to his neat new house. It was trim and fresh as a birdcage and almost as small, with its clean, green-and-white paint. He locked the car and mounted the porch and entered. His wife rose from a chair beside the reading lamp. McLendon stopped in the floor and stared at her until she looked down.

"Look at that clock," he said, lifting his arm, pointing. She stood before him, her face lowered, a magazine in her hands. Her face was pale, strained, and weary-looking. "Haven't I told you about sitting up like this, waiting to see when I come in?"

"John," she said. She laid the magazine down. Poised on the balls of his feet, he glared at her with his hot eyes, his sweating face.

"Didn't I tell you?" He went toward her. She looked up then. He caught her shoulder. She stood passive, looking at him.

"Don't, John. I couldn't sleep . . . The heat; something. Please, John. You're hurting me."

"Didn't I tell you?" He released her and half struck, half flung her across the chair, and she lay there and watched him quietly as he left the room.

He went on through the house, ripping off his shirt, and on the dark, screened porch at the rear he stood and mopped his head and shoulders with the shirt and flung it away. He took the pistol from his hip and laid it on the table beside the bed, and sat on the bed and removed his shoes, and rose and slipped his trousers off. He was sweating again already, and he stooped and hunted furiously for the shirt. At last he found it and wiped his body again, and, with his body pressed against the dusty screen, he stood panting. There was no movement, no sound, not even an insect. The dark world seemed to lie stricken beneath the cold moon and the lidless stars.

Discussion of Faulkner's "Dry September"

1. What is the effect of the razor in part I? Is it a sign of strength or impotence or what? What does the title suggest?

2. How do Minnie Cooper's clothes characterize her?

3. What is the effect of the structure, the cutting back and forth between the actions of the men and Minnie Cooper?

4. In stories that dramatize racial relationships, there are often analogies between racial exploitation and sexual exploitation. How does Faulkner's treatment of the theme differ from other authors'— for example, Wright's, Walker's, Betts's?

EDITH WHARTON

1862–1937

🌺 Born in New York City, Edith Wharton resided in Europe as an expatriate, like several American writers of her generation. Among her works are *The House of Mirth* (1905), *Ethan Frome* (1911), *The Age of Innocence* (1920), and *The Collected Stories of Edith Wharton* (1968, ed. R. W. B. Lewis). Her own assessment of her art and her life appear in *The Writing of Fiction* (1925) and her autobiography, *A Backward Glance* (1934). In his introduction to *Edith Wharton: A Collection of Critical Essays,* Irving Howe says that "no American novelist of our time—with the single exception of Nathanael West—has been so ruthless, so bitingly cold as Mrs. Wharton in assaulting the vulgarities and failures of our society" (Englewood Cliffs: Prentice-Hall, Inc., 1962, p. 4).

Permanent Wave

I

It gave Mrs. Vincent Craig a cold shiver to think how nearly she had missed her turn at Gaston's. Two women were already in the outer room, waiting to be waved, when she rushed in—"late as usual," (as her husband always said, in that irritating level voice of his).

The hairdresser looked at her with astonishment.

"But I expected you yesterday, Mrs. Craig."

"Yesterday? Oh, that's a mistake... I've got it written down here." She plunged into her bag for her engagement book, but brought up only a passport and a bunch of travelers' checks, which she didn't want seen, and thrust back hurriedly.

"I must have left my book at home. But I have the day written down. . . ."

The busy hairdresser shrugged. "So have I. But anyhow your appointment was for two."

"Well, what time is it now? Only a quarter past." After that it had taken all her arguments, persuasions, feigned indignations, fawning flattery even, to persuade the illustrious hairdresser that he had no right, absolutely no right, to give away her appointment simply because she was a few minutes late. ("Oh, half an hour? Really, Gaston, you exaggerate! Look at my watch . . . well, it was my husband who gave me that watch. Do you wonder if it's sometimes a little slow?") And finally, with a faint conniving smile, and a shrug at the two fuming women in the background, the artist had let Mrs. Craig slip into the tiled sanctuary.

Oh, the relief—the release from that cold immediate menace! It ran down Nalda Craig in little streams of retrospective fear, as if she had been sleepwalking, and suddenly opened her eyes just as she hung above a precipice. Think of it! If she had had to join Phil Ingerson at the station the next morning with a mop of lank irregular hair —for it wanted cutting as well as waving; and goodness knows, in the end-of-the-world places he and she were bound for, how soon she'd have another chance of being properly "done." Ah, how she'd always envied women with a natural wave! No difficulty for *them* in eloping with explorers. Of course they had to undergo the waving ordeal now and then too, but not nearly so often. . . . Well, if there were good hairdressers in Central America, she only hoped Phil wouldn't grouse about the expense, as Vincent had always done, playfully at first, then half irritably, then with that thin disparaging smile of his. "What, another barber's bill? Let's see if you've really been there this time." For, unless he scrutinized her closely, applied his mind to it, as well as his puzzled unseeing eyes, he never knew if her hair had been newly waved or not.

All the better, perhaps, in the present case. For her last wave was only three weeks old, and if Vincent had been a little more observant he might have said, when they met at dinner that evening: "Hello, hel-lo! Another twenty-dollar ripple already?" And as they were dining alone that night, and she could not dodge behind the general talk, it might have been awkward to explain. But as it was, he would sit there all the evening with his nose in his book, and if she should appear before him with her head shaved instead of waved he would never notice that either.

It was that which had been such a disillusionment when they were first married; his not being at every moment acutely conscious of her looks, her clothes, her graces, of what she was thinking or feeling. More than once she had nearly burst out: "If only you'd find fault with me!" But on the rare occasions when he did find fault she didn't like that either. Her mother and grandmother had brought her up with such different ideas of a husband's obligations toward his wife. "My husband was my lover to the end," her grandmother used to simper, turning on all her withered dimples; and Nalda's mother, though of course she didn't put it so romantically, always said: "Whatever your father's faults may have been," (it was hinted that conviviality was not the only one) "he was always the chivalrous gentleman where his wife was concerned."

It all sounded funny and old-fashioned; but if it meant anything at all, it meant, in modern lingo, that your husband was your pal, and that he backed up his little woman through thick and thin, and paid the bills without grumbling. Whereas Nalda had more than once had to borrow money in secret; and when she had that nasty dispute with the dressmaker about the price of her broadtail coat Vincent hadn't backed up his little woman for a cent. . . .

Well, she had on the broadtail when she first met Phil Ingerson. It was at that skating party on the river that the Pressly Normans had got up; and could she help it if she was prettier than the other women, and if her fur coat was out and away the smartest there, and if her hair had been "permed" the day before, and looked as lustrous as a chestnut just out of the burr? It was funny, perhaps, to date such an overwhelming event as her first encounter with Phil Ingerson by the fact of her having been waved the previous day; but then being waved gave one, as nothing else did, no, not even a new hat, that sense of security and power which a woman never needed more than at her first meeting with the man who was to remake her life....

II

Funny—she remembered now how bored and restless she used to get during the interminable waving *séance*. Four hours of immobility; "in the stocks," as Winna Norman called it. When you had run through Gaston's supply of picture papers, and exchanged platitudes with the other victims, if they happened to be acquaintances, there was simply nothing to do but to yawn and fidget, and think of all the worries and bothers which could be kept in abeyance at other times by bridge and golf and tennis, and rushing about, always a little late, to one's engagements. Yes; she had chafed at the imprisonment then: called it "serving a life sentence"; but since she had known Phil Ingerson (six months it must be, for this was her fourth wave since their first meeting) she had come to look forward to that four hours' immobility as a time for brooding over their friendship, taking stock of herself and of him. No leisure would have seemed too long for that, she thought. She looked at the driven faces of the other women, desperately enduring the four hours' imprisonment with their own thoughts; then she sank back into her secret bath of beatitude. There was so much to occupy her thoughts; every word of Phil's, every glance, his smile, his laugh, his comments on her dress and her looks (*he* never failed to notice when she had been newly waved!), and his odd paradoxical judgments of life and men, which were never exactly what one expected, and therefore so endlessly exciting—whereas with poor Vincent you could tell before he opened his mouth what he was going to say, and say it for him more quickly than he could get it out.

Not that (she interrupted herself parenthetically) she did not appreciate Vincent. Of course she did. She had always appreciated him. She knew how high he stood in his profession, how much the University esteemed him as a lecturer, and as an authority on his particular subject. And of course economics had become such an important branch of learning that Vincent Craig's name was known far beyond the University, and he sat up late writing learned articles for historical reviews and philosophical quarterlies; and she had even, at a New York reception, heard someone to whom she had been pointed out, eagerly rejoin; "What? The wife of *the* Vincent Craig? Is *he* here, by any chance?"

No one should dare to say she had not appreciated Vincent—she wasn't as stupid as all that! Only, when a man's life is wrapped up in economics, so little is left over for his wife. And had Vincent ever appreciated *her?* Hadn't he always taken her as much for granted as the cook, or the electric light, or the roof over his head? He had never seemed to be aware of her personality; and nothing was as humiliating to a woman as that. When he went out in the morning did it ever occur to him that he might not find his wife at the head of his table when he returned at night? What had he ever known of such palpitating anguish as she felt when, after every parting with Phil, she asked herself: "Shall I ever see him again?" or of the absurd boyish rapture with which, at every sight of her, Phil would exclaim: "I thought you were never coming! What on earth has kept you so long?"

Phil, in short, measured his hours by her comings and goings; Vincent measured his by college tasks, professional appointments, literary obligations, or interviewing people about gas and electricity and taxes. The two men lived in different worlds, between which, for the last months, Nalda had been swept on alternating currents of passion and compunction. . . .

For of course—again—she was sorry, by anticipation, for Vincent. He would hate to have her leave him, even though her presence made so little difference—or seemed to. For she could not but remember how, after her bad grippe and pneumonia, he had burst into tears the first day he was readmitted to her room, and the nurse had had to hurry him out again lest he should "bring back the fever." She smiled a little over the memory, self-complacently; and amusedly at the recollection of his re-appearing, the next day, with two-pound bag of *marrons glacés,* as the appropriate offering to a woman whose palate still shuddered at anything less ethereal than a grape! "Why, I thought you liked them," he had stammered. "Perhaps you'll fancy one later—" and left the sticky nauseating bag on her bed when he went out. . . . Old Vincent!

There hadn't been much time to conjecture as to how Phil would behave if she were very ill; but something already whispered to her that she had better not try the experiment. "He wouldn't know how . . ." she thought; and her lip curled with a sudden sense of their youth and power, and the mysterious security of their passion. . . .

III

Of course it was for her, and her alone, that Phil had turned up at Kingsbridge so often during the last months. He said the grave was a circus compared with a university town; and especially a New England university town. West of the Rockies academic life might have a little more ginger in it; but in the very capital of the Cut-and-Dried there was nothing doing for a young fellow of such varied ambitions and subversive views as Phil Ingerson, and he frankly confessed to Nalda that he had *dashed* down for a weekend with his aunt Miss Marcham (one of the social and financial pillars of the University) only because he was in pursuit, at the moment, of a good-looking girl he had run across on a West Indian cruise, and who kept house for her brother, a Kingsbridge professor. Poor Olive Fresno!—cutting her out had been part of the fun in the early days of Nalda's encounter with Phil. The girl had her points (Nalda was the first to admit it), and she had evidently been thawed out by the easy promiscuities of the cruise. But back under her brother's roof (he was Professor of Comparative Theology) she had turned icicle again, a blushing agonizing icicle, whom it was fun to taunt and tantalize; and to eclipse her with the easily bored Phil had been a walk-over for Mrs. Craig.

Now, as Nalda sat there, with her Medusa locks in the steel clutch of the waver, she felt, she couldn't tell why, a sudden pang of compunction about Olive Fresno. It wasn't Nalda's fault; of course, if the first sight of her (yes, that wonderful first day on the ice) had sealed poor Olive's fate. Nalda didn't for a moment imagine that, if she'd behaved differently, the Fresno girl might have got what she wanted; she simply shivered a little at the apparently inevitable cost of happiness. Life was so constituted that when you grabbed what you wanted you always left somebody else to pay the damages. All that was as old as the hills; but it had suddenly turned, in Nalda's mind, from a copybook axiom into a burning reality. . . .

Not indeed in terms of Olive Fresno. The person of whom Nalda was really thinking, under that disguise, was her husband. For the first time in her life she pictured to herself what he would suffer. Once, when she had spoken of it to Phil (just to see if it would make him jealous), he had vexed her by saying with a laugh: "Suffer—what for? Why shouldn't he marry Olive?"

It was not what she had meant him to say, and she had been distinctly offended. But she herself, at that time, had not been really sorry for her husband; she had simply been using him as a spice to whet Phil's appetite. Now it was different. Now that everything was irrevocably settled, even to the passport in her pocket, she knew for the first time what Vincent was feeling, seemed even, in a queer unexpected way, to be feeling it with him, to be not only the cause of his suffering but a sharer in it. . . .

A moment later a reaction of pity for Phil set in. Look at the difference between the careers of the two men! Vincent Craig had gone from achievement to achievement, from one academic honor to another. He had been "*the* Vincent Craig" for years now. And Phil (as he had often told her) had had the academic world against him from the start. Even his aunt, with all her influence at Kingsbridge, had never been able to interest the University authorities in what he called his discoveries, and they called his theories. And the articles he had published on his archaeological expedition in Central America, which his aunt had financed, had been passed over in silence in high quarters.

The woman nearest to Nalda said to her neighbor on the other side: "I never choose a day for this but just as I start there's a rumpus at home. This time it's the new girl. . . ."

The other responded drearily: "I don't have to have my hair waved to have trouble with the help."

There was a long silence. Then one of the two said: "I see they're going to wear those uncrushable velvets a good deal this winter."

"Well, all I can say is, mine was a rag when I took it out of the trunk—"

Nalda nestled down again into her own warm dream. Thank heaven she wasn't going to hear any more of that sort of talk—oh, not for ages, she hoped! Not that she wasn't interested in this new uncrushable velvet . . . she rather wished now she'd had her one good dress made of it, instead of a flowered chiffon. But chiffon took up so much less room, and Phil seemed to be as fussy as other men about too much luggage. . . . And after all, as they would have to do a good deal of flying. . . .

A sudden anxiety stirred in her. Miss Marcham, she knew, had given Phil the new airplane in which he was to explore the inaccessible ruins of Yucatan; the expedition which, if successful, would confirm his theory as to the introduction of Oriental culture to the Western hemisphere in—well, she simply never could remember whether it was B.C. something, or very early A.D. And Phil wouldn't mind her not remembering. He said he didn't want to elope with the *Encyclopedia Britannica*; on the contrary. . . . Only, if Miss Marcham, who was such an important figure at Kingsbridge, and took such a serious view of her standing in the university world—if Miss Marcham had known that the airplane she had paid for was to be used by her nephew to carry off the wife of Professor Vincent Craig. . . .

"What I always say is, it pays in the end to get your groceries sent from New York. But of course the cook hates it. . . . What they like is to have the grocer calling everyday for orders. . . ."

Nalda had imparted her scruples about the airplane to Phil: but he had only laughed. "If it's any comfort to you, my dear, I didn't make my first expedition alone. . . ." It was no comfort to her, but it silenced her protest. She didn't want him to think her what he called "Kingsbridgy." And, after all, to make a fuss about a trifle like an airplane, when her leaving was going to shatter a man's life! Yes—Vincent's life would be shattered! That cold current again, through the soft Gulf Stream of her broodings. . . .

"Well, when I come here to be waved I always say to myself before I open the door: 'Now, whatever you do, *don't worry!* Because no matter what's going on at home, you can't help it.' "

"No; but it does make it worse to have four hours to think things over."

Ah, yes; this time the woman was right! Four hours *were* too long to think over a plight like Nalda Craig's. It was never safe to turn any sentiment inside out; and happiness perhaps least of all. Happiness ought to be like a spring breeze blowing in at the window, coming from one didn't know where, bearing the scent of invisible flowers. You couldn't take it to pieces and put it together, like a sum in arithmetic. . . . She began to wish the waving were over.

"Well, I think you'll be satisfied with this job, Mrs. Craig," Gaston said, fluttering her chestnut ripples through his wizard fingers. The other women had been released, and gone their ways, and she had the room to herself, and could smile back complacently at her reflection, without risk of having the smile registered over her shoulder by envious eyes. Yes, she was satisfied! She leaned back and yielded her head to the hairdresser's rapid manipulations. The four hours didn't seem long now. . . .

"Well, I must fly. Oh, here, Gaston—" she drew the twenty dollar bill from her bag. Then, involuntarily, she paused and glanced about the familiar walls of Gaston's operating room, as Winna Norman called it. It made things look so funny when you knew you were seeing them for the last time. She noticed that the woman next to her had left a box of rouge on the washstand.

Her eyes traveled slowly about the room; then she stopped short with an exclamation.

"Ma'am?" queried Gaston, who was busy with his helper preparing for the next batch of victims.

Nalda gave a nervous laugh. She was pointing to a calendar on the wall. "You're a day ahead, Gaston."

He turned and followed her glance.

"Why, no. Today's Thursday."

She began to tremble inwardly. "Today's Wednesday, Gaston."

He shrugged. "I guess it's you who are behind the times, Mrs. Craig. I always pull off the leaf first thing every morning, myself. I don't trust anybody else to do it."

"Are you sure it's Thursday?" she repeated, with dry lips, as if he had not spoken. But one of the women she had ousted was coming back, sulkily, to be marcelled; and Gaston was already engaged in installing her.

Nalda walked blindly out of the shop. She did not know she had left it until she heard the door swing to behind her. It was Thursday . . . it was Thursday . . . Gaston said he always pulled the page off the calendar every morning himself. . . . Instead of letting days and days pass, as she did, and then tearing off a bunch haphazardly. How often her husband had laughed at her for that! "Nalda never knows the day of the week. She says it would only cramp her style if she did. . . . "

A busy man who kept a shop couldn't afford to be as careless as that. If Gaston said it was Thursday, then it was Thursday.

IV

She walked on unsteadily, deaf and blind to the noise and whirl of the street. She turned out of the business quarter into the residential part of the town without being conscious of the direction she was taking. She seemed to be following her feet instead of being carried by them.

Thursday—but then, if it was Thursday, Phil would have been waiting for her at the station at ten o'clock that morning! Slowly her stunned brain began to take it in. And when the time came for the start, and she was not there—what then? Wouldn't he have rushed to the house, or sent a message, or a telephone call? They always avoided telephoning in the mornings because her husband was sure to be in his study till twelve, and likely to emerge suddenly on the landing and unhook the receiver himself. But in any case, unless Phil decided to miss the train, there would be no time for telephoning. She was so notoriously unpunctual that till the very last minute he would be fuming up and down the platform, or leaning out watching for her; and when the train started he would start with it. Oh, she knew that as well as she knew her own name!

And how indeed could he do otherwise? The train they had fixed upon was the last which would get them to New York in time to catch the steamer—and the steamer was the only one to sail that month for Progreso. Dates and hours had been fitted together with the boyish nicety which characterized Phil when he was dealing with anything connected with his travels. Bent above maps and time-tables, his face grew as round and absorbed as a schoolboy's. And in New York, she knew, there would be just time to pick up his outfit: he'd talked to her enough about that famous outfit! Just time for that, and a taxi rush to the steamer. And the expedition came first in his mind—that fact had always been clear to Nalda. It was as it should be; as she wanted it to be. . . . And if a poor little woman, who had imagined she couldn't live without him, got cold feet at the last minute, and failed to turn up—well, with the exploring fever on him, he'd probably take even that with a shrug, for he was committed to the enterprise, and would have to go without her if she failed him.

And she *had* failed him—through sheer muddle-headedness, through unpardonable stupidity, the childish blunder of mistaking one day of the week for another, she had failed him; and of course he would always think it was because she hadn't had the pluck. . . .

"You'll see, my child, you'll funk it at the last minute. No woman really likes hardships; and this trip isn't going to be any season at Palm Beach," Phil had warned her, laughing and throwing out his chest a little.

She found herself on her own doorstep, and fumbled for her latch-key. It was not in her bag, and she rang the bell furiously.

"Is there a telegram?"

No; the maid who opened the door said there was none. Of course there was none; how should there be?

"I've mislaid my key," Nalda said, to say something.

The maid smiled. "Here it is. The Professor picked it up on the doorstep."

Of course—how like her again! Lucky she hadn't dropped the passport and the travelers' checks while she was about it.

She started up the stairs to her room. She thought: "If I hadn't mistaken the day I should have gone up these stairs tonight for the last time. I should never again have noticed that tear in the carpet, and said to myself: 'I must telephone at once to the upholsterer to send somebody to mend it.' "

Time and again her husband had said to her: "For heaven's sake get that tear in the stair carpet mended. It'll be the death of somebody. I caught my heel in it again last night." She had always said yes, and then forgotten; and it was because she had that kind of mind, with great holes in it like the hole in the stair carpet, that, instead of going up those stairs for the last time tonight, she would probably continue to go up them everyday for the rest of her life. It was queer, how unexpected things hung together. . . .

As she mounted the stairs her mind continued to rush through every possibility of retrieving the blunder of the date. But already she had the feeling that these dizzy feats of readjustment were being performed in the void, by some one who was not really herself. No; her real self was here, on this shabby familiar stair carpet, going up to the room which had been the setting of her monotonous married years. It was curious; she had no faith any longer in the reality of that other future toward which, a few hours ago, every drop of blood in her was straining. What if she should rush out again, and at least send off a wire to the steamer? No; that was not possible either. The steamer sailed at seven, and her bedroom clock (which always kept good time because Vincent saw to the clocks) told her that it was already past the hour.

But would she have telegraphed, even if there had been time? What could she have said? "Made a mistake in the day"? That was too humiliating. . . . Better let him think that her courage *had* failed her . . . or that a sense of duty. . . . But no; not that either. They had made too many jokes about that coward's pretext, the Sense of Duty. . . .

She tossed off her hat and sat down wearily. Her mind, sick of revolving in its endless maze, became suddenly cold and quiescent. This was the way things had been meant to happen, she supposed. . . .

Well, she thought, at any rate she would be alone this one evening. Thursday—the first Thursday of the month—was the night of her husband's Club dinner; the dinner which was the cause of so many pleasantries, and so much secret anxiety, among the ladies of the faculty, because of the late hour at which their husbands got home from it, but which had never troubled Nalda, since at eleven she could always count on hearing Vincent's punctual key in the lock.

Poor old Vincent—! She wondered what he would have said and done, if, returning home, he had found her gone?

There was a knock on the door and she started up. A telegram after all? "Yes?" she said.

"Dinner's ready, ma'am. The Professor sent me up to say—"

"Dinner?" She repeated the word slowly, trying to fit it into her mind. "I don't want any dinner. Mr. Craig's going out, isn't he?"

"Why, no; he hasn't mentioned it."

She stared at the woman, bewildered. It was extraordinary, incredible! Her husband, who never forgot anything, whose memory was so irritatingly retentive of every trifle, her husband had actually forgotten his famous Club dinner, the one social event which seemed to give him any pleasure, the one nonprofessional engagement with which nothing was allowed to interfere.

"Are you sure Mr. Craig hasn't gone out?"

"No, ma'am; Mr. Craig's in the library."

"But it's the night of his Club dinner. He must have forgotten. . . . I'll go down."

She sprang up, and then stood still, hesitating. She had been so thankful that she would not have to see her husband that night. What could have happened? Perhaps he had simply fallen asleep before the library fire. Daytime naps were not his habit—but she knew he had been very much overworked of late, and had reached a difficult controversial point in the course of lectures he was preparing. Even Winna Norman, who seldom noticed anything beyond the range of her personal interests, had said not long ago: "Look here, what's the matter with your domestic jailer? Looks as if he's been dug up. You'd better pack him off somewhere for a change."

Nalda had not paid any heed at the moment; she had no time to study Vincent's features, and she had fancied that Winna, who liked stirring up mud, and certainly suspected something about herself and Phil Ingerson, had simply wanted to give her a fright—or perhaps a warning. Fright or warning, Nalda had taken neither; she was too securely encased in her own bliss. But now she did remember being conscious that her husband of late had looked suddenly older, walked with a stoop. . . . She went slowly down the stairs, and slowly turned the handle of the library door.

"Vincent—?"

He was not asleep now, at any rate. He stood up quickly, and faced her with his dry smile. "Late, eh—as usual?" (Oh, why had he hit on that hated phrase?) "I'm rather disposed to dine, if you've no objection."

"But you're dining out tonight! Have you forgotten?" Even through the thick cloud of her misery it gave her a passing gleam of satisfaction to remind him, for once, of something he had forgotten.

His face clouded. "Dining out? Again? Good heavens! You promised solemnly only last week that you wouldn't accept another invitation for me till I'd finished this job. . . ."

"I haven't. Tonight is your Club dinner."

"Club dinner?" He looked relieved. "You're a day out, my child. My Club dinner's tomorrow."

"It always has been on a Thursday."

"Well—tomorrow's Thursday."

She gave a little nervous laugh. "No; today is."

"Today Thursday?" He smiled again. "I sometimes wonder how you ever keep your own engagements, let alone trying to keep mine for me."

"But this is Thursday—it *is* Thursday," she repeated vehemently, as though, after what she had undergone, it *had* to be Thursday now, for all time, if she said so.

"Bless your innocent heart, today's Wednesday."

"Wednesday?"

"Certainly. Why—what's wrong? Does it interfere with your plans, its being Wednesday?"

She stood before him, conscious that she was beginning to tremble. What on earth did his question mean? She clutched blindly at the back of the nearest chair. "With my plans?"

"I thought maybe you'd arranged to run round to Winna Norman's and talk about clothes," he joked.

She gave another little laugh, this time of relief; then she checked herself fiercely, as she felt the dangerous ripple prolonging itself in her throat. "It *is* Thursday, you know," she insisted with dry lips.

He lifted the calendar from his desk and held it out to her. "I turn it myself every morning. I don't trust anybody else to do it for me," he said, strangely echoing the hairdresser's words. She read: WEDNESDAY, in great staring block letters, and suddenly the uncontrollable ripple rose in her throat and forced its way through her clenched lips. She dropped down into the chair on which she had been leaning, and laughed and laughed and laughed. . . .

The last she remembered was seeing her husband's face above her, gray with fright, and saying to herself: "Winna was right. . . . Poor old Vincent—he looks like death. I'll have to take him away somewhere. . . ."

Then she knew that his arms were about her, and felt that with painful precautions he was lowering her slowly to the sofa, pushing back her suffocating hair, composing her limbs as if, with pious hands, he were preparing her for her final rest. . . .

"Poor old Vincent," she murmured again, as the fog closed in on her.

Discussion of Wharton's "Permanent Wave"

1. Compare the character of the husband in Wharton's story with that of the husband in Hemingway's "Cat in the Rain." Compare the wives in both stories. What epithet do both Vincent and Phil use when they address Nalda Craig? Does that epithet aid your comparison?

2. What specific language is used to describe the wave process in the beauty parlor? How does the language suggest a relationship between women and men? Include Gaston in your answer.

3. From the conversations and Mrs. Craig's thoughts, in what do women seem to be most interested? How does this interest relate to Mrs. Craig's attitude about her plans to escape her marriage?

KATHERINE MANSFIELD

1888–1923

❧ Katherine Mansfield was born in Wellington, New Zealand, attended school there as a girl, and went to Queen's College in London. Often traveling because of her health, she lived in many countries: England, France, Switzerland, and Italy, as well as her birthplace. Married only one day, she left her husband, George Bowden, but returned to him for a few months. She divorced him in 1918 and married John Middleton Murry, writer and critic. He became her literary executor when tuberculosis caused her death in 1923. In the introduction to *The Journal of Katherine Mansfield* (ed. John Middleton Murry [New York: Alfred A. Knopf, 1927]), Murry describes the quality of her work "as a kind of *purity*. It is as though the glass through which she looked upon life were crystal-clear" (p. xv). And that crystal vision created surprisingly lifelike characters: Murry tells us that a printer, setting the type for one of her stories, exclaimed, " 'My! but these kids are real!' " (p. xi). Her short fiction appears in several collections: *In a German Pension* (1911), *Bliss and Other Stories* (1920), *The Garden-Party and Other Stories* (1922), *The Doves' Nest and Other Stories* (1923), and *Something Childish and Other Stories* (1924).

Psychology

When she opened the door and saw him standing there she was more pleased than ever before, and he, too, as he followed her into the studio, seemed very very happy to have come.

"Not busy?"

"No. Just going to have tea."

"And you are not expecting anybody?"

"Nobody at all."

"Ah! That's good."

He laid aside his coat and hat gently, lingeringly, as though he had time and to spare for everything, or as though he were taking leave of them for ever, and came over to the fire and held out his hands to the quick, leaping flame.

Just for a moment both of them stood silent in that leaping light. Still, as it were, they tasted on their smiling lips the sweet shock of their greeting. Their secret selves whispered:

"Why should we speak? Isn't this enough?"

"More than enough. I never realized until this moment . . ."

"How good it is just to be with you. . . ."

"Like this. . . ."

"It's more than enough."

But suddenly he turned and looked at her and she moved quickly away.

"Have a cigarette? I'll put the kettle on. Are you longing for tea?"

"No. Not longing."

"Well, I am."

"Oh, you." He thumped the Armenian cushion and flung on to the *sommier.* "You're a perfect little Chinee."

"Yes, I am," she laughed. "I long for tea as strong men long for wine."

She lighted the lamp under its broad orange shade, pulled the curtains and drew up the tea table. Two birds sang in the kettle; the fire fluttered. He sat up clasping his knees. It was delightful—this business of having tea—and she always had the delicious things to eat—little sharp sandwiches, short sweet almond fingers, and a dark, rich cake tasting of rum—but it was an interruption. He wanted it over, the table pushed away, their two chairs drawn up to the light, and the moment came when he took out his pipe, filled it, and said, pressing the tobacco tight into the bowl: "I have been thinking over what you said the last time and it seems to me . . ."

Yes, that was what he waited for and so did she. Yes, while she shook the teapot hot and dry over the spirit flame she saw those other two, him leaning back, taking his ease among the cushions, and her, curled up *en escargot* in the blue shell arm-chair. The picture was so clear and so minute it might have been painted on the blue teapot lid. And yet she couldn't hurry. She could almost have cried: "Give me time." She must have time in which to grow calm. She wanted time in which to free herself from all these familiar things with which she lived so vividly. For all these gay things round her were part of her—her offspring—and they knew it and made the largest, most vehement claims. But now they must go. They must be swept away, shooed away—like children, sent up the shadowy stairs, packed into bed and commanded to go to sleep—at once—without a murmur!

For the special thrilling quality of their friendship was in their complete surrender. Like two open cities in the midst of some vast plain their two minds lay open to each other. And it wasn't as if he rode into hers like a conqueror, armed to the eyebrows and seeing nothing but a gay silken flutter—nor did she enter his like a queen walking soft on petals. No, they were eager, serious travellers, absorbed in understanding what was to be seen and discovering what was hidden—making the most of this extraordinary absolute chance which made it possible for him to be utterly truthful to her and for her to be utterly sincere with him.

And the best of it was they were both of them old enough to enjoy their adventure to the full without any stupid emotional complication. Passion would have ruined everything; they quite saw that.

Besides, all that sort of thing was over and done with for both of them—he was thirty-one, she was thirty—they had had their experiences, and very rich and varied they had been, but now was the time for harvest—harvest. Weren't his novels to be very big novels indeed? And her plays. Who else had her exquisite sense of real English Comedy? . . .

Carefully she cut the cake into thick little wads and he reached across for a piece.

"Do you realize how good it is," she implored. "Eat it imaginatively. Roll your eyes if you can and taste it on the breath. It's not a sandwich from the hatter's bag—it's the kind of cake that might have been mentioned in the Book of Genesis. . . . And God said: 'Let there be cake. And there was cake. And God saw that it was good.' "

"You needn't entreat me," said he. "Really you needn't. It's a queer thing but I always do notice what I eat here and never anywhere else. I suppose it comes of living alone so long and always reading when I feed . . . my habit of looking upon food as just food . . . something that's there at certain times . . . to be devoured . . . to be . . . not there." He laughed. "That shocks you. Doesn't it?"

"To the bone," said she.

"But—look here——" He pushed away his cup and began to speak very fast. "I simply haven't got any external life at all. I don't know the names of things a bit—trees and so on—and I never notice places or furniture or what people look like. One room is just like another to me—a place to sit and read or talk in—except," and here he paused, smiled in a strange naïve way, and said, "except this studio." He looked round him and then at her; he laughed in his astonishment and pleasure. He was like a man who wakes up in a train to find that he has arrived, already, at the journey's end.

"Here's another queer thing. If I shut my eyes I can see this place down to every detail—every detail. . . . Now I come to think of it— I've never realized this consciously before. Often when I am away from here I revisit it in spirit—wander about among your red chairs, stare at the bowl of fruit on the black table—and just touch, very lightly, that marvel of a sleeping boy's head."

He looked at it as he spoke. It stood on the corner of the mantelpiece; the head to one side down-drooping, the lips parted, as though in his sleep the little boy listened to some sweet sound. . . .

"I love that little boy," he murmured. And then they both were silent.

A new silence came between them. Nothing in the least like the satisfactory pause that had followed their greetings—the "Well, here we are together again, and there's no reason why we shouldn't go on from just where we left off last time." That silence could be contained in the circle of warm, delightful fire and lamplight. How many times hadn't they flung something into it just for the fun of watching the ripples break on the easy shores. But into this unfamiliar pool the head of the little boy sleeping his timeless sleep dropped—and the ripples flowed away, away—boundlessly far—into deep glittering darkness.

And then both of them broke it. She said: "I must make up the fire," and he said: "I have been trying a new . . ." Both of them escaped. She made up the fire and put the table back, the blue chair was wheeled forward, she curled up and he lay back among the cushions. Quickly! Quickly! They must stop it from happening again.

"Well, I read the book you left last time."

"Oh, what do you think of it?"

They were off and all was as usual. But was it? Weren't they just a little too quick, too prompt with their replies, too ready to take each other up? Was this really anything more than a wonderfully good imitation of other occasions? His heart beat; her cheek burned and the stupid thing was she could not discover where exactly they were or what exactly was happening. She hadn't time to glance back. And just as she had got so far it happened again. They faltered, wavered, broke down, were silent. Again they were conscious of the boundless, questioning dark. Again, there they were—two hunters, bending over their fire, but hearing suddenly from the jungle beyond a shake of wind and a loud, questioning cry. . . .

She lifted her head. "It's raining," she murmured. And her voice was like his when he had said: "I love that little boy."

Well. Why didn't they just give way to it—yield—and see what will happen then? But no. Vague and troubled though they were, they knew enough to realize their precious friendship was in danger. She was the one who would be destroyed—not they—and they'd be no party to that.

He got up, knocked out his pipe, ran his hand through his hair and said: "I have been wondering very much lately whether the novel of the future will be a psychological novel or not. How sure are you that psychology *qua* psychology has got anything to do with literature at all?"

"Do you mean you feel there's quite a chance that the mysterious non-existent creatures—the young writers of today—are trying simply to jump the psycho-analyst's claim?"

"Yes, I do. And I think it's because this generation is just wise enough to know that it is sick and to realize that its only chance of recovery is by going into its symptoms—making an exhaustive study of them—tracking them down—trying to get at the root of the trouble."

"But oh," she wailed. "What a dreadfully dismal outlook."

"Not at all," said he. "Look here . . ." On the talk went. And now it seemed they really had succeeded. She turned in her chair to look at him while she answered. Her smile said: "We have won." And he smiled back, confident: "Absolutely."

But the smile undid them. It lasted too long; it became a grin. They saw themselves as two little grinning puppets jigging away in nothingness.

"What have we been talking about?" thought he. He was so utterly bored he almost groaned.

"What a spectacle we have made of ourselves," thought she. And she saw him laboriously—oh, laboriously—laying out the grounds and herself running after, putting here a tree and there a flowery shrub and here a handful of glittering fish in a pool. They were silent this time from sheer dismay.

The clock struck six merry little pings and the fire made a soft flutter. What fools they were—heavy, stodgy, elderly—with positively upholstered minds.

And now the silence put a spell upon them like solemn music. It was anguish—anguish for her to bear it and he would die—he'd die if it were broken. . . . And yet he longed to break it. Not by speech. At any rate not by their ordinary maddening chatter. There was another way for them to speak to each other, and in the new way he wanted to murmur: "Do you feel this too? Do you understand it at all?" . . .

Instead, to his horror, he heard himself say: "I must be off; I'm meeting Brand at six."

What devil made him say that instead of the other? She jumped—simply jumped out of her chair, and he heard her crying: "You must rush, then. He's so punctual. Why didn't you say so before?"

"You've hurt me; you've hurt me! We've failed!" said her secret self while she handed him his hat and stick, smiling gaily. She wouldn't give him a moment for another word, but ran along the passage and opened the big outer door.

Could they leave each other like this? How could they? He stood on the step and she just inside holding the door. It was not raining now.

"You've hurt me—hurt me," said her heart. "Why don't you go? No, don't go. Stay. No—go!" And she looked out upon the night.

She saw the beautiful fall of the steps, the dark garden ringed with glittering ivy, on the other side of the road the huge bare willows and above them the sky big and bright with stars. But of course he would see nothing of all this. He was superior to it all. He—with his wonderful "spiritual" vision!

She was right. He did see nothing at all. Misery! He'd missed it. It was too late to do anything now. Was it too late? Yes, it was. A cold snatch of hateful wind blew into the garden. Curse life! He heard her cry "au revoir" and the door slammed.

Running back into the studio she behaved so strangely. She ran up and down lifting her arms and crying: "Oh! Oh! How stupid! How imbecile! How stupid!" And then she flung herself down on the *sommier* thinking of nothing—just lying there in her rage. All was over. What was over? Oh—something was. And she'd never see him again—never. After a long long time (or perhaps ten minutes) had passed in that black gulf her bell rang a sharp quick jingle. It was he, of course. And equally, of course, she oughtn't to have paid the slightest attention to it but just let it go on ringing and ringing. She flew to answer.

On the doorstep there stood an elderly virgin, a pathetic creature who simply idolized her (heaven knows why) and had this habit of turning up and ringing the bell and then saying, when she opened the door: "My dear, send me away!" She never did. As a rule she asked her in and let her admire everything and accepted the bunch of slightly soiled looking flowers—more than graciously. But today . . .

"Oh, I am sorry," she cried. "But I've got some one with me. We are working on some woodcuts. I'm hopelessly busy all evening."

"It doesn't matter. It doesn't matter at all, darling," said the good friend. "I was just passing and I thought I'd leave you some violets." She fumbled down among the ribs of a large old umbrella. "I put them down here. Such a good place to keep flowers out of the wind. Here they are," she said, shaking out a little dead bunch.

For a moment she did not take the violets. But while she stood just inside, holding the door, a strange thing happened. . . . Again she saw the beautiful fall of the steps, the dark garden ringed with glittering ivy, the willows, the big bright sky. Again she felt the silence that was like a question. But this time she did not hesitate. She moved forward. Very softly and gently, as though fearful of making a ripple in that boundless pool of quiet she put her arms round her friend.

"My dear," murmured her happy friend, quite overcome by this gratitude. "They are really nothing. Just the simplest little thrippenny bunch."

But as she spoke she was enfolded—more tenderly, more beautifully embraced, held by such a sweet pressure and for so long that the poor dear's mind positively reeled and she just had the strength to quaver: "Then you really don't mind me too much?"

"Good night, my friend," whispered the other. "Come again soon."

"Oh, I will. I will."

This time she walked back to the studio slowly, and standing in the middle of the room with half-shut eyes she felt so light, so rested, as if she had woken up out of a childish sleep. Even the act of breathing was a joy. . . .

The *sommier* was very untidy. All the cushions "like furious mountains" as she said; she put them in order before going over to the writing-table.

"I have been thinking over our talk about the psychological novel," she dashed off, "it really is interesting." . . . And so on and so on.

At the end she wrote: "Good night, my friend. Come again soon."

Discussion of Mansfield's "Psychology"

1. Notice the setting—its appointments that suggest gentility and coziness. How is the atmosphere that is established by the setting reinforced by the introduction of French words into the narrative?

2. What is the effect of such a setting in which to present the action of this story? Are the two characters' behaviors consistent with the setting?

3. Compare the actions and the attitudes of these characters with those of "Veronika," "Giving Blood," and "Beasts of the Southern Wild." What are the similarities and differences in the relationships between the men and the women and how do they manifest those relationships?

4. What do "Cicely's Dream," "A Painful Case," and "Psychology" show us about the unspoken bases of friendships between women and men?

RICHARD WRIGHT

1908–1960

🌷 When he was nineteen, Richard Wright left the American South, where he was born near Natchez, Mississippi. In Chicago he began his writing career, which included *Uncle Tom's Children: Four Novellas* (1938), republished in 1940 with the addition of a final story and an autobiographical piece, "The Ethics of Living Jim Crow." His biographer tells us that when Eleanor Roosevelt reacted with tears to his first work, Richard Wright was determined to make readers feel the necessity to act instead of merely to cry (Constance Webb, *Richard Wright: A Biography* [New York: Putnam, 1968], pp. 168–169). Among his novels are *Native Son* (1940), *The Outsider* (1953), and *The Long Dream* (1958); his short stories appear in *Eight Men* (1961). In addition to magazine articles and reviews, he published several books of nonfiction that include *12 Million Black Voices* (1941), *Pagan Spain* (1956), *White Man, Listen!* (1957), and his autobiography, *Black Boy: A Record of Childhood and Youth* (1945). "A Long Black Song" is from *Uncle Tom's Children*, a collection that reveals consciousness and the will to act emerging within a group of oppressed women and men.

Long Black Song

I

Go t sleep, baby
Papas gone t town
Go t sleep, baby
The suns goin down
Go t sleep, baby
Yo candys in the sack
Go t sleep, baby
Papas comin back . . .

Over and over she crooned, and at each lull of her voice she rocked the wooden cradle with a bare black foot. But the baby squalled louder, its wail drowning out the song. She stopped and stood over the cradle, wondering what was bothering it, if its stomach hurt. She felt the diaper; it was dry. She lifted it up and patted its back. Still it cried, longer and louder. She put it back into the cradle and dangled a string of red beads before its eyes. The little black fingers clawed them away. She bent over, frowning, murmuring: "Whuts the mattah, chile? Yuh wan some watah?" She held a dripping gourd to the black lips, but the baby turned its head and kicked its legs. She stood a moment, perplexed. Whuts wrong wid that chile? She ain never carried on like this this tima day. She picked it up and went to the open door. "See the sun, baby?" she asked, pointing to a big ball of red dying between the branches of trees. The baby pulled back and strained its round black arms and legs against her stomach and shoulders. She knew it was tired; she could tell by the halting way it opened its mouth to draw in air. She sat on a wooden stool, un-buttoned the front of her dress, brought the baby closer and offered it a black teat.

"Don baby wan suppah?" It pulled away and went limp, crying softly, piteously, as though it would never stop. Then it pushed its fingers against her breasts and wailed. Lawd, chile, what yuh wan? Yo ma cant hep yuh less she knows whut yuh wan. Tears gushed; four white teeth flashed in red gums; the little chest heaved up and down and round black fingers stretched floorward. Lawd, chile, whuts wrong wid yuh? She stooped slowly, allowing her body to be guided by the downward tug. As soon as the little fingers touched the floor the wail quieted into a broken sniffle. She turned the baby loose and watched it crawl toward a corner. She followed and saw the little fingers reach for the tail-end of an eight-day clock. "Yuh wan tha ol clock?" She dragged the clock into the center of the floor. The baby crawled after it, calling, "Ahh!" Then it raised its hands and beat on the top of the clock Bink! Bink! Bink! "Naw, yuhll hurt yo hans!" She held the baby and looked around. It cried and struggled. "Wait baby!" She fetched a small stick from the top of a rickety dresser. "Here," she said, closing the little fingers about it. "Beat wid this, see?" She heard each blow landing squarely on top of the clock. Bang! Bang! Bang! And with each bang the baby smiled and said, "Ahh!" Mabbe thall keep yuh quiet erwhile. Mabbe Ah kin git some res now. She stood in the doorway. Lawd, tha chiles a pain! She mus be teethin. Er something . . .

She wiped sweat from her forehead with the bottom of her dress and looked out over the green fields rolling up the hillsides. She sighed, fighting a feeling of loneliness. Lawd, its sho hard t pass the days wid Silas gone. Been mos a week now since he took the wagon outta here. Hope ain nothin wrong. He must be buyin a heapa stuff there in Colwatah t be stayin all this time. Yes; maybe Silas would remember and bring that five-yard piece of red calico she wanted. Oh, Lawd! Ah *hope* he don fergit it!

She saw green fields wrapped in the thickening gloam. It was as if they had left the earth, those fields, and were floating slowly sky-ward. The afterglow lingered, red, dying, somehow tenderly sad. And far away, in front of her, earth and sky met in a soft swoon of shadow. A cricket chirped, sharp and lonely; and it seemed she could hear it chirping long after it had stopped. Silas oughta c mon soon. Ahm tireda staying here by mahsef.

Loneliness ached in her. She swallowed, hearing Bang! Bang! Bang! Tom been gone t war mos a year now. N tha ol wars over n we ain heard nothing yit. Lawd, don let Tom be dead! She frowned into the gloam and wondered about that awful war so far away. They said it was over now. Yeah, Gowd had t stop em fo they killed everybody. She felt that merely to go so far away from home was a kind of death in itself. Just to go that far away was to be killed. Nothing good could come from men going miles across the sea to fight. N how come they wanna make blood? Killing was not what men ought to do. Shucks! she thought.

She sighed, thinking of Tom, hearing Bang! Bang! Bang! She saw Tom, saw his big black smiling face; her eyes went dreamily blank, drinking in the red afterglow. Yes, God; it could have been Tom instead of Silas who was having her now. Yes; it could have been Tom she was loving. She smiled and asked herself, Lawd, Ah wondah how would it been wid Tom? Against the plush sky she saw a white bright day and a green cornfield and she saw Tom walking in his overalls and she was with Tom and he had his arm about her waist. She remembered how weak she had felt feeling his fingers sinking into the flesh of her hips. Her knees had trembled and she had had a hard time trying to stand up and not just sink right there to the ground. Yes; that was what Tom had wanted her to do. But she had held Tom up and he had held her up; they had held each other up to keep from slipping to the ground there in the green cornfield. Lawd! Her breath went and she passed her tongue over her lips. But that was not as exciting as that winter evening when the grey skies were sleeping and she and Tom were coming home from church down dark Lover's Lane. She felt the tips of her teats tingling and touching the front of her dress as she remembered how he had crushed her against him and hurt her. She had closed her eyes and was smelling the acrid scent of dry October leaves and had gone weak in his arms and had felt she could not breathe any more and had torn away and run, run home. And the sweet ache which had frightened her then was stealing back to her loins now with the silence and the cricket calls and the red afterglow and Bang! Bang! Bang! Lawd, Ah wondah how would it been wid Tom?

She stepped out on the porch and leaned against the wall of the house. Sky sang a red song. Fields whispered a green prayer. And song and prayer were dying in silence and shadow. Never in all her life had she been so much alone as she was now. Days were never so long as these days; and nights were never so empty as these nights. She jerked her head impatiently, hearing Bang! Bang! Bang! Shucks! she thought. When Tom had gone something had ebbed so slowly that at first she had not noticed it. Now she felt all of it as though the feeling had no bottom. She tried to think just how it had happened. Yes; there had been all her life the long hope of white bright days and the deep desire of dark black nights and then Tom had gone.

Bang! Bang! Bang! There had been laughter and eating and singing and the long gladness of green cornfields in summer. There had
been cooking and sewing and sweeping and the deep dream of sleeping grey skies in winter. Always it had been like that and she had
been happy. But no more. The happiness of those days and nights,
of those green cornfields and grey skies had started to go from her
when Tom had gone to war. His leaving had left an empty black hole
in her heart, a black hole that Silas had come in and filled. But not
quite. Silas had not quite filled that hole. No; days and nights were
not as they were before.

She lifted her chin, listening. She had heard something, a dull
throb like she had heard that day Silas had called her outdoors to
look at the airplane. Her eyes swept the sky. But there was no plane.
Mabbe its behin the house? She stepped into the yard and looked upward through paling light. There were only a few big wet stars
trembling in the east. Then she heard the throb again. She turned,
looking up and down the road. The throb grew louder, droning; and
she heard Bang! Bang! Bang! There! A car! Wondah whuts a car
doin coming out here? A black car was winding over a dusty road,
coming toward her. Mabbe some white mans bringing Silas home
wida loada goods? But, Lawd, ah *hope* its no trouble! The car
stopped in front of the house and a white man got out. Wondah
whut he wans? She looked at the car, but could not see Silas. The
white man was young; he wore a straw hat and had no coat. He
walked toward her with a huge black package under his arm.

"Well, howre yuh today, Aunty?"

"Ahm well. How yuh?"

"Oh, so-so. Its sure hot today, hunh?"

She brushed her hand across her forehead and sighed.

"Yeah; it is kinda warm."

"You busy?"

"Naw, Ah ain doin nothin."

"Ive got something to show you. Can I sit here, on your porch?"

"Ah reckon so. But, Mistah, Ah ain got no money."

"Haven't you sold your cotton yet?"

"Silas gone t town wid it now."

"Whens he coming back?"

"Ah don know. Ahm waiting fer im."

She saw the white man take out a handkerchief and mop his face.
Bang! Bang! Bang! He turned his head and looked through the open
doorway, into the front room.

"Whats all that going on in there?"

She laughed.

"Aw, thas jus Ruth."

"Whats she doing?"

"She beatin tha ol clock."

"Beating a *clock*?"

She laughed again.

"She wouldn't go t sleep so Ah give her tha ol clock t play wid."

The white man got up and went to the front door; he stood a moment looking at the black baby hammering on the clock. Bang! Bang! Bang!

"But why let her tear your clock up?"

"It ain no good."

"You could have it fixed."

"We ain got no money t be fixin' no clocks."

"Haven't you got a clock?"

"Naw."

"But how do you keep time?"

"We git erlong widout time."

"But how do you know when to get up in the morning?"

"We jus git up, thas all."

"But how do you know what time it is when you get up?"

"We git up wid the sun."

"And at night, how do you tell when its night?"

"It gits dark when the sun goes down."

"Haven't you ever had a clock?"

She laughed and turned her face toward the silent fields. "Mistah, we don need no clock."

"Well, this beats everything! I don't see how in the world anybody can live without time."

"We just don need no time, Mistah."

The white man laughed and shook his head; she laughed and looked at him. The white man was funny. Jus like lil boy. Astin how do Ah know when t git up in the mawning! She laughed again and mused on the baby, hearing Bang! Bang! Bang! She could hear the white man breathing at her side; she felt his eyes on her face. She looked at him; she saw he was looking at her breasts. Hes jus lika lil boy. Acks like he cant understand *nothin!*

"But you need a clock," the white man insisted. "Thats what Im out here for. I'm selling clocks and graphophones. The clocks are made right into the graphophones, a nice sort of combination, hunh? You can have music and time all at once. Ill show you . . ."

"Mistah, we don need no clock!"

"You don't have to buy it. It wont cost you anything just to look."

He unpacked the big black box. She saw the strands of his auburn hair glinting in the afterglow. His back bulged against his white shirt as he stooped. He pulled out a square brown graphophone. She bent forward, looking. Lawd, but its pretty! She saw the face of a clock under the horn of the graphophone. The gilt on the corners sparkled. The color in the wood glowed softly. It reminded her of the light she saw sometimes in the baby's eyes. Slowly she slid a finger over a beveled edge; she wanted to take the box into her arms and kiss it.

"Its eight o'clock," he said.

"Yeah?"

"It only costs fifty dollars. And you dont have to pay for it all at once. Just five dollars down and five dollars a month."

She smiled. The white man was just like a little boy. Jus like a chile. She saw him grinding the handle of the box.

There was a sharp, scratching noise; then she moved nervously, her body caught in the ringing coils of music.

When the trumpet of the Lord shall sound . . .

She rose on circling waves of white bright days and dark black nights.

. . . and time shall be no more . . .

Higher and higher she mounted.

And the morning breaks . . .

Earth fell far behind, forgotten.

. . . eternal, bright and fair . . .

Echo after echo sounded.

When the saved of the earth shall gather . . .

Her blood surged like the long gladness of summer.

. . . over the other shore . . .

Her blood ebbed like the deep dream of sleep in winter.

And when the roll is called up yonder . . .

She gave up, holding her breath.

I'll be there . . .

A lump filled her throat. She leaned her back against a post, trembling, feeling the rise and fall of days and nights, of summer and winter; surging, ebbing, leaping about her, beyond her, far out over the fields to where earth and sky lay folded in darkness. She wanted to lie down and sleep, or else leap up and shout. When the music stopped she felt herself coming back, being let down slowly. She sighed. It was dark now. She looked into the doorway. The baby was sleeping on the floor. Ah gotta git up n put tha chile t bed, she thought.

"Wasn't that pretty?"

"It wuz pretty, awright."

"When do you think your husbands coming back?"

"Ah don know, Mistah."

She went into the room and put the baby into the cradle. She stood again in the doorway and looked at the shadowy box that had lifted her up and carried her away. Crickets called. The dark sky had swallowed up the earth, and more stars were hanging, clustered, burning. She heard the white man sigh. His face was lost in shadow. She saw him rub his palms over his forehead. Hes just lika lil boy.

"I'd like to see your husband tonight," he said. "Ive got to be in Lilydale at six o'clock in the morning and I wont be back through here soon. I got to pick up my buddy over there and we're heading North."

She smiled into the darkness. He was just like a little boy. A little boy selling clocks.

"Yuh sell them things alla time?" she asked.

"Just for the summer," he said. "I go to school in winter. If I can make enough money out of this Ill go to Chicago to school this fall . . ."

"Whut yuh gonna be?"

"*Be?* What do you mean?"

"Whut yuh goin to school fer?"

"Im studying science."

"Whuts tha?"

"Oh, er . . ." He looked at her. "Its about why things are as they are."

"Why things is as they *is?*"

"Well, its something like that."

"How come yuh wanna study tha?"

"Oh, you wouldn't understand."

She sighed.

"Naw, Ah guess Ah wouldnt."

"Well, I reckon Ill be getting along," said the white man. "Can I have a drink of water?"

"Sho. But we ain got nothin but well-watah, n yuhll have t come n git."

"Thats all right."

She slid off the porch and walked over the ground with bare feet. She heard the shoes of the white man behind her, falling to the earth in soft whispers. It was dark now. She led him to the well, groped her way, caught the bucket and let it down with a rope; she heard a splash and the bucket grew heavy. She drew it up, pulling against its weight, throwing one hand over the other, feeling the cool wet of the rope on her palms.

"Ah don git watah outa here much," she said, a little out of breath. "Silas gits the watah mos of the time. This buckets too heavy fer me."

"Oh, wait! Ill help!"

His shoulders touched hers. In the darkness she felt his warm hands fumbling for the rope.

"Where is it?"

"Here."

She extended the rope through the darkness. His fingers touched her breasts.

"Oh!"

She said it in spite of herself. He would think she was thinking about that. And he was a white man. She was sorry she had said that.

"Wheres the gourd?" he asked. "Gee, its dark!"

She stepped back and tried to see him.

"Here."

"I cant see!" he said, laughing.

Again she felt his fingers on the tips of her breasts. She backed away, saying nothing this time. She thrust the gourd out from her. Warm fingers met her cold hands. He had the gourd. She heard him drink; it was the faint, soft music of water going down a dry throat, the music of water in a silent night. He sighed and drank again.

"I was thirsty," he said. "I hadn't had any water since noon."

She knew he was standing in front of her; she could not see him, but she felt him. She heard the gourd rest against the wall of the well. She turned, then felt his hands full on her breasts. She struggled back.

"Naw, Mistah!"

"Im not going to hurt you!"

White arms were about her, tightly. She was still. But hes a *white* man. A *white* man. She felt his breath coming hot on her neck and where his hands held her breasts the flesh seemed to knot. She was rigid, poised; she swayed backward, then forward. She caught his shoulders and pushed.

"Naw, naw . . . Mistah, Ah cant do that!"

She jerked away. He caught her hand.

"Please . . ."

"Lemme go!"

She tried to pull her hand out of his and felt his fingers tighten. She pulled harder, and for a moment they were balanced, one against the other. Then he was at her side again, his arms about her.

"I wont hurt you! I wont hurt you . . ."

She leaned backward and tried to dodge his face. Her breasts were full against him; she gasped, feeling the full length of his body. She held her head far to one side; she knew he was seeking her mouth. His hands were on her breasts again. A wave of warm blood swept into her stomach and loins. She felt his lips touching her throat and where he kissed it burned.

"Naw, naw . . ."

Her eyes were full of the wet stars and they blurred, silver and blue. Her knees were loose and she heard her own breathing; she was trying to keep from falling. But hes a *white* man! A *white* man! Naw! Naw! And still she would not let him have her lips; she kept her face away. Her breasts hurt where they were crushed against him and each time she caught her breath she held it and while she held it it seemed that if she would let it go it would kill her. Her knees were pressed hard against his and she clutched the upper parts of his arms, trying to hold on. Her loins ached. She felt her body sliding.

"Gawd . . ."

He helped her up. She could not see the stars now; her eyes were full of the feeling that surged over her body each time she caught her breath. He held her close, breathing into her ear; she straightened, rigidly, feeling that she had to straighten or die. And then her lips felt his and she held her breath and dreaded ever to breathe again for fear of the feeling that would sweep down over her limbs. She held tightly, hearing a mountain tide of blood beating against her throat and temples. Then she gripped him, tore her face away, emptied her lungs in one long despairing gasp and went limp. She felt his hand; she was still, taut, feeling his hand, then his fingers. The muscles in her legs flexed and she bit her lips and pushed her toes deep into the wet dust by the side of the well and tried to wait until she could wait no longer. She whirled away from him and a streak of silver and blue swept across her blood. The wet ground cooled her palms and knee-caps. She stumbled up and ran, blindly, her toes flicking warm, dry dust. Her numbed fingers grabbed at a rusty nail in the post at the porch and she pushed ahead of hands that held her breasts. Her fingers found the door-facing; she moved into the darkened room, her hands before her. She touched the cradle and turned till her knees hit the bed. She went over, face down, her fingers trembling in the crumpled folds of his shirt. She moved and moved again and again, trying to keep ahead of the warm flood of blood that sought to catch her. A liquid metal covered her and she rode on the curve of white bright days and dark black nights and the surge of the long gladness of summer and the ebb of the deep dream of sleep in winter till a high red wave of hotness drowned her in a deluge of silver and blue and boiled her blood and blistered her flesh *bangbangbang* . . .

II

"Yuh bettah go," she said.

She felt him standing by the side of the bed, in the dark. She heard him clear his throat. His belt-buckle tinkled.

"Im leaving that clock and graphophone," he said.

She said nothing. In her mind she saw the box glowing softly, like the light in the baby's eyes. She stretched out her legs and relaxed.

"You can have it for forty instead of fifty. Ill be by early in the morning to see if your husbands in."

She said nothing. She felt the hot skin of her body growing steadily cooler.

"Do you think hell pay ten on it? Hell only owe thirty then."

She pushed her toes deep into the quilt, feeling a night wind blowing through the door. Her palms rested lightly on top of her breasts.

"Do you think hell pay ten on it?"

"Hunh?"

"Hell pay ten, wont he?"

"Ah don know," she whispered.

She heard his shoe hit against a wall; footsteps echoed on the wooden porch. She started nervously when she heard the roar of his car; she followed the throb of the motor till she heard it when she could hear it no more, followed it till she heard it roaring faintly in her ears in the dark and silent room. Her hands moved on her breasts and she was conscious of herself, all over; she felt the weight of her body resting heavily on shucks. She felt the presence of fields lying out there covered with night. She turned over slowly and lay on her stomach, her hands tucked under her. From somewhere came a creaking noise. She sat upright, feeling fear. The wind sighed. Crickets called. She lay down again, hearing shucks rustle. Her eyes looked straight up in the darkness and her blood sogged. She had lain a long time, full of a vast peace, when a far away tinkle made her feel the bed again. The tinkle came through the night; she listened, knowing that soon she would hear the rattle of Silas' wagon. Even then she tried to fight off the sound of Silas' coming, even then she wanted to feel the peace of the night filling her again; but the tinkle grew louder and she heard the jangle of a wagon and the quick trot of horses. Thas Silas! She gave up and waited. She heard horses neighing. Out of the window bare feet whispered in the dust, then crossed the porch, echoing in soft booms. She closed her eyes and saw Silas come into the room in his dirty overalls as she had seen him come in a thousand times before.

"Yuh sleep, Sarah?"

She did not answer. Feet walked across the floor and a match scratched. She opened her eyes and saw Silas standing over her with a lighted lamp. His hat was pushed far back on his head and he was laughing.

"Ah reckon yuh thought Ah waznt never comin back, hunh? Cant yuh wake up? See, Ah got that red cloth yuh wanted . . ." He laughed again and threw the red cloth on the mantel.

"Yuh hongry?" she asked.

"Naw, Ah kin make out till mawnin." Shucks rustled as he sat on the edge of the bed. "Ah got two hundred n fifty fer mah cotton."

"Two hundred n fifty?"

"Nothin different! N guess whut Ah done?"

"Whut?"

"Ah bought ten mo acres o lan. Got em from ol man Burgess. Paid im a hundred n fifty dollahs down. Ahll pay the rest next year ef things go erlong awright. Ahma have t git a man t hep me nex spring . . ."

"Yuh mean hire somebody?"

"Sho, hire somebody! Whut yuh think? Ain tha the way the white folks do? Ef yuhs gonna git anywheres yuhs gotta do just like they do." He paused. "What yuh been doin since Ah been gone?"

"Nothin. Cookin, cleanin, n . . ."

"How Ruth?"

"She awright." She lifted her head. "Silas, yuh git any lettahs?"

"Naw. But Ah heard Tom wuz in town."

"In *town*?"

She sat straight up.

"Yeah, thas whut folks wuz sayin at the sto."

"Back from the war?"

"Ah ast erroun t see ef Ah could fin im. But Ah couldnt."

"Lawd, Ah wish hed c mon home."

"Them white folks shos glad the wars over. But things wuz kinda bad there in town. Everywhere Ah looked wuznt nothin but black n white soljers. N them white folks beat up a black soljer yestiddy. He was jus in from France. Wuz still wearin his soljers suit. They claimed he sassed a white woman . . ."

"Who wuz he?"

"Ah don know. Never saw im befo."

"Yuh see An Peel?"

"Naw."

"Silas!" she said reprovingly.

"Aw, Sarah, Ah jus couldnt git out there."

"What else yuh bring sides the cloth?"

"Ah got yuh some high-top shoes." He turned and looked at her in the dim light of the lamp. "Woman, ain yuh glad Ah bought yuh some shoes n cloth?" He laughed and lifted his feet to the bed. "Lawd, Sarah, yuhs sho sleepy, ain yuh?"

"Bettah put tha lamp out, Silas . . ."

"Aw . . ." He swung out of the bed and stood still for a moment. She watched him, then turned her face to the wall.

"Whuts that by the windah?" he asked.

She saw him bending over and touching the graphophone with his fingers.

"Thasa graphophone."

"Where yuh git it from?"

"A man lef it here."

"When he bring it?"

"Today."

"But how come he t leave it?"

"He says hell be out in the mawnin t see ef yuh wans t buy it."

He was on his knees, feeling the wood and looking at the gilt on the edges of the box. He stood up and looked at her.

"Yuh ain never said yuh wanted one of these things."

She said nothing.

"Where wuz the man from?"

"Ah don know."

"He white?"

"Yeah."

He put the lamp back on the mantel. As he lifted the globe to blow out the flame, his hand paused.

"Whos hats this?"

She raised herself and looked. A straw hat lay bottom upwards on the edge of the mantel. Silas picked it up and looked back to the bed, to Sarah.

"Ah guess its the white mans. He must a lef it . . ."

"Whut he doing *in our room?*"

"He wuz talkin t me bout that graphophone."

She watched him go to the window again to the box. He picked it up, fumbled with the price-tag and took the box to the light.

"Whut this thing cos?"

"Forty dollahs."

"But its marked fifty here."

"Oh, Ah means he said fifty . . ."

He took a step toward the bed.

"Yuh lyin t me!"

"Silas!"

He heaved the box out of the front door; there was a smashing, tinkling noise as it bounded off the front porch and hit the ground.

"Whut in hell yuh lie t me fer?"

"Yuh broke the box!"

"Ahma break yo Gawddam neck ef yuh don stop lyin t me!"

"Silas, Ah ain lied t yuh!"

"Shut up, Gawddammit! Yuh did!"

He was standing by the bed with the lamp trembling in his hand. She stood on the other side, between the bed and the wall.

"How come yuh tell me that thing cos *forty* dollahs when it cos *fifty?*"

"Thas whut he tol me."

"How come he take *ten* dollars off fer yuh?"

"He ain took nothin off fer me, Silas!"

"Yuh lyin t me! N yuh lied t me bout Tom, too!"

She stood with her back to the wall, her lips parted, looking at him silently, steadily. Their eyes held for a moment. Silas looked down, as though he were about to believe her. Then he stiffened.

"Whos this?" he asked, picking up a short, yellow pencil from the crumpled quilt.

She said nothing. He started toward her.

"Yuh wan me t take mah raw-hide whip n make yuh talk?"

"Naw, naw, Silas! Yuh wrong! He wuz figgerin wid tha pencil!"

He was silent a moment, his eyes searching her face.

"Gawddam yo black soul t hell, don yuh try lyin t me! Ef yuh start layin wid white men Ahll hosswhip yuh t a incha yo life. Shos theres a Gawd in Heaven Ah will! From sunup t sundown Ah works mah guts out t pay them white trash bastards whut Ah owe em, n then Ah comes n fins they been in mah house! Ah cant go into their houses, n yuh know Gawddam well Ah cant! They don have no mercy on no black folks; wes jus like dirt under their feet! Fer ten years Ah slaves lika dog t git mah farm free, givin ever penny Ah kin t em, n then Ah comes fins they been in mah house . . ." He was speechless with outrage. "If yuh wans t eat at mah table yuhs gonna keep them white trash bastards out, yuh hear? Tha white ape kin come n git tha damn box n Ah ain gonna pay im a cent! He had no bisness leavin it here, n yuh had no bisness lettin im! Ahma tell tha sonofabitch something when he comes out here in the mawnin, so hep me Gawd! Now git back in tha bed!"

She slipped beneath the quilt and lay still, her face turned to the wall. Her heart thumped slowly and heavily. She heard him walk across the floor in his bare feet. She heard the bottom of the lamp as it rested on the mantel. She stiffened when the room darkened. Feet whispered across the floor again. The shucks rustled from Silas' weight as he sat on the edge of the bed. She was still, breathing softly. Silas was mumbling. She felt sorry for him. In the darkness it seemed that she could see the hurt look on his black face. The crow of a rooster came from far away, came so faintly that it seemed she had not heard it. The bed sank and the shucks cried out in dry whispers; she knew Silas had stretched out. She heard him sigh. Then she jumped because he jumped. She could feel the tenseness of his body; she knew he was sitting bolt upright. She felt his hands fumbling jerkily under the quilt. Then the bed heaved amid a wild shout of shucks and Silas' feet hit the floor with a loud boom. She snatched herself to her elbows, straining her eyes in the dark, wondering what was wrong now. Silas was moving about, cursing under his breath.

"Don wake Ruth up!" she whispered.

"Ef yuh say one mo word t me Ahma slap yuh inter a black spasm!"

She grabbed her dress, got up and stood by the bed, the tips of her fingers touching the wall behind her. A match flared in yellow flame; Silas' face was caught in a circle of light. He was looking downward, staring intently at a white wad of cloth balled in his hand. His black cheeks were hard, set; his lips were tightly pursed. She looked closer; she saw that the white cloth was a man's handkerchief. Silas' fingers loosened; she heard the handkerchief hit the floor softly, damply. The match went out.

"Yuh little bitch!"

Her knees gave. Fear oozed from her throat to her stomach. She moved in the dark toward the door, struggling with the dress, jamming it over her head. She heard the thick skin of Silas' feet swish across the wooden planks.

"Ah got mah raw-hide whip n Ahm takin yuh t the barn!"

She ran on tiptoe to the porch and paused, thinking of the baby. She shrank as something whined through the air. A red streak of pain cut across the small of her back and burned its way deep into her body, deeply.

"Silas!" she screamed.

She grabbed for the post and fell in dust. She screamed again and crawled out of reach.

"Git t the barn, Gawddammit!"

She scrambled up and ran through the dark, hearing the baby cry. Behind her leather thongs hummed and feet whispered swiftly over the dusty ground.

"C mere, yuh bitch! C mere, Ah say!"

She ran to the road and stopped. She wanted to go back and get the baby, but she dared not. Not as long as Silas had that whip. She stiffened, feeling that he was near.

"Yuh jus as well c mon back n git yo beatin!"

She ran again, slowing now and then to listen. If she only knew where he was she would slip back into the house and get the baby and walk all the way to Aunt Peel's.

"Yuh ain comin back in mah house till Ah beat yuh!"

She was sorry for the anger she knew he had out there in the field. She had a bewildering impulse to go to him and ask him not to be angry; she wanted to tell him that there was nothing to be angry about; that what she had done did not matter; that she was sorry; that after all she was still his wife and still loved him. But there was no way she could do that now; if she went to him he would whip her as she had seen him whip a horse.

"Sarah! Sarah!"

His voice came from far away. Ahm goin git Ruth. Back through dust she sped, going on her toes, holding her breath.

"Saaaarah!"

From far off his voice floated over the fields. She ran into the house and caught the baby in her arms. Again she sped through dust on her toes. She did not stop till she was so far away that his voice sounded like a faint echo falling from the sky. She looked up; the stars were paling a little. Mus be gittin near mawnin. She walked now, letting her feet sink softly into the cool dust. The baby was sleeping; she could feel the little chest swelling against her arm. She looked up again; the sky was solid black. Its gittin near mawnin. Ahma take Ruth t An Peels. N mabbe Ahll fin Tom . . . But she could not walk all that distance in the dark. Not now. Her legs were tired. For a moment a memory of surge and ebb rose in her blood; she felt her legs straining, upward. She sighed. Yes, she would go to the sloping hillside back of the garden and wait until morning. Then she would slip away. She stopped, listened. She heard a faint, rattling noise. She imagined Silas' kicking or throwing the smashed graphophone. Hes mad! Hes sho mad! Aw, Lawd! . . . She stopped stock still, squeezing the baby till it whimpered. What would happen when that white man came out in the morning? She had forgotten him. She would have to head him off and tell him. Yeah, cause Silas jus mad ernuff t kill! Lawd, hes mad erunff t kill!

III

She circled the house widely, climbing a slope, groping her way, holding the baby high in her arms. After awhile she stopped and wondered where on the slope she was. She remembered there was an elm tree near the edge; if she could find it she would know. She groped farther, feeling with her feet. Ahm gittin los! And she did not want to fall with the baby. Ahma stop here, she thought. When morning came she would see the car of the white man from this hill and she would run down the road and tell him to go back; and then there would be no killing. Dimly she saw in her mind a picture of men killing and being killed. White men killed the black and black men killed the white. White men killed the black men because they could, and the black men killed the white men to keep from being killed. And killing was blood. Lawd, Ah wish Tom wuz here. She shuddered, sat on the ground and watched the sky for signs of morning. Mabbe Ah oughta walk on down the road? Naw . . . Her legs were tired. Again she felt her body straining. Then she saw Silas holding the white man's handerchief. She heard it hit the floor, softly, damply. She was sorry for what she had done. Silas was as good to her as any black man could be to a black woman. Most of the black women worked in the fields as croppers. But Silas had given her her own home, and that was more than many others had done for their women. Yes, she knew how Silas felt. Always he had said he was as good as any white man. He had worked hard and saved his money and bought a farm so he could grow his own crops like white men. Silas hates white folks! Lawd, he sho hates em!

The baby whimpered. She unbuttoned her dress and nursed her in the dark. She looked toward the east. There! A tinge of grey hovered. It wont be long now. She could see ghostly outlines of trees. Soon she would see the elm, and by the elm she would sit till it was light enough to see the road.

The baby slept. Far off a rooster crowed. Sky deepened. She rose and walked slowly down a narrow, curving path and came to the elm tree. Standing on the edge of a slope, she saw a dark smudge in a sea of shifting shadows. That was her home. Wondah how come Silas didnt light the lamp? She shifted the baby from her right hip to her left, sighed, struggled against sleep. She sat on the ground again, caught the baby close and leaned against the trunk of a tree. Her eye-lids drooped and it seemed that a hard, cold hand caught hold of her right leg or was it her left leg—she did not know which —and began to drag her over a rough litter of shucks and when she strained to see who it was that was pulling her no one was in sight but far ahead was darkness and it seemed that out of the darkness some force came and pulled her like a magnet and she went sliding along over a rough bed of screeching shucks and it seemed that a wild fear made her want to scream but when she opened her mouth to scream she could not scream and she felt she was coming to a wide black hole and again she made ready to scream and then it was too late for she was already over the wide black hole falling falling falling . . .

She awakened with a start and blinked her eyes in the sunshine. She found she was clutching the baby so hard that it had begun to cry. She got to her feet, trembling from fright of the dream, re-membering Silas and the white man and Silas' running her out of the house and the white man's coming. Silas was standing in the front yard; she caught her breath. Yes, she had to go and head that white man off! Naw! She could not do that, not with Silas standing there with that whip in his hand. If she tried to climb any of those slopes he would see her surely. And Silas would never forgive her for something like that. If it were anybody but a white man it would be different.

Then, while standing there on the edge of the slope looking wonderingly at Silas striking the whip against his overall-leg—and then, while standing there looking—she froze. There came from the hills a distant throb. Lawd! The baby whimpered. She loosened her arms. The throb grew louder, droning. Hes comin fas! She wanted to run to Silas and beg him not to bother the white man. But he had that whip in his hand. She should not have done what she had done last night. This was all her fault. Lawd, ef anything happens t im its mah blame . . . Her eyes watched a black car speed over the crest of a hill. She should have been out there on the road instead of sleep-ing here by the tree. But it was too late now. Silas was standing in the yard; she saw him turn with a nervous jerk and sit on the edge of the porch. He was holding the whip stiffly. The car came to a stop. A door swung open. A white man got out. Thas im! She saw another white man in the front seat of the car. N thats his buddy . . . The white man who had gotten out walked over the ground, going to Silas. They faced each other, the white man standing up and Silas sitting down; like two toy men they faced each other. She saw Silas point the whip to the smashed graphophone. The white man looked down and took a quick step backward. The white man's shoulders were bent and he shook his head from left to right. Then Silas got up and they faced each other again; like two dolls, a white doll and a black doll, they faced each other in the valley below. The white man pointed his finger into Silas' face. Then Silas' right arm went up; the whip flashed. The white man turned, bending, flinging his hands to shield his head. Silas' arm rose and fell, rose and fell. She saw the white man crawling in dust, trying to get out of reach. She screamed when she saw the other white man get out of the car and run to Silas. Then all three were on the ground, rolling in dust, grappling for the whip. She clutched the baby and ran. Lawd! Then she stopped, her mouth hanging open. Silas had broken loose and was running toward the house. She knew he was going for his gun.

"Silas!"

Running, she stumbled and fell. The baby rolled in the dust and bawled. She grabbed it up and ran again. The white men were scrambling for their car. She reached level ground, running. Hell be killed! Then again she stopped. Silas was on the front porch, aiming a rifle. One of the white men was climbing into the car. The other was standing, waving his arms, shouting at Silas. She tried to scream, but choked; and she could not scream till she head a shot ring out.

"Silas!"

One of the white men was on the ground. The other was in the car. Silas was aiming again. The car started, running in a cloud of dust. She fell to her knees and hugged the baby close. She heard another shot, but the car was roaring over the top of the southern hill. Fear was gone now. Down the slope she ran. Silas was standing on the porch, holding his gun and looking at the fleeing car. Then she saw him go to the white man lying in dust and stoop over him. He caught one of the man's legs and dragged the body into the middle of the road. Then he turned and came slowly back to the house. She ran, holding the baby, and fell at his feet.

"Silas!"

IV

"Git up, Sarah!"

His voice was hard and cold. She lifted her eyes and saw blurred black feet. She wiped tears away with dusty fingers and pulled up. Something took speech from her and she stood with bowed shoulders. Silas was standing still, mute; the look on his face condemned her. It was as though he had gone far off and had stayed a long time and had come back changed even while she was standing there in the sunshine before him. She wanted to say something, to give herself. She cried.

"Git the chile up, Sarah!"

She lifted the baby and stood waiting for him to speak, to tell her something to change all this. But he said nothing. He walked toward the house. She followed. As she attempted to go in, he blocked the way. She jumped to one side as he threw the red cloth outdoors to the ground. The new shoes came next. Then Silas heaved the baby's cradle. It hit the porch and a rocker splintered; the cradle swayed for a second, then fell to the ground, lifting a cloud of brown dust against the sun. All of her clothes and the baby's clothes were thrown out.

"Silas!"

She cried, seeing blurred objects sailing through the air and hearing them hit softly in the dust.

"Git yo things n go!"

"Silas!"

"Ain no use yuh sayin *nothin* now!"

"But theyll kill yuh!"

"There ain nothin Ah kin do. N there ain nothin yuh kin do. Yuh done done too Gawddam much awready. Git yo things n go!"

"Theyll kill yuh, Silas!"

He pushed her off the porch.

"GIT YO THINGS N GO T AN PEELS!"

"Les *both* go, Silas!"

"Ahm stayin here till they come back!"

She grabbed his arm and he slapped her hand away. She dropped to the edge of the porch and sat looking at the ground.

"Go way," she said quietly. "Go way fo they comes. Ah didnt mean no harm . . ."

"Go way fer whut?"

"Theyll *kill* yuh . . ."

"It don make no difference." He looked out over the sun-filled fields. "Fer ten years Ah slaved mah life out t git mah farm free . . ." His voice broke off. His lips moved as though a thousand words were spilling silently out of his mouth, as though he did not have breath enough to give them sound. He looked to the sky, and then back to the dust. "Now, its all gone. *Gone* . . . Ef Ah run erway, Ah ain got nothin. Ef Ah stay n fight, Ah ain got nothin. It dont make no difference which way Ah go. Gawd! Gawd, Ah wish all them white folks wuz dead! *Dead*, Ah tell yuh! Ah wish Gawd would kill em *all!*"

She watched him run a few steps and stop. His throat swelled. He lifted his hands to his face; his fingers trembled. Then he bent to the ground and cried. She touched his shoulders.

"Silas!"

He stood up. She saw he was staring at the white man's body lying in the dust in the middle of the road. She watched him walk over to it. He began to talk to no one in particular; he simply stood over the dead white man and talked out of his life, out of a deep and final sense that now it was all over and nothing could make any difference.

"The white folks ain never gimme a chance! They ain never give no black man a chance! There ain nothin in yo whole life yuh kin keep from em! They take yo lan! They take yo freedom! They take yo women! N then they take yo life!" He turned to her, screaming. "N then Ah gits stabbed in the back by mah own blood! When mah eyes is on the white folks to keep em from killin me, mah own blood trips me up!" He knelt in the dust again and sobbed; after a bit he looked to the sky, his face wet with tears. "Ahm gonna be hard like they is! So help me, Gawd, Ah'm gonna be *hard!* When they come fer me Ahm gonna *be here!* N when they git me outta here theys gonna *know* Ahm gone! Ef Gawd lets me live Ahm gonna make em *feel* it!" He stopped and tried to get his breath. "But, Lawd, Ah don wanna be this way! I don mean nothin! Yuh die ef yuh fight! Yuh die ef yuh don fight! Either way yuh die n it don mean nothin . . ."

He was lying flat on the ground, the side of his face deep in dust. Sarah stood nursing the baby with eyes black and stony. Silas pulled up slowly and stood again on the porch.

"Git on t An Peels, Sarah!"

A dull roar came from the south. They both turned. A long streak of brown dust was weaving down the hillside.

"Silas!"

"Go on cross the fiels, Sarah!"

"We kin *both* go! Git the hosses!"

He pushed her off the porch, grabbed her hand, and led her to the rear of the house, past the well, to where a path led up a slope to the elm tree.

"Silas!"

"Yuh git on fo they ketch yuh too!"

Blind from tears, she went across the swaying fields, stumbling over blurred grass. It ain no use! She knew it was now too late to make him change his mind. The calves of her legs knotted. Suddenly her throat tightened, aching. She stopped, closed her eyes and tried to stem a flood of sorrow that drenched her. Yes, killing of white men by black men and killing of black men by white men went on in spite of the hope of white bright days and the desire of dark black nights and the long gladness of green cornfields in summer and the deep dream of sleepy grey skies in winter. And when killing started it went on, like a river flowing. Oh, she felt sorry for Silas! Silas. . . . He was following that long river of blood. Lawd, how come he wans t stay like tha? And he did not want to die; she knew he hated dying by the way he talked of it. Yet he followed the old river of blood, knowing that it meant nothing. He followed it, cursing and whimpering. But he followed it. She stared before her at the dry, dusty grass. Somehow, men, black men and white men, land and houses, green cornfields and grey skies, gladness and dreams, were all a part of that which made life good. Yes, somehow, they were linked, like the spokes in a spinning wheel. She felt they were. She knew they were. She felt it when she breathed and knew it when she looked. But she could not say how; she could not put her finger on it and when she thought hard about

it it became all mixed up, like milk spilling suddenly. Or else it
knotted in her throat and chest in a hard, aching lump, like the one
she felt now. She touched her face to the baby's face and cried again.

There was a loud blare of auto horns. The growing roar made her
turn round. Silas was standing, seemingly unafraid, leaning against
a post of the porch. The long line of cars came speeding in clouds
of dust. Silas moved toward the door and went in. Sarah ran down
the slope a piece, coming again to the elm tree. Her breath was slow
and hard. The cars stopped in front of the house. There was a
steady drone of motors and drifting clouds of dust. For a moment
she could not see what was happening. Then on all sides white
men with pistols and rifles swarmed over the fields. She dropped
to her knees, unable to take her eyes away, unable, it seemed, to
breathe. A shot rang out. A white man fell, rolling over, face
downward.

"Hes gotta gun!"

"Git back!'

"Lay down!"

The white men ran back and crouched behind cars. Three more
shots came from the house. She looked, her head and eyes aching.
She rested the baby in her lap and shut her eyes. Her knees sank
into the dust. More shots came, but it was no use looking now. She
knew it all by heart. She could feel it happening even before it happened. There were men killing and being killed. Then she jerked
up, being compelled to look.

"Burn the bastard out!"

"Set the sonofabitch on fire!"

"Cook the coon!"

"Smoke im out!"

She saw two white men on all fours creeping past the well. One
carried a gun and the other a red tin can. When they reached the
back steps the one with the tin can crept under the house and crept
out again. Then both rose and ran. Shots. One fell. A yell went up.
A yellow tongue of fire licked out from under the back steps.

"Burn the nigger!"

"C mon out, nigger, n git yos!"

She watched from the hill-slope; the back steps blazed. The white
men fired a steady stream of bullets. Black smoke spiraled upward
in the sunshine. Shots came from the house. The white men
crouched out of sight, behind their cars.

"Make up your mind, nigger!"

"C mon out er burn, yuh black bastard!"

"Yuh think yuhre white now, nigger?"

The shack blazed, flanked on all sides by whirling smoke filled
with flying sparks. She heard the distant hiss of flames. White men
were crawling on their stomachs. Now and then they stopped,
aimed, and fired into the bulging smoke. She looked with a tense
numbness; she looked, waiting for Silas to scream, or run out. But

the house crackled and blazed, spouting yellow plumes to the blue sky. The white men shot again, sending a hail of bullets into the furious pillars of smoke. And still she could not see Silas running out, or hear his voice calling. Then she jumped, standing. There was a loud crash; the roof caved in. A black chimney loomed amid crumbling wood. Flames roared and black smoke billowed, hiding the house. The white men stood up, no longer afraid. Again she waited for Silas, waited to see him fight his way out, waiting to hear his call. Then she breathed a long, slow breath, emptying her lungs. She knew now. Silas had killed as many as he could and stayed on to burn, had stayed without a murmur. She filled her lungs with a quick gasp as the walls fell in; the house was hidden by eager plumes of red. She turned and ran with the baby in her arms, ran blindly across the fields, crying, "Naw, Gawd!"

Discussion of Wright's "Long Black Song"

1. Notice the repetition of the sound "Bang! Bang! Bang!" What effects does the author achieve by the repetition? Do you find the placement of sounds significant? Where? Be specific.

2. How do the title and the repeated sound function as implicit comments upon each other? Where else is the "long black song" implied?

3. Compare this story with "Dry September" and with "Her Sweet Jerome." Violence appears in each. What does the violence express about human relationships—men and women, blacks and whites? Does Wright suggest any differences between men and women? The two races? What? How?

4. In the last story of *Uncle Tom's Children* the heroine does not submit to men, as does the heroine of "Long Black Song." What social comments does Wright imply by means of the sexual relationships in the latter story?

EUDORA WELTY

b. 1909

🌺 Eudora Welty was born in Jackson, Mississippi, which is still her home. She has published several collections of short stories: *A Curtain of Green* (1941), from which "Old Mr Marblehall" is taken; *The Wide Net* (1943); and *The Golden Apples* (1949). Of her novels—*Delta Wedding* (1946), *The Ponder Heart* (1954), *Losing Battles* (1970), and *The Optimist's Daughter* (1972)—the last named won a Pulitzer Prize. Her aesthetics may be inferred from her introduction to *One Time, One Place*, a collection of photographs she made during the Depression: "The human face and the human body are eloquent in themselves, and stubborn and wayward, and a snapshot is a moment's glimpse (as a story may be a long look, a growing contemplation) into what never stops moving, never ceases to express for itself something of our common feeling. Every feeling waits upon its gesture. Then when it does come, how unpredictable it turns out to be, after all" (Eudora Welty, *One Time, One Place* [New York: Random House, 1971], pp. 7–8). Her writings often portray the unexpected gestures of our common feeling. And that common feeling is many times a feeling of distances among people. In spite of these distances, Welty's men and women endure their loneliness, although—as in the following story—the author is seldom sentimental in presenting their endurance.

Old Mr Marblehall

Old Mr Marblehall never did anything, never got married until he was sixty. You can see him out taking a walk. Watch and you'll see how preciously old people come to think they are made—the way they walk, like conspirators, bent over a little, filled with protection. They stand long on the corners but more impatiently than anyone, as if they expect traffic to take notice of them, rear up the horses and throw on the brakes, so they can go where they want to go. That's Mr Marblehall. He has short white bangs, and a bit of snapdragon in his lapel. He walks with a big polished stick, a present. That's what people think of him. Everybody says to his face, "So well preserved!" Behind his back they say cheerfully, "One foot in the grave." He has on his thick, beautiful, glowing coat—tweed, but he looks as gratified as an animal in its own tingling fur. You see, even in summer he wears it, because he is cold all the time. He looks quaintly secretive and prepared for anything, out walking very luxuriously on Catherine Street.

His wife, back at home in the parlor standing up to think, is a large, elongated old woman with electric-looking hair and curly lips. She has spent her life trying to escape from the parlor-like jaws of self-consciousness. Her late marriage has set in upon her nerves like a retriever nosing and puffing through old dead leaves out in the woods. When she walks around the room she looks remote·and nebulous, out on the fringe of habitation, and rather as if she must have been cruelly trained—otherwise she couldn't do actual, immediate things, like answering the telephone or putting on a hat. But she has gone further than you'd think: into club work. Surrounded by other more suitably exclaiming women, she belongs to the Daughters of the American Revolution and the United Daughters of the Confederacy, attending teas. Her long, disquieted figure towering in the candlelight of other women's houses looks like something accidental. Any occasion, and she dresses her hair like a unicorn horn. She even sings, and is requested to sing. She even writes some of the songs she sings ("O Trees in the Evening"). She has a voice that dizzies other ladies like an organ note, and amuses men like a halloo down the well. It's full of a hollow wind and echo, winding out through the wavery hope of her mouth. Do people know of her perpetual amazement? Back in safety she wonders, her untidy head trembles in the domestic dark. She remembers how everyone in Natchez will suddenly grow quiet around her. Old Mrs Marblehall, Mr Marblehall's wife: she even goes out in the rain, which Southern women despise above everything, in big neat biscuit-colored galoshes, for which she "ordered off." She is only looking around—servile, undelighted, sleepy, expensive, tortured Mrs Marblehall, pinning her mind with a pin to her husband's diet. She wants to tempt him, she tells him. What would he like best, that he can have?

There is Mr Marblehall's ancestral home. It's not so wonderfully large—it has only four columns—but you always look toward it, the way you always glance into tunnels and see nothing. The river is after it now, and the little back garden has assuredly crumbled away, but the box maze is there on the edge like a trap, to confound the Mississippi River. Deep in the red wall waits the front door—it weighs such a lot, it is perfectly solid, all one piece, black mahogany. . . . And you see—one of *them* is always going in it. There is a knocker shaped like a gasping fish on the door. You have every reason in the world to imagine the inside is dark, with old things about. There's many a big, deathly-looking tapestry, wrinkling and thin, many a sofa shaped like an S. Brocades as tall as the wicked queens in Italian tales stand gathered before the windows. Everything is draped and hooded and shaded, of course, unaffectionate but close. Such rosy lamps! The only sound would be a breath against the prisms, a stirring of the chandelier. It's like old eyelids, the house with one of its shutters, in careful working order, slowly opening outward. Then the little son softly comes and stares out like a kitten, with button nose and pointed ears and little fuzz of silky hair running along the top of his head.

The son is the worst of all. Mr and Mrs Marblehall had a child! When both of them were terribly old, they had this little, amazing, fascinating son. You can see how people are taken aback, how they jerk and throw up their hands every time they so much as think about it. At least, Mr Marblehall sees them. He thinks Natchez people do nothing themselves, and really, most of them have done or could do the same thing. This son is six years old now. Close up, he has a monkey look, a very penetrating look. He has very sparse Japanese hair, tiny little pearly teeth, long little wilted fingers. Every day he is slowly and expensively dressed and taken to the Catholic school. He looks quietly and maliciously absurd, out walking with old Mr Marblehall or old Mrs Marblehall, placing his small booted foot on a little green worm, while they stop and wait on him. Everybody passing by thinks that he looks quite as if he thinks his parents had him just to show they could. You see, it becomes complicated, full of vindictiveness.

But now, as Mr Marblehall walks as briskly as possible toward the river where there is sun, you have to merge him back into his proper blur, into the little party-giving town he lives in. Why look twice at him? There has been an old Mr Marblehall in Natchez ever since the first one arrived back in 1818—with a theatrical presentation of Otway's *Venice*, ending with *A Laughable Combat between Two Blind Fiddlers*—an actor! Mr Marblehall isn't so important. His name is on the list, he is forgiven, but nobody gives a hoot about any old Mr Marblehall. He could die, for all they care; some people even say, "Oh, is he still alive?" Mr Marblehall walks and walks, and now and then he is driven in his ancient fringed carriage with the candle burners like empty eyes in front. And yes, he is supposed to travel for his health. But why consider his absence? There isn't any other place besides Natchez, and even if there were, it would hardly be likely to change Mr Marblehall if it were brought up against him. Big fingers could pick him up off the Esplanade and take him through the air, his old legs still measuredly walking in a dangle, and set him down where he could continue that same old Natchez stroll of his in the East or the West or Kingdom Come. What difference could anything make now about old Mr Marblehall—so late? A week or two would go by in Natchez and then there would be Mr Marblehall, walking down Catherine Street again, still exactly in the same degree alive and old.

People naturally get bored. They say, "Well, he waited till he was sixty years old to marry, and what did he want to marry for?" as though what he did were the excuse for their boredom and their lack of concern. Even the thought of his having a stroke right in front of one of the Pilgrimage houses during Pilgrimage Week makes them only sigh, as if to say it's nobody's fault but his own if he wants to be so insultingly and precariously well-preserved. He ought to have a little black boy to follow around after him. Oh, his precious old health, which never had reason to be so inspiring! Mr Marblehall has a formal, reproachful look as he stands on the corners arranging himself to go out into the traffic to cross the streets. It's as if he's thinking of shaking his stick and saying, "Well, look! I've done it, don't you see?" But really, nobody pays much attention to his look. He is just like other people to them. He could have easily danced with a troupe of angels in Paradise every night, and they wouldn't have guessed. Nobody is likely to find out that he is leading a double life.

The funny thing is he just recently began to lead this double life. He waited until he was sixty years old. Isn't he crazy? Before that, he'd never done anything. He didn't know what to do. Everything was for all the world like his first party. He stood about, and looked in his father's books, and long ago he went to France, but he didn't like it.

Drive out any of these streets in and under the hills and you find yourself lost. You see those scores of little galleried houses nearly alike. See the yellowing China trees at the eaves, the round flower beds in the front yards, like bites in the grass, listen to the screen door whining, the ice wagons dragging by, the twittering noises of children. Nobody ever looks to see who is living in a house like that. These people come out themselves and sprinkle the hose over the street at this time of day to settle the dust, and after they sit on the porch, they go back into the house, and you hear the radio for the next two hours. It seems to mourn and cry for them. They go to bed early.

Well, old Mr Marblehall can easily be seen standing beside a row of zinnias growing down the walk in front of that little house, bending over, easy, easy, so as not to strain anything, to stare at the flowers. Of course he planted them! They are covered with brown—each petal is a little heart-shaped pocket of dust. They don't have any smell, you know. It's twilight, all amplified with locusts screaming; nobody could see anything. Just what Mr Marblehall is bending over the zinnias for is a mystery, any way you look at it. But there he is, quite visible, alive and old, leading his double life.

There's his other wife, standing on the night-stained porch by a potted fern, screaming things to a neighbor. This wife is really worse than the other one. She is more solid, fatter, shorter, and while not so ugly, funnier looking. She looks like funny furniture —an unornamented stair post in one of these little houses, with her small monotonous round stupid head—or sometimes like a woodcut of a Bavarian witch, forefinger pointing, with scratches in the air all around her. But she's so static she scarcely moves, from her thick shoulders down past her cylindered brown dress to her short, stubby house slippers. She stands still and screams to the neighbors.

This wife thinks Mr Marblehall's name is Mr Bird. She says, "I declare I told Mr Bird to go to bed, and look at him! I don't understand him!" All her devotion is combustible and goes up in despair. This wife tells everything she knows. Later, after she tells the neighbors, she will tell Mr Marblehall. Cymbal-breasted, she fills the house with wifely complaints. She calls, "After I get Mr Bird to bed, what does he do then? He lies there stretched out with his clothes on and don't have one word to say. Know what he does?"

And she goes on, while her husband bends over the zinnias, to tell what Mr Marblehall (or Mr Bird) does in bed. She does tell the truth. He reads *Terror Tales* and *Astonishing Stories*. She can't see anything to them: they scare her to death. These stories are about horrible and fantastic things happening to nude women and scientists. In one of them, when the characters open bureau drawers, they find a woman's leg with a stocking and garter on. Mrs Bird had to shut the magazine. "The glutinous shadows," these stories say, "the red-eyed, muttering old crone," "the moonlight on her thigh," "an ancient cult of sun worshipers," "an altar suspiciously stained . . ." Mr Marblehall doesn't feel as terrified as all that, but he reads on and on. He is killing time. It is richness without taste, like some holiday food. The clock gets a fruity bursting tick, to get through midnight—then leisurely, leisurely on. When time is passing it's like a bug in his ear. And then Mr Bird—he doesn't even want a shade on the light, this wife moans respectably. He reads under a bulb. She can tell you how he goes straight through a stack of magazines. "He might just as well not have a family," she always ends, unjustly, and rolls back into the house as if she had been on a little wheel all this time.

But the worst of them all is the other little boy. Another little boy just like the first one. He wanders around the bungalow full of tiny little schemes and jokes. He has lost his front tooth, and in this way he looks slightly different from Mr Marblehall's other little boy—more shocking. Otherwise, you couldn't tell them apart if you wanted to. They both have that look of cunning little jugglers, violently small under some spotlight beam, preoccupied and silent, amusing themselves. Both of the children will go into sudden fits and tantrums that frighten their mothers and Mr Marblehall to death. Then they can get anything they want. But this little boy, the one who's lost the tooth, is the smarter. For a long time he supposed that his mother was totally solid, down to her thick separated ankles. But when she stands there on the porch screaming to the neighbors, she reminds him of those flares that charm him so, that they leave burning in the street at night—the dark solid ball, then, tongue-like, the wicked, yellow, continuous, enslaving blaze on the stem. He knows what his father thinks.

Perhaps one day, while Mr Marblehall is standing there gently bent over the zinnias, this little boy is going to write on a fence, "Papa leads a double life." He finds out things you wouldn't find out. He is a monkey.

You see, one night he is going to follow Mr Marblehall (or Mr Bird) out of the house. Mr Marblehall has said as usual that he is leaving for one of his health trips. He is one of those correct old gentlemen who are still going to the wells and drinking the waters —exactly like his father, the late old Mr Marblehall. But why does he leave on foot? This will occur to the little boy.

So he will follow his father. He will follow him all the way across town. He will see the shining river come winding around. He will see the house where Mr Marblehall turns in at the wrought-iron gate. He will see a big speechless woman come out and lead him in by the heavy door. He will not miss those rosy lamps beyond the many-folded draperies at the windows. He will run around the fountains and around the Japonica trees, past the stone figure of the pigtailed courtier mounted on the goat, down to the back of the house. From there he can look far up at the strange upstairs rooms. In one window the other wife will be standing like a giant, in a long-sleeved gathered nightgown, combing her electric hair and breaking it off each time in the comb. From the next window the other little boy will look out secretly into the night, and see him —or not see him. That would be an interesting thing, a moment of strange telepathies. (Mr Marblehall can imagine it.) Then in the corner room there will suddenly be turned on the bright, naked light. Aha! Father!

Mr Marblehall's little boy will easily climb a tree there and peep through the window. There, under a stark shadeless bulb, on a great four-poster with carved griffins, will be Mr Marblehall, reading *Terror Tales*, stretched out and motionless.

Then everything will come out.

At first, nobody will believe it.

Or maybe the policeman will say, "Stop! How dare you!"

Maybe, better than that, Mr Marblehall himself will confess his duplicity—how he has led two totally different lives, with completely different families, two sons instead of one. What an astonishing, unbelievable, electrifying confession that would be, and how his two wives would topple over, how his sons would cringe! To say nothing of most men aged sixty-six. So thinks self-consoling Mr Marblehall.

You will think, what if nothing ever happens? What if there is no climax, even to this amazing life? Suppose old Mr Marblehall simply remains alive, getting older by the minute, shuttling, still secretly, back and forth?

Nobody cares. Not an inhabitant of Natchez, Mississippi, cares if he is deceived by old Mr Marblehall. Neither does anyone care that Mr Marblehall has finally caught on, he thinks, to what people are supposed to do. This is it: they endure something inwardly—for a time secretly; they establish a past, a memory; thus they store up life. He has done this; most remarkably, he has even multiplied his life by deception; and plunging deeper and deeper he speculates upon some glorious finish, a great explosion of revelations . . . the future.

But he still has to kill time, and get through the clocking nights. Otherwise he dreams that he is a great blazing butterfly stitching up a net; which doesn't make sense.

Old Mr. Marblehall! He may have years ahead yet in which to wake up bolt upright in the bed under the naked bulb, his heart thumping, his old eyes watering and wild, imagining that if people knew about his double life, they'd die.

Discussion of Welty's "Old Mr Marblehall"

1. Listen to the voice that tells the story. What is the attitude of the narrator to her material? How can you tell?

2. Examine the language choices—the wife's "curly lips," for example, her "pinning her mind with a pin to her husband's diet." Would you describe these language choices as naturalistic? Why or why not? How do they affect your responses to the story?

3. Welty says in *One Time, One Place* that "my wish, indeed my continuing passion, would be not to point the finger in judgment but to part a curtain, that invisible shadow that falls between people, the veil of indifference to each other's presence, each other's wonder, each other's plight" (p. 8). Does this desire seem to have been fulfilled in this story?

4. Compare the marriages in "Old Mr Marblehall," "Daydreams of a Drunk Woman," and "Beasts of the Southern Wild." How do the authors of these stories counter our sentimental conceptions of marriage?

ELIZABETH BOWEN

b. 1899

🌷 Elizabeth Bowen was born in Dublin and brought up in England, leaving Ireland at age seven. She returned to Ireland for a short time during World War I, but lived most of her adult life in London, where she stayed during World War II. Thus she has seen the chaos of a war-torn twentieth century and the changes that occur rapidly in such a society. Praised for her polished and crafted style, Bowen often dramatizes lives that continue stolidly in the face of mutability and pain. Among her many novels are *The Death of the Heart* (1939), *The Heat of the Day* (1949), *The Little Girls* (1964), and *Eva Trout* (1969). Her short stories appear in several collections, among which are *Look at All Those Roses* (1941), *The Demon Lover* (1945), and *Stories by Elizabeth Bowen* (1959), her personal selection of eighteen stories and a preface.

Tears, Idle Tears

Frederick burst into tears in the middle of Regent's Park. His mother, seeing what was about to happen, had cried: "Frederick, you *can't*—in the middle of Regent's Park!" Really, this was a corner, one of those lively corners just inside a big gate, where two walks meet and a bridge starts across the pretty winding lake. People were passing quickly; the bridge rang with feet. Poplars stood up like delicate green brooms; diaphanous willows whose weeping was not shocking quivered over the lake. May sun spattered gold through the breezy trees; the tulips though falling open were still gay; three girls in a long boat shot under the bridge. Frederick, knees trembling, butted towards his mother a crimson convulsed face, as though he had the idea of burying himself in her. She whipped out a handkerchief and dabbed at him with it under his grey felt hat, exclaiming meanwhile in fearful mortification: "You really haven't got to be such a *baby!*" Her tone attracted the notice of several people, who might otherwise have thought he was having something taken out of his eye.

He was too big to cry: the whole scene was disgraceful. He wore a grey flannel knickerbocker suit and looked like a schoolboy; though in fact he was seven, still doing lessons at home. His mother said to him almost every week: "I don't know what they will think when you go to school!" His tears were a shame of which she could speak to no one; no offensive weakness of body could have upset her more. Once she had got so far as taking her pen up to write to the Mother's Advice Column of a helpful woman's weekly about them.

She began: "I am a widow; young, good tempered, and my friends all tell me that I have great control. But my little boy—" She intended to sign herself "Mrs. D., Surrey." But then she had stopped and thought no, no: after all, he is Toppy's son. . . . She was a gallant-looking, correct woman, wearing to-day in London a coat and skirt, a silver fox, white gloves and a dark-blue toque put on exactly right—not the sort of woman you ought to see in a Park with a great blubbering boy belonging to her. She looked a mother of sons, but not of a son of this kind, and should more properly, really, have been walking a dog. "Come on!" she said, as though the bridge, the poplars, the people staring were to be borne no longer. She began to walk on quickly, along the edge of the lake, parallel with the park's girdle of trees and the dark, haughty windows of Cornwall Terrace looking at her over the red may. They had meant to go to the Zoo, but now she had changed her mind: Frederick did not deserve the Zoo.

Frederick stumbled along beside her, too miserable to notice. His mother seldom openly punished him, but often revenged herself on him in small ways. He could feel how just this was. His own incontinence in the matter of tears was as shocking to him, as bowing-down, as annulling, as it could be to her. He never knew what happened—a cold black pit with no bottom opened inside himself; a red-hot bellwire jagged up through him from the pit of his frozen belly to the caves of his eyes. Then the hot gummy rush of tears, the convulsion of his features, the terrible square grin he felt his mouth take all made him his own shameful and squalid enemy. Despair howled round his inside like a wind, and through his streaming eyes he saw everything quake. Anyone's being there—and most of all his mother—drove this catastrophe on him. He never cried like this when he was alone.

Crying made him so abject, so outcast from other people that he went on crying out of despair. His crying was not just reflex, like a baby's; it dragged up all unseemliness into view. No wonder everyone was repelled. There is something about an abject person that rouses cruelty in the kindest breast. The plate-glass windows of the lordly houses looked at him through the may-trees with judges' eyes. Girls with their knees crossed, reading on the park benches, looked up with unkind smiles. His apathetic stumbling, his not seeing or caring that they had given up their trip to the Zoo, became more than Mrs. Dickinson, his mother, could bear. She pointed out, in a voice tense with dislike: "I'm not taking you to the Zoo."

"Mmmph-mmph-mmph," sobbed Frederick.

"You know, I so often wonder what your father would think."

"Mmmph-mmph-mmph."

"He used to be so proud of you. He and I used to look forward to what you'd be like when you were a big boy. One of the last things he ever said was: 'Frederick will take care of you.' You almost make me glad he's not here now."

"Oough-oough."

"What do you say?"

"I'm t-t-trying to stop."

"Everybody's looking at you, you know."

She was one of those women who have an unfailing sense of what not to say, and say it: despair, perversity or stubborn virtue must actuate them. She had a horror, also, of the abnormal and had to hit out at it before it could hit at her. Her husband, an R.A.F. pilot who had died two days after a ghastly crash, after two or three harrowing spaces of consciousness, had never made her ashamed or puzzled her. Their intimacies, then even his death, had a bold naturalness.

"Listen, I shall walk on ahead," said Frederick's mother, lifting her chin with that noble, decided movement so many people liked. "You stay here and look at that duck till you've stopped that noise. Don't catch me up till you have. No, I'm really ashamed of you."

She walked on. He had *not* been making, really, so very much noise. Drawing choppy breaths, he stood still and looked at the duck that sat folded into a sleek white cypher on the green grassy margin of the lake. When it rolled one eye open over a curve, something unseeing in its expression calmed him. His mother walked away under the gay tree-shadows; her step quickened lightly, the tip of her fox fur swung. She thought of the lunch she had had with Major and Mrs. Williams, the party she would be going to at five. First, she must leave Frederick at Aunt Mary's, and what would Aunt Mary say to his bloated face? She walked fast; the gap between her and Frederick widened: she was a charming woman walking by herself.

Everybody had noticed how much courage she had; they said: "How plucky Mrs. Dickinson is." It was five years since her tragedy and she had not remarried, so that her gallantness kept on coming into play. She helped a friend with a little hat shop called *Isobel* near where they lived in Surrey, bred puppies for sale and gave the rest of her time to making a man of Frederick. She smiled nicely and carried her head high. Those two days while Toppy had lain dying she had hardly turned a hair, for his sake: no one knew when he might come conscious again. When she was not by his bed she was waiting about the hospital. The chaplain hanging about her and the doctor had given thanks that there were women like this; another officer's wife who had been her friend had said she was braver than could be good for anyone. When Toppy finally died the other woman had put the unflinching widow into a taxi and driven back with her to the Dickinsons' bungalow. She kept saying: "Cry, dear cry: you'd feel better." She made tea and clattered about, repeating: "Don't mind me, darling: just have a big cry." The strain became so great that tears streamed down her own face. Mrs. Dickinson looked past her palely, with a polite smile. The empty-feeling bungalow with its rustling curtains still smelt of Toppy's pipe; his slippers were under a chair. Then Mrs. Dickinson's friend, almost tittering with despair, thought of a poem of Tennyson's she had learnt as a child. She said:

"Where's Frederick? He's quiet. Do you think he's asleep?" The widow, rising; perfectly automatic, led her into the room where Frederick lay in his cot. A nursemaid rose from beside him, gave them one morbid look and scurried away. The two-year-old baby, flushed, and drawing up his upper lip in his sleep as his father used to do, lay curved under his blue blanket, clenching one fist on nothing. Something suddenly seemed to strike his mother, who, slumping down by the cot, ground her face and forehead into the fluffy blanket, then began winding the blanket round her two fists. Her convulsions, though proper, were fearful: the cot shook. The friend crept away into the kitchen, where she stayed an half-hour, muttering to the maid. They made more tea and waited for Mrs. Dickinson to give full birth to her grief. Then extreme silence drew them back to the cot. Mrs. Dickinson knelt asleep, her profile pressed to the blanket, one arm crooked over the baby's form. Under his mother's arm, as still as an image, Frederick lay wide awake, not making a sound. In conjunction with a certain look in his eyes, the baby's silence gave the two women the horrors. The servant said to the friend: "You would think he knew."

Mrs. Dickinson's making so few demands on pity soon rather alienated her women friends, but men liked her better for it: several of them found in her straight look an involuntary appeal to themselves alone, more exciting than coquetry, deeply, nobly exciting: several wanted to marry her. But courage had given her a new intractable kind of virgin pride: she loved it too much; she could never surrender it. "No, don't ask me that," she would say, lifting her chin and with that calm, gallant smile. "Don't spoil things. You've been splendid to me: such a support. But you see, there's Frederick. He's the man in my life now. I'm bound to put him first. That wouldn't be fair, would it?" After that, she would simply go on shaking her head. She became the perfect friend for men who wished to marry but were just as glad not to, and for married men who liked just a little pathos without being upset.

Frederick had stopped crying. This left him perfectly blank, so that he stared at the duck with abstract intensity, perceiving its moulded feathers and porcelain-smooth neck. The burning, swirling film had cleared away from his eyes, and his diaphragm felt relief, as when retching has stopped. He forgot his focus of grief and forgot his mother, but saw with joy a quivering bough of willow that, drooping into his gaze under his swollen eyelids, looked as pure and strong as something after the Flood. His thought clutched at the willow, weak and wrecked but happy. He knew he was now qualified to walk after his mother, but without feeling either guilty or recalcitrant did not wish to do so. He stepped over the rail—no park keeper being at hand to stop him—and, tenderly and respectfully, attempted to touch the white duck's tail. Without a blink, with automatic uncoyness, the duck slid away from Frederick into the lake. Its lovely white china body balanced on the green glass water as it propelled itself gently round the curve of the bank. Frederick saw with a passion of observation its shadowy webbed feet lazily striking out.

"The keeper'll eat you," said a voice behind him.

Frederick looked cautiously round with his bunged-up eyes. The *individual* who had spoken sat on a park bench; it was a girl with a despatch case beside her. Her big bony knee-joints stuck out through her thin crepe-de-chine dress; she was hatless and her hair made a frizzy, pretty outline, but she wore spectacles, her skin had burnt dull red: her smile and the cock of her head had about them something pungent and energetic, not like a girl's at all. "Whatcher mean, eat me?"

"You're on his grass. And putting salt on his duck's tail."

Frederick stepped back carefully over the low rail. "I haven't got any salt." He looked up and down the walk: his mother was out of sight but from the direction of the bridge a keeper was approaching, still distant but with an awesome gait. "My goodness," the girl said, "what's been biting *you?*" Frederick was at a loss. "Here," she said, "have an apple." She opened her case, which was full of folded grease-paper that must have held sandwiches, and rummaged out an apple with a waxy, bright skin. Frederick came up, tentative as a pony, and finally took the apple. His breath was still hitching and catching; he did not wish to speak.

"Go on," she said, "swallow: it'll settle your chest. Where's your mother gone off to? What's all the noise about?" Frederick only opened his jaws as wide as they would go, then bit slowly, deeply into the apple. The girl re-crossed her legs and tucked her thin crepe-de-chine skirt round the other knee. "What had you done—cheeked her?"

Frederick swept the mouthful of apple into one cheek. "No," he said shortly. "Cried."

"I should say you did. Bellowed. I watched you all down the path." There was something ruminative in the girl's tone that made her remark really not at all offensive; in fact, she looked at Frederick as though she were meeting an artist who had just done a turn. He had been standing about, licking and biting the apple, but now he came and sat down at the other end of the bench. "How do you do it?" she said.

Frederick only turned away: his ears began burning again.

"What gets at you?" she said.

"Don't know."

"Someone coming it over you? I know another boy who cries like you, but he's older. He knots himself up and bellows."

"What's his name?"

"George."

"Does he go to school?"

"Oh, lord, no; he's a boy at the place where I used to work." She raised one arm, leaned back, and watched four celluloid bangles, each of a different colour, slide down it to her elbow-joint, where they stuck. "He doesn't know why he does it," she said, "but he's got to. It's as though he saw something. You can't ask him. Some people take him that way: girls do. I never did. It's as if he knew about something he'd better not. I said once, well, what just *is* it, and he said if he *could* tell me he wouldn't do it. I said, well, what's the *reason*, and he said, well, what's the reason not to? I knew him well at one time."

Frederick spat out two pips, looked round cautiously for the keeper, then dropped the apple-core down the back of the seat. "Whered's George live?"

"I don't know now," she said, "I often wonder. I got sacked from that place where I used to work, and he went right off and I never saw him again. You snap out of that, if you can, before you are George's age. It does you no good. It's all in the way you see things. Look, there's your mother back. Better move, or there'll be *more* trouble." She held out her hand to Frederick, and when he put his in it shook hands so cheerfully, with such tough decision, that the four celluloid bangles danced on her wrist. "You and George," she said. "Funny to meet two of you. Well, good-bye, Henry: cheer up."

"I'm Frederick."

"Well, cheer up, Freddie."

As Frederick walked away, she smoothed down the sandwich papers inside her despatch case and snapped the case shut again. Then she put a finger under her hair at each side to tuck her spectacles firmly down on her ears. Her mouth, an unreddened line across her harshly-burnt face, still wore the same truculent, homely smile. She crossed her arms under the flat chest, across her stomach, and sat there holding her elbows idly, wagging one foot in its fawn sandal, looking fixedly at the lake through her spectacles wondering about George. She had the afternoon, as she had no work. She saw George's face lifted abjectly from his arms on a table, blotchy over his clerk's collar. The eyes of George and Frederick seemed to her to be wounds in the world's surface, through which its inner, terrible, unassuageable, necessary sorrow constantly bled away and as constantly welled up.

Mrs. Dickinson came down the walk under the band of trees, carefully unanxious, looking lightly at objects to see if Frederick were near them: he had been a long time. Then she saw Frederick shaking hands with a sort of girl on a bench and starting to come her way. So she quickly turned her frank, friendly glance on the lake, down which, as though to greet her, a swan came swimming. She touched her fox fur lightly, sliding it up her shoulder. What a lovely mother to have. "Well, Frederick," she said, as he came into earshot, "coming?" Wind sent a puff of red mayflowers through the air. She stood still and waited for Frederick to come up. She could not think what to do now: they had an hour to put in before they were due at Aunt Mary's. But this only made her manner calmer and more decisive.

Frederick gave a great skip, opened his mouth wide, shouted: "Oo, I say, mother, I nearly caught a duck!"

"Frederick, dear, how silly you are: you couldn't."

"Oo, yes, I could, I could. If I'd had salt for its tail!" Years later, Frederick could still remember, with ease, pleasure and with a sense of lonely shame being gone, that calm white duck swimming off round the bank. But George's friend with the bangles, and George's trouble, fell through a cleft in his memory and were forgotten soon.

Discussion of Bowen's "Tears, Idle Tears"

1. How does Frederick react to his own crying? Why do you think the author introduces "a sort of girl" (whose phrase is that?) to tell Frederick about George? Compare the humor in Bowen's story with that of Edith Wharton. Compare the woman in Bowen's story with the one in "Permanent Wave."

2. Other than the literal meaning, what is suggested by the mother's widening a gap between herself and Frederick as she walks ahead of him? Does the narrator seem to mean it when she or he says, "What a lovely mother to have," at the end of the story?

3. As you have noticed, authors many times use setting or objects in order to imply more about an occasion or a character than they say. What is significant about the duck in "Tears, Idle Tears"? How does it suggest a socializing process predicted by the title? Compare the mother-and-son relationship in this story with those of "The Darling" and "The Rocking-Horse Winner."

JUAN RULFO

b. 1918

✿ Juan Rulfo's reputation—which is enormous—rests on two works: *Pedro Paramo* (1955), a novel about the fall of old Mexico, and *The Burning Plain* (1953), a collection of short stories related by theme. Rulfo's strength lies in his ability to get inside the heads of the poorest and most primitive Mexican peasants, and his stories recapture not only their language but also the way they see the world. All are brief, and in Spanish they are extremely difficult to read. Rulfo is an extremely slow and meticulous writer: A second novel has been awaited since 1960, as yet in vain. "We're Very Poor" does not, at first reading, seem to be as much about human beings as about poverty. It is only successive readings that force us to understand what poverty does to life, and what it does to the chances of young women to grow up and of families to flourish. The adolescent narrator's acceptance of his family's fate, his emphasis on the importance of animals over humans, reduces us to a world where there is little room for illusions, and apparently even less for love. This is frequently the lesson of Rulfo's other stories, an outstanding example being "Paso del Norte." But in none of the other stories is life quite as bleak, nor are the opportunities for men and women quite so barren, as in "We're Very Poor."

We're Very Poor

Everything is going from bad to worse here. Last week my Aunt Jacinta died, and on Saturday, when we'd already buried her and we started getting over the sadness, it began raining like never before. That made my father mad, because the whole rye harvest was stacked out in the open, drying in the sun. And the cloudburst came all of a sudden in great waves of water, without giving us time to get in even a handful; all we could do at our house was stay huddled together under the roof, watching how the cold water falling from the sky ruined that yellow rye so recently harvested.

And only yesterday, when my sister Tacha just turned twelve, we found out that the cow my father had given her for her birthday had been swept away by the river.

The river started rising three nights ago, about dawn. I was asleep, but the noise the river was making woke me up right away and made me jump out of bed and grab my blanket, as if the roof of our house was falling in. But then I went back to sleep, because I recognized the sound of the river, and that sound went on and on the same until I fell asleep again.

From *The Burning Plain and Other Stories* by Juan Rulfo, translated by George D. Schade. Copyright © 1967 Fondo de Cultura Económica. Part of the Texas Pan American Series published by the University of Texas Press. Reprinted by permission.

When I got up, the morning was full of black clouds and it looked like it had been raining without letup. The noise the river made kept getting closer and louder. You could smell it, like you smell a fire, the rotting smell of backwater.

When I went out to take a look, the river had already gone over its banks. It was slowly rising along the main street and was rushing into the house of that woman called La Tambora. You could hear the gurgling of the water when it entered her yard and when it poured out the door in big streams. La Tambora rushed in and out through what was already a part of the river, shooing her hens out into the street so they'd hide some place where the current couldn't reach them.

On the other side, where the bend is, the river must've carried off—who knows when—the tamarind tree in my Aunt Jacinta's yard, because now you can't see any tamarind. It was the only one in the village, and that's the reason why people realize this flood we're having is the biggest one that's gone down the river in many years.

My sister and I went back in the afternoon to look at that mountain of water that kept getting thicker and darker and was now way above where the bridge should be. We stood there for hours and hours without getting tired, just looking at it. Then we climbed up the ravine, because we wanted to hear what people were saying, for down below, by the river, there's a rumbling noise, and you just see lots of mouths opening and shutting like they wanted to say something, but you don't hear anything. That's why we climbed up the ravine, where other people are watching the river and telling each other about the damage it's done. That's where we found out the river had carried off La Serpentina, the cow that belonged to my sister Tacha because my father gave it to her on her birthday, and it had one white ear and one red ear and very pretty eyes.

I still don't understand why La Serpentina got it into her head to cross the river when she knew it wasn't the same river she was used to every day. La Serpentina was never so flighty. What probably happened is she must've been asleep to have let herself get drowned like that. Lots of times I had to wake her up when I opened the corral gate for her, because if I hadn't she would've stayed there all day long with her eyes shut, real quiet and sighing, like you hear cows sighing when they're asleep.

What must've happened then was that she went to sleep. Maybe she woke up when she felt the heavy water hit her flanks. Maybe then she got scared and tried to turn back; but when she started back she probably got confused and got a cramp in that water, black and hard as sliding earth. Maybe she bellowed for help. Only God knows how she bellowed.

I asked a man who saw the river wash her away if he hadn't seen the calf that was with her. But the man said he didn't know whether he'd seen it. He only said that a spotted cow passed by with her legs in the air very near where he was standing and then she turned over and he didn't see her horns or her legs or any sign of her again. Lots of tree trunks with their roots and everything were floating down the river and he was very busy fishing out firewood, so he couldn't be sure whether they were animals or trunks going by.

That's why we don't know whether the calf is alive, or if it went down the river with its mother. If it did, may God watch over them both.

What we're upset about in my house is what may happen any day, now that my sister Tacha is left without anything. My father went to a lot of trouble to get hold of La Serpentina when she was a heifer to give to my sister, so she would have a little capital and not become a bad women like my two older sisters did.

My father says they went bad because we were poor in my house and they were very wild. From the time they were little girls they were sassy and difficult. And as soon as they grew up they started going out with the worst kind of men, who taught them bad things. They learned fast and they soon caught on to the whistles calling them late at night. Later on they even went out during the daytime. They kept going down to the river for water and sometimes, when you'd least expect it, there they'd be out in the yard, rolling around on the ground, all naked, and each one with a man on top of her.

Then my father ran them both off. At first he put up with them as long as he could, but later on he couldn't take it any more and he threw them out into the street. They went to Ayutla and I don't know where else; but they're bad women.

That's why father is so upset now about Tacha—because he doesn't want her to go the way of her two sisters. He realized how poor she is with the loss of her cow, seeing that she has nothing left to count on while she's growing up so as to marry a good man who will always love her. And that's going to be hard now. When she had the cow it was a different story, for somebody would've had the courage to marry her, just to get that fine cow.

Our only hope left is that the calf is still alive. I hope to God it didn't try to cross the river behind its mother. Because if it did, then my sister Tacha is just one step from becoming a bad women. And Mamma doesn't want her to.

My mother can't understand why God has punished her so giving her daughters like that, when in her family, from Grandma on down, there have never been bad people. They were all raised in the fear of God and were very obedient and were never disrespectful to anybody. That's the way they all were. Who knows where those two daughters of hers got that bad example. She can't remember. She goes over and over all her memories and she can't see clearly where she went wrong or why she had one daughter after another with the same bad ways. She can't remember any such example. And everytime she thinks about them she cries and says, "May God look after the two of them."

But my father says there's nothing to be done about them now. The one in danger is the one still at home, Tacha, who is shooting up like a rod and whose breasts are beginning to fill out, promising to be like her sisters'—high and pointed, the kind that bounce about and attract attention.

"Yes," he says, "they'll catch the eye of anyone who sees them. And she'll end up going bad; mark my words, she'll end up bad."

That's why my father is so upset.

And Tacha cries when she realizes her cow won't come back because the river killed her. She's here at my side in her pink dress, looking at the river from the ravine, and she can't stop crying. Streams of dirty water run down her face as if the river had gotten inside her.

I put my arms around her trying to comfort her, but she doesn't understand. She cries even more. A noise comes out of her mouth like the river makes near its banks, which makes her tremble and shake all over, and the whole time the river keeps on rising. The drops of stinking water from the river splash Tacha's wet face, and her two little breasts bounce up and down without stopping, as if suddenly they were beginning to swell, to start now on the road to ruin.

Discussion of Rulfo's "We're Very Poor"

1. The young man in this story unconsciously constructs a set of values about human relationships. What are some of them?

2. The father in the story obviously is trying to live a moral life and improve his family's condition. Are his actions towards his daughters justified?

3. The story infers that among the poor people in this society prostitution becomes a necessary profession to which young women are driven by adversity. In the metaphorical sense, which other women in some of the stories you have read are prostitutes? What about some of the men in this anthology: Have they sold themselves to women? To social forces?

CLARICE LISPECTOR

b. 1925

🌷   Clarice Lispector emigrated to Brazil from the Ukraine
when she was two months old. A journalist and lawyer, she has
traveled widely and spent eight years in the United States. None of
her six novels has been translated into English. Her considerable
reputation in Brazil, however, is based largely on *Family Ties*
(1960), which has been translated and is a compilation of short
fiction written during the 1940s and 1950s. Her works are existential
in that they are removed from time and place and force the reader
to concentrate on the subjective consciousness of a particular individual whose thoughts, struggles, or actions reveal furious pas-
sions at war with one another. This is particularly true of her
feminine characters. But what differentiates them from women and
men portrayed by other authors to be in similar circumstances is
their ability to come close to an objective understanding of themselves—and their humor in so doing.

Daydreams of a Drunk Woman

It seemed to her that the trolley cars were about to cross through
the room as they caused her reflected image to tremble. She was
combing her hair at her leisure in front of the dressing table with
its three mirrors, and her strong white arms shivered in the cool-
ness of the evening. Her eyes did not look away as the mirrors
trembled, sometimes dark, sometimes luminous. Outside, from a
window above, something heavy and hollow fell to the ground.
Had her husband and the little ones been at home, the idea would
already have occurred to her that they were to blame. Her eyes did
not take themselves off her image, her comb worked pensively, and
her open dressing gown revealed in the mirrors the intersected
breasts of several women.

"Evening News" shouted the newsboy to the mild breeze in
Riachuelo Street, and something trembled as if foretold. She threw
her comb down on the dressing table and sang dreamily: "Who
saw the little spar-row . . . it passed by the window . . . and flew beyond Minho!"—but, suddenly becoming irritated, she shut up
abruptly like a fan.

She lay down and fanned herself impatiently with a newspaper
that rustled in the room. She clutched the bedsheet, inhaling its
odor as she crushed its starched embroidery with her red-lacquered
nails. Then, almost smiling, she started to fan herself once more.

From *Family Ties* by Clarice Lispector, translated by Giovanni Pontiero. Copyright ©
1972 by Clarice Lispector. Part of the Texas Pan American Series published by the
University of Texas Press. Reprinted by permission.

Oh my!—she sighed as she began to smile. She beheld the picture of her bright smile, the smile of a woman who was still young, and she continued to smile to herself, closing her eyes and fanning herself still more vigorously. Oh my!—she would come fluttering in from the street like a butterfly.

"Hey there! Guess who came to see me today?" she mused as a feasible and interesting topic of conversation. "No idea, tell me," those eyes asked her with a gallant smile, those sad eyes set in one of those pale faces that make one feel so uncomfortable. "Maria Quiteria, my dear!" she replied coquettishly with her hand on her hip. "And who, might we ask, would she be?" they insisted gallantly, but now without any expression. "You!" she broke off, slightly annoyed. How boring!

Oh what a succulent room! Here she was, fanning herself in Brazil. The sun, trapped in the blinds, shimmered on the wall like the strings of a guitar. Riachuelo Street shook under the gasping weight of the trolley cars which came from Mem de Sá Street. Curious and impatient, she listened to the vibrations of the china cabinet in the drawing room. Impatiently she rolled over to lie face downward, and, sensuously stretching the toes of her dainty feet, she awaited her next thought with open eyes. "Whosoever found, searched," she said to herself in the form of a rhymed refrain, which always ended up by sounding like some maxim. Until eventually she fell asleep with her mouth wide open, her saliva staining the pillow.

She only woke up when her husband came into the room the moment he returned from work. She did not want to eat any dinner nor to abandon her dreams, and she went back to sleep: let him content himself with the leftovers from lunch.

And now that the kids were at the country house of their aunts in Jacarepaguá, she took advantage of their absence in order to begin the day as she pleased: restless and frivolous in her bed . . . one of those whims perhaps. Her husband appeared before her, having already dressed, and she did not even know what he had prepared for his breakfast. She avoided examining his suit to see whether it needed brushing . . . little did she care if this was his day for attending to his business in the city. But when he bent over to kiss her, her capriciousness crackled like a dry leaf.

"Don't paw me!"

"What the devil's the matter with you?" the man asked her in amazement, as he immediately set about attempting some more effective caress.

Obstinate, she would not have known what to reply, and she felt so touchy and aloof that she did not even know where to find a suitable reply. She suddenly lost her temper. "Go to hell! . . . prowling round me like some old tomcat."

He seemed to think more clearly and said, firmly, "You're ill, my girl."

She accepted his remark, surprised, and vaguely flattered.

She remained in bed the whole day long listening to the silence of the house without the scurrying of the kids, without her husband who would have his meals in the city today. Her anger was tenuous and ardent. She only got up to go to the bathroom, from which she returned haughty and offended.

The morning turned into a long enormous afternoon, which then turned into a shallow night, which innocently dawned throughout the entire house.

She was still in bed, peaceful and casual. She was in love. . . . She was anticipating her love for the man whom she would love one day. Who knows, this sometimes happened, and without any guilt or injury for either partner. Lying in bed thinking and thinking, and almost laughing as one does over some gossip. Thinking and thinking. About what? As if she knew. So she just stayed there.

The next minute she would get up, angry. But in the weakness of that first instant she felt dizzy and fragile in the room which swam round and round until she managed to grope her way back to bed, amazed that it might be true. "Hey, girl, don't you go getting sick on me!" she muttered suspiciously. She raised her hand to her forehead to see if there was any fever.

That night, until she fell asleep, her mind became more and more delirious—for how many minutes?—until she flopped over, fast asleep, to snore beside her husband.

She awoke late, the potatoes waiting to be peeled, the kids expected home that same evening from their visit to the country. "God, I've lost my self-respect, I have! My day for washing and darning socks. . . . What a lazy bitch you've turned out to be!" she scolded herself, inquisitive and pleased . . . shopping to be done, fish to remember, already so late on a hectic sunny morning.

But on Saturday night they went to the tavern in Tiradentes Square at the invitation of a rich businessman, she with her new dress which didn't have any fancy trimmings but was made of good material, a dress that would last her a lifetime. On Saturday night, drunk in Tiradentes Square, inebriated but with her husband at her side to give her support, and being very polite in front of the other man who was so much more refined and rich— striving to make conversation, for she was no provincial ninny and she had already experienced life in the capital. But so drunk that she could no longer stand.

And if her husband was not drunk it was only because he did not want to show disrespect for the businessman, and, full of solicitude and humility, he left the swaggering to the other fellow. His manner suited such an elegant occasion, but it gave her such an urge to laugh! She despised him beyond words! She looked at her husband stuffed into his new suit and found him so ridiculous! . . . so drunk that she could no longer stand, but without losing her self-respect as a woman. And the green wine from her native Portugal slowly being drained from her glass.

When she got drunk, as if she had eaten a heavy Sunday

lunch, all things which by their true nature are separate from each other—the smell of oil on the one hand, of a male on the other; the soup tureen on the one hand, the waiter on the other —became strangely linked by their nature and the whole thing was nothing short of disgraceful . . . shocking!

And if her eyes appeared brilliant and cold, if her movements faltered clumsily until she succeeded in reaching the toothpick holder, beneath the surface she really felt so far quite at ease . . . there was that full cloud to transport her without effort. Her puffy lips, her teeth white, and her body swollen with wine. And the vanity of feeling drunk, making her show such disdain for everything, making her feel swollen and rotund like a large cow.

Naturally she talked, since she lacked neither the ability to converse nor topics to discuss. But the words that a woman uttered when drunk were like being pregnant—mere words on her lips which had nothing to do with the secret core that seemed like a pregnancy. God, how queer she felt! Saturday night, her every-day soul lost, and how satisfying to lose it, and to remind her of former days, only her small, ill-kempt hands—and here she was now with her elbows resting on the white and red checked tablecloth like a gambling table, deeply launched upon a degrading and revolting existence. And what about her laughter? . . . this outburst of laughter which mysteriously emerged from her full white throat, in response to the polite manners of the businessman, an outburst of laughter coming from the depths of that sleep, and from the depths of that security of someone who has a body. Her white flesh was as sweet as lobster, the legs of a live lobster wriggling slowly in the air . . . that urge to be sick in order to plunge that sweetness into something really awful . . . and that perversity of someone who has a body.

She talked and listened with curiosity to what she herself was about to reply to the well-to-do businessman who had so kindly invited them out to dinner and paid for their meal. Intrigued and amazed, she heard what she was on the point of replying, and what she might say in her present state would serve as an augury for the future. She was no longer a lobster, but a harsher sign— that of the scorpion. After all, she had been born in November.

A beacon that sweeps through the dawn while one is asleep, such was her drunkenness which floated slowly through the air.

At the same time, she was conscious of such feelings! Such feelings! When she gazed upon that picture which was so beautifully painted in the restaurant, she was immediately overcome by an artistic sensibility. No one would get it out of her head that she had really been born for greater things. She had always been one for works of art.

But such sensibility! And not merely excited by the picture of grapes and pears and dead fish with shining scales. Her sensibility irritated her without causing her pain, like a broken fingernail.

And if she wanted, she could allow herself the luxury of becoming even more sensitive, she could go still further, because she was protected by a situation, protected like everyone who had attained a position in life. Like someone saved from misfortune. I'm so miserable, dear God! If she wished, she could even pour more wine into her glass, and, protected by the position which she had attained in life, become even more drunk just so long as she did not lose her self-respect. And so, even more drunk, she peered round the room, and how she despised the barren people in that restaurant. Not a real man among them. How sad it really all seemed. How she despised the barren people in that restaurant, while she was plump and heavy and generous to the full. And everything in the restaurant seemed so remote, the one thing distant from the other, as if the one might never be able to converse with the other. Each existing for itself, and God existing there for everyone.

Her eyes once more settled on that female whom she had instantly detested the moment she had entered the room. Upon arriving, she had spotted her seated at a table accompanied by a man and all dolled up in a hat and jewelry, glittering like a false coin, all coy and refined. What a fine hat she was wearing! . . . Bet you anything she isn't even married for all that pious look on her face . . . and that fine hat stuck on her head. A fat lot of good her hypocrisy would do her, and she had better watch out in case her airs and graces proved her undoing! The more sanctimonious they were, the bigger frauds they turned out to be. And as for the waiter, he was a great nitwit, serving her, full of gestures and finesse, while the sallow man with her pretended not to notice. And that pious ninny so pleased with herself in that hat and so modest about her slim waistline, and I'll bet she couldn't even bear her man a child. All right, it was none of her business, but from the moment she arrived she felt the urge to give that blonde prude of a woman playing the grand lady in her hat a few good slaps on the face. She didn't even have any shape, and she was flat-chested. And no doubt, for all her fine hats, she was nothing more than a fishwife trying to pass herself off as a duchess.

Oh, how humiliated she felt at having come to the bar without a hat, and her head now felt bare. And that madam with her affectations, playing the refined lady! I know what you need, my beauty, you and your sallow boy friend! And if you think I envy you with your flat chest, let me assure you that I don't give a damn for you and your hats. Shameless sluts like you are only asking for a good hard slap on the face.

In her holy rage, she stretched out a shaky hand and reached for a toothpick.

But finally, the difficulty of arriving home disappeared; she now bestirred herself amidst the familiar reality of her room, now seated on the edge of the bed, a slipper dangling from one foot.

And, as she had half closed her blurred eyes, everything took on the appearance of flesh, the foot of the bed, the window, the suit her husband had thrown off, and everything became rather painful. Meanwhile, she was becoming larger, more unsteady, swollen and gigantic. If only she could get closer to herself, she would find she was even larger. Each of her arms could be explored by someone who didn't even recognize that they were dealing with an arm, and someone could plunge into each eye and swim around without knowing that it was an eye. And all around her everything was a bit painful. Things of the flesh stricken by nervous twinges. The chilly air had caught her as she had come out of the restaurant.

She was sitting up in bed, resigned and sceptical. And this was nothing yet, God only knew—she was perfectly aware that this was nothing yet. At this moment things were happening to her that would only hurt later and in earnest. When restored to her normal size, her anesthetized body would start to wake up, throbbing, and she would begin to pay for those big meals and drinks. Then, since this would really end up by happening, I might as well open my eyes right now (which she did) and then everything looked smaller and clearer, without her feeling any pain. Everything, deep down, was the same, only smaller and more familiar. She was sitting quite upright in bed, her stomach so full, absorbed and resigned, with the delicacy of one who sits waiting until her partner awakens. "You gorge yourself and I pay the piper," she said sadly, looking at the dainty white toes of her feet. She looked around her, patient and obedient. Ah, words, nothing but words, the objects in the room lined up in the order of words, to form those confused and irksome phrases that he who knows how will read. Boredom . . . such awful boredom. . . . How sickening! How very annoying! When all is said and done, heaven help me—God knows best. What was one to do? How can I describe this thing inside me? Anyhow, God knows best. And to think that she had enjoyed herself so much last night! . . . and to think of how nice it all was—a restaurant to her liking—and how she had been seated elegantly at table. At table! The world would exclaim. But she made no reply, drawing herself erect with a bad-tempered click of her tongue . . . irritated . . . "Don't come to me with your endearments" . . . disenchanted, resigned, satiated, married, content, vaguely nauseated.

It was at this moment that she became deaf: one of her senses was missing. She clapped the palm of her hand over her ear, which only made things worse . . . suddenly filling her eardrum with the whirr of an elevator . . . life suddenly becoming loud and magnified in its smallest movements. One of two things: either she was deaf or hearing all too well. She reacted against this new suggestion with a sensation of spite and annoyance, with a sigh of resigned satiety. "Drop dead," she said gently . . . defeated.

"And when in the restaurant . . ." she suddenly recalled when she had been in the restaurant her husband's protector had pressed his foot against hers beneath the table, and above the table his face was watching her. By coincidence or intentionally? The rascal. A fellow, to be frank, who was not unattractive. She shrugged her shoulders.

And when above the roundness of her low-cut dress—right in the middle of Tiradentes Square! she thought, shaking her head incredulously—that fly had settled on her bare bosom. What cheek!

Certain things were good because they were almost nauseating . . . the noise like that of an elevator in her blood, while her husband lay snoring at her side . . . her chubby little children sleeping in the other room, the little villains. Ah, what's wrong with me! she wondered desperately. Have I eaten too much? Heavens above! What *is* wrong with me?

It was unhappiness.

Her toes playing with her slipper . . . the floor not too clean at that spot. "What a slovenly, lazy bitch you've become."

Not tomorrow, because her legs would not be too steady, but the day after tomorrow that house of hers would be a sight worth seeing: she would give it a scouring with soap and water which would get rid of all the dirt! "You mark my words," she threatened in her rage. Ah, she was feeling so well, so strong, as if she still had milk in those firm breasts. When her husband's friend saw her so pretty and plump he had immediately felt respect for her. And when she started to get embarrassed she did not know which way to look. Such misery! What was one to do? Seated on the edge of the bed, blinking in resignation. How well one could see the moon on these summer nights. She leaned over slightly, indifferent and resigned. The moon! How clearly one could see it. The moon high and yellow gliding through the sky, poor thing. Gliding, gliding . . . high up, high up. The moon! Then her vulgarity exploded in a sudden outburst of affection; "you slut," she cried out, laughing.

Discussion of Lispector's "Daydreams of a Drunk Woman"

1. Although both the title and the context imply inebriation, to what extent are these "daydreams" idle dreams and to what extent are they rather profound meditations about the difficulties of life?

2. Are there some ways in which Lispector's heroine is simply a more modern version of Machado de Assis's? If Conceição were to speak, what would she say that could be similar?

3. Typically, such extended meditations as the one in this story reveal certain tensions within the speaker. Some of these are obvious enough, but in what ways does the heroine seem at ease with herself? Compare her with the heroine of "Beasts of the Southern Wild."

DORIS LESSING

b. 1919

❧ Besides *The Golden Notebook* (1962), *The Summer Before the Dark* (1969), and *Memoirs of a Survivor* (1975), Doris Lessing's novels include *Briefing for a Descent into Hell* (1971) and the five-volume Martha Quest series entitled *Children of Violence* (1952–1964). Lessing has also written several plays, many articles and personal narratives, and poetry. Among her short story collections are *The Habit of Loving* (1957), *A Man and Two Women* (1963), and *African Stories* (1964). Born of British parents in Persia, growing up in Southern Rhodesia, and settling in England in 1949, Doris Lessing is perhaps speaking for herself through her character Molly: " 'It's coming back to England again—everybody so shut up, taking offense, I feel like breaking out and shouting and screaming whenever I set foot on this frozen soil. I feel locked up the moment I breathe our sacred air' " (*The Golden Notebook* [New York: Simon and Schuster, 1962], p. 17). Post–World War II society, its political dreams and abstractions form the language environment in which her characters attempt to survive. Said Josephine Hendin in a review of *The Summer Before the Dark*, "None of Mrs. Lessing's women can flourish in the world as it is, none can resist the engulfing power of others."

Wine

A man and woman walked toward the boulevard from a little hotel in a side street.

The trees were still leafless, black, cold; but the fine twigs were swelling toward spring, so that looking upward it was with an expectation of the first glimmering greenness. Yet everything was calm, and the sky was a calm, classic blue.

The couple drifted slowly along. Effort, after days of laziness, seemed impossible; and almost at once they turned into a café and sank down, as if exhausted, in the glass-walled space that was thrust forward into the street.

The place was empty. People were seeking the mid-day meal in the restaurants. Not all: that morning crowds had been demonstrating, a procession had just passed, and its straggling end could still be seen. The sounds of violence, shouted slogans and singing, no longer absorbed the din of Paris traffic; but it was these sounds that had roused the couple from sleep.

A waiter leaned at the door, looking after the crowds, and he reluctantly took an order for coffee.

The man yawned; the woman caught the infection; and they laughed with an affectation of guilt and exchanged glances before their eyes, without regret, parted. When the coffee came, it remained untouched. Neither spoke. After some time the woman yawned again; and this time the man turned and looked at her critically, and she looked back. Desire asleep, they looked. This remained: that while everything which drove them slept, they accepted from each other a sad irony; they could look at each other without illusion, steady-eyed.

And then, inevitably, the sadness deepened in her till she consciously resisted it; and into him came the flicker of cruelty.

"Your nose needs powdering," he said.

"You need a whipping boy."

But always he refused to feel sad. She shrugged, and, leaving him to it, turned to look out. So did he. At the far end of the boulevard there was a faint agitation, like stirred ants, and she heard him mutter, "Yes, and it still goes on. . . ."

Mocking, she said, "Nothing changes, everything always the same. . . ."

But he had flushed. "I remember," he began, in a different voice. He stopped, and she did not press him, for he was gazing at the distant demonstrators with a bitterly nostalgic face.

Outside drifted the lovers, the married couples, the students, the old people. There the stark trees; there the blue, quiet sky. In a month the trees would be vivid green; the sun would pour down heat; the people would be brown, laughing, bare-limbed. No, no, she said to herself, at the vision of activity. Better the static sadness. And, all at once, unhappiness welled up in her, catching her throat, and she was back fifteen years in another country. She stood in blazing tropical moonlight, stretching her arms to a landscape that offered her nothing but silence; and then she was running down a path where small stones glinted sharp underfoot, till at last she fell spent in a swathe of glistening grass. Fifteen years.

It was at this moment that the man turned abruptly and called the waiter and ordered wine.

"What," she said humorously, "already?"

"Why not?"

For the moment she loved him completely and maternally, till she suppressed the counterfeit and watched him wait, fidgeting, for the wine, pour it, and then set the two glasses before them beside the still-brimming coffee cups. But she was again remembering that night, envying the girl ecstatic with moonlight, who ran crazily through the trees in an unsharable desire for—but that was the point.

"What are you thinking of?" he asked, still a little cruel.

"Ohhh," she protested humorously.

"That's the trouble, that's the trouble." He lifted his glass, glanced at her, and set it down. "Don't you want to drink?"

"Not yet."

He left his glass untouched and began to smoke.

These moments demanded some kind of gesture—something slight, even casual, but still an acknowledgment of the separateness of those two people in each of them; the one seen, perhaps, as a soft-staring never-closing eye, observing, always observing, with a tired compassion; the other, a shape of violence that struggled on in the cycle of desire and rest, creation and achievement.

He gave it her. Again their eyes met in the grave irony, before he turned away, flicking his fingers irritably against the table; and she turned also, to note the black branches where the sap was tingling.

"I remember," he began; and again she said, in protest, "Ohhh!"

He checked himself. "Darling," he said drily, "you're the only woman I've ever loved." They laughed.

"It must have been this street. Perhaps this café—only they change so. When I went back yesterday to see the place where I came every summer, it was a *pâtisserie*, and the woman had forgotten me. There was a whole crowd of us—we used to go around together—and I met a girl here, I think, for the first time. There were recognized places for contacts; people coming from Vienna or Prague, or wherever it was, knew the places—it couldn't be this café, unless they've smartened it up. We didn't have the money for all this leather and chromium."

"Well, go on."

"I keep remembering her, for some reason. Haven't thought of her for years. She was about sixteen, I suppose. Very pretty—no, you're quite wrong. We used to study together. She used to bring her books to my room. I liked her, but I had my own girl, only she was studying something else, I forget what." He paused again, and again his face was twisted with nostalgia, and involuntarily she glanced over her shoulder down the street. The procession had completely disappeared, not even the sounds of singing and shouting remained.

"I remember her because. . . ." And, after a preoccupied silence: "Perhaps it is always the fate of the virgin who comes and offers herself, naked, to be refused."

"What!" she exclaimed, startled. Also, anger stirred in her. She noted it, and sighed. "Go on."

"I never made love to her. We studied together all that summer. Then, one weekend, we all went off in a bunch. None of us had any money, of course, and we used to stand on the pavements and beg lifts, and meet up again in some village. I was with my own girl, but that night we were helping the farmer get in his fruit, in payment for using his barn to sleep in, and I found this girl Marie was beside me. It was moonlight, a lovely night, and we were all singing and making love. I kissed her, but that was all. That night she came to me. I was sleeping up in the loft with another lad. He was asleep. I sent her back down to the others. They were all together down in the hay. I told her she was too young. But she was no younger than my own girl." He stopped; and after all these years his face was rueful and puzzled. "I don't know," he said. "I don't know why I sent her back." Then he laughed. "Not that it matters, I suppose."

"Shameless hussy," she said. The anger was strong now. "You had kissed her, hadn't you?"

He shrugged. "But we were all playing the fool. It was a glorious night—gathering apples, the farmer shouting and swearing at us because we were making love more than working, and singing and drinking wine. Besides, it was that time: the youth movement. We regarded faithfulness and jealousy and all that sort of thing as remnants of bourgeois morality." He laughed again, rather painfully. "I kissed her. There she was, beside me, and she knew my girl was with me that weekend."

"You kissed her," she said accusingly.

He fingered the stem of his wineglass, looking over at her and grinning. "Yes, darling," he almost crooned at her. "I kissed her."

She snapped over into anger. "There's a girl all ready for love. You make use of her for working. Then you kiss her. You know quite well. . . ."

"What do I know quite well?"

"It was a cruel thing to do."

"I was a kid myself. . . ."

"Doesn't matter." She noted, with discomfort, that she was almost crying. "Working with her! Working with a girl of sixteen, all summer!"

"But we all studied very seriously. She was a doctor afterwards, in Vienna. She managed to get out when the Nazis came in, but. . . ."

She said impatiently, "Then you kissed her, on *that* night. Imagine her, waiting till the others were asleep, then she climbed up the ladder to the loft, terrified the other man might wake up, then she stood watching you sleep, and she slowly took off her dress and. . . ."

"Oh, I wasn't asleep. I pretended to be. She came up dressed. Shorts and sweater—our girls didn't wear dresses and lipstick—more bourgeois morality. I watched her strip. The loft was full of moonlight. She put her hand over my mouth and came down beside me." Again, his face was filled with rueful amazement. "God knows, I can't understand it myself. She was a beautiful creature. I don't know why I remember it. It's been coming into my mind the last few days." After a pause, slowly twirling the wineglass: "I've been a failure in many things, but not with. . . ." He quickly lifted her hand, kissed it, and said sincerely: "I don't know why I remember it now, when. . . ." Their eyes met, and they sighed.

She said slowly, her hand lying in his: "And so you turned her away."

He laughed. "Next morning she wouldn't speak to me. She started a love affair with my best friend—the man who'd been beside me that night in the loft, as a matter of fact. She hated my guts, and I suppose she was right."

"Think of her. Think of her at that moment. She picked up her clothes, hardly daring to look at you. . . ."

"As a matter of fact she was furious. She called me all the names she could think of; I had to keep telling her to shut up, she'd wake the whole crowd."

"She climbed down the ladder and dressed again, in the dark. Then she went out of the barn, unable to go back to the others. She went into the orchard. It was still brilliant moonlight. Everything was silent and deserted, and she remembered how you'd all been singing and laughing and making love. She went to the tree where you'd kissed her. The moon was shining on the apples. She'll never forget it, never, never!"

He looked at her curiously. The tears were pouring down her face.

"It's terrible," she said. "Terrible. Nothing could ever make up to her for that. Nothing, as long as she lived. Just when everything was most perfect, all her life, she'd suddenly remember that night, standing alone, not a soul anywhere, miles of damned empty moonlight. . . ."

He looked at her shrewdly. Then, with a sort of humorous, deprecating grimace, he bent over and kissed her and said: "Darling, it's not my fault; it just isn't my fault."

"No," she said.

He put the wineglass into her hands; and she lifted it, looked at the small crimson globule of warming liquid, and drank with him.

Discussion of Lessing's "Wine"

1. Compare the setting of this story with that of "Cat in the Rain." Do the settings suggest similar marital relationships?

2. Compare the couple in "Wine" with the couple in "Giving Blood." What do these stories dramatize about the bonds of marriage, about subtle cruelties and kindnesses?

3. What is the metaphoric function of the wine in this story?

GABRIEL GARCÍA MÁRQUEZ

b. 1928

❧ García Márquez is a Columbian journalist whose fifth book, *One Hundred Years of Solitude* (1967), is in its forty-fifth printing in Latin America alone. Three of his other books—*Leaf Storm* (1955), *No One Writes to the Colonel* (1961), and *The Funeral of Mama Grande* (1962)—have been translated into English. His latest work, the novel *El Otoño del Patriarca,* was published in 1975 and translated as *The Autumn of the Patriarch* (1976). García Márquez was born in Aractaca, Columbia, a small town on the Caribbean side of the country. Nearby was the even smaller town of Macondo, which is the locale of all his stories, thus suggesting inevitable comparisons by North Americans to William Faulkner, whose stories also depend on intricately constructed worlds based on real regions. García Márquez is in fact an admirer of Faulkner and shares with him an emphasis on the simple men and women whose ability to endure captures the reader's imagination. Although the short stories contained in *No One Writes to the Colonel*—in which "Tuesday Siesta" appears—become extremely complex, each begins with an image rather than a phrase, idea, or concept. In this story the image of the mother's quiet train ride leads to her defense of her son and her quiet courage to face the street alone. One of García Márquez's recurrent themes is the responsibility of women in society. It is they who keep it going and who sustain the family. Behind the apparent innocence of "Tuesday Siesta" lies a powerful analysis of how women sustain society.

Tuesday Siesta

The train emerged from the quivering tunnel of sandy rocks, began to cross the symmetrical, interminable banana plantations, and the air became humid and they couldn't feel the sea breeze any more. A stifling blast of smoke came in the car window. On the narrow road parallel to the railway there were oxcarts loaded with green bunches of bananas. Beyond the road, in uncultivated spaces set at odd intervals there were offices with electric fans, red-brick buildings, and residences with chairs and little white tables on the terraces among dusty palm trees and rosebushes. It was eleven in the morning, and the heat had not yet begun.

"You'd better close the window," the woman said. "Your hair will get full of soot."

The girl tried to, but the shade wouldn't move because of the rust.

They were the only passengers in the lone third-class car. Since the smoke of the locomotive kept coming through the window, the girl left her seat and put down the only things they had with them: a plastic sack with some things to eat and a bouquet of flowers wrapped in newspaper. She sat on the opposite seat, away from the window, facing her mother. They were both in severe and poor mourning clothes.

The girl was twelve years old, and it was the first time she'd ever been on a train. The woman seemed too old to be her mother, because of the blue veins on her eyelids and her small, soft, and shapeless body, in a dress cut like a cassock. She was riding with her spinal column braced firmly against the back of the seat, and held a peeling patent-leather handbag in her lap with both hands. She bore the conscientious serenity of someone accustomed to poverty.

By twelve the heat had begun. The train stopped for ten minutes to take on water at a station where there was no town. Outside, in the mysterious silence of the plantations, the shadows seemed clean. But the still air inside the car smelled like untanned leather. The train did not pick up speed. It stopped at two identical towns with wooden houses painted bright colors. The woman's head nodded and she sank into sleep. The girl took off her shoes. Then she went to the washroom to put the bouquet of flowers in some water.

When she came back to her seat, her mother was waiting to eat. She gave her a piece of cheese, half a corn-meal pancake, and a cookie, and took an equal portion out of the plastic sack for herself. While they ate, the train crossed an iron bridge very slowly and passed a town just like the ones before, except that in this one there was a crowd in the plaza. A band was playing a lively tune under the oppressive sun. At the other side of town the plantations ended in a plain which was cracked from the drought.

The woman stopped eating.

"Put on your shoes," she said.

The girl looked outside. She saw nothing but the deserted plain, where the train began to pick up speed again, but she put the last piece of cookie into the sack and quickly put on her shoes. The woman gave her a comb.

"Comb your hair," she said.

The train whistle began to blow while the girl was combing her hair. The woman dried the sweat from her neck and wiped the oil from her face with her fingers. When the girl stopped combing, the train was passing the outlying houses of a town larger but sadder than the earlier ones.

"If you feel like doing anything, do it now," said the woman. "Later, don't take a drink anywhere even if you're dying of thirst. Above all, no crying."

The girl nodded her head. A dry, burning wind came in the window, together with the locomotive's whistle and the clatter of the old cars. The woman folded the plastic bag with the rest of the food and put it in the handbag. For a moment a complete picture of the town, on that bright August Tuesday, shone in the window. The girl wrapped the flowers in the soaking-wet newspapers, moved a little farther away from the window, and stared at her mother. She received a pleasant expression in return. The train began to whistle and slowed down. A moment later it stopped.

There was no one at the station. On the other side of the street, on the sidewalk shaded by the almond trees, only the pool hall was open. The town was floating in the heat. The woman and the girl got off the train and crossed the abandoned station—the tiles split apart by the grass growing up between—and over to the shady side of the street.

It was almost two. At that hour, weighted down by drowsiness, the town was taking a siesta. The stores, the town offices, the public school were closed at eleven, and didn't reopen until a little before four, when the train went back. Only the hotel across from the station, with its bar and pool hall, and the telegraph office at one side of the plaza stayed open. The houses, most of them built on the banana company's model, had their doors locked from inside and their blinds drawn. In some of them it was so hot that the residents ate lunch in the patio. Others leaned a chair against the wall, in the shade of the almond trees, and took their siesta right out in the street.

Keeping to the protective shade of the almond trees, the woman and the girl entered the town without disturbing the siesta. They went directly to the parish house. The woman scratched the metal grating on the door with her fingernail, waited a moment, and scratched again. An electric fan was humming inside. They did not hear the steps. They hardly heard the slight creaking of a door, and immediately a cautious voice, right next to the metal grating: "Who is it?" The woman tried to see through the grating.

"I need the priest," she said.

"He's sleeping now."

"It's an emergency," the woman insisted.

Her voice showed a calm determination.

The door was opened a little way, noiselessly, and a plump, older woman appeared, with very pale skin and hair the color of iron. Her eyes seemed too small behind her thick eyeglasses.

"Come in," she said, and opened the door all the way.

They entered a room permeated with an old smell of flowers. The woman of the house led them to a wooden bench and signaled them to sit down. The girl did so, but her mother remained standing, absent-mindedly, with both hands clutching the handbag. No noise could be heard above the electric fan.

The woman of the house reappeared at the door at the far end of the room. "He says you should come back after three," she said in a very low voice. " He just lay down five minutes ago."

"The train leaves at three-thirty," said the woman.

It was a brief and self-assured reply, but her voice remained pleasant, full of undertones. The woman of the house smiled for the first time.

"All right," she said.

When the far door closed again, the woman sat down next to her daughter. The narrow waiting room was poor, neat, and clean. On the other side of the wooden railing which divided the room, there was a worktable, a plain one with an oilcloth cover, and on top of the table a primitive typewriter next to a vase of flowers. The parish records were beyond. You could see that it was an office kept in order by a spinster.

The far door opened and this time the priest appeared, cleaning his glasses with a handkerchief. Only when he put them on was it evident that he was the brother of the woman who had opened the door.

"How can I help you?" he asked.

"The keys to the cemetery," said the woman.

The girl was seated with the flowers in her lap and her feet crossed under the bench. The priest looked at her, then looked at the woman, and then through the wire mesh of the window at the bright, cloudless sky.

"In this heat," he said. "You could have waited until the sun went down."

The woman moved her head silently. The priest crossed to the other side of the railing, took out of the cabinet a notebook covered in oilcloth, a wooden penholder, and an inkwell, and sat down at the table. There was more than enough hair on his hands to account for what was missing on his head.

"Which grave are you going to visit?" he asked.

"Carlos Centeno's," said the woman.

"Who?"

"Carlos Centeno," the woman repeated.

"He's the thief who was killed here last week," said the woman in the same tone of voice. "I am his mother."

The priest scrutinized her. She stared at him with quiet self-control, and the Father blushed. He lowered his head and began to write. As he filled the page, he asked the woman to identify herself, and she replied unhesitatingly, with precise details, as if she were reading them. The Father began to sweat. The girl unhooked the buckle of her left shoe, slipped her heel out of it, and rested it on the bench rail. She did the same with the right one.

It had all started the Monday of the previous week, at three in the morning, a few blocks from there. Rebecca, a lonely widow who lived in a house full of odds and ends, heard above the sound of the drizzling rain someone trying to force the front door from outside. She got up, rummaged around in her closet for an ancient revolver that no one had fired since the days of Colonel Aureliano Buendía, and went into the living room without turning on the lights. Orienting herself not so much by the noise at the lock as by a terror developed in her by twenty-eight years of loneliness, she fixed in her imagination not only the spot where the door was but also the exact height of the lock. She clutched the weapon with both hands, closed her eyes, and squeezed the trigger. It was the first time in her life that she had fired a gun. Immediately after the explosion, she could hear nothing except the murmur of the drizzle on the galvanized roof. Then she heard a little metallic bump on the cement porch, and a very low voice, pleasant but terribly exhausted: "Ah, Mother." The man they found dead in front of the house in the morning, his nose blown to bits, wore a flannel shirt with colored stripes, everyday pants with a rope for a belt, and was barefoot. No one in town knew him.

"So his name was Carlos Centeno," murmured the Father when he finished writing.

"Centeno Ayala," said the woman. "He was my only boy."

The priest went back to the cabinet. Two big rusty keys hung on the inside of the door; the girl imagined, as her mother had when she was a girl and as the priest himself must have imagined at some time, that they were Saint Peter's keys. He took them down, put them on the open notebook on the railing, and pointed with his forefinger to a place on the page he had just written, looking at the woman.

"Sign here."

The woman scribbled her name, holding the handbag under her arm. The girl picked up the flowers, came to the railing shuffling her feet, and watched her mother attentively.

The priest sighed.

"Didn't you ever try to get him on the right track?"

The woman answered when she finished signing.

"He was a very good man."

The priest looked first at the woman and then at the girl, and realized with a kind of pious amazement that they were not about to cry. The woman continued in the same tone:

"I told him never to steal anything that anyone needed to eat, and he minded me. On the other hand, before, when he used to box, he used to spend three days in bed, exhausted from being punched."

"All his teeth had to be pulled out," interrupted the girl.

"That's right," the woman agreed. "Every mouthful I ate those days tasted of the beatings my son got on Saturday nights."

"God's will is inscrutable," said the Father.

But he said it without much conviction, partly because experience had made him a little skeptical and partly because of the heat. He suggested that they cover their heads to guard against sunstroke. Yawning, and now almost completely asleep, he gave them instructions about how to find Carlos Centeno's grave. When they came back, they didn't have to knock. They should put the key under the door; and in the same place, if they could, they should put an offering for the Church. The woman listened to his directions with great attention, but thanked him without smiling.

The Father had noticed that there was someone looking inside, his nose pressed against the metal grating, even before he opened the door to the street. Outside was a group of children. When the door was opened wide, the children scattered. Ordinarily, at that hour there was no one in the street. Now there were not only children. There were groups of people under the almond trees. The Father scanned the street swimming in the heat and then he understood. Softly, he closed the door again.

"Wait a moment," he said without looking at the woman.

His sister appeared at the far door with a black jacket over her nightshirt and her hair down over her shoulders. She looked silently at the Father.

"What was it?" he asked.

"The people have noticed," murmured his sister.

"You'd better go out by the door to the patio," said the Father.

"It's the same there," said his sister. "Everybody is at the windows."

The woman seemed not to have understood until then. She tried to look into the street through the metal grating. Then she took the bouquet of flowers from the girl and began to move toward the door. The girl followed her.

"Wait until the sun goes down," said the Father.

"You'll melt," said his sister, motionless at the back of the room. "Wait and I'll lend you a parasol."

"Thank you," replied the woman. "We're all right this way."

She took the girl by the hand and went into the street.

Discussion of García Márquez's "Tuesday Siesta"

1. The action of this story, like that of the stories by Hemingway and Chopin, is full of puzzles and major moral issues. One such issue is the woman's devotion to her dead son. Is it mere reflex or is it conscious? If reflexive, is it still admirable?

2. "Tuesday Siesta" is the first story in a collection of short stories that are widely regarded as being thematically linked so that each one in some sense is a sequel to the one before it. What sort of sequel can you envision?

3. Although you are given very few details as to why, there seems to be something incredibly courageous in the woman's behavior. What aspects of the story seem designed to give you this impression?

MURIEL SPARK

b. 1918

❧ Muriel Spark's novels focus on the relationships between men and women in a variety of unusual and always concrete situations: teachers and students (*The Prime of Miss Jean Brodie*, 1961), the elderly and middle-aged (*Memento Mori*, 1959), Europeans and Asians (*The Mandelbaum Gate*, 1965). Among her more recent works the same diversity and imagination are at work: *The Abbess of Crewe* (1975), for example, is a parable of Watergate transposed into a Roman Catholic convent. It is typical of Spark's interest in the theological dimensions of modern life that such a juxtaposition would occur to her. "The Fathers' Daughters" gives the reader considerable insight into Spark's concern with the moral significance of human relationships. It also stands as an expression of her interest in the interplay between illusion and reality and the surprising extent to which human beings mistake the one for the other.

The Fathers' Daughters

She left the old man in his deck-chair on the front, having first adjusted the umbrella awning with her own hand, and with her own hand, put his panama hat at a comfortable angle. The beach attendant had been sulky, but she didn't see why one should lay out tips only for adjusting an umbrella and a panama hat. Since the introduction of the new franc it was impossible to tip less than a franc. There seemed to be a conspiracy all along the coast to hide the lesser coins from the visitors, and one could only find franc pieces in one's purse, and one had to be careful not to embarrass Father, and one . . .

She hurried along the Rue Paradis, keeping in the hot shade, among all the old, old smells of Nice, not only garlic wafting from the cafés, and of the hot invisible air itself, but the smells from her memory, from thirty-five summers at Nice in apartments of long ago, Father's summer salon, Father's friends' children, Father's friends, writers, young artists dating back five years at Nice, six, nine years; and then, before the war, twenty years ago—when we were at Nice, do you remember, Father? Do you remember the pension on the Boulevard Victor Hugo when we were rather poor? Do you remember the Americans at the Negresco in 1937—how changed, how demure they are now! Do you remember, Father, how in the old days we disliked the thick carpets—at least, you disliked them, and what you dislike, I dislike, isn't it so, Father?

Yes, Dora, we don't care for luxury. Comfort, yes, but luxury, no.

I doubt if we can afford to stay at an hotel on the front this year, Father.

What's that? What's that you say?

I said I doubt if we ought to stay on the front this year, Father; the Promenade des Anglais is becoming very trippery. Remember you disliked the thick carpets. . . .

Yes, yes, of course.

Of course, and so we'll go, I suggest, to a little place I've found on the Boulevard Gambetta, and if we don't like that there's a very good place on the Boulevard Victor Hugo. Within our means, Father, modest and . . .

What's that you say?

I said it wasn't a vulgar place, Father.

Ah. No.

And so I'll just drop them a note and book a couple of bedrooms. They may be small, but the food . . .

Facing the sea, Dora.

They are all very vulgar places facing the sea, Father. Very distracting. No peace at all. Times have changed, you know.

Ah. Well, I leave it to you, dear. Tell them I desire a large room, suitable for entertaining. Spare no expense, Dora.

Oh, of course not, Father.

And I hope to God we've won the lottery, she thought, as she hurried up the street to the lottery kiosk. Someone's got to win it out of the whole of France. The dark-skinned blonde at the lottery kiosk took an interest in Dora, who came so regularly each morning rather than buy a newspaper to see the results. She leaned over the ticket, holding her card of numbers, comparing it with Dora's ticket, with an expression of earnest sympathy.

'No luck,' Dora said.

'Try again tomorrow,' said the woman. 'One never knows. Life is a lottery . . .'

Dora smiled as one who must either smile or weep. On her way back to the sea front she thought, tomorrow I will buy five hundred francs' worth. Then she thought, no, no, I'd better not, I may run short of francs and have to take Father home before time. Dora, the food here is inferior.—I know, Father, but it's the same everywhere in France now, times have changed.—I think we should move to another hotel, Dora.—The others are all very expensive, Father.—What's that? What's that you say?—There are no other rooms available, Father, because of the tourists, these days.

The brown legs of lovely young men and girls passed her as she approached the sea. I ought to appreciate every minute of this, she thought, it may be the last time. This thoroughly blue sea, these brown limbs, these white teeth and innocent inane tongues, these palm trees—all this is what we are paying for.

'Everything all right, Father?'

'Where have you been, dear?'

'Only for a walk round the back streets to smell the savours.'

'Dora, you are a chip off the old block. What did you see?'

'Brown limbs, white teeth, men in shirt sleeves behind café windows, playing cards with green bottles in front of them.'

'Good—you see everything with my eyes, Dora.'

'Heat, smell, brown legs—it's what we are paying for, Father.'

'Dora, you are becoming vulgar, if you don't mind my saying so. The eye of the true artist doesn't see life in the way of goods paid for. The world is ours. It is our birthright. We take it without payment.'

'I'm not an artist like you, Father. Let me move the umbrella—you mustn't get too much sun.'

'Times have changed,' he said, glancing along the pebble beach, 'the young men today have no interest in life.'

She knew what her father meant. All along the beach, the young men playing with the air, girls, the sun; they were coming in from the sea, shaking the water from their heads; they were walking over the pebbles, then splashing into the water; they were taking an interest in their environment with every pore of their skin, as Father would have said in younger days when he was writing his books. What he meant now, when he said, 'the young men of today have no interest in life' was that his young disciples, his admirers, had all gone, they were grown old and preoccupied, and had not been replaced. The last young man to seek out Father had been a bloodless-looking youth—not that one judged by appearances—who had called about seven years ago at their house in Essex. Father had made the most of him, giving up many of his mornings to sitting in the library talking about books with the young man, about life and the old days. But this, the last of Father's disciples, had left after two weeks with a promise to send them the article he was going to write about Father and his works. Indeed he had sent a letter: 'Dear Henry Castlemaine,—Words cannot express my admiration . . .' After that they heard no more. Dora was not really sorry. He was a poor specimen compared with the men who, in earlier days, used to visit Father. Dora in her late teens could have married one of three or four vigorous members of the Henry Castlemaine set, but she had not done so because of her widowed father and his needs as a public figure; and now she sometimes felt it would have served Father better if she had married, because of Father—one could have contributed from a husband's income, perhaps, to his declining years.

Dora said, 'We must be going back to the hotel for lunch.'

'Let us lunch somewhere else. The food there is . . .'

She helped her father from the deck-chair and, turning to the sea, took a grateful breath of the warm blue breeze. A young man, coming up from the sea, shook his head blindly and splashed her with water; then noticing what he had done he said—turning and catching her by the arm—'Oh, I'm so sorry.' He spoke in English, was an Englishman, and she knew already how unmistakably she was an Englishwoman. 'All right,' she said, with a quick little laugh. The father was fumbling with his stick, the incident had passed, was immediately forgotten by Dora as she took his arm and propelled him across the wide hot boulevard where the white-suited policemen held up the impetuous traffic. 'How would you like to be arrested by one of those, Dora? He gave his deep short laugh and looked down at her. 'I'd love it, Father.' Perhaps he wouldn't insist on lunching elsewhere. If only they could reach the hotel it would be all right; Father would be too exhausted to insist. But already he was saying, 'Let's find somewhere for lunch.'

'Well, we've paid for it at the hotel, Father.'

'Don't be vulgar, my love.'

In the following March, when Dora met Ben Donadieu for the first time, she had the feeling she had seen him somewhere before, she knew not where. Later she told him of this, but he could not recall having seen her. But this sense of having seen him somewhere remained with Dora all her life. She came to believe she had met him in a former existence. In fact, it was on the beach at Nice that she had seen him, when he came up among the pebbles from the sea, and shook his hair, wetting her, and took her arm, apologising.

'Don't be vulgar, my love. The hotel food is appalling. Not French at all.'

'It's the same all over France, Father, these days.'

'There used to be a restaurant—what was its name?—in one of those little streets behind the Casino. Let's go there. All the writers go there.'

'Not any more, Father.'

'Well, so much the better. Let's go there in any case. What's the name of the place?—Anyway, come on, I could go there blindfold. All the writers used to go . . .'

She laughed, because, after all, he was sweet. As she walked with him towards the Casino she did not say—Not any more, Father, do the writers go there. The writers don't come to Nice, not those of moderate means. But there's one writer here this year, Father, called Kenneth Hope, whom you haven't heard about. He uses our beach, and I've seen him once—a shy, thin, middle-aged man. But he won't speak to anyone. He writes wonderfully, Father. I've read his novels, they open windows in the mind that have been bricked-up for a hundred years. I have read *The Inventors*, which made great fame and fortune for him. It is about the inventors of patent gadgets, what lives they lead, how their minds apply themselves to invention and to love, and you would think, while you were reading *The Inventors*, that the place they live in was dominated by inventors. He has that magic, Father—he can make you believe anything. Dora did not say this, for her father had done great work too, and deserved a revival. His name was revered, his books were not greatly spoken of, they were not read. He would not understand the fame of Kenneth Hope.

Father's novels were about the individual consciences of men and women, no one could do the individual conscience like Father. 'Here we are, Father—this is the place, isn't it?'

'No, Dora, it's further along.'

'Oh, but that's the Tumbril; it's wildly expensive.'

'Really, darling!'

She decided to plead the heat, and to order only a slice of melon for lunch with a glass of her father's wine. Both tall and slim, they entered the restaurant. Her hair was drawn back, the bones of her face were good, her eyes were small and fixed ready for humour, for she had decided to be a spinster and do it properly; she looked forty-six and she did not look forty-six; her skin was dry; her mouth was thin, and growing thinner with the worry about money. The father looked eighty years old, as he was. Thirty years ago people used to turn round and say, as he passed, 'That's Henry Castlemaine.'

Ben lay on his stomach on his mattress on the beach enclosure. Carmelita Hope lay on her mattress, next to him. They were eating rolls and cheese and drinking white wine which the beach attendant had brought to them from the café. Carmelita's tan was like a perfect garment, drawn skintight over her body. Since leaving school she had been in numerous jobs behind the scenes of film and television studios. Now she was out of a job again. She thought of marrying Ben, he was so entirely different from all the other men of her acquaintance, he was joyful and he was serious. He was also good looking: he was half-French, brought up in England. And an interesting age, thirty-one. He was a school teacher, but Father could probably get him a job in advertising or publishing. Father could do a lot of things for them both if only he would exert himself. Perhaps if she got married he would exert himself.

'Did you see your father at all yesterday, Carmelita?'

'No; as a matter of fact he's driven up the coast. I think he's gone to stay at some villa on the Italian border.'

'I should like to see more of him,' said Ben. 'And have a talk with him. I've never really had a chance to have a talk with him.'

'He's awfully shy,' said Carmelita, 'with my friends.'

Sometimes she felt a stab of dissatisfaction when Ben talked about her father. Ben had read all his books through and through—that seemed rather obsessive to Carmelita, reading books a second time and a third, as if one's memory was defective. It seemed to her that Ben loved her only because she was Kenneth Hope's daughter, and then, again, it seemed to her that this couldn't be so, for Ben wasn't attracted by money and success. Carmelita knew lots of daughters of famous men, and they were beset by suitors who were keen on their father's money and success. But it was the books that Ben liked about her father.

'He never interferes with me,' she said. 'He's rather good that way.'

'I would like to have a long talk with him,' Ben said.

'What about?—He doesn't like talking about his work.'

'No, but a man like that. I would like to know his mind.'

'What about my mind?'

'You've got a lovely mind. Full of pleasant laziness. No guilè.' He drew his forefinger from her knee to her ankle. She was wearing a pink bikini. She was very pretty and had hoped to become a starlet before her eighteenth birthday. Now she was very close to twenty-one and was thinking of marrying Ben instead, and was relieved that she no longer wanted to be an actress. He had lasted longer than any other boy-friend. She had often found a boy exciting at first but usually went off him quite soon. Ben was an intellectual, and intellectuals, say what you like, seemed to last longer than anyone else. There was more in them to find out about. One was always discovering new things—she supposed it was Father's blood in her that drew her towards the cultivated type, like Ben.

He was staying at a tiny hotel in a back street near the old quay. The entrance was dark, but the room itself was right at the top of the house, with a little balcony. Carmelita was staying with friends at a villa. She spent a lot of time in Ben's room, and sometimes slept there. It was turning out to be a remarkably happy summer.

'You won't see much of Father,' she said, 'if we get married. He works and sees nobody. Perhaps he'll get married again and—'

'That's all right,' he said, 'I don't want to marry your father.'

Dora Castlemaine had several diplomas for elocution which she had never put to use. She got a part-time job, after the Christmas holidays that year, in Basil Street Grammar School in London, and her job was to try to reform the more pronounced Cockney accents of the more promising boys into near-standard English. Her father was amazed.

'Money, money, you are always talking about money. Let us run up debts. One is nobody without debts.'

'One's credit is limited, Father. Don't be an old goose.'

'Have you consulted Waite?' Waite was the publisher's young man who looked after the Castlemaine royalties, diminishing year by year.

'We've drawn more than our due for the present.'

'Well, it's a bore, you going out to teach.'

'It may be a bore for you,' she said at last, 'but it isn't for me.'

'Dora, do you really mean you want to go to this job in London?'

'Yes, I want to. I'm looking forward to it.'

He didn't believe her. But he said, 'I suppose I'm a bit of a burden on you, Dora, these days. Perhaps I ought to go off and die.'

'Like Oates at the South Pole,' Dora commented.

He looked at her and she looked at him. They were shrewd in their love for each other.

She was the only woman teacher in the school, with hardly the status of a teacher. She had her own corner of the common room and, anxious to reassure the men that she had no intention of intruding upon them, would, during free periods, spread out on the table one of the weekly journals and study it intently, only looking up to say good morning or good afternoon to the masters who came in with piles of exercise books under their arms. Dora had no exercise books to correct, she was something apart, a reformer of vowel sounds. One of the masters, and then another, made conversation with her during morning break, when she passed round the sugar for the coffee. Some were in their early thirties. The ginger-moustached science master was not long graduated from Cambridge. Nobody said to her, as intelligent young men had done as late as fifteen years ago, 'Are you any relation, Miss Castlemaine, to Henry Castlemaine the writer?'

Ben walked with Carmelita under the trees of Lincoln's Inn Fields in the spring of the year, after school, and watched the children at their games. They were a beautiful couple. Carmelita was doing secretarial work in the City. Her father was in Morocco, having first taken them out to dinner to celebrate their engagement.

Ben said, 'There's a woman at the school, teaching elocution.'

'Oh?' said Carmelita. She was jumpy, because since her father's departure for Morocco Ben had given a new turn to their relationship. He would not let her stay overnight in his flat in Bayswater, not even at the week-ends. He said it would be nice, perhaps, to practise restraint until they were married in the summer, and that would give them something to look forward to. 'And I'm interested to see,' said Ben, 'what we mean to each other without sex.'

This made her understand how greatly she had become obsessed with him. She thought perhaps he was practising a form of cruelty to intensify her obsession. In fact, he did want to see what they meant to each other without sex.

She called at his flat unexpectedly and found him reading, with piles of other books set out on the table as if waiting to be read.

She accused him: You only want to get rid of me so that you can read your books.

'The fourth form is reading Trollope,' he explained, pointing to a novel of Trollope's among the pile.

'But you aren't studying Trollope just now.'

He had been reading a life of James Joyce. He banged it down and said. 'I've been reading all my life, and you won't stop me, Carmelita.'

She sat down. 'I don't want to stop you,' she said.

'I know,' he said.

'We aren't getting on at all well without sex,' she said, and on that occasion stayed the night.

He was writing an essay on her father. She wished that her father had taken more interest in it. Father had taken them out to dinner with his party face, smiling and boyish. Carmelita had seen him otherwise—in his acute dejection, when he seemed hardly able to endure the light of day.

'What's the matter, Father?'

'There's a comedy of errors going on inside me, Carmelita.' He sat at his desk most of the day while he was in these moods, doing nothing. Then, during the night, he would perhaps start writing, and sleep all the next morning, and gradually in the following days the weight would pass.

"There's a man on the phone wants you, Father—an interview.'

'Tell him I'm in the Middle East.'

'What did you think of Ben, Father?'

'A terribly nice man, Carmelita. You've made the right choice, I think.'

'An intellectual—I do like them the best, you know.'

'I'd say he was the student type. Always will be.'

'He wants to write an essay about you, Father. He's absolutely mad about your books.'

'Yes.'

'I mean, couldn't you help him, Father? Couldn't you talk to him about your work, you know?'

'Oh, God, Carmelita. It would be easier to write the bloody essay myself.'

'All right, all right. I was only asking.'

'I don't want any disciples, Carmelita. They give me the creeps.'

'Yes, yes, all right. I know you're an artist, Father, there's no need to show off your temperament. I only wanted you to help Ben. I only . . .'

I only, she thought as she walked in Lincoln's Inn Fields with Ben, wanted him to help me. I should have said, 'I want you to talk more to Ben, to help me.' And Father would have said, 'How do you mean?' And I would have said, 'I don't know, quite.' And he would have said, 'Well, if you don't know what you mean, how the hell do I?'

Ben was saying, 'There's a woman at the school, teaching elocution.'

'Oh?' said Carmelita jumpily.

'A Miss Castlemaine. She's been there four months, and I only found out today that she's the daughter of Henry Castlemaine.'

'But he's dead!' said Carmelita.

'Well, I thought so too. But apparently he isn't dead, he's very much alive in a house in Essex.'

'How old is Miss Castlemaine?' said Carmelita.

'Middle-aged. Middle forties. Perhaps late forties. She's a nice woman, a classic English spinster. She teaches the boys to say "How now brown cow." You could imagine her doing wood-engravings in the Cotswolds. I only found out today—'

'You might manage to get invited to meet him, with any luck,' Carmelita said.

'Yes, she said I must come and see him, perhaps for a week-end. Miss Castlemaine is going to arrange it. She was awfully friendly when she found I was a Castlemaine admirer. A lot of people think he's dead. Of course, his work belongs to a past world, but it's wonderful. Do you know *The Pebbled Shore?*—that's an early one.'

'No, but I've read *Sin of Substance*, I think. It—'

'You mean *The Sinner and the Substance*. Oh, it has fine things in it. Castlemaine's due for a revival.'

Carmelita felt a sharp stab of anger with her father, and then a kind of despair which was not yet entirely familiar to her, although already she wondered if this was how Father felt in his great depressions when he sat all day, staring and enduring, and all night miraculously wrote the ache out of his system in prose of harsh merriment.

Helplessly, she said, 'Castlemaine's novels aren't as good as Father's, are they?'

'Oh, there's no comparison. Castlemaine is quite different. You can't say one type is *better* than another—goodness me!' He was looking academically towards the chimney stacks of Lincoln's Inn. This was the look in which she loved him most. After all, she thought, the Castlemaines might make everything easier for both of us.

'Father, it's really absurd. A difference of sixteen years. . . . People will say—'

'Don't be vulgar, Dora dear. What does it matter what people say? Mere age makes no difference when there's a true affinity, a marriage of true minds.'

'Ben and I have a lot in common.'

'I know it,' he said, and sat a little higher in his chair.

'I shall be able to give up my job, Father, and spend my time here with you again. I never really wanted that job. And you are so much better in health now . . .'

'I know.'

'And Ben will be here in the evenings and the weekends. You get on well with Ben, don't you?'

'A remarkably fine man, Dora. He'll go far. He's perceptive.'

'He's keen to revive your work.'

'I know. He should give up that job, as I told him, and devote himself entirely to literary studies. A born essayist.'

'Oh, Father, he'll have to keep his job for the meantime, anyhow. We'll need the money. It will help us all; we—'

'What's that? What's that you say?'

'I said he finds work in the grammar school stimulating, Father.'

'Do you love the man?'

'It's a little difficult to say, at my age, Father.'

'To me, you both seem children. Do you love him?'

'I feel,' she said, 'that I have known him much longer than I have. Sometimes I think I've known him all my life. I'm sure we have met before, perhaps even in a former existence. That's the decisive factor. There's something of *destiny* about my marrying Ben; do you know what I mean?'

'Yes, I think I do.'

'He was engaged, last year for a short time, to marry quite a young girl,' she said. 'The daughter of a novelist called Kenneth Hope. Have you heard of him, Father?'

'Vaguely,' he said. 'Ben,' he said, 'is a born disciple.'

She looked at him and he looked at her, shrewd in their love for each other.

Discussion of Spark's "The Fathers' Daughters"

1. Why the emphasis on Father at the beginning? How would you characterize that daughter's relationship with her father?

2. What is the effect of there being no quotation marks around the conversation on the first few pages of the story?

3. Do you find significance in where the scene changes from Dora and Henry Castlemaine to Carmelita Hope and Ben Donadieu? What is the effect? For example, what can the author achieve by beginning the story with the Castlemaines rather than the Hopes? What is achieved by Spark's cutting back and forth between the two sets of lives?

4. Whose point of view does this story emphasize? How do you know? What is the effect of the title?

JOHN UPDIKE

b. 1932

Born in Shillington, Pennsylvania, John Updike now lives in Ipswich, Massachusetts. A prolific writer since he graduated from Harvard, he has published over seventy stories and several novels as well as poetry, essays, and reviews. His novels include *The Poorhouse Fair* (1959); *Rabbit, Run* (1960); *The Centaur* (1963), which won the National Book Award; *Couples* (1968); and, more recently, *Bech: A Book* (1970), *Rabbit Redux* (1971), and *Marry Me* (1977). Some of his collections of short stories are *The Same Door* (1959), *Pigeon Feathers* (1962), and *The Music School* (1966), from which "Giving Blood" was taken. In *The Music School* appear the Maples, who were introduced in *The Same Door.* Much of Updike's writing concentrates on married couples, on their conflicts with one another and their concern with growing old. Moments of loving provide temporary counterforces to the lack of permanence in life.

Giving Blood

The Maples had been married now nine years, which is almost too long. "Goddammit, goddammit," Richard said to Joan, as they drove into Boston to give blood, "I drive this road five days a week and now I'm driving it again. It's like a nightmare. I'm exhausted. I'm emotionally, mentally, physically exhausted, and she isn't even an aunt of mine. She isn't even an aunt of *yours*."

"She's a sort of cousin," Joan said.

"Well hell, every goddam body in New England is some sort of cousin of yours; must I spend the rest of my life trying to save them *all?*"

"Hush," Joan said. "She might die. I'm ashamed of you. Really ashamed."

It cut. His voice for the moment took on an apologetic pallor. "Well I'd be my usual goddam saintly self if I'd had any sort of sleep last night. Five days a week I bump out of bed and stagger out the door past the milkman and on the one day of the week when I don't even have to truck the blasphemous little brats to Sunday school you make an appointment to have me drained dry thirty miles away."

"Well it wasn't *me,*" Joan said, "who had to stay till two o'clock doing the Twist with Marlene Brossman."

"We weren't doing the Twist. We were gliding around very chastely to 'Hits of the Forties.' And don't think I was so oblivious I didn't see you snoogling behind the piano with Harry Saxon."

"We weren't behind the piano, we were on the bench. And he was just talking to me because he felt sorry for me. Everybody there felt sorry for me; you could have at *least* let somebody else dance *once* with Marlene, if only for show."

"Show, show," Richard said. "That's your mentality exactly."

"Why, the poor Matthews or whatever they are looked absolutely horrified."

"Matthiessons," he said. "And that's another thing. Why are idiots like that being invited these days? If there's anything I hate, it's women who keep putting one hand on their pearls and taking a deep breath. I thought she had something stuck in her throat."

"They're a perfectly pleasant, decent young couple. The thing you resent about their coming is that their being there shows us what we've become."

"If you're so attracted," he said, "to little fat men like Harry Saxon, why didn't you marry one?"

"My," Joan said calmly, and gazed out the window away from him, at the scudding gasoline stations. "You honestly *are* hateful. It's not just a pose."

"Pose, show, my Lord, who are you performing for? If it isn't Harry Saxon, it's Freddie Vetter—all these dwarves. Every time I looked over at you last night it was like some pale Queen of the Dew surrounded by a ring of mushrooms."

"You're too absurd," she said. Her hand, distinctly thirtyish, dry and green-veined and rasped by detergents, stubbed out her cigarette in the dashboard ashtray. "You're not subtle. You think you can match me up with another man so you can swirl off with Marlene with a free conscience."

Her reading his strategy so correctly made his face burn; he felt again the tingle of Mrs. Brossman's hair as he pressed his cheek against hers and in this damp privacy inhaled the perfume behind her ear. "You're right," he said. "But I want to get you a man your own size; I'm very loyal that way."

"Let's not talk," she said.

His hope, of turning the truth into a joke, was rebuked. Any implication of permission was blocked. "It's that *smugness*," he explained, speaking levelly, as if about a phenomenon of which they were both disinterested students. "It's your smugness that is really intolerable. Your stupidity I don't mind. Your sexlessness I've learned to live with. But that wonderfully smug, New England—I suppose we needed it to get the country founded, but in the Age of Anxiety it really does gall."

He had been looking over at her, and unexpectedly she turned and looked at him, with a startled but uncannily crystalline expression, as if her face had been in an instant rendered in tinted porcelain, even to the eyelashes.

"I asked you not to talk," she said. "Now you've said things that I'll always remember."

Plunged fathoms deep into the wrong, his face suffocated with warmth, he concentrated on the highway and sullenly steered. Though they were moving at sixty in the sparse Saturday traffic, he had travelled this road so often its distances were all translated into time, so that they seemed to him to be moving as slowly as a minute hand from one digit to the next. It would have been strategic and dignified of him to keep the silence; but he could not resist believing that just one more pinch of syllables would restore the fine balance with which each wordless mile slipped increasingly awry. He asked, "How did Bean seem to you?" Bean was their baby. They had left her last night, to go to the party, with a fever of 102.

Joan wrestled with her vow to say nothing, but guilt proved stronger than spite. She said, "Cooler. Her nose is a river."

"Sweetie," Richard blurted, "will they hurt me?" The curious fact was that he had never given blood before. Asthmatic and underweight, he had been 4-F, and at college and now at the office he had, less through his own determination than through the diffidence of the solicitors, evaded pledging blood. It was one of those tests of courage so trivial that no one had ever thought to make him face up to it.

Spring comes carefully to Boston. Speckled crusts of ice lingered around the parking meters, and the air, grayly stalemated between seasons, tinted the buildings along Longwood Avenue with a drab and homogeneous majesty. As they walked up the drive to the hospital entrance, Richard nervously wondered aloud if they would see the King of Arabia.

"He's in a separate wing," Joan said. "With four wives."

"Only four? What an ascetic." And he made bold to tap his wife's shoulder. It was not clear if, under the thickness of her winter coat, she felt it.

At the desk, they were directed down a long corridor floored with cigar-colored linoleum. Up and down, right and left it went, in the secretive, disjointed way peculiar to hospitals that have been built annex by annex. Richard seemed to himself Hansel orphaned with Gretel; birds ate the bread crumbs behind them, and at last they timidly knocked on the witch's door, which said BLOOD DONATION CENTER. A young man in white opened the door a crack. Over his shoulder Richard glimpsed—horrors!—a pair of dismembered female legs stripped of their shoes and laid parallel on a bed. Glints of needles and bottles pricked his eyes. Without widening the crack, the young man passed out to them two long forms. In sitting side by side on the waiting bench, remembering their middle initials and childhood diseases, Mr. and Mrs. Maple were newly defined to themselves. He fought down that urge to giggle and clown and lie that threatened him whenever he was asked—like a lawyer appointed by the court to plead a hopeless case—to present, as it were, his statistics to eternity. It seemed to mitigate his case slightly that a few of these statistics (present address, date of marriage) were shared by the hurt soul scratching beside him, with his own pen. He looked over her shoulder. "I never knew you had whooping cough."

"My mother says. I don't remember it."

A pan crashed to a distant floor. An elevator chuckled remotely. A woman, a middle-aged woman top-heavy with rouge and fur, stepped out of the blood door and wobbled a moment on legs that looked familiar. They had been restored to their shoes. The heels of these shoes clicked firmly as, having raked the Maples with a defiant blue glance, she turned and disappeared around a bend in the corridor. The young man appeared in the doorway holding a pair of surgical tongs. His noticeably recent haircut made him seem an apprentice barber. He clicked his tongs and smiled. "Shall I do you together?"

"Sure." It put Richard on his mettle that this callow fellow, to whom apparently they were to entrust their liquid essence, was so clearly younger than they. But when Richard stood, his indignation melted and his legs felt diluted under him. And the extraction of the blood sample from his middle finger seemed the nastiest and most needlessly prolonged physical involvement with another human being he had ever experienced. There is a touch that good dentists, mechanics, and barbers have, and this intern did not have it; he fumbled and in compensation was too rough. Again and again, an atrociously clumsy vampire, he tugged and twisted the purpling finger in vain. The tiny glass capillary tube remained transparent.

"He doesn't like to bleed, does he?" the intern asked Joan. As relaxed as a nurse, she sat in a chair next to a table of scintillating equipment.

"I don't think his blood moves much," she said, "until after midnight."

This stab at a joke made Richard in his extremity of fright laugh loudly, and the laugh at last seemed to jar the panicked coagulant. Red seeped upward in the thirsty little tube, as in a sudden thermometer.

The intern grunted in relief. As he smeared the samples on the analysis box, he explained idly, "What we ought to have down here is a pan of warm water. You just came in out of the cold. If you put your hand in hot water for a minute, the blood just pops out."

"A pretty thought," Richard said.

But the intern had already written him off as a clowner and continued calmly to Joan, "All we'd need would be a baby hot plate for about six dollars, then we could make our own coffee too. This way, when we get a donor who needs the coffee afterward, we have to send up for it while we keep his head between his knees. Do you think you'll be needing coffee?"

"No," Richard interrupted, jealous of their rapport.

The intern told Joan, "You're O."

"I know," she said.

"And he's A positive."

"Why that's very good, Dick!" she called to him.

"Am I rare?" he asked.

The boy turned and explained, "O positive and A positive are the most common types." Something in the patient tilt of his close-cropped head as its lateral sheen mixed with the lazily bright mid-morning air of the room sharply reminded Richard of the days years ago when he had tended a battery of teletype machines in a room much this size. By now, ten o'clock, the yards of copy that began pouring through the machines at five and that lay in great crimped heaps on the floor when he arrived at seven would have been harvested and sorted and pasted together and turned in, and there was nothing to do but keep up with the staccato appearance of the later news and to think about simple things like coffee. It came back to him, how pleasant and secure those hours had been when, king of his own corner, he was young and newly responsible.

The intern asked, "Who wants to be first?"

"Let me," Joan said. "He's never done it before."

"Her full name is Joan of Arc," Richard explained, angered at this betrayal, so unimpeachably selfless and smug.

The intern, threatened in his element, fixed his puzzled eyes on the floor between them and said, "Take off your shoes and each get on a bed." He added, "Please," and all three laughed, one after the other, the intern last.

The beds were at right angles to one another along two walls. Joan lay down and from her husband's angle of vision was novelly foreshortened. He had never before seen her quite this way, the combed crown of her hair so poignant, her bared arm so silver and long, her stocking feet toed in so childishly and docilely. There were no pillows on the beds, and lying flat made him feel tipped head down; the illusion of floating encouraged his hope that this unreal adventure would soon dissolve in the manner of a dream. "You O.K.?"

"Are you?" Her voice came softly from the tucked-under wealth of her hair. From the straightness of the parting it seemed her mother had brushed it. He watched a long needle sink into the flat of her arm and a piece of moist cotton clumsily swab the spot. He had imagined their blood would be drained into cans or bottles, but the intern, whose breathing was now the only sound within the room, brought to Joan's side what looked like a miniature plastic knapsack, all coiled and tied. His body cloaked his actions. When he stepped away, a plastic cord had been grafted, a transparent vine, to the flattened crook of Joan's extended arm, where the skin was translucent and the veins were faint blue tributaries shallowly buried. It was a tender, vulnerable place where in courting days she had liked to be stroked. Now, without visible transition, the pale tendril planted here went dark red. Richard wanted to cry out.

The instant readiness of her blood to leave her body pierced him like a physical pang. Though he had not so much as blinked, its initial leap had been too quick for his eye. He had expected some visible sign of flow, but from the mere appearance of it the tiny looped hose might be pouring blood *into* her body or might be a curved line added, irrelevant as a mustache, to a finished canvas. The fixed position of his head gave what he saw a certain flatness.

And now the intern turned to him, and there was the tiny felt prick of the novocain needle, and then the coarse, half-felt intrusion of something resembling a medium-weight nail. Twice the boy mistakenly probed for the vein and the third time taped the successful graft fast with adhesive tape. All the while, Richard's mind moved aloofly among the constellations of the stained cracked ceiling. What was being done to him did not bear contemplating. When the intern moved away to hum and tinkle among his instruments, Joan craned her neck to show her husband her face and, upside down in his vision, grotesquely smiled.

It was not many minutes that they lay there at right angles together, but the time passed as something beyond the walls, as something mixed with the faraway clatter of pans and the approach and retreat of footsteps and the opening and closing of unseen doors. Here, conscious of a pointed painless pulse in the inner hinge of his arm but incurious as to what it looked like, he floated and imagined how his soul would float free when all his blood was underneath the bed. His blood and Joan's merged on the floor, and together their spirits glided from crack to crack, from star to star on the ceiling. Once she cleared her throat, and the sound made an abrasion like the rasp of a pebble loosened by a cliff-climber's boot.

The door opened. Richard turned his head and saw an old man, bald and sallow, enter and settle in a chair. He was one of those old men who hold within an institution an ill-defined but consecrated place. The young doctor seemed to know him, and the two talked, softly, as if not to disturb the mystical union of the couple sacrificially bedded together. They talked of persons and events that meant nothing—of Iris, of Dr. Greenstein, of Ward D, again of Iris, who had given the old man an undeserved scolding, of the shameful lack of a hot plate to make coffee on, of the rumored black bodyguards who kept watch with scimitars by the bed of the glaucomatous king. Through Richard's tranced ignorance these topics passed as clouds of impression, iridescent, massy—Dr. Greenstein with a pointed nose and almond eyes the color of ivy, Iris eighty feet tall and hurling sterilized thunderbolts of wrath. As in some theologies the proliferant deities are said to exist as ripples upon the featureless ground of Godhead, so these inconstant images lightly overlay his continuous awareness of Joan's blood, like his own, ebbing. Linked to a common loss, they were chastely conjoined; the thesis developed upon him that the hoses attached to them somewhere out of sight met. Testing this belief, he glanced down and saw that indeed the plastic vine taped to the flattened crook of his arm was the same dark red as hers. He stared at the ceiling to disperse a sensation of faintness.

Abruptly the young intern left his desultory conversation and moved to Joan's side. There was a chirp of clips. When he moved away, she was revealed holding her naked arm upright, pressing a piece of cotton against it with the other hand. Without pausing, the intern came to Richard's side, and the birdsong of clips repeated, nearer. "Look at that," he said to his elderly friend. "I started him two minutes later than her and he's finished at the same time."

"Was it a race?" Richard asked.

Clumsily firm, the boy fitted Richard's fingers to a pad and lifted his arm for him. "Hold it there for five minutes," he said.

"What'll happen if I don't?"

"You'll mess up your shirt." To the old man he said, "I had a woman in here the other day, she was all set to leave when all of a sudden, pow!—all over the front of this beautiful linen dress. She was going to Symphony."

"Then they try to sue the hospital for the cleaning bill," the old man muttered.

"Why was I slower than him?" Joan asked. Her upright arm wavered, as if vexed or weakened.

"The woman generally is," the boy told her. "Nine times out of ten, the man is faster. Their hearts are so much stronger."

"Is that really so?"

"Sure it's so," Richard told her. "Don't argue with medical science."

"Woman up in Ward C," the old man said, "they saved her life for her out of an auto accident and now I hear she's suing because they didn't find her dental plate."

Under such patter, the five minutes eroded. Richard's upheld arm began to ache. It seemed that he and Joan were caught together in a classroom where they would never be recognized, or in a charade that would never be guessed, the correct answer being Two Silver Birches in a Meadow.

"You can sit up now if you want," the intern told them. "But don't let go of the venipuncture."

They sat up on their beds, legs dangling heavily. Joan asked him, "Do you feel dizzy?"

"With my powerful heart? Don't be presumptuous."

"Do you think he'll need coffee?" the intern asked her. "I'll have to send up for it now."

The old man shifted forward in his chair, preparing to heave to his feet.

"I do *not* want any *coffee*"—Richard said it so loud he saw himself transposed, another Iris, into the firmament of the old man's aggrieved gossip. *Some dizzy bastard down in the blood room, I get up to get him some coffee and he damn near bit my head off.* To demonstrate simultaneously his essential good humor and his total presence of mind, Richard gestured toward the blood they had given—two square plastic sacks filled solidly fat—and declared, "Back where I come from in West Virginia sometimes you pick a tick off a dog that looks like that." The men looked at him amazed. Had he not quite said what he meant to say? Or had they never seen anybody from West Virginia before?

Joan pointed at the blood too. "Is that us? Those little doll pillows?"

"Maybe we should take one home to Bean," Richard suggested.

The intern did not seem convinced that this was a joke. "Your blood will be credited to Mrs. Henryson's account," he stated stiffly.

Joan asked him, "Do you know anything about her? When is she—when is her operation scheduled?"

"I think for tomorrow. The only thing on the tab this after is an open heart at two; that'll take about sixteen pints."

"Oh . . ." Joan was shaken. "Sixteen . . . that's a full person, isn't it?"

"More," the intern answered, with the regal handwave that bestows largess and dismisses compliments.

"Could we visit her?" Richard asked, for Joan's benefit. ("Really ashamed," she had said; it had cut.) He was confident of the refusal.

"Well, you can ask at the desk, but usually before a major one like this it's just the nearest of kin. I guess you're safe now." He meant their punctures. Richard's arm bore a small raised bruise; the intern covered it with one of those ample, salmon, unhesitatingly adhesive bandages that only hospitals have. That was their specialty, Richard thought—packaging. They wrap the human mess for final delivery. Sixteen doll's pillows, uniformly dark and snug, marching into an open heart: the vision momentarily satisfied his hunger for cosmic order.

He rolled down his sleeve and slid off the bed. It startled him to realize, in the instant before his feet touched the floor, that three pairs of eyes were fixed upon him, fascinated and apprehensive and eager for scandal. He stood and towered above them. He hopped on one foot to slip into one loafer, and then on this foot to slip into the other loafer. Then he did the little shuffle-tap, shuffle-tap step that was all that remained to him of dancing lessons he had taken at the age of seven, driving twelve miles each Saturday into Morgantown. He made a small bow toward his wife, smiled at the old man, and said to the intern, "All my life people have been expecting me to faint. I have no idea why. I never faint."

His coat and overcoat felt a shade queer, a bit slithery and light, but as he walked down the length of the corridor, space seemed to adjust snugly around him. At his side, Joan kept an inquisitive and chastened silence. They pushed through the great glass doors. A famished sun was nibbling through the overcast. Above and behind them, the King of Arabia lay in a drugged dream of dunes and Mrs. Henryson upon her sickbed received like the comatose mother of twins their identical gifts of blood. Richard hugged his wife's padded shoulders and as they walked along leaning on each other whispered, "Hey, I love you. Love love *love* you."

Romance is, simply, the strange, the untried. It was unusual for the Maples to be driving together at eleven in the morning. Almost always it was dark when they shared a car. The oval of her face was bright in the corner of his eye. She was watching him, alert to take the wheel if he suddenly lost consciousness. He felt tender toward her in the eggshell light, and curious toward himself, wondering how far beneath his brain the black pit did lie. He felt no different; but then the quality of consciousness perhaps did not bear introspection. Something certainly had been taken from him; he was less himself by a pint and it was not impossible that like a trapeze artist saved by a net he was sustained in the world of light and reflection by a single layer of interwoven cells. Yet the earth, with its signals and buildings and cars and bricks, continued like a pedal note.

Boston behind them, he asked, "Where should we eat?"

"Should we eat?"

"Please, yes. Let me take you to lunch. Just like a secretary."

"I do feel sort of illicit. As if I've stolen something."

"You too? But what did we steal?"

"I don't know. The morning? Do you think Eve knows enough to feed them?" Eve was their sitter, a little sandy girl from down the street who would, in exactly a year, Richard calculated, be painfully lovely. They lasted three years on the average, sitters; you got them in the tenth grade and escorted them into their bloom and then, with graduation, like commuters who had reached their stop, they dropped out of sight, into nursing school or marriage. And the train went on, and took on other passengers, and itself became older and longer. The Maples had four children: Judith, Richard Jr., poor oversized, angel-faced John, and Bean.

"She'll manage. What would you like? All that talk about coffee has made me frantic for some."

"At the Pancake House beyond 128 they give you coffee before you even ask."

"Pancakes? Now? Aren't you gay? Do you think we'll throw up?"

"Do you feel like throwing up?"

"No, not really. I feel sort of insubstantial and gentle, but it's

probably psychosomatic. I don't really understand this business of
giving something away and still somehow having it. What is it—
the spleen?"

"I don't know. Are the splenetic man and the sanguine man
the same?"

"God. I've totally forgotten the humors. What are the others—
phlegm and choler?"

"Bile and black bile are in there somewhere."

"One thing about you, Joan. You're educated. New England
women are educated."

"Sexless as we are."

"That's right; drain me dry and then put me on the rack." But
there was no wrath in his words; indeed, he had reminded her of
their earlier conversation so that, in much this way, his words might
be revived, diluted, and erased. It seemed to work. The restaurant
where they served only pancakes was empty and quiet this early. A
bashfulness possessed them both; it had become a date between
two people who have little as yet in common but who are nevertheless sufficiently intimate to accept the fact without chatter. Touched
by the stain her blueberry pancakes left on her teeth, he held a
match to her cigarette and said, "Gee, I loved you back in the
blood room."

"I wonder why."

"You were so brave."

"So were you."

"But I'm supposed to be. I'm paid to be. It's the price of having
a penis."

"Shh."

"Hey. I didn't mean that about your being sexless."

The waitress refilled their coffee cups and gave them the check.

"And I promise never never to do the Twist, the cha-cha, or the
schottische with Marlene Brossman."

"Don't be silly. I don't care."

This amounted to permission, but perversely irritated him. That
smugness; why didn't she *fight*? Trying to regain their peace,
scrambling uphill, he picked up their check and with an effort of
acting, the pretense being that they were out on a date and he was
a raw dumb suitor, said handsomely, "I'll pay."

But on looking into his wallet he saw only a single worn dollar
there. He didn't know why this should make him so angry, except
the fact somehow that it was only *one*. "Goddammit," he said.
"Look at that." He waved it in her face. "I work like a bastard all
week for you and those insatiable brats and at the end of it what do
I have? One goddam crummy wrinkled dollar."

Her hands dropped to the pocketbook beside her on the seat, but
the gaze stayed with him, her face having retreated, or advanced,
into that porcelain shell of uncanny composure. "We'll both pay,"
Joan said.

Discussion of Updike's "Giving Blood"

1. Whose point of view guides this story? How do you know?

2. Why the emphasis on Joan's hand—its age and its history? On Richard's seeing Joan in a new way as they prepare to give blood?

3. What is the significance of the title? The name of the couple— the Maples? Support your answers.

4. What evidence of a "power play" do you find in the story? If so, what does Updike suggest about it? How might it compare with the one in "Tears, Idle Tears"? In "Wine"? In the nineteenth-century stories "Ligeia" and "The Birthmark"?

JOYCE CAROL OATES

b. 1938

🌿 Joyce Carol Oates is one of the most prolific contemporary writers, so prolific that it is difficult to single out any one piece of work. *A Garden of Earthly Delights* (1967) and *Them* (1969) are two of her novels that have earned national awards, while *The Wheel of Love* (1970) and *Marriages and Infidelities* (1972) represent excellent collections of her short fiction. Oates's works excite considerable controversy, caused largely by her tendency to hold her characters up to intense scrutiny and criticism and her continuing interest in plots and situations that are reminiscent of popular fiction and soap operas. Oates's people are, in fact, frequently dissected with a scalpel. Often the women, like Pauline in "Bodies," are substantially stronger than the men, but this strength, like that of Duffy in Joyce's "Painful Case," is usually obtained only at considerable cost. At the same time, her stories attempt to deal with those melodramatic, stereotyped, and somewhat hysterical levels of belief that may constitute what film directors Arnaldo Jabor and Nelson Pereira dos Santos have called the thematic basis for a popular art, that is, one that speaks to the emotions of a majority of people and not just to a cultural elite. If this is true, Oates's tales are popular fiction as nightmare, where men and women are caught up in their own stereotypes and then trapped by their inabilities to respond to the needs of others around them.

Bodies

She met him in the cafeteria of the Art Museum, on a Thursday. His name was Draier, Drayer—she couldn't quite make it out. "Please call me Anthony," he said, leaning forward against the wrought-iron table, jarring it, and his attempt at intimacy was blocked by the formality of that name also. Pauline's friend, their mutual friend, hadn't figured much in her life for several years, and she wondered where his loneliness was leading him—he had been reluctant to introduce Anthony to her, she could see that. Her friend's name was Martin. He had something to do with an art gallery; his art galleries were always failing, disappearing and returning again with new names. Pauline wondered if Anthony was an artist.

"I'm not an artist. I'm not anything," he said. He smiled a sad, quick smile. She was startled by his frankness, distrusting it. He had a striking face, though he had not shaved for several days, his eyes set clearly beneath the strong, clear line of his eyebrows. Beside him, Martin was silent. Students from Pauline's art class were carrying their trays past this table with serious faces; their faces, like the work they did, were intense and prematurely aged.

"Pauline does beautiful work," Martin said. He seemed to be talking to no one in particular. "But it's very difficult to talk about art, or about anything. I can't explain her work."

"Why should you explain it?" Pauline said. She stood to leave: she never took much time for lunch. The noise of the cafeteria annoyed her. Formally, with a smile, she put out her hand to Anthony. "It was very nice to meet you," she said.

He looked surprised. "Yes, very nice. . . ."

She was out of the restaurant before he caught up with her. Before turning, she heard footsteps and it flashed through her mind, incredibly, that this man was following her—then she turned to face him, and her expression was curious rather than alarmed. "I thought I'd walk with you. Are you going to look at the pictures?" he said.

Look at the pictures. "No," she said. "I have a class at two."

His face, in the mottled light of the broad, marble-floored hall, looken sullen. She had thought he was fairly young, in his mid-twenties; now she supposed he was at least ten years older. His hair was curly, black but tinged with gray, and it fell down around the unclean neck of his sweater lazily, making her think of one of the heads she herself had done a few years ago . . . in imitation of a Greek youth, the head of a sweetly smiling child. This man stared at her rudely. She could not bear to face him.

"I have to teach a class at two . . ." she said.

They walked awkwardly together. Not far away were the stairs to the first floor, and once upstairs she could escape . . . the side of her face tingled from his look, she thought it foolish and degrading, she wondered what he thought of her face . . . was he thinking anything about her face?

"Do you live around here?" he said.

"No. Out along the lake."

"Out there?" His tone was suspicious, as if she had been deceiving him until now. This was her own fault—though she wore her pale blond hair in a kind of crown, braided tightly, and though her face was cool, slow to awaken to interest, held always in a kind of suspension, she wore the standard casual clothes of girls who were artists or wanted to be, living alone, freely, sometimes recklessly, down here in the center of the city. She wore dark stockings, leather shoes that had been ruined by this winter's icy, salted sidewalks, a dark, rather shapeless skirt, and a white blouse that had once been an expensive blouse but now looked as old as Anthony's sweater and blue jeans, its cuffs rolled up to her elbows, its first button hanging by a thread. Her hands were not stubby, but there was nothing elegant about them—short, colorless fingernails, slightly knobby knuckles, small wrists. She was anxious to get back to work, her fingers actually itching to return to work, and this man was a pull in the edge of her consciousness, like something invisible but deadly blown into her eye.

"I have to leave," she said abruptly.

"You don't have a place down here? In town?"

"I have a studio. But I live at home with my mother."

She faced him and yet was not facing him; her eyes were moving coldly behind his head. He had no interest for her, not even as someone whose head she might copy; she had done a head like his once, she had no desire to repeat herself. She felt very nervous beneath his frank, blunt scrutiny, but her face showed nothing. Like the head of an Amazon on a stand near the stairs—a reproduction of an Etruscan work—she was vacuous, smooth-skinned, patient. From art she had learned patience, centuries of patience. The man, Anthony, was humming nervously under his breath, sensing her desire to get away and yet reluctant to let her get away.

"Do you come around here often?" he said.

"No."

"Why are you so ... unfriendly?" He smiled at her, his face grown suddenly shabby and appealing, his eyes dark with wonder. *Tell the truth,* he was pleading. It occurred to her that he was insane. But she laughed, looking from the inhuman composed face of that Amazon to his face, hearing him say again, *Are you going to look at the pictures?*

"Come over here. Can I show you something?" he said. He took her arm with a sudden childish familiarity that annoyed her. In the noisy confusion of this part of the museum, at noon, she had to give herself up to anything that might happen; it was part of coming here at all. When she had begun teaching at the Art Institute across the street, years ago, she had brought her own lunch and eaten in her studio, she had thrown herself into her work and that had been, maybe, the best idea. Meeting people down here was a waste of time. The people she spent time with socially were friends of her mother's, most of them older than she, a careful, genteel network of people who could never harm her. Down here, the city was open. Anything could happen. This stranger, whose name was Anthony Drayer, whose rumpled clothes told her everything she needed to know about him, now took her by the arm and led her over to a reproduction of another Etruscan work she had been looking at for years with no more than mild interest.

"Did you ever see this?" Anthony said. He was very excited. The piece was a tomb monument, showing a young man lying on a cushion with a winged woman at his side. The man's hair was bound up tightly, in a kind of band; his face was very strong, composed. Pauline had the idea that Anthony saw himself in that face, though his own was soft, sketchy, as if done with a charcoal pencil, not shaped vividly in stone. His smile moved from being

gentle to being loose, almost out of control. "Who are these people?" he said, glancing at her.

She saw that his fingers were twitching. Her eye was too intimate, too quick to take in shameful details—it was a fault in her.
She could not help noticing that the skin around his thumbnails
was raw from his digging at it. "I moved down here a few months
ago and almost every day I come to the museum," Anthony said.
He spoke in a rapid, low murmur, as if sensing her coldness but
unable to stop his words. He picked at his thumbnail. "I like to
look at the pictures but especially the statues. You do statues? That
must be expensive, isn't it, to buy the stone and all that . . . ? I
could never do anything like this, my hands are too shaky, my
judgment isn't right, I can't stand still long enough, but I love to
look at these things; it makes me happy to know that they exist. . . .
Are those two in love? Is that why she's reaching out toward him?"

"No, they're not in love," Pauline said, wondering if her tone
could rid her of this man forever. "The man is dead. You see how
her hand is broken off—she was holding out to him a scroll with
his fate written on it. This is a monument to adorn a tomb. It isn't
about life, it's about death. They're both dead."

Anthony stared at the figures.

"But they look alive . . . their faces look alive. . . ."

"Do you see how their bodies are twisted around? The demon's
body is organically impossible, it's out of shape from the waist
down, and the man's body is almost as unnatural. . . . That's a
typical Etruscan characteristic."

"Why?"

"I don't know why," she said, avoiding his melancholy stare.
"The artists weren't interested in that part of the body, evidently
their interest was in the head, the face, the torso. . . ."

"Why is that?"

He scratched at his own head, at the dusky, graying curls. She
could smell about him an odor of something stale, sad—cigarette
smoke, unwashed flesh, the gritty deposit of decades in some
walk-up room. Her own odor clean and impersonal. Her hands
smelled whitely of the clay in which she worked. Anthony looked
sideways at her. His look was pleading, intense, threatening . . . for
the first time in years she was afraid of another person.

"I have to leave," she said.

"Can I see you again?"

She was already walking away. Her heart was pounding. He was
calling after her—she nearly collided with an elderly man making
his way slowly down the stairs—she had the excuse of apologizing
to this man, helping him, saying something about the danger of
such wide stairs. "And outside it ain't no better, all that goddamn
ice," the old man said angrily, as if blaming her for that too.

She escaped them both.

It is a festival of some kind. Mules with muddy bellies and legs; a young man with a bare chest leading one of the mules. He is laughing. His head falls back with drunken laughter, as if loose on his shoulders. Another man is riding a mule, slipping off into the mud, laughing. Garlands of flowers are woven in the manes of these mules. What is happening? Women run by . . . their shouts are hilarious, drunken. I see what it is—someone is being pulled in a wagon. The wagon's railings are decorated with bruised white flowers, the man inside the wagon is speechless, his face dark with a look of terror, as if blood has settled heavily in his face and will never flow out again. Now a soldier appears on a black horse, the horse's belly is splashed with mud. The leather of his complicated saddle creaks. . . .

She woke suddenly. Her head pounded. The dream was still with her—the raucous laughter in the room with her, the whinnying of a horse. She looked around wildly, for a moment suspended of all personal existence, of thinking, not even afraid. The wagon's wheels made a creaking noise and so perhaps it was the wheels, not the soldier's gear, that was creaking. . . . Then the dream faded and she felt only a dull, aching fear. For a while she lay unthinking in bed and felt the cool, contented length of her body beneath the covers, not thinking.

Twenty-nine years old, she had a sense of being much older, of being ageless. So many years of patience, the shaping of clay and stone, the necessity for patience had aged her magically; she was content in her age. Her work was heads. She was interested only in the human head. Out in the street she could not help but stare at the heads of strangers, at their unique, mysterious, miraculous shapes; sometimes their heads were a threat to her, unnerving her. She couldn't explain. But most of the time she brought back to her work a sense of excitement, as if her blood, in flowing out at the instant of glimpsing some rare sight, had returned again to her heart exhilarated and blessed. She felt at times an almost uncontrollable excitement, and she would spend hours at her work, feverish, unaware of time.

She and her mother had breakfast together every morning. They ate in the dining room, enjoying its size, undiminished by its high ceiling. The house was very large, very old, a house meant to store collections—paintings, manuscripts, first editions, antiques. Her father, now dead, had collected things. The house had become a small museum, but polished and sprightly, ruled by her mother's bustling efficiency. A woman with a firm place in local society, her days filled with luncheons and committee meetings and her weekends given over to entertaining or to being entertained, Pauline's mother was that kind of middle-aged, generous, busy woman who becomes impersonal around the middle of her life. She too collected things, antiques and jewels, and kept up what she thought to be an enthusiastic interest in "culture"; it was something to talk about with enthusiasm. "We're stopping at the auction after lunch," she told Pauline. She chattered at breakfast, her rich, rosy face ready for the day that would never disappoint her, being a complicated day filled with women like herself, the making out of checks, endless conversations. . . . "You look a little pale. Are you well? Did you sleep well?"

"I had a strange dream, but I slept well. I'm fine."

"I still think you should give up that job. . . . I wish the weather would change. April is almost here and everything is still frozen, it depresses me when winter lasts so long. . . ." she said vaguely. She wore a dark dress, she wore pearls and pearl earrings; a slightly heavy woman, yet with a curious grace, a girlish flutter at the wrists and ankles, which Pauline herself had never had. She was in the mold of her father: tall, lean, composed, with a patient, cool kind of grace, never hurried. Pauline had never been able to accept the memory of her father in the hospital after his stroke, suddenly an elderly man, trembling, with tiny broken veins in his face. . . .

RITES TO BE HELD FOR PROMINENT
FINANCIER, PHILANTHROPIST

"Are you sure you're well?" her mother said suddenly.

"Yes. Please."

They parted for the day. Pauline's mother approved of her "work," though she did not like her teaching down at the Art Institute; she feared the city. She did not exactly approve of Pauline's clothes and her tendency to wear the same outfit day after day, but her daughter had a profession, a career, she was an *artist*, unlike the daughters of her friends. Every few years the newspapers did stories on her when she won some new award or had a new show for the art page or the splashy women's page, the daughter of the late Francis Ressner, with large photographs that showed her standing beside one of her stark, white heads, her own head beautiful as a work of art. There was a certain stubbornness in both her and in her work. She had very light blond hair that fell past her shoulders, but she wore it braided around her head, giving her a stiff, studied look; she had worn it like that since the age of fifteen. Her cheekbones were a little prominent because her face was too thin, but she attended to her face with some of the respect for clarity and precision that she applied to her work—though she wore no make-up, she kept her eyebrows plucked to a delicate, arched thinness, and she saw that her face was smoothed by oils and creams, protected against the city's sooty wind. She was pleased to have a kind of beauty, pale and unemphatic; her father too had been a beautiful man. Her mother, florid and conversational, had been startlingly pretty until recent years, a perfumed and likeable woman, but Pauline was another kind of woman altogether and pleased with herself. Sometimes, in the privacy of her studio, she sat on a stool before a mirror, her long legs stretched out before her, and contemplated herself as if contemplating a work of art. She could remain like this for an hour, without moving. It pleased her to be so complete; unlike other women, she did not want to turn into anyone else.

That morning, entering the Institute, she saw one of the girl students talking to the man she had met the day before, Anthony—they were standing just inside the door, and both looked around at her. She smiled and said hello, not waiting for any reply. Her heart had jumped absurdly at the sight of him and she had no desire to hear his voice . . . she was afraid he would hurry after her, take hold of her arm. . . . Safe in her class, she put on a shapeless, soiled smock. She directed eight students in their own work with clay. She was efficient with them, not friendly, not unfriendly, never called anything except *Miss Ressner*. She felt no interest in her students' lives, no jealousy for the girls with their engagement rings and wedding bands. The girl who had been talking with Anthony had long black hair and an annoying eagerness. She had a small, minimal talent, but she was one of those students who want to be told, at once, whether they will succeed or not, whether their talent is great enough to justify work, as if the future could be handed to them on a scroll, everything figured out by a superior mind, determined permanently. . . . And she felt no interest in the men, who were both older and younger than she; their pretensions, their sincerity, their private feverish plans did not interest her.

After class the girl said to her, "Miss Ressner, that man was asking about you. Out there. Did you notice him?"

Pauline showed no curiosity. "I saw you talking to someone."

"He asked a lot of questions about you. . . . I know him a little, not well, he hangs around down here in the bars and places. . . . " Then, embarrassed, she said quickly, "But of course I didn't tell him anything."

Pauline felt tension rising in her. She dropped her paper cup into a wastebasket, conscious of spilling coffee in the basket, onto napkins . . . coarse paper napkins that soaked up the liquid at once. . . . It was ugly, a mess. She went out into the drafty corridor. That dream was still with her. . . . She was tempted suddenly to go over to the museum to see if anything there could explain it, surely it had an origin in something she had seen and forgotten. . . . *Why a procession of mules, why garlands of flowers, why a bare-chested victim in a wagon?*

Later that day she saw Anthony again. He was standing in front of a restaurant, doing nothing, as if waiting for her. . . . She had left her studio, restless, wanting to get away from students who dropped in to talk with her. She was too polite to discourage visits.

Why did people waste her time talking to her? Why did they ask her vulgar, personal questions, about where she got her ideas, about whose work she admired most . . . ? Why did people talk to one another, drawn together mysteriously, fatally, helpless to break the spell? She had sensed, in certain men and in a few women, a strange attraction for her—something she had never understood or encouraged. Gentle, withdrawing, but withdrawing permanently, she backed out of people's lives, turning aside from offers of friendship, from urgency, intensity, the admiration of men who did not know her at all. She liked all these people well enough, she just did not want to be close to them. And now this Anthony, whom she would not have liked anyway, was hanging around her, a dragging tug at the corner of her eye, a threat. Her mother's first command would be to call the police, but Pauline, being more sensible, knew that was not necessary.

It would have been a mistake to ignore him. She said, "Hello, how are you?" Her smile was guarded and narrow in the cold sunlight.

"Hello," he said. His voice sounded uneven, as if he was so surprised by her attention that he could not control it. "Where are you going? Would you like some coffee?"

"I don't have time," she said, side-stepping him. She felt her face shape into a polite smile of dismissal. Anthony smiled back at her, mistaking the smile . . . or was he pretending to mistake it? Was he really very arrogant? She felt again a sense of fear, a suffocating pounding of her heart.

He rubbed his hands together suddenly, warmly, as if pleased by her. Today he looked more robust; he had shaved, his black curls fell more neatly down onto his collar; he wore a short, sporty coat that was imitation camel's hair, only a little soiled; he wore leather boots, cracked and marred like her own shoes.

"I'd like to talk with you," he said. "It's very important."

"Not today—"

"But I won't hurt you. I only want to talk." He smiled a dazzling smile at her—he was about to move toward her, about to take her arm again. She jumped back, frightened. But he only said, "I want to talk about different kinds of living, I want to know you . . . how it is for you, your life, a woman who looks like you. . . . I spend my time watching things, or listening to things, music, in a bar or in somebody's apartment, listening to records. . . ."

"I have to leave," she said thinly, bowing her head. She could not look up at him.

"Yesterday, when I saw you, I thought . . . I thought that I would like to meet you. . . . Why does that offend you?"

She said nothing.

"I asked him, what's-his-name, to introduce us. He didn't want to. It was very important to me, something gave me a feeling about you, meeting you, I was very nervous . . . last night I couldn't sleep. . . ."

She stared at his boots. Strong lines and faint lines, a pattern made by the salted ice in leather, ruining it. The pattern was interesting. One of her own shoes was coming apart. . . . What if friends of her mother's saw her standing here, on Second Avenue, talking to this man? His long, shabby curls, his striking face, the slouch of his shoulders and the urgent line of his leg, bent dancerlike from the hip, even the stupid cowboy boots, would upset and please them probably: looking like that, he must be an artist of some kind.

Stammering, embarrassed, she interrupted him, "I'm older than you think . . . I'm over thirty . . . I don't have time to talk to you, I don't go out with people, I'm not the way you think. . . ."

"How do you know what I think?" he said angrily.

His anger frightened her. She was silent. Why was she here quarreling with a man she didn't know? She never quarreled with anyone at all. She never quarreled.

"If you're so anxious to leave, leave," he said.

Released, she could not move. For a moment she had not even heard him.

"Don't run—I won't follow you!" he said angrily.

Back for her two-o'clock class, trying to control herself. She had another cup of coffee. Shaking inside. The coffee tasted bad. Everything down here was cheap, her students' talent was cheap, common, their faces had no interest for her, she could not use them in her work, why was she pretending to need a job? She should quit. Move her studio out. There were only two genuinely talented students in her class, both men, and she guessed from their nervousness and the frequency with which they cut class that they would never achieve anything, they would disintegrate . . . other talented students of hers had appeared and disappeared over the years, where did they all end up? And yet when former students did come back to visit, most of them art teachers in high school, she was unable to show more than a perfunctory interest in their careers; why did people surround her, clamor into her ears, what did they want from her? What secret?

"He's crazy," she thought.

During the next several days, aware of him at a distance out on the street, she sometimes felt terror, sometimes a kind of dizzy, abandoned excitement. It was necessary for her to be afraid; she knew the police should be notified, barriers raised, bars put into place; yet she wondered idly why she should be afraid, why . . . ? She could not believe that anything might happen to her. She was safe in her composure, her strength, she had been taking care of herself for years, and so why should she be afraid of that man, why should she even think about him. . . ?

Getting into her car one afternoon, late, she saw him at the edge of the faculty parking lot, watching her. She was tempted to raise her hand casually in a greeting. Would that dispel the danger or make it worse? She imagined him leaping over the low wire fence and galloping up to her. . . . She did not wave. She did not give any sign of seeing him. But when she drove by him she saw him take several quick steps, faltering steps, after the car, in the street . . . his action was ludicrous, sad, crazy. . . . She wondered if she herself had become a little crazy.

> Bodies in a field. The field is sandy, a wasteland, but great
> spiky weeds grow in it, needing no water. The end of
> winter, not yet spring. The bodies come to life: a man and
> a woman. The woman has long, ratty hair, the man's hair
> is mussed. It is confused with his face. Their bodies are
> twisted and their faces in shadow. They laugh loudly,
> waking, they embrace right on the sand, in the open field.
> . . . Near them is something dead. Is it a dog or a large rat?
> Let it be a large rat. Frozen hard from winter, not decayed.
> . . . In the presence of that thing the man and woman
> embrace violently, tearing at each other's skin, their
> laughter sharp and wild. . . . They make love right there in
> the open, among the spiky weeds and the dead rat, aware
> of nothing around them.

She woke with a headache again, unable to remember what had wakened her. A dream? It was still dark. Only six o'clock. She got out of bed, her body suddenly aching. She dragged herself to her closet, put on a warm robe, stood in a kind of perplexed slouch, wondering what to do next. . . . Her shoulders and thighs ached, her head ached. Her eyes in their sockets were raw and burning, as if someone had been sticking his thumbs in them. Nearby, on a handsome old table, was a head she had done recently, in white; the model had been an old man, but very clean, dignified. He had had a light fringe of hair, almost like frost, but she had dismissed that and the head was bold, an exacting skull. It interested her strangely. The head of an old man, a dignified shape of bone, interlocking bone. Ingenious work of art, the human skull. His forehead was solid, bony, broad. The nose was rather flat, but broad at the bridge; a strong nose. The eyes were stern, the eyebrows strong and clear, the mouth slightly surprised, but withdrawing from surprise. She had wanted to convey a certain emotion—terror, really, but at the same time the refusal to accept this terror, even to allow the surface of the skin to register it. She ran her hand over the top of the head, over the face. Cold lead. Cold skin. She pressed her cheek against the top of the head. A completed work.

In her bathroom the light was too strong. It was reflected from the cream-colored porcelain of the skin. The house was old but the bathrooms and kitchen had been remodeled at great expense; Pauline had never liked the change. She had liked the old-fashioned fixtures with their heavy, exaggerated handles, the mirror beginning to show lead beneath it—like the gray bones beneath a skull's skin, without shame—and the old, creaky shower, the worn black and white tile. Now everything was new and clean, as if in a motel. It had no history.

She peered at herself in the mirror. In a few weeks she would be thirty years old, which seemed to her suprisingly young. Surely she had lived more than three decades . . . ? Yet her face looked very young. It was pale, untouched, soft and baffled from sleep, as if with a child's apprehension. What had she dreamed? She took a jar of night cream out of the cabinet and smoothed it onto her face. It was necessary to lubricate her skin, she had to take care of herself. It was a duty. One day, twenty years ago, her father had told her bluntly that she was dirty—disheveled hair, socks running down into her shoes. "I don't want you to look ugly," he had said. It was a command she took seriously, because she had his face, a striking, beautiful face, and that face brought with it a certain responsibility. There is a terrible weight in all kinds of beauty.

> Skin is an organ of the body. It consists of many layers of cells. No one could have invented it. Cells absorb moisture and lose moisture; they pulsate in their own secret rhythm, in their own private time. Invisible, elastic. Each human being has his own skin, unique to him. It is a mystery. Someday a dead woman will wear the skin that belonged to a living woman, and it is the same skin exactly. Then it decomposes. . . . The skin is the most impermeable barrier of the body. It is always thirsty. Its thirst is insatiable. Human thirsts are satisfied from time to time, but the thirst of the human skin is never satisfied so long as it lives.

She wandered aimlessly through the house. Downstairs, she looked out of the window down the slope of their long front lawn, at car lights on the avenue, a distance away. Where were all those people going? It surprised her to see the cars out there, people driving all night, into the dawn, with secret, private destinations. . . . Something moved out on the lawn. She did not look at it. Then, feeling helpless, she looked at it . . . she saw nothing, only shadow . . . it was not possible that anything had been there.

If that man followed her home?

Years ago, a student in London, she had modeled for a class. They were sketching heads, torsos. The instructor had been a peculiar man —middle-aged, wheedling, argumentative, but enormously talented, a big man with hairy arms. He had always spilled coffee on the floor, knocked ashes everywhere. Pauline had sat there in the center of a circle, motionless. She had never been shy or self-conscious. Her face, protected by its film of impersonality, was invulnerable. . . . The instructor's name was Julius. She had sat on a stool, relaxed,

and he had stood wrenching her into shape, turning her face one
way, then another. "Remain like that. Don't complicate our lives,"
he had said. Somewhere on the other side of the silent, working
students he had stood, smoking, staring at her. He had a large, ungainly, gracefully clumsy body. He never talked to anyone per-
sonally, he never bothered to look anyone in the eye. She loved
him, with rushes of enthusiasm that did not last, imagining him
kneeling before her, kissing her knees, in the pose of a certain
decadent painting . . . and her staring down through mild, half-
closed eyelids at him, uncomprehending. But nothing happened.
One day she imagined he was about to embrace her—they were
alone for some reason in the studio—she had an uncanny, terrifying
moment when she was certain he was going to embrace her, pressing her face against his, his large hands wild in her hair. . . . But he
only opened a drawer and some objects inside rattled around. She
had gone out into the wet air relieved, ready to weep, feeling totally
herself once more.

Since that time she had thought herself in love with two other
men, one of them a painter who still lived in this city but whom she
no longer bothered to see, another a lawyer, the son of a wealthy
couple in her parents' set of friends. But nothing had happened.
Nothing. She had approached them as if in a dance, she had noticed
something in their faces, a certain intense yearning, and she had
gracefully, shyly, permanently withdrawn, not even allowing the
surface of her skin to register the excitement and dread she had felt.
So it had ended. She was complete in herself, like the heads she
made, and like them she felt her skin a perfect organ, covering her,
a surface that was impregnable because it was so still and cold.

> Statue of Mars. Brandishing a spear, attacking. The
> muscular body is in contrast with the graceful pose, almost
> a dancer's pose. One hand holds the lance, the other
> probably holds a libation bowl. Lips are inlaid in copper
> and eyes in some colored material; helmet separate and
> attached. Gently modeled eyes, strange expression of
> mouth, almost a smile. Tension of body: elegance of face.
> Small, tight, careful curls descending around ear, down
> onto cheek.
>
> EMERGENCY NUMBERS:
> FIRE   POLICE   SHERIFF   DOCTOR
> STATE POLICE   COAST GUARD
> or dial Operator in any emergency and say "I want to
> report a fire at ———" or "I want a
> policeman at ———"

She was walking with a friend of hers, another art instructor,
down a street of bookstores and bars and restaurants, student hang-
outs. While the man talked, her eyes darted about frantically. It was

still cold. She had forgotten her gloves. Her fingers ached with something more than cold, because it was not that cold. He friend—a married man with four children, a safe man—was talking about something she couldn't concentrate on when Anthony appeared in a doorway ahead of them. He looked out of breath, as if he had just been running. Pauline had the strange idea that he had run around the block just to head them off. He was staring at them, but her friend noticed nothing, and as if this were a scene carefully rehearsed, everyone between them—students in sloppy overcoats, a Negro woman with her children—moving away, clearing the view. Pauline and her friend were going to pass Anthony by a few feet, pass right by him. There was nothing she could do. She stared at him, unable to look away, catching the full angry glare of his eyes, the tension in his head. Cords in his neck were prominent. His coat was open, his hands thrust in his pockets. He glared at her, his glare surrounding her as if the coldness were forming a halo, magically, about her body. The line of his jaw was very hard, his mouth was slightly open as if he were breathing with great difficulty. . . .

He jumped out at them, grabbing her arm. She tried to break loose. In silence he swung a knife, the blade suddenly bright and decorative, and slashed at his own throat. Pauline screamed. Her friend yanked her away, but not before Anthony's blood had splashed onto her. "What are you doing? What—what is this?" the man cried. Anthony, staggering, caught her around the hips, the thighs, as he fell heavily, and she had not the power to break herself loose from him; she stared down at the top of his head, paralyzed.

In a few minutes it was over.

He was taken away; it was over. Her friend answered the policeman's questions. An ambulance had come with its lights and siren but now it was gone. "It's all over. Don't think about it," her friend said, as if speaking to one of his own children. Pauline was not thinking about anything. She walked woodenly, looking down at her blood-splattered shoes. Her coat was smeared with blood in front. Her stockings might have been bloody also, but she could not see; she walked stiffly, not bending at the waist, her shoulders rigid.

"You'd think they would catch people like that before they do something violent," her friend said.

Teen-aged girls, passing them on the sidewalk, stared in amazement at Pauline.

MAN SLASHES OWN THROAT IN UNIVERSITY AREA

Anthony Drayer, 35, of no fixed address, slashed his own throat with a butcher knife this noon on Second Avenue. He is in critical condition at Metropolitan Hospital. No motive was given for the act.

TEMPERATURE HOVERS AT 32°; WEATHERMEN
PREDICT FAIR AND WARMER THIS WEEKEND

When she got home, she went right up to her bathroom, avoiding the maid. Safe. She tore off her coat, sobbing, she threw it onto the floor, and stared at her legs—blood still wet on her knees, on her legs, splattered onto her shoes. As if paralyzed, she stared down at her legs; she could not think what this meant. She kept seeing him in the doorway, his chest heaving, waiting, and she kept reliving that last moment when she knew unmistakably that she dare not pass him, it could not be done; and yet she had said nothing to the man she was with, had kept on walking as if in a trance. Why? Why had she walked straight toward him?

She was shivering. In horror, she raised her skirt slowly. More blood on her stockings. On the inside of her thigh, smeared there. It was a puzzle to her, she could not think. Why was that man's blood on her, what had happened? Had he really stabbed himself with a knife? How could a man bring himself to draw a blade hard across his own throat, why wouldn't the muscles rebel at the last instant, freezing?

She took off her stockings and threw them away. In a ball squeezed in her fist, they seemed harmless. Blood on her legs, thighs. She stared. What must she do next?

She took a bath. She scrubbed herself.

She fell onto her bed and slept heavily, as if drugged.

> On the table are four heads in a white material, a ceramic material. It shines, gleams cheaply, light glares out of the eyes of the heads. . . . The first head is my own. A blank white face. The next face is my own, but smaller, pinched. Shocked. The next head, also white, is my own head again . . . my own face . . . the lips drawn back in a look of hunger or revulsion, the eyes narrowed. Can that be my face, so ugly a face? The fourth head is also mine. White, stark white. A band tight around the head has emphasized a vein on my temple, a small wormlike vein in white, standing out. The eyes are stern and empty, like the eyes in Greek statues, gazing inward, fulfilled. The head is in a trance-like sleep, like the sleep of a pregnant woman. I walk around and around the table as if choosing. My hands are itching for work of my own. I can feel the white clay beneath my fingernails, but when I look down it is not clay but blood, hardening in the cracks of my hands.

Driving to the Institute, she was overcome by a sudden attack of nausea and had to pull her car over to the side. Now it was April. She sat for a while behind the wheel, too faint to get out, helpless. The nausea passed. Still she did not drive on for a while but remained there, sitting, listening intently to the workings of her body.

> The doctor stands above me. I am lying on an old-fashioned table, he is holding a large pair of tweezers, his glasses are rimmed by metal, he is bald, the formation of his forehead

shines, bumps shine in the light, I am ready to scream but the straps that hold down my legs also hold back my screams. . . . This happened centuries ago. A slop pail is beneath the sink. The doctor holds up his tweezers to the light and blows at a curly dark hair that is stuck to them . . . the hair falls slowly, without weight. . . .

While teaching her class, she felt a sudden urgency to get out of the room. She went to the women's rest room. Safe, she stared at herself in the mirror, seeing a tired, pale, angry face. Dull splotches of the metal that backed the mirror showed through, giving her a leprous look. She recalled a mirror like this in a public rest room, herself a girl of thirteen, pale and scared and very ignorant. She had thought she was pregnant. At that time she had thought pregnancy could happen to any woman, like a disease. Like cancer, it could happen.

For weeks she had imagined herself pregnant. Her periods had been irregular and very painful. She struck at her stomach, weeping, she went without eating until she was faint. . . . One day, kneeling with her forehead pressed against her old bathtub, thinking for the five-thousandth time of the terrible secret she held within her, she had felt the first painful tinge of cramps and then a slight, reluctant flow of blood. . . . So she was not pregnant after all . . . ?

How did a woman get pregnant?

She lifted her skirt again to stare at the smooth white skin of her leg. Blank. Blood had been smeared there, but now it was clean; she showered every morning and took a hot bath every night, anxious to be clean and soothed and free of his blood.

> The living cells of the blood, insatiably hungry for more life, flow upward. They rise anxiously, viciously upward . . . in test tubes they may be observed defying the well-known law of gravity. Also, blood splashed onto bread mould will devour it and be nourished by it. Also, blood on foreign skin or fur will harden into a scab and work its way into the new flesh, draining life from it. Also, blood several days old, dropped into tubes containing female reproductive cells, will unite with these cells and form new life.

At a dinner party one Saturday in April. Her escort was a bachelor, a lawyer. She rose suddenly from the table, trembling, careful to pull back her chair without catching it in the rug, her head bowed, demure, her diamond earrings brushing coldly against her cheeks. Not all the candlelight of this room could warm those earrings or those cheeks. She hurried to the bathroom, she clutched at her face, she realized with a stunning certainty that she was pregnant.

She was sick to her stomach, as if trying to vomit that foreign life out of her.

On Monday, not wanting to worry her mother, she drove out
though she had no intention of teaching her class. She parked
around the university and walked for hours. She was looking for
him, for evidence of him. Her breasts felt sore, her thighs and
shoulders ached. She knew that she could not be pregnant and yet
she was certain she was pregnant. Her face burned. After hours of
walking, exhausted, she called a cab and went back home, abandon-
ing her car. She wept.

"I just found out about Drayer," Martin said, stammering. "They
said he cut himself and attacked a woman, and I knew it would be
you, I knew it. . . ." Pauline was silent, holding the telephone to her
ear without expression. "I knew something like that would happen!
He was very strange, he never appreciated what I did for him, he
was forgetful, like a child—he was always forgetting my name and
he had no gratitude—he was like a criminal—I would never have
introduced you but he insisted upon it, he said he couldn't take his
eyes off your face—I knew I shouldn't have done it, please, do you
forgive me? Pauline? Do you forgive me?"
She hung up.

> A woman in a stiff brocade dress, wearing jewels.
> Evening. Candlelight. Her face is shadowed . . . is it my
> mother, my aunt? She opens the window, which is a door,
> and a large dog appears. It is a greyhound, elegant and
> spoiled and lean, with a comely head. The woman takes
> hold of the dog's head in both hands, staring into its
> eyes. The dog begins to shake its head . . . its teeth flash
> . . . foam appears on its mouth. . . . I turn away with a
> scream, slamming my hand flat on the keyboard of a
> piano: the notes crash and bring everything to a stop.

Her mother was packing the large suitcase with the blue silk
lining. Weeping, her mother. Her back is shaking. A friend of her
mother's talks patiently to Pauline, who lies hunched up in bed,
rigid. "If you would try to relax. If you would let us dress you," the
woman says. Her own son, at the age of seventeen, once tried to kill
her: so she has had experience with this sort of thing. No doubt why
Pauline's mother called upon her.

"You understand that you cannot be pregnant and that you are
not pregnant," the doctor says. He shapes his words for her to read,
as if she might be deaf. She feels the foreign life inside her, hard as
stone.

Bleeding from the loins, she aches with cramps, coils of cramps.

The blood seeps through the embryonic sack, not washing it free. How to get it free? She has a sudden vision, though she is not sleeping, of a tweezers catching hold of that blood-swollen little sack and dragging it free. . . .

Dr. Silverman, a friend of her father's, visits her in this expensive hospital. He talks to her kindly, lovingly, holding her stone fingers. He is a very cultured man who, having lost most of his family in a Nazi death camp, is especially suited to talk to her, arguing her out of madness and death. No doubt why her mother called upon him.
Her hair has been cut off short. She cannot hear him.

The nurse says sourly, "You'll get over it." She is lying in warm water, frightened by a terrible floating sensation, as if her organs are floating free inside her, buoyed up by the water. Only the embryo is hard, hard as stone, fixed stubbornly to her arteries. She tries to scream but cannot scream. Anyway, it is dangerous to open her mouth: they feed her that way, tearing open her mouth and inserting a tube.

> . . . He is an ancient Chinese, his face unclear. He stands
> fishing in a delicate stream, his heavy, coarse robe pulled
> up and tucked in his belt. He catches a fish and pulls it out
> of the water, pulls it off the hook with one jerk of his
> hand . . . he tosses the fish onto the bank where the
> other fish lay, bleeding at the mouth, unable to close
> their eyes. . . .

Her mother brings a box of candy. Cheeks haggard, spring coat not festive. She is a widow, and now it is beginning to show. She sits by the bedside weeping, weeping. . . . "Do you hear me? Why don't you talk to me? Do you hate me unconsciously? Why do you hate me?" Her mother weeps, words are all she knows, she turns them over and over again in her mind. "That man . . . you know . . . the one who stabbed himself, well, it was in the paper that he finally killed himself, in the hospital where he was being kept. . . . Why don't you hear me, Pauline? I said that man did away with himself. He won't bother you any more, he can't bother you. Are you listening? Why aren't you listening?"
She lies listening.

> It is a monument in dark stone. A body is being cremated.
> Birds in the air, crows. It is finally spring and everything
> is loose. Children are running around the base of the
> monument, with no eye for it. What do children care
> about the monuments of the world! They throw flowers

at one another. . . . Atop the monument is a statue, two figures. One is a youth with curly hair, a thick torso, protruding blank eyes. The set of his mouth shows him both angry and frightened. The other figure is an angel of death, a beautiful woman with outspread wings, though her body is shaped unnaturally from the waist down. She holds out her hand to the young man.

I am standing before him. He sinks to his knees and embraces me, he presses his face against me. Leaning over him, with lust and tenderness that is violent, like pain, I clutch him to me, I feel the tight muscles of his shoulders, I press my face against the top of his head. . . .

We kneel together. We press our faces together, our tears slick and warm. . . .

Discussion of Oates's "Bodies"

1. The "reality" of Pauline's life becomes steadily punctuated by fantasies. The presence of these fantasies becomes increasingly hard to detect. Try to separate them from the waking life of the heroine. Compare the technique here and in "Beasts of the Southern Wild" and "Daydreams of a Drunk Woman."

2. The story seems to embody a paradox, in that what can't possibly be true becomes the most real experience of Pauline's life. Is this the most likely reading of the story?

3. Many of the heroines of the stories in this anthology seem far stronger than the men they are involved with—as is certainly the case of Pauline and Anthony. Pauline's strength seems to be achieved at tremendous cost. Are there other, equally strong but more balanced heroines in these stories?

4. This story appears to be one about a woman who has tried to free herself in order to devote her life to intellectual pursuits, only to be broken by a man. To what extent is Pauline's freedom real, and to what extent is it a refuge from reality?

DORIS BETTS

b. 1932

❦ Born in Statesville, North Carolina, Doris Betts lives now near Chapel Hill, where she teaches at the University of North Carolina. She has written several novels, *Tall Houses in Winter* (1957), *The Scarlet Thread* (1964), and *The River to Pickle Beach* (1972). Her collected short stories appear in three volumes, *The Gentle Insurrection* (1954), *The Astronomer and Other Tales* (1966), and *Beasts of the Southern Wild and Other Stories* (1973), which was nominated for a National Book Award. As an instructor of creative writing, she comments, "Most of the students tend to rebel against form—which I think is very healthy, but it's not very good for a short story writer who first has to learn the form, and then how he can break it" ("The Unique Voice: Doris Betts," *Kite-Flying and Other Irrational Acts*, ed. John Carr [Baton Rouge: Louisiana University Press, 1972], p. 159). When asked to define the short story, she responds, "I wouldn't, but I would steal from the letter of Chekhov in which he said, 'I can speak briefly on long subjects.' That's my favorite definition of the short story and of what it can do." (p. 173). Many of her long subjects are people poised in the crisis of living: feeling its pain and anticipating its pleasures. Never sentimental, her writing generally is characterized by a humorous, even sardonic, tone that suggests her own and her characters' dignity and courage in the face of crises.

Beasts

of the Southern Wild

. . . I have been in this prison a long time, years, since the Revolution. They have made me an animal. They drive us in and out our cells like cattle to stalls. Our elbows and knees are jagged and our legs and armpits swarm with hair.

We are all women, all white, bleached whiter now and sickly as blind moles. All our jailers, of course, are black.

So much has been done to us that we are bored with everything, and when they march me and six others to the Choosing Room, we make jokes about it and bark with laughter. I am too old to be chosen—thirty when I came. And now? Two hundred. It is not clear to me what has happened to my husband and my sons. Like a caged chicken on a truck, I have forgotten the cock and the fledglings.

We file into the Choosing Room and from dim instinct stand straighter on the concrete floors and lift our sharp chins. The Chooser sits on an iron stool. Negro, of course, in his forties, rich, his hair like a halo that burned down to twisted cinders. Jim Brown used to look like him; there's a touch of Sidney Poitier— but he has thin lips. I insist on that: thin lips.

They line us up and he paces out of sight to examine our ankles and haunches. He will choose Wilma, no doubt, who still has some shape to her and whose hair is yellow.

The Chooser steps back to his seat and picks up our stacked files and asks the guard a few soft questions while a brown finger is pointed at first this one of us and then that. This procedure is un-usual. The dossiers are always there, containing every detail of our past lives. Usually they are consulted only after the field has been narrowed and two finalists checked for general health, sound teeth.

He speaks to the guard, who looks surprised, then beckons to me. The others, grumbling, are herded out and I am left standing in front of the Chooser. He is very tall. I say to his throat, "Why me?" He taps my dossier against some invisible surface in the air and goes out to sign my contract.

"You're lucky," says the guard through his thick lips.

I am beginning to be afraid. That's strange. I've been beaten now, been raped, other things. These are routine. But something will change now and I fear any changes. I ask who the man is who will take me to his house for whatever use he wants, and the guard says, "Sam Porter." He takes me out a side door and puts me in the back seat of a long car and tells me to be quiet and not move around. And I wait for Sam Porter like a mongrel bitch he has bought from the pound.

When the alarm clock rang, she dragged herself upright and hung on the bookcase. She loved to sleep—a few more seconds prone and she'd be gone again, with the whole family late for work and school. She balanced on one foot and kicked Rob lightly in the calf. "Up, Rob. Rob? Up!"

Fry bacon, cook oatmeal, scramble eggs, make coffee. There was a tiny box, transistorized, under her mastoid bone. All day long it gave her orders, and between times it hummed like a tuning fork deep in her ear. Set table. Bring in milk and newspaper. Spoons, forks. Sugar bowl, cream.

She yelled, "Breakfast!"

Nobody came and the shower was still running. Down the hall both boys quarreled over who got to keep the pencil with the eraser. When the shower stopped, she yelled again, "Breakfast!" (I'm Rob's transistor box.)

Her husband and sons came in and ate. Grease, toast, crumbs, wet rings on the table. Egg yolk running on one plate, a liquefied eye. If thine eye offend thee, pluck it out.

"Don't forget my money," Michael said, and Robbie, "Me, too."

"How much you need?" She counted out lunch money, a subscription to *Weekly Reader*. Rob said he'd leave the clothes at the cleaners, patted her, and went off to the upholstery shop. She drove the boys to school, then across town to the larger one where she taught English, Grade 12, which she liked, and Girls' Hygiene, which she despised. It was November, and the girls endured nutrition charts only because they could look ahead to a chapter on human reproduction the class should reach before Christmas.

Today's lesson was on the Seven Basic Foods, and one smartmouth, as usual, had done her essay on eating all of one type each day, then balancing the diet in weekly blocks. The girl droned her system aloud to the class. "So on Wednesday we indulge in the health-giving green and yellow vegetables group, which may be prepared in astonishing variety, from appetizing salads to delicious soups to assorted nourishing casseroles."

None of the students would use a short word when three long ones would do. They loved hyperbole. Carol Walsh wanted to say, "There's no variety, none at all," but this was not part of their education. She was very sleepy. When she looked with half-closed eyes out the schoolroom window, the landscape billowed like a silk tapestry and its folds blew back in her face like colored veils.

In the hall later, a student asked, "Miz Walsh? What kind of essay you want on Coleridge? His life and all?"

"No, no. His poetry."

"I can't find much on his poetry." The boy was bug-eyed and gasping, helpless as a fish. Couldn't find some library book to tell him in order what each line of the poems *meant*.

She said, "Just think about the poems, George. Experience them. Use your imagination." Flap your wings, little fish. She went into English class depressed. There was nothing to see out this window but a wall of concrete blocks and, blurred, it looked like a dirty sponge.

"Before we move to today's classwork, I'm getting questions about your Coleridge essay. I'm not interested in a record of the man's biography. I don't even want a paper on what kind of poet he might have been without an opium addiction." A flicker of interest in the back row. "I want you to react to the poems, emotionally. To do what Coleridge did, put your emphasis on imagination and sensibility, not just reason." She saw the film drop over thirty-five gazes, like the extra eyelids of thirty-five reptiles. "Mood, feeling," she said. The class was integrated, and boredom did the same thing to a black face as to a white.

The Potter girl raised her hand. "I've done a special project on Coleridge and I wondered if that would count instead?"

Count, count. They came to her straight from math and waited for the logarithms of poetry. Measure me, Miz Walsh. Am I sufficient?

She said. "See me after class, Ann. Now, everybody, turn in your text to the seven poems you read by Thomas Lovell Beddoes." They whispered and craned in their desks, although the section had been assigned for homework. Dryly she said, "Page 309. First of all, against the definition we've been using for the past section, is Beddoes a romantic poet?"

Evelina dropped one choked laugh like a porpoise under water. Romantic, for her, had only one definition.

"Ralph?"

Ralph dragged one shoe on the floor and stared at the scrape it left. "Sort of in between." His heel rasped harder when she asked why. "He was born later? There's a lot of nature in his poems, though." He studied her face for clues. "But not as much as Wordsworth?"

His girl friend raised her hand quickly to save him and blurted, "I like the one that goes, 'If there were dreams to sell,/What would you buy?'" In the back, one of the boys made soft, mock-vomit noises in his throat.

After class Ann Potter carried to the front of the room and unrolled on the desk a poster of a huge tree painted in watercolor. Its roots were buried in the soil of Classicism and Neoclassicism; "18th Century," it said in a black parenthesis. Dryden, Swift, and Pope had been written in amongst the root tangle. James Thomson vertically on the rising trunk. Then there were thick limbs branching off assigned to Keats, Shelley, Byron . . .

When Ann smiled, she showed two even rows of her orthodontist's teeth. "This sort of says it all, doesn't it, Miz Walsh!"

"You could probably be a very successful public schoolteacher."

"It's got dates and everything."

"Everything." Blake's *Songs of Innocence* branched off to one side, where Byron would not be scraped in a high wind. "Tintern Abbey." There was a whole twig allotted to "Kubla Khan."

"I thought you might count this equal to a term paper, Miz Walsh. I mean, I had to look things up. I spent just days on it."

"Ann, why not write the paper anyway? Then this can be extra credit if you need it." She'd need it. There was nothing in her skull but filtered air, stored in a meticulous honeycomb.

"My talents lie more in art, I think. I had to mix and mix to get just that shade of green, since England's a green country. I read that someplace. The Emerald Isle and all. I read a lot."

"It's a very attractive tree."

For last period, Carol Walsh gave a writing assignment; they could keep their textbooks open. Compare Beddoes and Southey. She sat at her desk making bets with herself about how many first sentences would state when each man was born. I'm good at dates, Miz Walsh. That Poe *looks* crazy. Well, Blake had this vision of a tiger, burning bright. He was this visionary. And he wrote this prayer about it.

That night she graded health tests until she herself could hardly remember what part of the digestive tract ran into what other part and whether the small or the large intestine came first. She chewed up an apple as she worked, half expecting its residue to drop, digested, out her left ear. Who knew what a forbidden fruit might take it in its—in *her* head to do?

"You're going to bed this early?" Rob glanced up from the magazine he was skimming during TV commercials.

"Not to sleep. Just to rest my eyes. Leave the TV on. I might decide to watch that movie." She got into bed and immediately curled up facing the wall. She was drowsy but curious, not ready for sleep; and there was nothing on television to compare with the pictures she could make herself. The apple had left her teeth feeling tender, and she had munched out the pulp from every dark seed, cyanide and all. Once she'd read of a man who loved apple seeds and saved up a cupful for a feast and it killed him.

She smiled when the story started.

. . . The car is moving. Its chauffeur is white, a free white who could buy off his contract. Sam Porter has said nothing. He does not even look at me but out the window. For years I have seen no city streets and I long to get off the floor and look, too; but he might strike me with that cane. A black cane, very slim, with a knob of jasper. The tops of buildings glimpsed do not look new. It's hard to rebuild after revolutions.

We stop at last. I follow him through a narrow gate, bordered with a clipped yew hedge. A town house, narrow and high, like the ones they used to build in Charleston. This one is blue. A white man is raking in the tulip beds—spring, then. I had forgotten. Sam Porter walks straight through the foyer and up the stairs and shows me a bedroom. "Clean up and dress." He opens a closet with many dresses, walks through a bathroom and out a door on the far side. So. Our rooms adjoin. Mine seems luxurious.

I do not look at myself until I am deep in the soapy water. My body is a ruin. No breasts at all. I can rake one fingernail down my ribs as if along a picket fence. The flesh which remains on my legs is strung there, loose, like a curtain swag. I am crying. I soak my head but lice do not drown; and finally I find a shampoo he has left for me which makes them float on the water and speckle the ring around the tub. I scrub it and wash myself again.

The dresses are made of soft material, folded crêpes and draped jerseys, and I do not look so thin in the red one, although it turns my face white as a china plate. He may prefer that. I wonder if there is a Mrs. Porter; I hope not. They have grown delicate since the war and faint easily and some of the prison women have been poisoned by them. I pin up my wet hair and redden my lips, so thin now I no longer have a mouth, only a hole in my jaw. He knocks on the door. "We'll eat. Downstairs." His voice is very deep. I have lived so long with the voices of women that his sound makes a bass vibration on my skin.

Practicing the feel of shoes again, I go down alone to find him. The table is large, linen-covered. I am set at his right. There's soup and a wine. It's hard not to dribble. The white housekeeper changes our plates for fish and a new wine. She looks at me with pity. She must be sixty-five. Where is my mother keeping house? At what tables do my sisters sit tonight?

"Carol Walsh," he says suddenly, looking down as if he can read me off his tablecloth.

The wine has changed me. "Sam Porter," I say in the same tone, to surprise him. He lifts his face and his forehead glistens from heat on its underside. His eyes are larger than mine, wetter, even the tiny veins seem brown.

"What do you expect of me?" I ask, but he shakes his head and begins eating the pale fish meat. I put it in my mouth and it disappears. Only the sweet taste but no bulk, and I am hungry, hungry.

After dinner he waves one hand and I follow him to a sitting room with bookshelves and dark walls. "Your file indicates you are literate, a former English teacher." He has no trouble taking down a book from a very high shelf. "Read to me. Your choice."

I choose Yeats. I choose "Innisfree" and "Sleuth Wood." To him I read aloud: "Be secret and exult/Because of all things known/That is most difficult." He sits in his big chair listening, a cold blue ring on his finger. I turn two pages and read, "Sailing to Byzantium."

When that is done, Sam Porter says, "What poem did you skip? And why?"

I have hurried past the page which has "Leda and the Swan." The lines are in my head but I cannot read them here: ". . . the staggering girl, her thighs caressed/By the dark webs . . ."

I say aloud, "I'll go back and read it, then," but the poem I substitute is "Coole Park," and he knows; he knows. He smiles in his chair and offers me brandy, which turns my sweat gold. He says, "You look well."

"Not yet. I look old and fresh from prison."

He rises, very tall, and does not look at me. "Shall we go up?"

I follow on the stairs, watching his thighs when he lifts each leg, how the muscles catch. He passes through my room and I follow; but he stops at the door to his and shakes his frizzed head. "When you come to me," he says, "it will not be with your shoulders squared."

He closes the door while I am still saying "Thank you." I cannot even tell if what I feel is gratitude or disappointment.

They drove Sunday afternoon to look at a new house in the town's latest subdivision. "Wipe your feet, boys," said Carol. The foyer

was tiled with marbleized vinyl, and in the wallpaper mural a bird
—half Japanese and half Virginian—flew over bonsai magnolias.

"If the interest rates weren't so damn high," Rob said, muffled in
a closet. "That's one more thing George Wallace would have done.
Cut down that interest."

"It's got a fireplace. Boys, stay off those steps. They don't have a
railing yet."

"Bedrooms are mighty little. Not much way to add on, either.
Maybe the basement can be converted."

There were already plastic logs in the fireplace and a jet for a gas
flame. Their furniture, all of it old and recovered by Rob's upholster-
ers, seemed too wide to go through the doorways. He called to her
from the kitchen, "Built-in appliances!" She could see the first
plaster crack above the corner of the kitchen door. Rob had gone
down into the basement and yelled for them to stay out, too many
nails and lumber piles. "Lots of room, though," called his hollow
voice. "I could have myself a little shop. Build a rumpus room?"

Carol stood in the kitchen turning faucets on and off—though
there were no water lines to the house yet—and clicking the wall
switches that gave no light. I could get old here, in this house.
Stand by this same sink when I'm forty and fifty and sixty. Die in
that airtight bedroom with its cedar closets when I'm eighty-two. By
the time they roll me out the front walk, the boxwoods will be high.

"Drink of water?"

"Not working, Robbie. See?"

"Well, Michael peed in the toilet!"

"It'll evaporate," she said. They were handsome boys, and Robbie
was bright. Michael had been slower to talk and slower to read;
nothing bothered him. Robbie was born angry and had stayed angry
most of his life. Toys broke for him; brothers tattled; bicycles threw
boys on gravel. Balls flew past his waiting glove. Robbie could
think up a beautiful picture and the crayons ruined it. She'd say to
him, "Thinking's what matters," and doubt if that were true.

"We move in this house, I want a room by myself," he announced
now, and punched at the hanging light fixture. "Michael's a baby.
Michael wets in the bed."

In the doorway Michael stretched his face with all fingers and
stuck out his dripping tongue and roared for the fun of it.

"Michael gets in my things all the time. He marked up my zoo
book. He tore the giraffe."

Rob's head rose out of the stairwell. "No harm in asking the price
and what kind of mortgage deal we could get. You agree, Carol? It's
got a big back yard. We could build a fence."

"Could we get a dog?" Michael yelled.

Robbie pinched his arm. "I want my own dog. I want a big dog
with teeth. I'll keep him in my room to bite you if you come in
messing things up."

Carol made both boys be quiet, and in the car agreed the house was far better than the one they rented now. Rob smiled and swung the wheel easily, as if the car were an extension of his body, something he wore about him like familiar harness.

"I like that smell of raw wood and paint," he said. "Yesterday we had a nigger couch to cover, a fold-out couch, and it smelled so bad Pete moved it in the back lot and tore it down out there. Beats me why they smell different. It's in the sweat, I guess."

Robbie was listening hard from the back seat, and she was afraid tomorrow he would be sniffing around his school's only Negro teacher. "There's no difference," she said, putting her elbow deep in Rob's side.

"You college people kill me."

They drove in silence while she set up in her mind two columns: His thoughts and Hers. He was thinking how tired he was of a know-it-all wife, who'd have been an old maid if Rob Walsh hadn't come along, a prize, a real catch. With half-interest in his daddy's business just waiting for them. Gave Carol everything, and still she stayed snooty. Didn't drink, didn't gamble, didn't chase women—but by God he might! He might yet! He was two years younger. He was better-looking. He didn't have to keep on with this Snow Queen here, with Miss Icebox. Old Frosty Brain, Frozen Ass. Who needed it?

And Her thoughts, accusing. Who do I think I am? What options did I ever have? Was I beautiful, popular, a genius? Once when we quarreled, Rob said to me, "Hell, you've been in menopause since you were twenty." I'll never forgive him for that. For being mediocre, maybe; but never for saying that.

Turning in to their driveway, Rob said in a sullen voice, "You college people can't be bothered believing your noses. All you believe is books." He got out of the car and went into the house and left them sitting there.

Robbie said to his brother, "I warned you not to pee in that toilet."

After supper of leftover roast, Carol read the boys another chapter from *Winnie the Pooh*. When she had heard their flippant prayers and turned out the light, she stood in the hall and smiled as they whispered from bed to bed. I can love them till my ribs ache, but it still seems like an afterthought. She dreaded to go downstairs and watch the cowboys fight each other on a little screen, one in the white hat, one in the black.

While she was ironing Rob a clean work shirt for tomorrow, she wondered if there were some way she could ask Sam Porter about an odor without offending him. She decided against it.

. . . I have been here two weeks and Sam has never laid a hand on me. Yet I am treated like a favorite concubine. I dine at his table; he dresses me as though the sight of me gave him pleasure. The housekeeper mourns over what she imagines of our nights together. Every

evening, I read to him—one night he asked for Othello *just to laugh
at my startled face. One other evening, he had friends over and
made me play hostess from a corner chair. He encouraged me to join
in the talk, which was of new writers unknown to me. One of the
men—a runt with a chimpanzee's face—looked me over as if I might
be proffered to him along with the cigars. Plainly, he could do better
on his own. He made one harem joke, a coarse one, and jerked his
thumb toward me and up. Sam Porter tapped him atop his spine.
"Not in my house," he said. I was looking away, grinding my teeth.
To me he said, "Sit straight. There's nothing in your contract which
says . . . Some things you need not endure."*

*"He isn't worth my anger." Sam laughed, but the others worried
and took him off in the front hall to offer advice.*

*Tonight as we sit down with our brandy, he says to me, "You
were happy in the old days? As a woman?"*

"Sometimes."

"My color and hair. Perhaps they disgust you?"

*"No. Although in prison we were often . . . forced. I cannot forget
those times."*

"And you never had pleasure? From a black?"

"No. None. What shall I read tonight?"

"From yourself, perhaps? Or the women prisoners?"

*"Not much," I say quickly, and, "Should we read some of the new
things your friends like?"*

"What subject did you choose for your Master's thesis?"

*By now I know Sam Porter is no quick-rich, quick-cultured black.
He is Provost at New Africa University, which I attended under its
old name. And my dusty thesis must be stored there, in the prewar
stacks. If he wished to know my subject, then he already knows it. I
answer truthfully anyway, "John Donne."*

*He hands me a book of collected writings, from the library at
school. "Perhaps the early work?" I reach for it and my fingers graze
his. His hand is warmer than mine—unscientific, I know; but I can
feel old sunlight pooled in his flesh and my hand feels wintry by his.*

*I am sorry to have the book again. The blue veins on my hands
are high as the runs of moles; when I held Donne last, I had no
veins at all and my skin was soft. I was twenty-three then, and not
in menopause. No! I felt isolated from all things and swollen with
myself as a tree hangs ripe with unplucked fruit. I was ugly, if the
young are ever ugly; and sat alone in the caves and tunnels of the
library, at a desk heaped high with Donne's mandrake root. Sam
Porter says, "When you tire of staring at the cover, perhaps you will
read?"*

*"The Sunne Rising." I look to a different page and, perversely,
read aloud, "I can love both faire and brown/Her whom abundance melts and her whom want betraies."*

Sam is watching me; I feel it though I do not look up. Sometimes

*his eye lens seems wide as a big cat's, and it magnifies the light and
throws it in perforations onto me. I swallow, read, "Her who loves
lonenesse best, and her who makes and plaies." My voice is thin
through my dry mouth. I ask Donne's question, "Will it not serve
your turn to do as did your mothers?/Or have you all vices spent,
and now would finde out others?/Or doth a fear, that men are true,
torment you?"*

*When the poem is done, there is silence. He drinks his brandy; I
drink mine; is it as warm going down inside him as in me? His glass
clicks on the table. "You sit awhile. The brandy's there, and the
book. I'm tired tonight."*

*I sit numb in my chair. He passes, then, with one swoop, bends
down and touches my mouth with his, and his lips are not thin—not
thin at all. He walks out quickly and I sit with the book and the
snifter tight in my hands, for there is a smell; yes, it is sweetish, like
a wilted carnation fermenting on an August grave. Even a mouthful
of brandy does not wash out his scent. My lungs are rich with it.
And I do not go upstairs for a long time, until Sam Porter is asleep
in the other room.*

All evening she had been marking the participles which hung
loose in the Coleridge essays like rags; and all evening Rob kept in-
terrupting her work. He talked of the new house and what their
monthly payments would be if they took a ten-year mortgage, or
twenty. Or thirty—like a judge considering sentence.

"I'm leaving that up to you," she said, trying to figure out on
which page Ann Potter had changed Kubla Khan to Genghis Khan
in her paper, "The Tree of Romanticism."

Rob said if she'd give less written work she wouldn't have to
waste so much time marking papers. One of the themes—George's
—appeared to be copied from an encyclopedia. Symptoms of opiate
intoxication. There followed a list of Coleridge's poems. "These,"
George wrote, "show clearly the effects of the drug on his mind."
She turned the page but there wasn't a word more.

Rob said, "If the federal government would just quite raising the
minimum wage. How can I tell how much I'll earn in a year or two
years, the way they eat into profits more and more? You know how
much I got to pay a guy just to put chairs on a truck and drive them
across town?"

"Umm." Ralph's paper was "Nature in Wordsworth and Coleridge" and how Wordsworth had more of it and wrote prettier.

"The harder I work, the more I send to Washington to keep some
shiftless s.o.b. drawing welfare," Rob said, and rattled his newspaper. "And next year they raise my taxes to build back the big cities
the bums are burning down. So everybody can draw welfare in new
buildings, for Christ's sake. My daddy would turn over in his grave."

There's life, she thought, in the old boy yet. She read an essay on an albatross, a harmless bird feeding on fish and squid, and no need for anybody to fear it.

Rob was asleep when she marked the last red letter grades and slipped between the sheets like an otter going under the surface without a ripple. She lay wide-eyed in the dark. The streetlight shone through the window blinds, and threw stripes across their bed and her face. After a while she slid one hand under the covers and closed her eyes.

. . . Sam is sick. The doctor who came was the chimpanzee man and he pinched in the air at me—but I moved. There is something of me to pinch now, after Sam's food and his wines and my long, lazy days in his handsome house. The doctor says he has flu, not serious; and for two days I have been giving him capsules and citrus juices. The housekeeper sees I am worried and has lost all her pity. She turns her face from me when I draw near, as if my gaze would leave a permanent stain.

> *"Are Sunne, Moone, or Starres by law forbidden*
> *To smile where they list, or lend away their light?*
> *Are birds divorc'd, or are they chidden*
> *If they leave their mate, or lie abroad at night?"*

He fell asleep from his fever and I read alone and sometimes laid my hand on his blazing forehead. Against his color, my hand had more shape and weight than it has ever had.

Tonight he is much better and sips hot lemonade and listens with half his attention to old favorites. "Come live with me and be my love."

He asks once, "You don't sing, do you?"

"No."

He falls asleep. I tiptoe into my own room. Perhaps in the Choosing Room there is someone new, who sings. I pace on my carpet, John Donne's poems open on my dressing table like a snare. He hooks me with his frayed old line, "For thee, thou needst no such deceit/For thou thy selfe are thine own bait." I close the book; I spring his trap; I leap away.

In the mirror I see who I really am . . . my hair grown long and brown, my eyes brown, my skin toasted by the sun on Sam Porter's noonday roof. I will never be pretty, but this is the closest I have ever come, and I pinch my own cheeks and look at myself sideways. I have grown round again from eating at his table, and my breasts are distended with his brandy. I put on the red robe and walk softly into the next room. Sam sleeps, turned away from me, with one dark hand half open on the pillow as if something should alight in it.

I return to my room and brush out my hair. My body has a foreign fragrance—perhaps from these bottles and creams. Perhaps I absorb it from the air.

I pass through to the next room and drop my robe on the floor. I turn off the lamp and he is darker than the room. I slide in against his back, the whole length of him hot from fever. I reach around to hold him in my right hand. He is soft as flowers. He makes some sound and stirs; then he lies still and I feel wakefulness rise in him and his skin prickles. He turns; his arms are out. I am taken into his warm darkness and lie in the lion's mouth.

The bed shook and she opened her eyes and stared at the luminous face of the clock. Rob said, "You asleep?" She lay very still, breathing deep and careful, pressing her hand tight between her thighs as if to hold back an outcry. The air was thick with Old Spice shaving lotion—a bad sign. A hand struck her hip like a flyswatter. "Carol? You can't be asleep." The ghostly face of the clock showed 1 A.M. "Honey?"

She jerked her hand free just in time for his. "Ah," he said with satisfaction against her shoulder blades. He curled around her from behind. "Picked a good time, huh?" She moved obediently so it would be quickly done, and he rolled away from her and slept with one arm over hers like a weighted chain.

. . . Sam bends over the bed where I have been crying and now lie weary, past crying. "Who was it, Carol? Tell me who it was?"

I roll my head away from him and he kisses one damp temple, then the other. He whispers, "This isn't prison anymore, hear me, Carol? No more endurance is required. Understand that. You are home, here; and that was rape. Whoever it was, I'll punish him."

I am a single bruise. "No." I run my hand under his shirt. "I didn't encourage him, Sam, I didn't. He broke in here—I was alone. I called for you. I never wanted him.

"If you do," says Sam, "I'll tear up your contract and let you go."

"No." I look in his eyes. "He was never my desire. An intruder. A thief. He forced himself on me. I swear it."

"Tell me one thing." He lies by me and his heat comes through the blanket. "Was he a white man?"

"Yes. He was white."

Gently he holds me, says, "I can have him killed, then. You know that. Did you know him?"

"I know his name. That's all we know, each other's names."

His hair is black and jumbled. "If you tell me his name, I can have him killed. But I won't ask you to do that. You must choose. You'll not be blamed if you choose silence." His hands are so pale on one side, so dark on the other.

"Rob Walsh," I whisper. "Rob Walsh."

"We'll hunt him down," he says, and gets up and goes downstairs.

He does not come back for hours and I wake near dawn to see him stripping off the black suit, the black mask, the black cloak. I sit up in bed. "It's done," he says, sounding tired, maybe sick. He comes naked and curly to me and falls away on the far side. "There's no love left in me tonight."

But I am there, my hands are busy, and I can devour him; he will yield to me. The room is dark and he is so dark, and all I can see is the running back and forth of my busy hands, like pale spiders who have lived underground too long.

Discussion of Betts's "Beasts of the Southern Wild"

1. What do the italicized portions of the story signal? What is the effect of the story's beginning and ending with italicized narrative?

2. Describe Carol Walsh's daytime life.

3. What, if anything, seems to be significant about Carol Walsh's fantasy centering on a black man? Compare the racial and sexual relationships with "Dry September" and "Long Black Song."

4. Compare the relationship between married men and women in "Beasts" with those in "Giving Blood," "Daydreams of a Drunk Woman," and "Permanent Wave." Do the points of view make a difference?

5. Compare the use of humor here and in "Old Mr Marblehall," "Giving Blood," and "Permanent Wave."

6. Who might the "beasts of the southern wild" be?

ALICE WALKER

b. 1944

❦ Born of sharecropping parents in Eatonton, Georgia, Alice Walker now makes her home in New York City. She graduated from Sarah Lawrence College and was writer-in-residence at Tougaloo College in Mississippi. Her first volume of poetry, *Once*, was published in 1968; her second, *Revolutionary Petunias and Other Poems*, in 1972. She has also written two novels, *The Third Life of Grange Copeland* (1970) and *Meridian* (1976); a biography of the poet Langston Hughes; and a collection of short stories, *In Love and Trouble* (1973), from which "Her Sweet Jerome" was taken. Her dedicatory preface to *Revolutionary Petunias* applies also to her short stories: "These poems are about Revolutionaries and Lovers; and about the loss of compassion, trust, and the ability to expand in love that marks the end of hopeful strategy. Whether in love or revolution. They are also about (and for) those few embattled souls who remain painfully committed to beauty and to love even while facing the firing squad."

Her Sweet Jerome

1

Ties she had bought him hung on the closet door, which now swung open as she hurled herself again and again into the closet. Glorious ties, some with birds and dancing women in grass skirts painted on by hand, some with little polka dots with bigger dots dispersed among them. Some red, lots red and green, and one purple, with a golden star, through the center of which went his gold mustang stickpin, which she had also given him. She looked in the pockets of the black leather jacket he had reluctantly worn the night before. Three of his suits, a pair of blue twill work pants, an old gray sweater with a hood and pockets lay thrown across the bed. The jacket leather was sleazy and damply clinging to her hands. She had bought it for him, as well as the three suits: one light blue with side vents, one gold with green specks, and one reddish that had a silver imitation-silk vest. The pockets of the jacket came softly outward from the lining like skinny milktoast rats. Empty. Slowly she sank down on the bed and began to knead, with blunt anxious fingers, all the pockets in all the clothes piled around her. First the blue suit, then the gold with green, then the reddish one that he said he didn't like most of all, but which he would sometimes wear if she agreed to stay home, or if she promised not to touch him any-where at all while he was getting dressed.

She was a big awkward woman, with big bones and hard rubbery flesh. Her short arms ended in ham hands, and her neck was a squat roll of fat that protuded behind her head as a big bump. Her skin was rough and puffy, with plump molelike freckles down her cheeks. Her eyes glowered from under the mountain of her brow and were circled with expensive mauve shadow. They were nervous and quick when she was flustered and darted about at nothing in particular while she was dressing hair or talking to people.

Her troubles started noticeably when she fell in love with a studiously quiet schoolteacher, Mr. Jerome Franklin Washington III, who was ten years younger than her. She told herself that she shouldn't want him, he was so little and cute and young, but when she took into account that he was a schoolteacher, well, she just couldn't seem to get any rest until, as she put it, "I were Mr. and Mrs. Jerome Franklin Washington the third, *and that's the truth!*"

She owned a small beauty shop at the back of her father's funeral home, and they were known as "colored folks with money." She made pretty good herself, though she didn't like standing on her feet so much, and her father let anybody know she wasn't getting any of his money while he was alive. She was proud to say she never asked him for any. He started relenting kind of fast when he heard she planned to add a schoolteacher to the family, which consisted of funeral directors and bootleggers, but she cut him off quick and said she didn't want anybody to take care of her man but her. She had learned how to do hair from an old woman who ran a shop on the other side of town and was proud to say that she could make her own way. And much better than some. She was fond of telling schoolteachers (women schoolteachers) that she didn't miss her "eddicashion" as much as some did who had no learning and no money both together. She had a low opinion of women school-teachers, because before and after her marriage to Jerome Franklin Washington III, they were the only females to whom he cared to talk.

The first time she saw him he was walking past the window of her shop with an armful of books and his coat thrown casually over his arm. Looking so neat and *cute*. What popped into her mind was that if he was hers the first thing she would get him was a sweet little red car to drive. And she worked and went into debt and got it for him, too—after she got him—but then she could tell he didn't like it much because it was only a Chevy. She had started right away to save up so she could make a down payment on a brand-new white Buick deluxe, with automatic drive and whitewall tires.

Jerome was dapper, every inch a gentleman, as anybody with half an eye could see. That's what she told everybody before they were married. He was beating her black and blue even then, so that every time you saw her she was sporting her "shades." She could not open her mouth without him wincing and pretending he couldn't stand it, so he would knock her out of the room to keep her from talking to him. She tried to be sexy and stylish, and was, in her fashion, with a predominant taste for pastel taffetas and orange shoes. In the summertime she paid twenty dollars for big umbrella hats with bows and flowers on them and when she wore black and white together she would liven it up with elbow-length gloves of red satin. She was genuinely undecided when she woke up in the morning whether she really outstripped the other girls in town for beauty, but could convince herself that she was equally good-looking by the time she had breakfast on the table. She was always talking with a lot of extra movement to her thick coarse mouth, with its hair tufts at the corners, and when she drank coffee she held the cup over the saucer with her little finger sticking out, while she crossed her short hairy legs at the knees.

If her husband laughed at her high heels as she teetered and minced off to church on Sunday mornings, with her hair greased and curled and her new dress bunching up at the top of her girdle, she pretended his eyes were approving. Other times, when he didn't bother to look up from his books and only muttered curses if she tried to kiss him good-bye, she did not know whether to laugh or cry. However, her public manner was serene.

"I just don't know how some womens can stand it, honey," she would say slowly, twisting her head to the side and upward in an elegant manner. "One thing my husband does not do," she would enunciate grandly, "he don't beat me!" And she would sit back and smile in her pleased oily fat way. Usually her listeners, captive women with wet hair, would simply smile and nod in sympathy and say, looking at one another or at her black eye, "You say he don't? Hummmm, well, hush your mouf." And she would continue curling or massaging or straightening their hair, fixing her face in a steamy dignified mask that encouraged snickers.

2

It was in her shop that she first heard the giggling and saw the smirks. It was at her job that gossip gave her to understand, as one woman told her, "Your cute little man is sticking his finger into somebody else's pie." And she was not and could not be surprised, as she looked into the amused and self-contented face, for she had long been aware that her own pie was going—and for the longest time had been going—strictly untouched.

From that first day of slyly whispered hints, "Your old man's puttin' something *over* on you, sweets," she started trying to find out who he was fooling around with. Her sources of gossip were malicious and mean, but she could think of nothing else to do but believe them. She searched high and she searched low. She looked in taverns and she looked in churches. She looked in the school where he worked.

She went to the whorehouses and to prayer meetings, through parks and outside the city limits, all the while buying axes and pistols and knives of all descriptions. Of course she said nothing to her sweet Jerome, who watched her maneuverings from behind the covers of his vast supply of paperback books. This hobby of his she had heartily encouraged, relegating reading to the importance of scanning the funnies; and besides, it was something he could do at home, if she could convince him she would be completely silent for an evening, and, of course, if he would stay.

She turned the whole town upside down, looking at white girls, black women, brown beauties, ugly hags of all shades. She found nothing. And Jerome went on reading, smiling smugly as he shushed her with a carefully cleaned and lustred finger. "Don't interrupt me," he was always saying, and he would read some more while she stood glowering darkly behind him, muttering swears in her throaty voice, and then tramping flatfooted out of the house with her collection of weapons.

Some days she would get out of bed at four in the morning after not sleeping a wink all night, throw an old sweater around her shoulders, and begin the search. Her firm bulk became flabby. Her eyes were bloodshot and wild, her hair full of lint, nappy at the roots and greasy on the ends. She smelled bad from mouth and underarms and elsewhere. She could not sit still for a minute without jumping up in bitter vexation to run and search a house or street she thought she might have missed before.

"You been messin' with my Jerome?" she would ask whomever she caught in her quivering feverish grip. And before they had time to answer she would have them by the chin in a headlock with a long knife pressed against their necks below the ear. Such bloodchilling questioning of its residents terrified the town, especially since her madness was soon readily perceivable from her appearance. She had taken to grinding her teeth and tearing at her hair as she walked along. The townspeople, none of whom knew where she lived— or anything about her save the name of her man, "Jerome"—were waiting for her to attempt another attack on a woman openly, or, better for them because it implied less danger to a resident, they hoped she would complete her crack-up within the confines of her own home, preferably while alone; in that event anyone seeing or hearing her would be obliged to call the authorities.

She knew this in her deranged but cunning way. But she did not let it interfere with her search. The police would never catch her, she thought; she was too clever. She had a few disguises and a thousand places to hide. A final crack-up in her own home was impossible, she reasoned contemptuously, for she did not think her husband's lover bold enough to show herself on his wife's own turf.

Meanwhile, she stopped operating the beauty shop, and her

patrons were glad, for before she left for good she had the unnerving habit of questioning a woman sitting under her hot comb—"You
the one ain't you?!"—and would end up burning her no matter what
she said. When her father died he proudly left his money to "the
schoolteacher" to share or not with his wife, as he had "learnin'
enough to see fit." Jerome had "learnin' enough" not to give his
wife one cent. The legacy pleased Jerome, though he never bought
anything with the money that his wife could see. As long as the
money lasted Jerome spoke of it as "insurance." If she asked insurance against what, he would say fire and theft. Or burglary and
cyclones. When the money was gone, and it seemed to her it vanished overnight, she asked Jerome what he had bought. He said,
Something very big. She said, Like what? He said, Like a tank. She
did not ask any more questions after that. By that time she didn't
care about the money anyhow, as long as he hadn't spent it on some
woman.

As steadily as she careened downhill, Jerome advanced in the
opposite direction. He was well known around town as a "shrewd
joker" and a scholar. An "intellectual," some people called him, a
word that meant nothing whatever to her. Everyone described
Jerome in a different way. He had friends among the educated,
whose talk she found unusually trying, not that she was ever invited
to listen to any of it. His closest friend was the head of the school
he taught in and had migrated south from some famous university in
the North. He was a small slender man with a ferociously unruly
beard and large mournful eyes. He called Jerome "brother." The
women in Jerome's group wore short kinky hair and large hoop
earrings. They stuck together, calling themselves by what they
termed their "African" names, and never went to church. Along
with the men, the women sometimes held "workshops" for the
young toughs of the town. She had no idea what went on in these;
however, she had long since stopped believing they had anything
to do with cabinetmaking or any other kind of woodwork.

Among Jerome's group of friends, or "comrades," as he sometimes
called them jokingly (or not jokingly, for all she knew), were two or
three whites from the community's white college and university.
Jerome didn't ordinarily like white people, and she could not understand where they fit in the group. The principal's house was the
meeting place, and the whites arrived looking backward over their
shoulders after nightfall. She knew, because she had watched this
house night after anxious night, trying to rouse enough courage to
go inside. One hot night, when a drink helped stiffen her backbone,
she burst into the living room in the middle of the evening. The
women, whom she had grimly "suspected," sat together in debative
conversation in one corner of the room. Every once in a while a
phrase she could understand touched her ear. She heard "slave
trade" and "violent overthrow" and "off de pig," an expression she'd
never heard before. One of the women, the only one of this group to

acknowledge her, laughingly asked if she had come to "join the revolution." She had stood shaking by the door, trying so hard to understand she felt she was going to faint. Jerome rose from among the group of men, who sat in a circle on the other side of the room, and, without paying any attention to her, began reciting some of the nastiest-sounding poetry she'd ever heard. She left the room in shame and confusion, and no one bothered to ask why she'd stood so long staring at them, or whether she needed anyone to show her out. She trudged home heavily, with her head down, bewildered, astonished, and perplexed.

3

And now she hunted through her husband's clothes looking for a clue. Her hands were shaking as she emptied and shook, pawed and sometimes even lifted to her nose to smell. Each time she emptied a pocket, she felt there was something, *something*, some little thing that was escaping her.

Her heart pounding, she got down on her knees and looked under the bed. It was dusty and cobwebby, the way the inside of her head felt. The house was filthy, for she had neglected it totally since she began her search. Now it seemed that all the dust in the world had come to rest under her bed. She saw his shoes; she lifted them to her perspiring cheeks and kissed them. She ran her fingers inside them. Nothing.

Then, before she got up from her knees, she thought about the intense blackness underneath the headboard of the bed. She had not looked there. On her side of the bed on the floor beneath the pillow there was nothing. She hurried around to the other side. Kneeling, she struck something with her hand on the floor under his side of the bed. Quickly, down on her stomach, she raked it out. Then she raked and raked. She was panting and sweating, her ashen face slowly coloring with the belated rush of doomed comprehension. In a rush it came to her: "It ain't no woman." Just like that. It had never occurred to her there could be anything more serious. She stifled the cry that rose in her throat.

Coated with grit, with dust sticking to the pages, she held in her crude, indelicate hands, trembling now, a sizeable pile of paperback books. Books that had fallen from his hands behind the bed over the months of their marriage. She dusted them carefully one by one and looked with frowning concentration at their covers. Fists and guns appeared everywhere. "Black" was the one word that appeared consistently on each cover. *Black Rage, Black Fire, Black Anger, Black Revenge, Black Vengeance, Black Hatred, Black Beauty, Black Revolution.* Then the word "revolution" took over. *Revolution in the Streets, Revolution from the Rooftops, Revolution in the Hills, Revolution and Rebellion, Revolution and Black People in the*

United States, Revolution and Death. She looked with wonder at the books that were her husband's preoccupation, enraged that the obvious was what she had never guessed before.

How many times had she encouraged his light reading? How many times been ignorantly amused? How many times had he laughed at her when she went out looking for "his" women? With a sob she realized she didn't even know what the word "revolution" meant, unless it meant to go round and round, the way her head was going.

With quiet care she stacked the books neatly on his pillow. With the largest of her knives she ripped and stabbed them through. When the brazen and difficult words did not disappear with the books, she hastened with kerosene to set the marriage bed afire. Thirstily, in hopeless jubilation, she watched the room begin to burn. The bits of words transformed themselves into luscious figures of smoke, lazily arching toward the ceiling. "Trash!" she cried over and over, reaching through the flames to strike out the words, now raised from the dead in glorious colors. "I kill you! I kill you!" she screamed against the roaring fire, backing enraged and trembling into a darkened corner of the room, not near the open door. But the fire and the words rumbled against her together, overwhelming her with pain and enlightenment. And she hid her big wet face in her singed then sizzling arms and screamed and screamed.

Discussion of Walker's "Her Sweet Jerome"

1. What attitude does the author seem to have towards her character? What is the effect of Mrs. Washington's grotesqueness? Her attempts to overcome it? Her husband's responses to her?

2. Compare the effect of violence in this story with the violence in "Dry September," and "Long Black Song" or with the subtle cruelties of "Wine" and "The Birthmark."

3. Knowing that this story is from a collection entitled *In Love and Trouble,* can you assess the effects of love in "Her Sweet Jerome"? What is the nature of love as dramatized in this story? How does cruelty in many of these stories become an effective means of presenting relationships among women and men, parents and children?

4. Think of other stories in which politics and human relationships are implicitly compared. In what way does Walker's story resemble them?